MIMA ROSENFELD

THE PATH OF A LOGICAL LOVER

This is a work of fiction. Names, places, characters and incidents are either the product of the author's imagination or are used fictitiously and are not to be construed as real. Any resemblance to any actual persons, living or dead, organizations, events or locales is entirely coincidental.

The Path of a Logical Lover. Copyright 2022 by Mima Rosenfeld, All rights reserved.

Printed in the United Stated of America. No part of this book may be reproduced or transmitted in any form or by any means, electronic or mechanical, including photocopying and recording, or by any information storage retrieval system, without permission in writing from the publisher.

FIRST U.S. EDITION

Designed by Books and Moods

ISBN: 979-8-218-02829-9

To Isaac.
You're my person.

CHAPTER ONE

AVA

He's here.
I know it, and as ridiculous as it sounds, I can feel him in the room.

I'm seated on stage at Radio City Music Hall for my graduation ceremony. My entire family is here to celebrate. My oldest brother, Devon, got some signing bonus from his new job in Brooklyn and flew everyone out. He wanted all of us here together since it's my birthday tomorrow.

I'll be twenty-two.

My name finally gets called. On the right side of the room, I can hear my brothers' noisy hollering and, on the left, I can hear a slightly louder clap than the rest of the room's. My eyes dart rapidly to spot him, and as soon as my brown eyes meets his green ones, I gasp.

The bomb-blasting, earthquake, vibrating, ground-shattering, emotional burst inside of my chest chokes me. It's like whiplash that I have to turn away immediately. I stumble slightly when I walk off the stage and toward a seat in the audience.

He came. He came to my graduation.

Fifteen months. I haven't seen this man in fifteen months.

I ask myself how he got an invitation, but the realization hits me humorously. College sponsors get invitations. He was invited because of me.

I somehow spot my best friend and roommate, Chloe, in the sea of people surrounding us and give her that wide-eyed *holy shit* look.

"What?" she mouths.

"He's here!" I mouth back.

"Who?"

My expression says it all; my eyes pop cartoonishly out of my face. Her jaw drops. "What the fuck?"

"I have no idea."

When the ceremony is over, I head straight for my family, hoping to distract them.

Several kisses, hugs, and *I'm so proud of you*s later, I hand my graduation cap to my mother then tug at Devon's arm to pull him aside.

"He's here, Devon," I whisper shakily, inching into my brother for protection or comfort, or maybe both.

My brother, however, doesn't pick up on my anxiety and is confused. "Who is?"

"Grant." Devon's head leans back in surprise. "Don't tell Mom," I beg. "She's going to get all Spanish and embarrass everybody."

"Too late, Indiana," Devon tells me, nodding toward my family and *him*.

I tighten my grasp on Devon's forearm when I study every moment of their exchange. He shakes my father's hand, gives my mother a hug. *Get off of them*, I want to say. *Don't touch my family*.

My heart beats fast, hands perspiring madly at the range of emotions that encompass my body when I see him again. When he's only a few feet away from me, my breathing turns irregular.

I hold my breath as he turns to glance at me, dismisses himself from the huddle of my family members, and walks over in my direction.

Keeping eye contact with him proves impossible. It's enough that a simple glance from a darkened audience can knock me off kilter, but if I look into his eyes, I might pass out.

Grant stops two feet in front of me and lifts his left hand up from out of his pocket. I immediately fixate my gaze on his ring finger, his *bare* ring finger, and all I can do is stare at it. When he notices what I'm looking at and why, he slips his hand back out of sight.

"Hi," he says gruffly.

"Why did you come?" I ask in a near whisper.

"I wanted to congratulate you."

I gulp and exhale shakily. "Um… You shouldn't be here."

"I know. I'll go."

He rocks back on his heels and stands up straighter, buttons the top button of his suit jacket.

"One more thing," he mutters. He has something else to say before he walks away for good. "Happy birthday, Ava."

CHAPTER TWO

GRANT

"That's fine, Hannah," I mumble at my kitchen sink.

"Great," she calls out from the doorway of my bedroom. "I'll have Bobby call it in in the morning."

She is going to send the suit I wore today to the cleaners in our building. She is adding a couple of her dresses to the pile, too.

I hum an affirmative sound, then focus back on the dishes in the sink from dinner tonight. Hannah requested an organic salad. I made myself a steak. Oftentimes, we eat separately. Both time wise and the contents of our dinners. Most of our life together is pretty separate, actually. That's never how I envisioned my future to look, but then again, Hannah isn't who I envisioned for my future either.

"You okay?" Hannah asks tenderly. I gulp, dismissing her. When she pushes, I snap, "I'm fine."

"What's your deal?" she snaps back a moment later. "What's with all of your moodiness tonight?"

I can't tell you why. I can't tell you because I don't want to hurt you.

I ask her what she means. She scoffs, says, "You know exactly what I mean."

I take a deep breath, rub my eyes with my forearm, hands wet with soapy suds. "I'm just tired, Hannah. It's been a long day."

Exhaustion has been my choice of excuse for over a year now. It isn't a lie.

Ten minutes later, as I'm starting up the dishwasher, I can feel Hannah suddenly appear by my side. She throws something on the counter opposite me, then stomps back into the bedroom.

New York University
Graduation Program 2019

Fuck. My suit jacket pocket. The cleaners bag.

I swallow the guilt that lives in my chest, wipe my hands, then follow my fiancée into my room, ready myself for war.

War. A silent, passive-aggressive war that Hannah is oh so good at.

I sigh. "Say what you want to say, Hannah."

"You're a dick. Does that work?"

"Yeah." I swallow thickly, dart my eyes to hide that painful shame that lives within me, that's lived within me for the last couple of years. "That's fine, Hannah."

"I think that's what'll be written on your tombstone for the number of times you say it. That's fine, Hannah. It wouldn't kill you to have an opinion. To look alive sometimes."

She stands on the other side of my bed, long arms crossed. She pins me with that sapphire glare, blonde hair knotted in a messy bun. Lululemon shorts and a sports bra. She's what I should be attracted to. She's what I tell myself I'm attracted to.

I want her to end it. I want her to end this fucked up engagement for her own fucking sake.

"I'm sorry, Hannah. I don't want to hurt you. You have to understand."

She laughs bitterly, shakes her head. "You're not hurting me.

You're just wasting my time. You went to her graduation? Really?"

I blink away from her knowing, judgmental gaze, but she has every reason to judge me.

I don't know why I went today. It benefitted nobody, not Ava, not myself, and certainly not Hannah. It was a mistake. But when the alert sounded on my Google calendar an hour before the ceremony started, I battled within myself whether or not to go. I decided, against my better judgement, that I was going.

I stood at the exit as if I wasn't really there. Like me not taking a seat in the audience meant I wasn't actually in attendance, but when Ava saw me, it marked said attendance. I clapped loudly. I couldn't not.

I was so proud of her; *I am so proud of her.*

She could barely look at me. That's the difference between Hannah and Ava. Hannah stares at me with hatred. Ava avoids my eyes with that same hatred.

"Why'd you go?" Hannah interrupts my train of thought. "And an honest answer would be nice, Grant."

"I was invited."

"She invited you? Because I swear to God, if she—"

"*No,*" I stress, my voice strong. "I was invited through NYU. She didn't know I was coming."

"Did you see her?"

"Yes."

"Did you talk to her?"

"I'm sorry," I whisper, pleading. "I swear, I don't want to hurt you. It won't happen again. I'm not going to see her ever again."

My stomach bottoms out at the truth in my statement. A painful, concrete truth. Any lingering acquaintance that remained between Ava and I ended today with her graduation. I am no longer funding her college tuition. I am no longer sponsoring her last year of college. After today, I have zero connection to her at all.

The finiteness in that reality burns in my chest.

"I'm not asking for you to love me like you love her. I'm just asking for you to make a decision and stick to it." Hannah's stark-white teeth clench, nostrils flare with tears I assume she's holding in. "Me or her. Not whether you're going to love me like you love her. Just me or her. Choose."

"I did. I chose. I chose you."

"No. You didn't choose me. *She* just didn't choose *you*."

Her words break my heart. I'm ruining her. She doesn't deserve any of this bullshit.

I walk over to Hannah, who's standing at my bedside. I hug her, then take a deep breath. "I'm sorry. Please believe me," I whisper into Hannah's hair. "I never want to hurt you. I don't want this. Okay?"

Hannah hugs me back, rubs up and down my back. "I believe you."

"I chose you, Han, okay?" I repeat, trying to convince myself just as much I'm trying to convince her.

Hannah nods. I kiss her head, then head straight for the shower.

CHAPTER THREE

AVA

"Where were you?!" Chloe shouts in my face, above the loud music.

After a celebratory dinner with my family, Chloe, Derek, and the rest of our friend group met up at a nightclub in Chelsea. It's bachelor degree etiquette.

I face Chloe and shout, "To pee!"

"Come dance with me!" she demands, like she knows that she'll get her way, because that's just who she is. No one says no to Chloe.

She pulls me by the hand through the wild crowd; sweaty bodies, sloshing drinks, throbbing lights. Once we've made it to the middle of the dance floor, she faces me.

"How many more minutes?" she shouts directly into my ear. I check my watch and holler, "Four!"

My birthday is in four minutes.

When Derek squeezes his way through the mob of dancegoers and stands flush against me, Chloe dismisses herself, tells us she'll be right back. I smile up at Derek. Derek with his blonde hair and blue eyes. Derek with his baby face.

He bends to speak in my ear. "Can I dance with you?" he asks.

With a grin and laugh, I kiss Derek's cheek. "What kind of question is that?"

Grabbing his hand, I follow his lead. I pay no mind to the way I'm dancing because that's the best kind.

"Hey, hey, hey!" the DJ shouts into the mic, interrupting his well-played soundtrack. He points directly at me in the crowd. "Shoutout to the birthday girl! Give it up for Ava, everybody!"

Chloe sprints toward me and crashes into my chest. She's singing 50 Cent at the top of her lungs, and I have no doubt that she coerced the DJ to play this birthday song with her doe eyes and giant personality.

Chloe envelops me in the tightest hug imaginable and brings her lips to my ear. "I'm so happy we found each other. You're the strongest person I know, Ava. You deserve the motherfucking world, you hear me? *The world.* You're my bitch. I love you so much."

I grab her face and kiss her sweaty cheek. "I love you more! You're my bitch, too!"

We continue dancing, and at one point, Derek slips his hand into mine. His confidence, boldness, makes me smile, so I squeeze his hand. When he looks down at me, his eyes turn serious.

"I want to kiss you," he mouths, pointing to his lips.

Oh, what the hell!

I nod without thinking twice. He goes for it. He slips an arm around my waist, his hand cups my cheek, and he leans in to kiss me deeply but I freeze. I freeze in place as if I've never done this before. As if the action of kissing is so foreign to me that I am completely dumbfounded and clueless about what to do.

I feel blindsided from the influx of feelings that overcome me when Derek puts his mouth to mine, and because of it, I rip myself from his grasp and shake my head.

"I can't. I'm so sorry!" I shout. My voice wavers. "I can't kiss you,

Derek! I'm sorry!"

I maneuver between swaying bodies until I'm outside. Bending my head and gripping my knees, I heave until my stomach muscles ache. When I straighten again, Chloe is right behind me because Chloe is always there.

"You good?" she asks, rubbing my back. I don't reply. "What happened? I saw Derek kissing you."

"That's what happened," I breathe. The taste of him still remains on my lips, despite my body's violent rejection of him.

"I don't understand."

"Me neither, Chloe. I don't understand why I couldn't…" I shake my head. "I gotta go."

She takes my hand, tugs on it a little, and makes me look her dead in the eye. "Promise me you won't go there." She knows what I'm thinking, what I'm always thinking.

I shake my head. *Of course I won't. I can't.*

"Promise me, Ava."

"I promise."

"Does he still live here?" I ask Bobby, the building's long-time doorman.

I slipped into the back of an Uber by the club, ready to recite the address to my dorm, but instead found myself rattling off Grant's address from memory. I hadn't said the street name in over a year, but it somehow, regardless of my drunken state, came as easily to me as my own apartment.

Bobby replies to my question with a curt nod and motions for me to enter the building.

I stumble into the elevator, lean my head against one of the glass walls, and insert the security code into the keypad without any fumbling or second-guessing. It doesn't strike me as odd that it comes so easily to me until about ten seconds later.

Fifteen months, and it's like I was here yesterday.

I reach his floor within a matter of seconds, and the familiarity of it—the wooden grain and paint color of his door—fills me with inexplainable fury. Balling my hand into a fist, I bang on the door. The face he gives me when the door opens is one of pure disbelief.

CHAPTER FOUR

AVA

The shock is like a light tap on my warm, flushed cheeks as soon as I see her robe: silk, purple, floral.

It completely smacks me in the face when I notice her hair: perfect, long, blonde.

An audible gasp escapes me when I see them standing together, when it dawns on me that he's still engaged, that the reason there wasn't a ring on his finger earlier tonight is because Grant isn't married *yet*.

It's really true. They got engaged. I stare at the proof of that gossip website. And when I see her with him, that beautiful woman, I sober up.

"*Oh my God.* I'm so sorry. I didn't know you guys were... *Oh my God.*"

Before disappearing, I can't stop myself from taking a peek in Grant's direction to find his expression varying between trepidation, shock, and pity.

I detest that last one.

I whip around and head to the elevator toward my hasty exit but turn when I hear him murmur, "Give me a minute," into his apartment and shut the door behind him. My eyes widen. I glance between him and the door, but my gaze never lands on him for long. I can't face him. I can't face myself.

Homewrecker.

"Are you insane?! Go back in there right now," I whisper-shout, point a wobbly limb to his penthouse door. He doesn't listen to me. He just keeps standing there, watching me, with his hands in his sweatpants pockets. "What? Don't...don't look at me like that. Go back in there." My voice is tough, angry, but that's just a mask for the fear and shame I feel.

"I will," he states with that deep voice, but I don't recognize it. It's low and reserved. It's so different from the way he used to be with me. Happy. Alive. And with that thought, something tugs in my chest, a longing I am not allowed to feel.

I shake my head to clear my thoughts. He continues to speak quietly.

"But... How are you getting home? Let me drive you."

Tears immediately burn behind my eyelids. I bite my lip to keep from crying.

"You can't... I didn't know... I wouldn't have come here if I had known, I swear. But please go back in there. Go. You're hurting her more with every second you're out here with me. Please." I plead with him. I put myself in her shoes, and I die inside.

Grant nods, so I turn away, but the sound of his voice catches me again. I can hear his hard swallow.

"Uh... Happy birthday, Ava," he tells me softly, strongly. "Again. The happiest."

The elevator doors open with the simultaneous sound of Grant's apartment door closing behind him. What I do next is something I know that I'll have to pray to God for forgiveness tomorrow, but I do it anyway. I don't get into the elevator. No, I do something positively insane.

I tiptoe to Grant's apartment door and seat myself outside of it. Putting my ear to the door, I can hear Grant's every word.

CHAPTER FIVE

GRANT

It'll take more than a measly minute to process what just happened. *Who* just happened.

For now, I brace myself to apologize for the second time today.

Hannah isn't upset when I walk back into the penthouse, leaving Ava to fend for herself. Hannah doesn't seem hurt or angry like she did earlier. She's just...curious.

"I'm sorry, Hannah," I say to her from across the room. "I shouldn't have left you...I shouldn't have gone after her. Again, I'm sorry."

My fiancée remains silent. Her eyes aren't murderous like I suspected them to be. She isn't furious at what I did, and that somehow both shocks and terrifies me. I'd almost rather her yell like she did earlier, the sensible response, than look so...indifferent.

"So, it's true. I wasn't just saying it based on some self-inflicted insecurity. You really want her," Hannah finally tells me through a sigh of surrender. "I'm not the one you want. You want to be with her."

Now, I *really* wish she hadn't said that. It hasn't been easy sterilizing my brain of Ava in the last fifteen months, so to prevent Hannah's words from penetrating inside of me, from allowing myself to feel them and to yearn for the girl I'll never again have, I create a mental barrier in my mind. I take a deep breath and tell my fiancée, "Hannah, I'm engaged to you, not her. We went through this. I chose you."

Hannah tilts her head and watches me. I am under a figurative microscope. I am being studied right now, the effects of Ava coming here surely on my face. There is no escaping it. I know that.

"But you'd rather marry her, if you had a choice."

But I don't. I don't have a choice. Hannah is my fiancée, so here we are.

I reply to Hannah with the one thing I've been telling myself on repeat, trying to dampen the blow when I allow myself to remember that Ava will forever be in my past.

"I can't marry her, Hannah. She can't have children."

The taste of metallic blood forms on my tongue when the lie leaves my mouth. To avoid the guilt that festers inside me, I nod toward my bedroom and follow Hannah back into our bed.

CHAPTER SIX

AVA

I suppress the urge to vomit until I reach the front of Grant's building.

When I am comfortably hunched over the cold metal, I let it all out into the public trash bin a few yards from the lobby door. Retching violently while holding back tears, I squeeze my eyes shut and convince myself that the lump in my throat is from the nausea and not from what I heard upstairs.

I can't marry her, Hannah. She can't have children.

I don't expect it to hurt more than when I initially heard his voice utter those words, but every minute that passes, my lungs feel like they're being pressed on. My heart feels like it's being pressed on.

Even though what he said is the truth, it paralyzes me. I am stunned, embarrassed, hurt.

Days later, and I still overhear it in my head like I'm seated outside his door. How nine words could affect a person this way, I'll never know.

But just like I could admit the pain that Grant's words caused, and the reality of them, I also understand that I am not defined by my pain. I am not defined by my circumstances. I am me, and I'm in a good place now. In the last fifteen months, I've improved. I'm better. Healthy. The worst part of what happened that night isn't what he said. It isn't seeing her in his apartment. The part that stings the most is how uncharacteristic it was of me to go there after what I accomplished this past year.

Self-growth. Self-worth. *Self-fucking-sufficiency.*

It's like I regressed into the girl from last year the moment I saw him again. I can't bear the idea that Hannah now likely thinks the same of me as he does: that I'm broken, that I need fixing. Something about that urges me to prove myself.

I don't like what I'm about to do, but I also don't sit around waiting for shit to happen anymore.

I'm not sure if her number is the same, but when I click her contact and it *is* Grant's sister, Annie, who answers the call, I sigh in relief.

"Ava? Ava Campbell?" I've stumped her by calling.

"Hi, Annie. Yeah, it's me. I'm sorry for calling you out of the blue, but I'll be quick. Can I please ask you to send me Hannah's number?"

The other end of the line is dead. Looks like I've rendered her speechless.

Her brother's ex-girlfriend is asking for his current fiancée's number. I am a walking telenovela.

"Uh… Can I ask why?" I explain that I owe Hannah an apology. Annie doesn't react because I'm sure Grant told her all about what happened.

She showed up hammered. She was acting crazy. Hannah was pissed.

I end the call once Annie accepts my explanation, and I immediately type out an apology that I know can't possibly suffice. I do it anyway.

Me: Hi. It's Ava Campbell. I wanted to apologize for the other night. It is not an excuse, but I was very drunk. It was a huge invasion of privacy, and I did not mean to disrespect you in any way. I really am sorry. I hope you can forgive me.

She replies almost immediately. Astonishment overcomes me when I read her single-worded response.

Hannah: Forgiven.

CHAPTER SEVEN
AVA

Yesterday was move-in day.
Chloe and I finally moved in together into a two-bedroom apartment in Midtown. I feel really good about it. I feel proud.

I got a job with Mr. Homer at the beginning of my last semester at NYU, which is how I was able to save up for this big move. He's a lawyer. Cue the mention of irony because *I know*, but my boss is decent and honest. He practices real estate law. I'm his assistant.

On my way home from work today, lugging my knitted tote bag in million-degree weather, I burst through the front door of my apartment and welcome the air conditioning. I sigh happily then turn to my roommate in the kitchen.

"Hey. In case you were wondering, I am the biggest loser to ever live. Your roommate is a record breaker, Chloe Danes."

She rolls her blue eyes at me from her seat at the kitchen stool. She reaches out to hand me a Twizzler. When I chomp on it, she squeaks like I've murdered a kitten.

"You're supposed to peel it, you witch!" she exclaims. " Anyway, aside from the obvious, why are you a loser?"

I flick her cheek. Then admit, "I texted Hannah Butch soon-to-be-Wilder."

Chloe freezes and becomes quiet.

Chloe Danes is never quiet.

"Nice. I've rendered you speechless, too," I mumble, picking Twizzler bits out of my molars with my pinky nail. "Also, we should probably go to the dentist."

Chloe and I are both junk food fiends. I have found my sugar-lover match. Grant would have an aneurism if he looked through our pantry. Not an organic item in sight.

"Ava. Ruth. Campbell. I am still processing what you just told me. Shut your ever-loving trap *up!*" she whines in a high-pitch yell. I stand at the kitchen counter across from her.

"I asked Grant's sister for her number, so I could apologize after that night. I am so embarrassed, Chlo." I look up at the ceiling and groan.

Chloe laughs at me. She also rolls her eyes. "Your guilty conscience is going to be the death of you, Ruthie. I cannot believe you did that."

I open the fridge, bend to browse the contents, then close it knowingly. There is nothing of nutritional value in here. I turn at the fridge to glare at my best friend.

"I hate you," I say. "A little bit."

"Good, because I hate you a little bit, too. Just for the hell of it. Pizza or burgers?" she asks regarding dinner. Chloe grabs her purse while I change my work flats into sneakers before we seek a relatively healthy meal.

"Sushi," I reply, hooking my arm through hers at the door. "And since I'm the epic loser in this duo, you're paying."

CHAPTER EIGHT
GRANT

"Would you be okay with that?"

I sit at Annie's breakfast nook and try to process her question, stunned that she's even asked. Is my sister serious right now? Because I have no idea if I would be okay with Annie asking Ava to nanny for her.

When I have yet to reply, Annie continues. "I'm desperate, Grant. And she's a good kid. For all I know, she could be unavailable. She might not even live in New York anymore. She could say no immediately, but I had to ask you first before trying. Please?"

Her blue eyes blink at me from across the table. I flip her off then tell her yes, only because of how sure I am that Ava will decline the job offer. There is just no way she'll accept. Not after what we've been through.

"You owe me big time. And I want her on speaker when you ask."

It's instant. With Ava, it's always instant. That burst of intense emotion in my chest when I hear her voice or see her face.

"Hello?" Her voice is questioning. I can't imagine what she's thinking. Probably about how to get as far away from my family as she can.

My sister does what she does best: small talk. I enjoy eavesdropping. What I love even more is the sound of Ava's soft voice.

I learn that she works part time.

I learn that she, in fact, does live in New York.

I learn that she lives with a girl named Chloe in Midtown.

"Okay," Annie exclaims. "So, the reason I called."

Ava chuckles, and my stomach tightens, then rolls. I stiffen at my body's unexpected reaction to my ex-girlfriend's laugh.

"You mentioned you work part-time, and I was wondering if you're in the market…for…*another job?*"

"Oh," Ava says, her tone surprised. "Um, okay…I wasn't looking for anything. Why do you ask?"

The phone sits on the table between Annie and me. My older sister hunches into the marble, squeezes her eyes shut, and crosses both fingers, holding them up in the air. Then, she tells Ava, "Because I'm looking for a nanny and I would literally give you my left kidney if you said yes."

Ava doesn't laugh at Annie's joke. Ava doesn't say anything at all. I glance at the phone to find the screen still counting every second of the call. She didn't hang up.

"Uh…" she rasps. "Um, I don't know… Uh, sorry, do you think that would be appropriate?"

She isn't saying no. Across the table, Annie mouths, "That's not a no!"

I can't possibly imagine Ava accepting this job, but I'll let Annie have hope. She hates me too much to agree to being around my family. I also feel terrible about this call. She's clearly uncomfortable that Annie is asking.

"Well, if you're referring to my brother, I would *never* put you in a position where you'd be uncomfortable. He won't be allowed to come over when you're here, and—"

Ava interrupts her. "Annie, I appreciate it, but—"

"I'll pay you $500 a day!" *Fucking Annie.* If she knew Ava at all, she'd know that the prospect of money won't change her mind.

"Um… No way. That is way too much money." Ava sighs heavily. "If you really need the help, I'll do it for free. We can figure out the… *other stuff* later."

Fuck, I love her.

I still love her.

Annie fists her phone and puts her lipstick-painted mouth close to the tiny mic. "I am *not* letting you work for free. I'm only letting you watch my kids if you agree to get paid."

Ava replies with a quiet and skeptical, "Okay?"

Before Annie can discuss logistics, Ava calls out, "Wait! I'm not doing it for $500 a day!"

Holy shit, I really do love her.

I continue to eavesdrop on the logistics because I want to hear her voice for as long as possible. When the conversation finally ends and Annie hangs up the call, she looks at me with hearts in her eyes. I force myself to say something about the doubt I have that Ava will stick to this job. She'll see a photo of me at Annie's and bolt.

"Annie, you're a little too excited about this. Calm down."

"Grant, Madison is getting older. She wants someone who could hang out with her like she does with me, and I know Ava. I know she's a good girl, and I won't have to worry about making her sign an NDA. I can trust that she'd never go to the press. This is a big deal for me," she whines. "Don't ruin it."

Annie kicks me under the table, then rummages around the kitchen, cleaning up absolutely nothing.

I kiss my sister's head and say goodnight before leaving her brownstone. I stare out the windshield like I'm on autopilot on my drive home.

Ava. Working for Annie. *Ava.*

Something tells me I should have told Annie no.

CHAPTER NINE
AVA

"Chloe, if I have to see Grant and Hannah being all over each other and shit, I'm going to projectile vomit."

I'm too nice. Annie sounded desperate, and I know she wouldn't have called me unless it was important, so I said yes to nannying her kids. I'm scheduled to work every day from three to eight. We discussed the arrangement in detail, and now, it's too late to back out.

"Set your boundary. You know how to do that now, babe. Be upfront with Annie when you go over there today."

Boundaries. Limits. All the things in my life that needed tweaking have been tweaked. The boundaries Chloe is referring to are the ones I seemed to have been missing when Grant was pushy about us being together, forcing me to tell him things I didn't want to. I didn't stand my ground last year. I barely had boundaries with him because he made it impossible. The guy had a goal in mind, and nothing was going to stop him. Nothing *did* stop him.

But I hope he's happy. Truly. That's all I could do for myself at this point. I forgive him because holding onto what once weighed me down so heavy is over and done with. I hope him and Hannah are happy, I really do. I want him to have everything his heart desires. I want him to have kids.

I can't marry her, Hannah. She can't have children.

I inhale and exhale to get my head out of the gutter. Then, Annie texts me.

> Annie: Thibault will be there in twenty minutes. Thank you!!!!!!!!!

Annie's driver picks me up outside of my apartment at three o'clock sharp. I don't bother addressing him by name since I have all of zero guesses on how to pronounce it.

It's a twenty-minute drive to Annie and Jackson's brownstone. The street they live on is quiet, green, and gorgeous.

That blue-eyed beauty swings the front door open and rushes toward me with opened arms. Thank God she doesn't look like Julia Wilder. Babysitting for Grant's clone would make me physically ill.

After a lively (*obviously*) welcome, Annie gives me a tour of the house. I am not mad about spending five hours a day here. The furniture, the wallpaper, the hardware; it's all rich, immaculate, stunning. My apartment doesn't hold a candle to this gorgeous house.

Madison's bedroom is a little girl's dream—canopy bed, butterfly wallpaper, pink *everything*. I guess it pays off to be the oldest kid in the family.

Annie's youngest, Josh, wakes up from a nap during the tour that's still going on because this house is massive. His cheeks are red, his hair is a mess, and his head lays on Annie's shoulder with his eyes on me.

"Put your arms out. I want to see if he'll go to you," she says.

I follow Annie's directions and laugh at her excited expression when Josh climbs into my arms.

"No, you don't understand. He doesn't let *anyone* hold him."

I believe I have secured this job indefinitely.

I agree to a $500 a day compensation since Annie refuses to pay me anything less. That's *$100 an hour.* I can't be sure if accepting this job makes me lucky or unfortunate. She said she won't let her brother come over when I'm here, but how realistic is that? I'm sure one of the kids will have a birthday party or Annie will host a dinner for her family. Grant and Hannah will attend. And there I'll be—single, with a kid on my hip who could never, ever be mine.

I hear those words every single night before I go to bed.

I can't marry her, Hannah. She can't have children.

I wonder if that excuse was sufficient for Hannah. I wonder if she realized that Grant being with me *is* ridiculous since I can't have kids. I wonder if it was enough for her to keep her dresser drawers full.

Annie asked me to stay late tonight since her and Jackson have an event to go to.

I've only been working here for a week, which is why she was desperately apologetic. I said yes, of course. I'm not sure what it is, but I genuinely enjoy helping Annie. I feel useful.

It helps that her kids are obsessed with me.

Josh doesn't ever let me put him down, so I'm certain carpal tunnel is in my future. Jack insists I build Jenga structures with him and every night, Madison waits patiently for the hour she gets me all to herself since the boys' bedtime is at 7:00 and hers is at 8:00.

"Boys or Barbies," Madison says once we're comfortably seated across from each other on her pink bed. "Take your pick."

I bite the inside of my cheek to keep from laughing. This nine-year-old is giving me options for conversation.

I steer clear of the discussion about boys and choose Barbies. I was not a Barbie kid growing up, but I am ready to pretend as if that's all I played with.

"Ugh. I was really hoping you'd say boys," Madison groans.

"But Barbies are way more fun to talk about."

"In what world?" she sasses. I snicker. After too much time discussing a doll that I have zero recollection of ever playing with, Madison takes matters into her own hands and loudly asks, "So, what happened between you and Uncle Grant?"

Whoops.

My eyes laser focus on the clock on Madison's night table. 7:57. I spring off of the floral comforter.

"Would you look at the time, Miss Madison? It is time for you to go to bed!"

"Nu-uh," she whines. "I have three more minutes. You came over for Thanksgiving last year and then...?"

I bop her nose, kiss her cheek, and say, "I'll need a lot longer than three minutes for that story. Night, cutes."

Closing Madison's bedroom door, I head over to the laundry room to fold my stuff that just finished in the dryer. I do my laundry here because it's infinitely cleaner and easier than the basement laundromat in my building. When Chloe is running out of underwear and is too lazy to do a proper load, she hands them to me in a mesh bag and says, *"Wash these at your rich boss's house, will ya?"*

Once I've arranged my folded laundry in a big Ikea bag, I go downstairs to check my phone. Annie texted less than ten minutes ago that she'll be home in an hour, so when the front door begins to unlock while I'm killing time on my phone, I panic. *Literally panic.*

I shake as I tiptoe to the kitchen and remove a fork from the kitchen sink, wielding it like a weapon. I hold it close to my chest and hide behind the kitchen island. I am the world's worst babysitter.

Finally, a deep voice rumbles, "Hello?" into the empty kitchen.

No.

Oh God, this is worse than an intruder. I'd rather an intruder!

Heavy footsteps grow louder as he walks toward me. He stops at my feet. I stare at Grant's black loafers.

"Ava?" he asks from eight stories above me. "Uh… what are you doing here? Where is—give me the fork." Handing it to him without making eye contact, I come to terms with the sheer embarrassment I feel at the fact that I was holding a kitchen utensil as a weapon and about what happened the last time I saw him.

Mostly about what happened the last time I saw him.

"Sorry," I mumble. I can feel my cheeks heat. "I thought you were an intruder."

He is apologetic when he rushes to say, "Shit. My bad. I came over to drop something off for the kids. I thought Annie would be here. Sorry."

"Um," I croak. "Okay."

I haven't looked into his eyes yet. He must notice because he asks, "You can't bear the thought of looking me in the eyes? It's that bad?"

"What's that bad?" I rasp.

"Your hatred toward me."

Hate him? Never. I never hated him!

But we shouldn't be discussing anything to do with him and me right now. This man is engaged to another woman. Us being alone in the same room together is inappropriate, but I'm not going to ask him to leave his own sister's house to avoid talking to him.

"I…" I swallow hard. "I don't think this conversation is appropriate. I could leave early, and you'll babysit until Annie and Jackson get home. It shouldn't be more than forty-five minutes."

"No," he grunts. "You stay. I'll go."

His footsteps fall as he aims for the front door. Before leaving, he calls out, "Make sure Thibault drives you home. Goodnight, Ava."

(Tee-bow! That's how it's pronounced!)

"Night," I mumble back.

CHAPTER TEN

AVA

Nine-year-olds these days are really something else. Madison's line of questioning has the maturity threshold of a forty-year-old woman.

"Are you an attorney, or you just work for one?" she asks when glancing at my computer.

I've been sending out a few emails for Mr. Homer from Annie's living room sofa. Madison seems to enjoy my company and won't leave my side, even when her mom is in the next room. I don't mind hanging out with her, though. I kind of love it, actually. My inner child feels cool that she's friends with the popular girl whose bed has a canopy.

I tell her that I work for a lawyer, and on her own, she translates lawyer to attorney.

"I just work for one."

"What's your boss's name?" she asks.

"Mr. Homer. Are you enjoying this interrogation?"

"Yes. Moving on," she states with a wave of her Rubix-Cube-sized hand. "Where are you from?"

"I'm from Northern California."

"Frisco or Berkeley?"

I laugh. "How do you even know that?"

Madison rolls her eyes at me. "An answer, Ava. Please. I don't have all day." *This kid.*

I laugh out loud again. "Neither. I'm from a place called Arcata."

"Is that close to Napa Valley?"

"It's not too far from there."

"Aww. I think Uncle Grant's wedding was going to be there!"

Gut. Wrenching.

I don't probe this Benjamin Button nine-year-old for more information. Instead, I say, "That sounds cool!" Thankfully, her questions stop when it's time for her to go to sleep.

When Annie comes back downstairs after putting Madison to bed, she faces me with a remorseful and apprehensive expression. She's about to ask me something Grant-related.

"I offered Grant to come over for leftovers after you leave for the day, but because Thibault is running late tonight, we both agreed I should ask if you're okay with it first."

Annie and Jackson don't ever let me take the subway, a cab, or an Uber back home. They insist on having their driver take me back to Midtown every night. Tonight is no exception, although Thibault is picking Jackson up from the airport and won't be back until closer to nine. I guess when Annie invited Grant, she hadn't known yet that Jackson's flight was delayed.

"I can run outside and give him a Tupperware if it's—"

"No way," I interrupt. "That's so depressing. Let him come. I'll just hang out in the living room, if that's okay."

So much for not being put in a situation that would make me uncomfortable, boss.

We give each other tight smiles when Grant gets to Annie's. I won't lie and say that I feel neutral about seeing him because I don't. I don't think I'll ever feel neutral when it comes to him. I think a part of me will always enjoy having him near me. But Grant isn't even a little bit happy to see me.

I showed up to his apartment when he and his fiancée were lying in bed together.

He must hate me.

He *totally* hates me.

I bury myself in the crevices of the furthest couch from the kitchen where I assume Grant is eating Annie's delicious leftover dinner. So far, two out of four Wilder kids cook immaculately.

After working for another half hour, I sign out of the law firm's server, shut my laptop, and slowly walk toward the kitchen. I halt mid-step when I hear my name being said in a quiet murmur. I can hardly make anything out, so I walk a little closer until I do.

"What about Ava?" Annie asks.

Grant grunts and replies, "Don't tell her."

Junior Year Ava would never have confronted the situation. This Ava does.

I turn the corner of the dining room. Immediately, Grant and Annie's whispers come to a silent hush.

"Don't tell me what?" I talk to Grant and try to glare at him, but his back faces me, so I stare at his hair.

I hate his hair.

"Hello?" I say into the kitchen when no one replies.

"Nothing," Grant replies passively.

Nothing? The feeling of embarrassment is so strong in my chest that it morphs into anger, and I'm anxious to know what he was referring to. I get that I made a mistake, but God, I'm still a person. *Don't tell Ava?* I won't stand for that. I'm going to stand up for myself now that I finally know how to.

If Annie wasn't witness, I'd give him a piece of my goddamn mind. For now, I grit out, "If you're going to talk about me, at least have the decency to be discreet about it, asshole."

CHAPTER ELEVEN
GRANT

Four encounters.

Four times I've seen Ava since the breakup, and awe fills me, each time greater than the last. I'm taken aback that she called me an asshole the other night, that she has it in her to be so bold, but I'm coming to realize that Ava changed. I no longer have any idea who she is anymore. I don't know who she is when she isn't broken.

I don't know who she is when she is all blaze.

Annie's voice on our phone call brings me back to reality, the contracts on my desk posing as an easy excuse for distraction. I don't want to think about, or answer, Annie's question, but she isn't getting the hint.

"Grant, when I asked if I could hire Ava, you said yes. This is part of it! I'm not missing this trip, and I'm not going without her!"

I lean against my desk before replying to Annie with gritted teeth. I rub my temples in frustration and take a longer than necessary moment before losing it on my sister.

I won't survive it. I can't let her do this.

"Annie, you're not bringing my ex-girlfriend to Montauk. I'm not spending a week at the beach house with her in a fucking bikini."

Spit flies out of my mouth at my terse words. My chest tightens from nothing other than fear. Fear at being near someone for days, someone who is a forbidden temptation, one who will possibly be half-naked.

"I'll tell her to wear a one-piece," Annie replies sarcastically. It infuriates me.

"That's not the point!" I shout into the receiver. I hang up the call, then toss the phone onto my desk. Dina must hear the commotion behind the glass separating us, so she enters the office without warning and sits herself across from me. She doesn't have to ask for me to know she'd like an explanation.

"Remember when I told you that Ava works for Annie now?" Dina nods once. "Well, Annie wants her to come to the beach house next week."

We spend a few weeks every summer at my parents' beach house up in Montauk. Our entire family goes, including Annie's kids. Typically, she brings her nanny to help watch them. However, this year, her nanny is my ex-girlfriend.

Dina gives her two cents because she always does. "You agreed to let Annie hire Ava. I think it's only fair for you to allow Ava to go and for you to decide whether or not you're going to come with."

I put my face in my hands, take a deep breath. "Dina," I whisper. My voice is pleading. "I can't be around her. It's too hard."

"Have we established if Ava even wants to come?"

"She asked me before asking Ava."

"Talk to Annie in person," Dina instructs in level manner. "Have her ask Ava, then go from there."

I park outside of Annie's brownstone the next morning in a bitter mood. I don't bother with formalities when I make it to the breakfast nook and find Annie sipping coffee, staring at her MacBook.

"Tell me you didn't invite her yet," I state as soon as I slide onto the bench opposite her.

"I didn't. I'm waiting on you." Not bothering to hide my desperation, I look at Annie. I look her in the eyes, and she sees exactly what she needs to in them.

"What's your best-case scenario?" she asks. I don't bother to give a verbal answer, just shoot her an obvious glare. She shakes her head and mutters, "Okay, don't answer that. Do you want to at least try being friends with her?"

I scoff like she's being stupid. Ava would never agree to being my friend. And me, her *friend*? How could I just… No, it's impossible.

"That'll never happen, An."

"I'm asking you, if it's a possibility, would you want that?" Annie pushes.

How could I be friends with her? How could I be in her life when I know I'd do anything to be with her again? Being Ava's friend threatens every ounce of self-control I have in me.

I'll want to kiss her. I'll want to have her, and I know that I can't.

But then I wonder, what if we *could* be friends? What if it's enough? What if that small piece is enough to satiate the real desire that I have for her?

I decide, hypothetically speaking, that having Ava in my life as a friend is better than having nothing of her at all. It's better than the hostility and hatred I've been getting from her lately.

I tell Annie yes. Then we do that same thing we did a few weeks ago where we place Annie's phone between us, on speakerphone.

"Hey, girl!" she exclaims cheerfully when Ava answers the call.

"So…here's the deal. My family goes to Montauk every summer, and we're going next week. I was hoping you'd come with?"

She gets right to it. I'm sure Ava's eyes are widened after hearing Annie's proposal.

"Annie…" Ava's voice is uncertain, raspy. "That's a lot."

I want to hug her through the phone. Annie is quite literally torturing Ava with all of this. I'm almost mad that she's even asking.

"I know, I know! I just love having you, and the kids adore you, so I figured it was worth a shot since—"

"Stop pushing her," I whisper to Annie, anger filling me unexpectedly. I try to be as quiet as possible, but Ava hears me.

"Oh," she says. "You."

I hate the hostile tone in her voice. I hate how much she hates me. "Me. The asshole."

Ava takes a deep breath. "Are you going to be there?" she asks, her voice nervous and a little shaky. "Is Hannah going to…"

"No," I reply immediately. I would never do that to her, to either of them.

It helps that she is no longer my fiancée.

Ava pauses, then says, "I'm assuming I'm on speaker, so, Annie, could you find a backup? If not, let me think about it… And for the record, I don't think you're an asshole. Sorry I said that."

When Ava hangs up, Annie gives me the eyebrows, surely reading my shocked expression.

Did that really just happen? Did Ava just *apologize*?

CHAPTER TWELVE
AVA

I lay on the floor with the worst period cramps of my entire life when Chloe gets home from Broadway.

She was a theater major at NYU. If anyone belongs on a stage, it's my roommate.

She dumps her Mary Poppins bag on the couch, then lays beside me on the hardwood. "Why are we on the ground? You okay?" she asks, concerned.

I explain that my periods have gotten so insanely painful the last couple of months. I feel like I'm dying.

"Here if you need me."

"I know. How was work?"

"It was good. Busy, per usual. How was your day?"

Chloe lifts herself off of the floor and heads to the kitchen for a snack. She hands me one of two bags of Cheese-Itz before laying back down beside me.

"My day was weird. Annie wants me to vacation with Grant."

Chloe always seems to react in the best most appropriate way, no matter what I tell her. It must be a theater kid thing that she illustrates exactly what she's feeling with her beautiful face, and it's glorious. It's a mixture of surprise and genuine confusion when I tell her about the conversation surrounding Montauk.

"Do you want to go?" Chloe's voice is soft, caring. She gets how big of an ask this is.

"Yeah," I reply honestly. Who am I kidding? Of course I want to go.

That's the problem, isn't it? Even if Hannah won't be there, I shouldn't do this. I shouldn't spend a week with him. "But it just feels like cheating."

In between bites of Cheese-Itz, Chloe says, "You're not cheating on anybody. That's his fight, not yours. Your boss is asking for you to come on a family trip with her to the beach. Dude, there's no question. It's a free vacation. *Go!*"

I feel like the worst type of person for deciding to do this, but after leaving Homer's office the next day and stopping at a one-dollar pizza parlor for a quick slice, I head over to Annie's a little earlier than usual. The kids aren't back from school yet, so it's just Annie and me.

"So…" Annie looks all impish.

"I'll do it," I mumble.

"YEAH?" She sees my fearful and hesitant expression. She leans over the kitchen island and squeezes my shoulder.

"It's going to be okay. I promise. I'll take up all of your time. You'll be too busy to even look at him."

ANYONE DESCRIBING THIS property as a house is clearly blind. The beach house in Montauk is a mansion. A beach *mansion*.

I follow Annie down the outdoor stairs to the backyard after having just got here. We drove the two hours altogether, stopping several times for Madison to pee. Apparently, she recently learned the benefits of drinking water and is on a bender.

The Wilders are lounging on the chaises and the outdoor furniture placed throughout the lush backyard. Julia and Layla are in the giant pool; Callum and Ben are shirtless, playing chess at a mosaic-tiled table. Grant is lying on a chaise alone at the far end of the backyard. I let myself look for a split second before he picks his head up and notices that I'm here. That I joined his family vacation like this isn't the most bizarre thing in the world.

It's shady where Grant is laying down, ankles crossed, eyebrows furrowed. He's immersed in a book about business, I think. He's got a summer tan that you wouldn't know was a tan unless you knew how pale he usually is. A subtle print decorates his bathing suit, but I can't see what it is from here. He's wearing a white linen shirt. It has short sleeves, is unbuttoned, and reveals his naked chest.

His naked chest.

Annie saunters toward her family, holding Josh on her floral-clad hip. To catch her family's attention, she shouts, "Why is there no music playing?!"

Splashes sound as Julia and Layla hurriedly emerge out of the pool to give Annie and me soaking wet hugs. Julia leans her head back, and I gasp to myself at how similar she looks to Grant, those striking eyes piercing mine. She tells me with sincerity, seemingly reading the hesitation on my face, that she's happy I'm here and that she's looking forward to spending time with me. Layla greets me with a paper-white smile.

"Ava. You look amazing. How are you?" she asks after hugging me tightly.

"I'm doing good," I reply casually, matching her smile. Quickly, I deem Layla an ally, so I lean into her and whisper, "Hey, is it really weird that I'm here?"

She winks mischievously. "No. It'll be an adventure."

I couldn't agree more.

I greet Ben, then Callum, and finally, brace myself to face the edge of the backyard where I know he's sitting. His serious gaze is already on me when my eyes find him. I lift my right hand and wave it lazily. He leans forward to get off the chaise and come over.

My heart immediately panics. Starting to sweat, I do anything but watch him walk over to me with all his attractiveness and his stupid, naked chest. When he hugs Annie, he kisses her head. I've always loved when he did that with his sisters.

"Hey, An," he greets with his signature, deep tone. He nods at me. "Ava."

"Hello."

"Welcome to Montauk."

"Thanks."

It suddenly gets quieter than it was before Grant said anything to me. Everyone stares at us having our little chat. I'd stare too if it weren't me in this awkward exchange. I glance around with a neutral smile and nonchalantly wait for someone to do something.

After what seems like an unnecessary long time, Annie tells me to follow her into the house, so she could show me to my room. I can feel Grant watching us walk inside the house.

Once I'm indoors and positive no one can see me, I turn to observe their *real* reactions to me coming here. He talks to the twins and his parents. Julia says something to him, and he responds with a shrug, his palms facing up. It's like a *What can I do about it?* shrug.

I follow Annie up two flights of stairs and let my jaw drop when I see the bedroom that they've put me in. I turn to her.

"This is way too much. I don't need this nice of a room, Annie!"

She deadpans. "There are another four empty ones just like it. Get comfy."

Okay, boss. If you insist.

I put my bags down on the lilac, velvet bench at the foot of the bed. I sprawl my arms out to my sides, bounce back on the bed, and sigh. The stream of questions come immediately.

Does everyone in this house assume that I hate Grant? Does Hannah know that I'm here? Does Hannah care *that I'm here?*

What have I gotten myself into?

CHAPTER THIRTEEN
GRANT

She can barely look at me, and it's driving me insane.

How do I feel extra shitty right now about something I've known for over a year? But watching it happen in real-time hits harder than I thought it would.

She despises me. She hates my guts.

We're grilling outside for dinner tonight. I am manning the grill when my family members slowly trickle into the backyard. The dining table is set flawlessly, and the weather is perfect. The sunset creates that perfect ambiance. It's gotten cooler since this afternoon, the lack of sun forming the salty winds you could only get from being seaside.

Contrary to how I feel today, this is my favorite place in the world.

Ava carries the baby on her hip when she follows Annie's two other kids to the back. I overhear Madison demanding she be placed beside Ava for dinner, making me smile.

I text Annie while we're seated and feasting.

> Me: Does she have everything she needs?
>
> Annie: Yeah. She's in good hands, bro.

Me: I know. Just making sure. Thank you.

When I look up, I catch Ava looking between Annie and me. We're both hunched over our phones, so it's apparent that we're texting. When Ava thinks I'm not looking, she blows out a heavy breath through her O-shaped lips. It's like she has to brace herself to get through this week with me.

I don't know how I let Annie let her come. I can't imagine what this feels like for her.

What does *it feel like for her?*

Does she look at my family and feel glad to be here, or does she see the differences and feel like an outcast?

The last thing I want is for Ava to feel uncomfortable being here, stuck with us for the next week.

Everyone's phones vibrate and ring at the same time when I, without thinking, text our family group chat to remind them to make Ava feel comfortable and included. They all look at me. Ava pretends to be focused on the steak on her plate, but she blushes hard. She's embarrassed.

Fuck.

She murmurs to Annie that she's going inside to the bathroom. I watch her rake her dainty fingers through her short hair when she walks toward the house.

She cut it. Her golden-brown hair isn't long anymore.

"You're so dumb!" Annie whisper-shouts to me across the table.

"I know. I wasn't thinking. I'm going to go apologize."

I catch Ava on the way out of the bathroom and attempt at an immediate apology. "I'm really sorry. I—"

"At least try to be subtle about it," she mumbles. Her tone is sarcastic, but she's serious.

"I was just asking them to make you feel welcome. That's it, I swear," I explain, antsy for her to believe me. This trip is becoming even more awkward than I thought it would.

"They've always made me feel welcome, but even if they didn't, I can take care of myself," she snaps. "Don't do that again."

Holy hell. Who is this girl?

Ava is all fire. Ava is *different*.

CHAPTER FOURTEEN
AVA

I slept better than I have in my entire life last night.
I showered and watched a movie on the giant flat screen TV before drifting into a sun-induced coma.

How to Lose a Guy in Ten Days.

I'm hoping they film *How to Go on Vacation with Your Engaged Ex-boyfriend for Seven Days* next.

God, yesterday sucked. And for no reason! I knew what I signed up for when I told Annie I would come to Montauk with her family. It was my choice to come, and I'm fine.

I'm fine.

So what if we dated! He's just another guy, is what I tell myself. He's just my boss's brother. I'm just his sister's employee. That's all.

Now, we're on the sidewalk exiting the four cars it took to get the family here. Grandpa (Callum) promised Madison some ice cream, so we all decided to go into town to get some.

After getting Josh situated in his stroller with only a small scoop of vanilla to prevent him from dirtying his linen overalls, I return inside the novelty ice cream parlor to collect my ice cream from the pick-up counter. Once I'm done, I head onto the sidewalk toward the rest of the Wilder family holding my double scoop. Grant snickers immediately once he notices me but turns his head to try to hide it. I park myself beside him.

"What?" He shakes his head but doesn't respond. "Why are you laughing at me?"

"Why am I not surprised that you chose the ice cream flavor with the most food dye in it?"

I look down at my Dynamite Destruction Sherbet. "It's eye-catching."

"Yes. Which is why it's made for children." He holds back a smile or a laugh or both. His eyes are dancing. I suddenly want to swim in those bright green swirls, but instead, I quickly blink away.

This feels like cheating.

I snatch his scoop from his hand, put his ice cream cup beside my own, and look at him pointedly. He got Rocky Road.

"Just admit you're boring, and I'll be on my merry way."

Grant chuckles deeply.

We're *talking*. This feels *normal*. I don't hate it. I kind of love it.

I never said that.

"Let me have some," he says, nodding at my sherbet.

I pinch my eyebrows when I look at him. "Of my ice cream?" I ask. He nods. "Even with all of the food dye?"

He shrugs, then reaches his hand out. He instantly grimaces when he tastes it. "Oh my God, Ava," he laughs, handing the sherbet back to me. "That is terrible."

I nod curtly. "So, you're boring. You're admitting it."

He belts out a loud laugh, causing a tickling sensation to sprout in my middle. Butterflies, the kind I used to have with him last year, return.

What am I doing? He's *taken*. I can't be crushing on a guy who is unavailable for so many reasons.

I can't marry her, Hannah. She can't have children.

But he isn't making this easy when he mumbles, "Weirdo," ignoring his family's curious gazes and returning to his ice cream. I bite the inside of my cheek to hide my smile at the endearing name.

I love the way he's teasing me. I should not love the way he's teasing me.

CHAPTER FIFTEEN
AVA

Kids will be kids
Madison will be Madison.

It's nothing short of weird and awkward when she stands eye-to-eye with my scar. Granted, we're in bikinis on the beach, but I didn't think I'd have to worry about getting comments when I put this red bikini on. The scar is small.

Then again, Madison notices everything. She cocks her head.

"What is that?" she inquires curiously. She studies the shiny line in detail. I wonder what her nine-year-old mind is thinking.

I bloom red. I can feel my cheeks heat because she isn't quiet, and I'm pretty sure everyone heard that.

Before I have a chance to explain or stutter or laugh it off, Madison continues. "Did you have a baby?"

"HEY!" I slowly close my eyes when I hear his booming voice. "Mads. Hey, come here."

"Why?" she wonders.

"Now, Madison." His tone is strict and curt and unlike anything I've heard him use with his niece before.

I eye Madison's path toward her uncle and avoid eye contact with everyone who have presumably the same questions that she does. I slip my earbuds in, but I don't play anything. My mind is overflowing right now, and music will overwhelm me more. I can also overhear when Grant berates Madison several feet behind me. He doesn't speak too quietly, but that's probably because he sees the earbuds in my ears.

"Don't ask her that. Ever, Madison. That's private information. You know better."

"Ava doesn't care. She's my friend," Madison replies to his rebuke.

"Of course she's your friend, but it's about respect, Mads. That's called intrusiveness. It's not welcome, okay?"

My phone pings a minute later with a text. Grant's number is still blocked on my phone, so it seems he used Annie's phone to text me.

> Annie: It's Grant. I'm sorry about that. I'll make sure it doesn't happen again.

I swallow thickly and brace myself to face him. When my eyes find Grant's, I nod and offer up a small smile.

"Thank you," I mouth. Grant nods, and with his pouty lips, mouths back, "Of course."

I'M DOWNSTAIRS. I didn't have much of an appetite after what happened with Madison earlier, so I barely ate dinner. I'm here for a snack.

Grant sits at the dining table out on the back patio where we typically eat all of our meals. He's with friends I've never met before. Pretty ones. Handsome ones. Rich-looking ones.

I'm pretty sure they are smoking cigars. I'm sure because every year on my dad's birthday, Devon, Cooper, Connor, and I buy him a case of Cuban cigars that we all pitch in for. Well, my brothers never take my money, but it's been a tradition in the Campbell family for a while. I'd recognize that smell anywhere.

Grant is smiling with his friends. He's smiling, and it makes me happy. I guess that happens when you care about someone so much. Their happiness ensures your own.

I try to go unnoticed since I'm wildly intimidated by anyone who resembles Grant. Me being in his life for the meager six months we dated was an anomaly. Everyone knew it. I knew it. He knew it.

That's why I'm happy for him and Hannah. He found someone that makes sense. I sure as hell didn't.

I quickly shuffle through the dairy drawer in the wall-to-wall refrigerator and grab a Go-Gurt tube. Madison's favorite is strawberry, so I snatch a blueberry one. When I hear the back door open, I start for the stairs.

"Hey," he calls out after me. *Busted, Campbell.* I pause. Grant clears his throat. "Are you okay?"

I turn and feel my cheeks heat when I see him. He looks handsome. His face is sun-kissed and...

He's engaged. I really have to stop this.

I nod. With a raspy voice, I mutter, "Yeah, just..." I hold up the yogurt. His lips twitch, but he suppresses whatever smile he's tempted to give me.

"Do you want something to eat? There's a really good meat board outside. You're more than welcome to join. It's just a couple buddies of mine."

"Oh... Um, I'm okay. I don't know anybody."

"You know me...?" His voice is hesitant. He's not sure if that means anything anymore.

It does.

I miss him.

I shuffle my feet in a nervous tick.

"I'm kind of scared of your friends." I laugh awkwardly. "But thanks." Grant nods, so I dismiss myself. Before ascending the staircase, though, I hurry back to the kitchen and catch him halfway outside.

"Wait! Um…" He immediately comes back inside and shuts the door behind him. He gives me his full, undivided attention.

"Thanks for what you did earlier," I say sincerely. "With Madison. That was really nice of you."

His eyebrows pinch when he studies me for several long seconds. Finally, in a low voice, he states, "You don't have to thank me for that."

I shrug. "Well, I am anyway. Thanks. Again." I swallow and nervously curl my hair behind my ears. His eyes observe me, and they look pleased. He likes how nervous I am.

I slowly walk backwards.

"Um… have fun? Good night. Enjoy the meat board." I chuckle awkwardly. I groan and shake my head at myself.

"Good night, Ava," his deep voice rasps.

CHAPTER SIXTEEN
GRANT

Heartbreak followed by an unintentional reunion is a bizarre experience.

I knew I'd see her the night of her graduation, but I didn't expect to see her a single time afterwards. Now, this. She's at my family's vacation house. I stand next to her, and we act normal, and we get ice cream, and I'm in love with her.

I stand beside Ava casually when there is nothing casual about how I feel in my chest toward this beautiful girl. That, to me, is bizarre. How you can have so much love for someone while you can't do anything about it.

You can tease them about ice cream and defend them when they're uncomfortable, but you can't...*love* them. Act on the love. *God*, it's *weird*. And I don't mean anything sexual. Not at all. With Ava, the thing I desire most is hugging her. Holding her. It feels like my arms are empty, as is my chest, since she left. I've made love to her, and I've kissed her, but nothing compares to the fullness I'd feel every time Ava was in my arms. Like I had a duty. Like my life boiled down to these moments that genuinely felt like I was fulfilling my purpose in life.

Loving her. Taking care of her. Protecting her.

The bottom line is, I really miss holding Ava.

Annie's second, Jack, wanders into the living room where I'm sprawled out on the couch. Dina sent over some docs via email that I'm lightly perusing. I vowed to leave work alone until I'm back in the city—I don't need to review these documents right now—but finding ways to keep busy here has been difficult. She's everywhere.

I lay in bed, I hear her laughing down the hall.

I sit outside, I watch her with my niece and nephews with love in her eyes. She loves my family. We love the same people. Something about that feels…significant. And don't get me started on the bikini situation.

One piece, my ass.

"What's up, Mr. Jack? Come over here."

"*Shhhhhhhhh.*" It sounds more like *Thhhhhhhhhh.*

I lean my head back and stifle a laugh. "Okay," I whisper. "Why are we whispering?"

"We're playing hide and go seek."

"Who's trying to find you? Mads?"

Jack shakes his head when he cases the living room to find a hiding spot. Then, I hear Ava loudly count down from twenty from the backyard. Finally, he looks at me to answer.

"Aunty Ava. Can you help me?"

Aunty Ava?!

Mimicking Jack, I sit up on the couch and scan the living room, landing on a good hiding spot. The most obvious one. I nod my head toward the big living room window, the view of the ocean breathtaking every time even after all these years, and lead Jack to his hiding spot behind the curtain. I situate his tiny body directly behind mine and stand in front of him to help hide him better.

When Ava finally strolls into the living room, I stand straight. After all, I have a job to do.

"Hey, um…" She blushes. I love when she does that. *Why do I love when Ava is shy with me?* "Have you seen Jack?"

"Who?"

"Jack. Little Jack."

"Never heard of him in my life."

"Wha…?"

"I have no idea who you're talking about."

Ava's face is painted with confusion, but when I nod my head to where Jack is hiding, it dawns on her. She snickers.

Ava positions her hand to an approximation of Jack's height. "Yay high? Jack Wilson. His mom is Annie Wilder-Wilson?"

"No," I mutter. "Sorry. If I meet someone of the sort, I'll let you know."

Ava can't contain her poker face any longer, but she doesn't want Jack to know she knows, so she squeezes her eyes shut, scrunches her entire face, and stifles a laugh.

I'm in awe. I'm in fucking awe watching her like this.

She looks so beautiful. She is the most endearing human being I've ever met.

My heart feels fuller in this moment than it has the last eighteen months.

Naturally, Jack is bored at this point. He jumps out from behind me and shouts, "AUNTY AVA! I'M RIGHT OVER HERE!"

"Ahhhhh!" Ava feigns a frightened scream. "Jack! You scared me!"

I laugh at their exchange. I laugh harder when he happy dances to put on a show for us.

"I win! I win! Aunty Ava loses!"

"Good job, Jacky boy." Ava looks up at me and returns my smile with a small one of her own.

I gulp and quietly ask, "They call you Aunty Ava?"

Ava's face blooms pink, but she just shrugs.

"Why are you so shy around me?" I can't help it. It comes out of my mouth before I realize I probably shouldn't have said that. Luckily, though, she doesn't seem taken aback. Her reply is another shrug, but it's followed by a chuckle.

"Sorry if it's weird that I'm… I don't know, intrusive with your family and stuff. If Annie didn't need me, I wouldn't have… She seemed really desperate for someone to hire. I know I'm the wrong person for this job, but—"

"No way. Don't say that. Don't apologize. You're not intrusive. I see how much they love you. You're the perfect person for this job. Are you happy?" When Ava colors at my question, I quickly interject, "I mean, happy with the job."

"Yes to both. I'm gonna head back outside, 'kay?"

Ava smiles genuinely at me and waves before leaving the living room for the backyard, leaving me completely slack-jawed.

CHAPTER SEVENTEEN
AVA

"You are so great with those children, I commend you," Julia tells me with a kind smile.

We clean up the remnants of dinner, a roast Julia made that melted in my mouth. At the fridge where I'm reshelving the homemade lemonade she's made, I swivel and return her smile.

"Thanks for saying that. They're great. They make my job easy," I chuckle.

"Girl, you're going to be the best mom one day," Annie calls out, unaware that her compliment is baseless and impossible.

A block of lead forms in my throat, tightening, that pressure building with nowhere to go. I'm not exactly going to cry about it.

I flush red, my cheeks blister, beads of sweat form under the chunks of hair that haven't made it into my ponytail. I do a fairly good job at hiding my reaction because Annie continues, oblivious to my unease.

"That is, if you want kids? But I assume you do. How could you not? It's like you were born for motherhood." She meanders her way around the kitchen preparing a peanut butter and honey sandwich for Jack.

Her boisterous voice, genuine and excited, makes my middle somersault. Beads of sweat now form under my boobs from shame. Shame that I'm still ashamed after all this time, with no reason to be.

"Uh...," I croak, clearing my throat then swallowing. I put on a smile, and with the shake of my head, stutter, "I can't... Um, I can't—"

"What is it?" she asks, looking up at me with the bottle of honey between her two fists. "You can't what?"

I jump when he bellows from behind me, "Leave her alone, Annie! Get your daughter to do the same. Leave her be."

"What? I didn't—"

"I don't care," he spits furiously, interrupting her. "Just stop being intrusive. Give her some privacy, *holy shit*."

She doesn't know. She doesn't know about my past, so she is clueless that her comment means anything other than the implication that I'm good with kids, but he knows. Of course he does, and he defends me. This is the second time he's done that on this trip.

I turn to face him and shake my head. "It's fine," I mumble with an awkward half-smile. "It's fine. They didn't—"

"Don't defend them," he demands angrily.

"It's really okay. Seriously," I say quietly. I turn to Julia and Annie and smile, take a deep breath, put on a brave face. When my lips part, ready to explain, Grant interjects.

"Ava." He clears his throat. "Can I talk to you privately?"

Uh oh.

Julia and Annie's faces have that same look. *Uh oh.*

Aside from the obvious and painful awkwardness, this makes me want to laugh, the sheer hilarity that is this conversation. I've given myself away with the uncontrollable snicker that comes out of my mouth once Grant leads me to the outdoor patio and stands so we're face to face. His eyebrows furrow; he narrows his curious eyes.

"Why are you laughing?"

"It's just… What you did in there. It's okay. You care about this more than I do. It's fine. They didn't know. Thanks. I mean, it's really fine. I'm over it."

"What…what do you mean, over it?" He clears his throat. In a quiet voice, he mumbles, "Sorry. Now, I'm the one who is being intrusive."

I bite my bottom lip to keep myself from smiling, taming the happy burst in my chest at how much he still cares, despite him being with somebody else.

"Why do you care so much about it anyway?" I chuckle to mask the shakiness of my voice, nerves encompassing me. The feeling of shame because I'm being wrong in asking him, a taken man, that question.

His face softens. "Because I always will. I'm sorry if that upsets you. It seems that I can't help it when it comes to you."

Don't let yourself have hope. He's not available. He's just being decent because we have history.

I shake my head. For the third time today, my cheeks heat.

"It doesn't," I croak. I take a small step backward until I'm leaning against the wall behind me. I need some sort of support because I feel a little winded.

It's kind of crazy how I feel right now, actually, because I really shouldn't. I shouldn't like this. I shouldn't love this as much as I do.

He's with another woman. Another woman claims him as her own. If I allow myself to feel the happiness this conversation brings me, I break my own heart. I give myself that whiplash kind of disappointment that I already feel, so what's the point?

To go through this twice makes no sense.

"I appreciate it."

Grant gives me a small nod, straightens his already perfect posture, and slips his tanned, hairy hands into pressed, linen pockets. I slowly gaze up at him, from his hands to his face, then quickly look away. A small gasp exits my throat when I memorize what he looks like right now. The way he looks at me. The way his eyes roam my face. The way…

I don't know. I'm not going to bother trying to put a name to it.

Instead of being a mature adult and managing this awkward conversation between exes casually, I cover my face with my hands, so he can't see me smile. From ear to ear, in the palms of my clammy hands, I grin because I can't help it. I give myself hope with that grin. I let myself enjoy something that isn't mine to enjoy.

Hannah isn't the only barrier between us. The words he said to her when he didn't know I was listening is a huge part of it. I think it's the biggest part of it, actually.

My face remains hidden in my hands. Through the slips between my fingers, I manage to speak with a muffled sound. "Don't look at me like that."

"Like what?" he wonders, softening his voice.

"I don't know. Just… I don't know." I shake my head, trying to find the explanatory words but failing.

"Move your hands." His voice is husky, demanding. It's insanely hot.

When I don't listen right away, I can feel him take a step toward me. He circles both my wrists and moves my hands from my face for me.

I hold my breath in shock. My eyes are wide when I look up at him.

"There you are," he mutters deeply. He nods like this is the way it's supposed to be. Him having a perfect view of my face. *Finally* having a perfect view of my face.

I think I do the opposite of blush. I think the color drains from my face entirely.

"You're engaged," I whisper to the ground.

"I…" Grant closes his eyes slowly. When he opens them, they're guarded. "I'm sorry."

"'Kay," I rasp.

"For a lot of things." He lowers his voice significantly, even inches a little closer. "I really, really hope you know that."

I'm mute. He's caused the vocal cords in my throat to take a vacation. In response, I nod, and his lips twitch with a small sense of satisfaction.

I do know. I see it in the way you look at me. Like I'm an enigma. Like you can't believe I'm actually here.

When he dismisses himself almost professionally, my shoulders finally lower after having been raised for so long with nerves. When I slump them and release a sharp exhale, my mind goes haywire.

CHAPTER EIGHTEEN

AVA

"You could put Ava beside Grant!" Julia calls out to Layla before breakfast the next morning.

Layla is setting the table with fine china, and Annie brings out platters of food from the house before sitting down beside her husband. Callum always sits at the head of the table, and Julia sits opposite him. Ben is permanently seated beside his father. Grant moves around.

"Mom!" Layla shouts at her mother. She gives Annie a *Can you believe this?* look and I immediately want to crawl under the table and disappear.

I chuckle awkwardly, wave my hand around. "It's fine! He's *engaged*." The chuckle I conclude with sounds unusually loud because it's suddenly silent.

Everyone, every single member of this family, freezes.

I smile when I look around, but no one matches it. They all just stare at Grant.

"What?" I ask. My laughter wavers almost immediately. Again, no one matches my tone.

Layla finally perks up. "You didn't tell her?" she spits at Grant. Her eyes are squinted. She's furious. Layla spins around to face Annie.

"*You* didn't tell her?"

"I…" Annie stutters. She's guilty of something.

"Tell me what?" I ask hesitantly.

Grant's brother and sisters look amongst each other. Callum and Julia stay silent but observant. When Annie looks at Layla for assistance, she lifts her palms up and says, "Don't look at me. I'm not doing it."

"Not it!" Ben chimes in.

I face Grant then. His hands are tucked into the pockets of his swim trunks. These ones have tiny flamingos all over them.

He stares at the ground between his feet. His broad shoulders are hunched; his long black hair dangles off of his forehead when he bows his head. I have not heard a single word leave his mouth yet. When Annie orders him to tell me, he shakes his head.

What's going on?

"Um… I'm sorry. Did I say something out of line?" I ask hesitantly.

Annie mumbles, "Fuck it. Fine. I'll do it." She comes to stand in front of me. She clears her throat, and with an even tone, says, "Grant is not engaged."

My stomach bottoms out. I shake my head. "I don't understand."

Annie stands to my side, and we both look at Grant. He doesn't look up, so to catch his attention, Annie says, "Your turn," even though I'm sure he's been paying real good attention for the last five minutes. He shakes his head yet again.

The feeling of that last day, the day I found out who he was, when I discovered that he'd been dishonest, penetrates my skin until unhealthy anger festers.

"Tell me," I stress. I feel like I have to start reeling it in, so I don't yell at him in front of everybody.

"Ava—"

"Tell me," I repeat.

God, why couldn't this happen at Annie's? Why do *his parents* have to witness this drama?

"Annie told you," he mumbles. His voice is extremely tight and low, like he's purposefully being incoherent so I can't hear what he's saying.

"You're not engaged anymore?" I ask. My voice is disbelieving because I quite literally do not believe it.

"No," he responds deeply.

My heart stops at the confirmation. I feel like I'm going to vomit.

"You're not getting married?" I could ask this same question in a million different ways, and I still won't believe it.

"No."

I swallow thickly. I need a minute to process what in the world I just learned, but I can't do it with everyone watching this exchange. I just stand there and wait for somebody to make the next move. Thankfully, Annie pulls at my arm and brings me to a quiet corner. Before she says anything to me, she shouts over her shoulder, "Show's over! Everybody, eat!" into the backyard. I can hear shuffling behind me.

"I am so confused," I whisper to Annie. It's still really quiet, so I have to be ten times quieter.

Annie squeezes my shoulder. "I'm sorry I didn't tell you. He asked me not to."

That's what I overheard the night at Annie's house.

"What about Ava?"

"Don't tell her."

I take a giant breath and rub up my face. I shake my head.

"I think he was just embarrassed." Annie eyes me with remorse, but it isn't aimed at me. It's aimed at her brother. She feels sorry for him. I ask her why he would be embarrassed. "Maybe you guys should talk…"

Immediately, I say, "I can't. I don't know how to talk to him." I rake my fingers through my hair, wishing that things uncomplicate themselves between Grant and me on their own.

Annie demands that I take a breather, that she'll save me food.

I head straight for the beach.

CHAPTER NINETEEN
GRANT

I stare at nothing but her when I set my sights on where I'm going, drudging through the heavy sand.

I stop behind Ava's curled frame; knees resting against her chest, tanned arms enveloping her long legs tightly.

"Did she break up with you because I came to your apartment?" Her voice is small, timid.

The guilt in her question slays me. I instantly explain, "No. I ended it."

"Why?" she whispers. When I don't reply for fear of freaking her out, she asks, "Did you do it because of me?"

Ava's voice is soft, but when the words leave her mouth, there is a certain edge to them. I think she's hesitant to ask that question because of its implications.

Of course it was because of you, I want to tell her. I want to confess every part of love I still have for this woman, but I don't want to push her away.

Instead of replying the way I truly want to, I say a simple, "Yes."

I watch Ava directly below me as she lays her forehead into the crook between her knees. I watch her shake her head over and over. I don't know how right this is, but I do it anyway; I sit beside her on the warm sand and mimic the way she's sitting. We both place our gazes on the water, the vast ocean, the openness.

"That's crazy," she says after minutes of the waves being the soundtrack to this impending conversation. "I hope you know that."

"You make me crazy," I confess quietly. Ava inhales a sharp breath. I wait for her to say something. It's too long before she finally speaks.

"You broke off your engagement with Hannah," she says slowly, clarifying. "You are no longer marrying Hannah because of me." This time, she says it in a different way with sharper, genuine understanding in her voice.

I remain silent because there is nothing to object to. It's true. I left Hannah for Ava.

"You made a big mistake. We both know that."

"What part was a mistake?" I ask. When Ava finally gains the courage to look at me beside her, it only lasts for a second before she turns away again.

This girl still can't look me in the eye.

"*You walked away from your future,*" she whimpers.

"In pursuit of the one I really want."

I knew I wasn't over Ava. I knew when after seven, eight months had passed and her toothbrush still lived in the cup beside my left sink. When I couldn't bring myself to throw it away. When I called her every day since the breakup to apologize only to get her voicemail each time. She blocked my number.

I knew I wasn't over Ava when the guilt ate me up inside, *has been eating me up inside*, since it happened. Since I saw what I did to her. Since I witnessed the way that her face contorted in the most hurt, betrayed look when she found out what I did.

Who I was.

Who I represented.

I knew something had to give. I knew it couldn't go on like this. I couldn't function, and it was affecting every single area of my life.

Hannah proposed to me. Well, she suggested we move forward with that dumb pact we made before we turned thirty. I said yes almost immediately. I said yes because I had hoped it would help me get over Ava. I had hoped it would bring me back to life, steer my focus away from a girl I thought that I would never see again.

But then I *did* see her again. She came to my house.

Seeing her that night changed everything.

Ava's voice interrupts my thoughts. "You know that we can't be together, Grant," she says, her voice stern like she's stating an accepted fact.

And the crazy thing is, *I know that.* I *always* knew it.

I never thought that Ava would take me back, but that's not why I ended it with Hannah. I ended it because I couldn't marry someone when I had another girl perpetually consuming my brain, my mind, and my heart.

I couldn't do that to Hannah anymore. I *wouldn't* do that to Hannah anymore.

"Okay," I reply gruffly.

"We can't," she says again.

"I know that. I didn't think you'd take me back." The breath she releases is shaky. She swallows hard, unsure of what to say next. I hate that I've stumped her like this.

With a small voice, she asks, "You…you wanted me to take you back?"

"Is that a serious question?" I ask, brows furrowed.

She shakes her head, shock painting her features. How is this news to her? How does she question my need for her? Especially after admitting that I ended my engagement because of the five minutes I saw her that night.

"You have to win her back," Ava demands, the shock now gone from her voice and face. "Tell her you made a mistake."

"Do you want to be friends?" I ask, cocking my head while studying her reaction to my proposition. I want to smile at the cute way her eyebrows arch at my abrupt question.

"What?" she squeaks.

"Do you want to be friends?" I repeat.

Ava blinks rapidly. "Me and you?"

I nod. "One and the same."

"How would that even…" Ava shakes her head again, this time to clear the thoughts clogging her mind. She must think this idea is insane: being my friend after everything I've done to her. She ignores my question and repeats, "You have to win her back, Grant."

"I'm not interested."

Ava jumps up from her seated position and spins to face me. My face is even when I look back at her. I remain seated in the sand. She watches me for a long moment. She shakes her head *again*.

The wavering chuckle that comes out of her mouth speaks volumes. It's like she wants to laugh and scream and cry all at the same time. I want to hug her.

Fuck, I want to hold her.

"When did you end it?" I had hoped she wouldn't ask me that. I purposefully take my time replying. "Oh my God, I'm a homewrecker. When?" she nudges.

"Your birthday," I admit quietly. I clear my throat. "The morning after you came over. And you're not a homewrecker. It was a long time in the making."

I did it quickly. Honestly, I didn't have to say much.

Hannah and I woke up the next morning with this palpable tension in the air. She still didn't give me a piece of her mind like I thought she would, and I waited. All morning, I just waited until it came, but it never did.

Not when she got ready for the day or sipped her coffee or made breakfast.

But then, she got the suitcase out of the storage closet. That got the conversation rolling.

"Hannah—" She put her palm up to stop me. She shook her head.

"I'm not mad. Not at anyone but myself. You will never love me like you love her. I think I've always known that."

It hurt to say the next part. I had tears in my eyes. "I can't go through with this, Hannah."

She nodded in understanding. "I know."

She took a deep breath. In silence, I helped her pack the clothing and shoes that she kept at my apartment. She gave me a small smile, slipped the engagement ring off of her finger, and placed it on the console table beside the front door.

And I knew it was the right decision when I didn't feel even a fraction of the pain I did when Ava left.

CHAPTER TWENTY
AVA

Is it possible to be angry at the feeling of grief?

Because being told that Hannah and Grant aren't getting married, that my heartache from finding out about their engagement was for nothing, angers me. It still doesn't matter. With all factors at play, feeling anything that resembles hope about us is moot. I still overheard those nine words he said the night of my graduation.

"Say something," Grant begs from his placement in the sand behind me.

I stand a few feet away from him, close to the shore. Gazing out at the water, I can't possibly comprehend how far the ocean goes. I try to imagine it. I look as far out as I can, see that hazy grey line that marks the end of my visual of the water. Somehow, watching the water this way is therapeutic for me. It's life-altering, actually. It brings me a sense of peace and understanding that only comes with perspective.

With my focus on the white, foamy waves, a lighthouse I can barely see unless I squint my eyes, I make a choice, a choice I know is the right one.

No matter what happens next, no matter that we're both single, no matter what Grant says he wants following his break-up, those nine words were his truth. So, without Grant ever finding out that I overheard him, I will stand my ground. I will reject the idea of us getting back together. *You're my ex for a reason. You hurt me. I can't forgive you for what you did.*

False.

And there will always be so much more behind *why* we can't be together.

But I'll let Grant believe the obvious because it's the sensible option. After hearing what I did, I have to put the thought of us in a box, throw away the key, and throw the box into this humongous ocean.

I won't drag him down with me. I won't ask him to forfeit fatherhood for me.

Okay. Relax, Casanova.

"You want to be my friend," I finally say to Grant. We maintain eye contact, but I gnaw at my bottom lip. He nods once. "Why?"

"Because I like being around you? Because you're amazing? Because…you're a weirdo?"

I turn around, so I can hide my smile. I can feel myself blushing. I hear his rough voice from behind me say, "Don't hide your smile from me."

I turn back around to study his face. This man, this perfect and stupid man, is asking me to be his friend. He's calling me amazing. He doesn't even seem sad about his broken engagement.

But if he really wants to do this, if Grant really wants to move on together as just friends, I need my questions answered first. After all, I can't wipe my memory as much as I wish I could.

"Before anything, I want some answers," I tell him, making sure to keep my voice even.

"Ask your questions." His voice is smooth. After everything he did to me, to us, Grant doesn't seem uneasy about what I'm going to ask. He seems confident in his accountability, but I don't think I'm ready for the hard stuff. I kind of just want to put it behind me and forget it ever happened. Tell him I forgive him and never revisit the whole Pat thing again.

"Why did you come to my graduation?" I begin.

"Because I couldn't not. I knew where you'd be. I needed to see you."

My God, the assurance in his voice. I gulp.

"What law school did you go to?"

"Harvard," he states as factually as one would say the sky is blue.

"Of course you did," I mumble, rolling my eyes. Grant waits patiently for my next question.

"Why did you hug my mom at my graduation?"

In response to my inquiry, Grant leans forward, creating a cave of his limbs to almost hide from me. Whatever answer follows my question is one he has to mentally prepare himself to give me.

"Wait. Did you speak to my mom in the last year or so?"

"Only once," he mumbles.

I lean my head back in surprise, narrow my eyes at him. "Why?" I ask, my voice strong.

"I…" Grant looks up at me, seeming insecure. "Could I hug you?"

"Huh?"

"Just one hug. In case you never want to speak to me again." I wave him off, nudge him to explain what the hell he's so nervous about.

He takes a deep breath. "What did your parents tell you about the case?"

"That we won." He nods into his lap. I take it as a sign to ask my next question. "Why? Why are you nodding all weird?"

"You…" Grant clears his throat into his large fist. "You didn't win."

"Yes, we did."

Grant looks up at me from his loose placement in the mounded sand. He watches for something in my expression, some sort of revelation, but I have none. I am hollow for another thing to say. I am an empty can of Pringles. "Okay, stop being so quiet. What am I missing?"

"How do you know that you won?" he asks.

"Because we settled? Because the bills were…" *No. No!* The realization hits me like a boulder, like a foul ball.

No, that can't be.

"You paid?" He says nothing. "You spoke to my parents?" I question, anxiety causing my voice to rise in pitch.

I watch his even expression, the way his face calms, reverts back to being the same confident Grant. Zero wrinkles, pretty eyes. His shirt is opened, chest hair peeking through.

"Yes."

The only thing I could think of right now is about the jealousy I feel that my mom and my dad got to speak to him in those fifteen months while I didn't.

"Why didn't you…why didn't you say hi, or at least send regards? Why did you hide that from me? What did you say to them? And please tell me the truth," I whisper, begging.

Grant deflates in guilt at my vulnerability, at my small assumption that he might lie because he's done that before.

"I called them before it had a chance to go to trial," he begins. "McCall wanted to keep fighting, but it was pointless, and that was the last thing I wanted for you. I would never…" His voice wavers. He braces himself to continue. "I told them that there was no end in sight, that I'm not letting you step foot in a court room with him. I told them that I'm covering the bills, that they should drop the case."

"What about me?" I ask. A fire sparks in me, it always does, when I remember the girl who I used to be. The girl who I was with him. I huff. "Did you even care about how I was doing, or were you too busy picking out a ring?"

"*Ava*," he whispers tightly. I've broken his heart with my question. "Of course I cared about how you were doing. I always care about you."

Grant takes a deep breath, recalls the events of what feels like so long ago. "I asked your parents how you were doing, and they said you were coping; that you were managing and you were going to be okay. I didn't want to interfere with what seemed like progress, so I didn't want to come back into your life in any capacity, even with a simple hello. I asked them to keep this from you, so you wouldn't have to…I guess so you wouldn't have to think about me?"

I scoff, look at him with a stunned expression. "As if I didn't think about you," I mutter.

Grant rubs his bottom lip in contemplation. He shifts in his seat.

"What, so you told them you wanted to cover the bills and that they shouldn't tell me?"

"I told them I *was* covering the bills and that I think it'd be best to keep it between us and tell you that McCall agreed on a settlement."

"It was over a hundred grand, Grant. You just…*poof*? That's it?" I turn away from him when he shrugs nonchalantly, like a hundred grand is nothing to fuss over.

This is crazy. I rub my eyes and groan, irritation washing over me. So much money. Then, now. *Fuck*.

I swivel to face him. "Goddammit, Grant. Why? Why all of this money? What is it with you and me and money? You don't have to buy me. You never did. I don't understand what drives you to throw money at me like this. And it's a lot of money, it's tuition and rent and bills and—"

Grant interrupts me. He shakes his head rapidly and hunches forward to push himself off the sand to be level with me. He doesn't want to be on the floor for this, but when he stands before me and my heart beats faster, I say, "No. No, you're too tall. Sit back down. You're…you're crowding me."

Grant slowly inches down and settles on the sand. He bends to meet my eye because what he wants to say is important for me to hear. I give it to him.

"It has never, ever been about money, Ava. Ever. I paid for the bills, so you'd have one less thing to worry about, so you'd get some good news in the moments following our break up."

I didn't only mention bills. I mentioned rent and tuition, too. He bought an apartment for me to live in. He paid for my full tuition for two years of college.

"And what about NYU?" I test him.

"It was about opportunity. I never tried buying you. I never wanted you to know that I was paying for all of this stuff, I just wanted you to have it." He is so sincere. Holy shit, he means all of it, but *how*? He can't possibly have assumed I'd never find out.

"You knew I'd find out about the college sponsorship."

He shakes his head and laughs awkwardly. "I actually didn't. I knew you'd find out about McCall and the case because of the scheduled deposition, but I didn't know you'd go through the files. That hadn't crossed my mind when I initially sponsored and met you."

He gave his clients what they wanted, knowing that he'd take care of me anyway. I wonder at what point he decided he was going to pay for all of my hospital bills.

"What else did you pay for that I don't know about?"

"Your lawyer fees. Ellison."

I tip my head back. Relief for my parents fills me, and I just want nothing more than to hug my mom right now. I swallow the lump down, homesickness encompassing me, and sigh.

"How much money do you have?" I rasp. Grant snickers at my question. I laugh a little, too. "You…I feel like I'm supposed to thank you."

Nervous, I can't help but bite my lip again. Grant lifts his face to look me in the eyes and says, "Hug me. I don't want you to thank me. I just want to hug you again."

"So, stand up."

He pauses before diving forward to push himself off the sand. He inches closer, and as he does, my tired eyes dart to my side. I'm *really* nervous. I'm nervous to touch him. I'm nervous at what I'll feel.

His long arms spread open, inviting me but not forcing me. Like he's giving me a choice to back out by not stepping any closer, by not hugging me himself.

I imagine my short self cradled into this little haven that he's created, against his skin's heat and his massively long body. I imagine his strong arms holding me against his chest and his chin resting on my head. I imagine the way it used to be between us. I inch forward slowly. Once Grant confirms that I want to hug him just as badly as he wants to hug me, he takes a single step forward. That's all he has to do to reach me. He wraps those amazing arms around me and squeezes as hard as he can. I grunt from the pressure, and he loosens his hold. His chuckle reverberates through his hard chest. I feel it cause goosebumps to rapidly erupt across my body. Just hearing his throaty chuckle makes my nipples harden.

I never said that.

I hug him back. I hug him like I've been missing him for the last year because I have. I've missed him so much, it hurt. It doesn't feel like it did last year, though. It's weird now.

"This feels…interesting."

I can feel Grant shrug above me. "You're still my former girlfriend. We still have history. All that doesn't erase itself after a lousy year and a half. I missed you."

"I missed you, too," I say quietly, like I'm trying to hide the reality from Grant and me alike.

He pulls me back, so we're face to face, and grips my shoulders hard enough to ground me. I need it. Hugs from Grant take me to another place, and I'm sure my eyes are glazed over. I feel woozy.

"Friends?" There is hope in those pretty green eyes. I can't fathom the idea of that, of us being friends, *just friends*.

"This is crazy."

He nods. "I know."

"You and me. Friends. Just friends."

He nods again. "Yes."

"I don't know what it's like to be friends with you."

His eyes hold hope, hope that I'm not shunning him. Hope that I will be his friend. Hope that I'll take him up on his offer. Hope that maybe I want to be friends, too.

I watch him think it over. He's so handsome.

"I guess what I'm asking is… Are you open to trying?"

CHAPTER TWENTY ONE
AVA

I am the worst at drinking water, and because it's summer, I am in a constant state of dehydration.

I quietly tiptoe downstairs to get a bottle of water or two from the pantry. The house is still and quiet, which is how I prefer it. I'm a little nervous around the Wilders.

I halt mid-step when I make it into the kitchen and find Grant sitting by the marble island, similar to the one he has at his place. A white t-shirt pulls slightly at his chest. He's wearing a pair of gray sweatpants with a matching zip-up, the thick cotton sleeves pulled up to his elbows. The bar stool he's sitting on only makes his already giant frame taller. His body crowds the entire room. I feel him everywhere.

"Hey, you," Grant greets me softly. A captivated look shines in his pretty green eyes when he looks at me. The hardness to his face disappears, one I hadn't noticed was there until it softened after our conversation on the beach earlier.

Grant hiding his broken engagement from me must have been tough for him to navigate through. Now that the impending conversation is over, it's like he can finally breathe.

"You okay?" he asks sincerely.

I nod and tell him that I was just thirsty.

"Are you hungry? Do you want to eat something?"

"Depends if it's organic or not," I reply playfully.

He chuckles, then steps off the bar stool, aiming for the pantry. He begins to shuffle through the never-ending shelves, bins of every snack imaginable front and center for the taking. A minute later, he struts over to me with Oreos and Swedish Fish in each of his massive hands. I let out a quiet laugh.

"Is that a mainstream cookie brand you're about to serve me? How dare you!" I mock. He's always been a health freak.

Grant rolls his eyes at me. He places the junk food on the kitchen island and motions for me to join him. I turn to face him once I've hopped onto a stool with an unpleasant grunt.

"Are you going to eat some, too?" He reaches for an Oreo and opens it in response. I gasp in feigned horror. "Don't tell me you get rid of the cream. Why do I feel like you get rid of the cream?"

"I eat the cream first, smartass."

Grant chuckles with me, then licks more Oreo cream off of the cookies with a thick tongue. I reach for my own Oreo. Without opening it first, I take a bite. Grant gasps.

"You're eating it wrong, Campbell. One must always take apart an Oreo before consumption. It's textbook."

I giggle like a school girl. I properly *giggle*.

I am nearly hypnotized watching Grant eat this cookie, his pouty lips moist, tongue swirling to clean off every bit of cream. My eyes are glued to his mouth as he rubs a thick thumb across his bottom lip, dusting off black pieces of cookie. He reaches for my water bottle with a long, hairy arm and takes a big gulp; his Adam's apple bobs down his long, tanned neck. I stare at his veined forearm.

Is it obvious that I haven't gotten laid in way too long?

I am a mess.

We sit in silence, focus on the Oreos in our hands since we're both pretty clueless on how to do this. Being friends with an ex. Having casual conversations with said ex.

It's somehow both comforting and concerning that I can still read Grant as well as I can. Beside me, he prepares himself to tell me something, or perhaps ask me a question, but he stops himself. It happens a few times until I finally put him out of his misery.

"You can tell me anything, you know. I don't bite."

His shy laugh tugs at my chest. "I just… I want to hear about your life. The last year and a half. You've…you're different. In a good way!" he frantically adds. "Like, the best way."

I ask him what he wants to know. He tells me everything, instructs me not to leave a single detail out. He's jumpy on his chair when I nod and recall what stands out enough to tell him.

Mr. Homer and my apartment with Chloe are some of the things I mention. And with every new item on my list of experiences he had nothing to do with, he's proud of me. Genuine pride fills his features when he smiles, hanging on to my every word, and it warms me.

Fuck me sideways—I think I have a full-on crush on my ex-boyfriend. My completely unavailable, impossible, zero-future ex-boyfriend.

"What about you?" I ask, leaning forward for the bag of Swedish Fish. I pop one in my mouth. "Aside from almost getting married, that is," I joke.

He clears his throat, shifts nervously in his seat.

"Yeah, not much, honestly. Been pretty quiet since you left."

Since I left? I had every reason to leave!

My phone vibrates just in time to stop any of my irritation to seep through. I pull it out of the elastic of my leggings. Mom is FaceTiming me.

I ease off the bar stool, face Grant, and tell him, "It's my mom. I'm—"

"Of course. Go for it." He *doesn't* tell me to send his regards. Hm.

Once I'm safely secure on the other side of the patio doors, I answer the call. Mom is confused that the background of this video call isn't my bedroom wall, that my face is not fluorescently lit.

"Hi, baby. Where are you?"

I hold my breath, then proceed to release a complete and chaotic ramble about where I am, thus admitting to taking a job with Annie, thus admitting to being in the presence of Grant Wilder again. Her eyes are wide; my mother doesn't believe I'd ever be okay with this.

"Baby, no money is worth this. I can ask your father to send you some money on the bank app. I don't want you to be hurt."

"It's not the money. I'm good, Mom. We're going to try being friends."

That Spanish gasp never ceases to make my eyes roll. You'd think I told her I'm pregnant again.

Whoop. That's *never going to happen.*

"Are you sure this is what you want, baby?" Mom asks, her voice careful and soft. Her eyes study mine for any hint of depression, I think, but it's not there. Nothing about being friends with Grant hurts. In fact, it's quite frightening how excited I am about the prospect.

Shit, why *am* I so excited about this?

"You know you have nothing to prove, yes? It is okay if you do not want to like him," she says, coercing an epiphany to swarm through my mind.

Is that it? Did my mother unintentionally decipher what it is that makes me happy about this friendship, despite what Grant did to me? That somehow, subconsciously, I feel like I need to prove something to him—perhaps that he didn't win when he tried to break me or maybe that I picked myself up and gave myself the feeling of contentment and happiness, without his help?

Shit, that's kind of fucked up. When I think about it, I know it's senseless, but this new discovery doesn't want to be a passing thought. It wants to simmer on my brain.

Grant looks at me like he's proud of me. He seems authentically happy that I prevailed.

"Baby, I really do not think this is a good idea," my mother continues. Heat rises inside me, an inexplicable anger at the forefront of my mind. "I do not think it is healthy for you to—"

"I told you I could handle it," I spit, my teeth gritted.

"Sometimes your mother knows what is better for you to do."

"This is not one of those times, Mom. If I tell you I'm fine with it, that I'm actually happy about it, believe me." I scoff and run my fingers through my hair. I laugh without humor. "I don't get it. You're the one who isn't letting me move on, Mom. You're constantly hinting that if I do something in my life that saddens me, oh shit, back on the pills, she goes! Just *trust me*!"

Mom is stunned into silence by my angry retort. My brother, Connor, pops his head into the camera with his goofy smile, ready to tame me with something funny or perhaps by changing the conversation. I interject before he has a chance to do any of those things.

"I don't want to hear it, Con."

"Hear what? That I love my sister? Okie dokie. Have it your way, Indiana."

I roll my eyes. A small smile peaks through my pursed lips.

Connor walks into another room holding my mom's phone, away from earshot. At the same time, a metal sound catches my attention from behind me. I swivel my head to find Grant standing at the kitchen window, leaning over to close the door separating the outdoors and the screen.

With a curt nod and once the window is fully closed, he steps away from the glass, disappearing from view.

He heard everything. He's giving me privacy.

"He just heard everything," I groan. *Oh, God.* I face the screen. "What did you want to say?"

My brother tilts his head and smiles sweetly at me. I'm so lucky to have him, all three of them. I don't say it enough.

"I trust you, and I'm proud of you. Mom is just being overbearing—"

"Which is—"

Connor nods once. "Which is wrong. I know. It's not okay. You're more than capable of taking care of yourself. I swear, it's just coming from a little bit of PTSD. She loves you. She wants to protect you."

"I just want her to believe I'm healthy enough to be friends with my ex," I say, my voice tightening with the urge to cry. I swallow hard. "I want her to stop keeping me in that box. It's insulting, Con, okay? It's like, *Ava will never* not *be fragile.*"

"I get it. I'll talk to her. You're strong and resilient, we all know that. And I love you, okay?" I pout at the camera, my eyes tearing up from the loving words. I would do anything for a big bear hug from him right now. I don't even care if he noogies me, I just miss him.

"I love you, too," I choke. "I miss you."

"I miss you, too. Call me more, will ya?" Con chuckles.

I promise to keep in touch more, end the call, then swipe at my eyes to remove the evidence that I've unexpectedly cried.

Grant peacefully reads a book at the dining room table when I sneak back into the house. I match the small smile that he gives me. I also blush wildly because of what he overheard.

...oh shit, back on the pills, she goes!

"Hi," he utters, dog earring his book and placing it on the silk tablecloth in front of him.

"Hi. Long time no see," I tease lightly.

"I'm sorry," he says. "I probably wasn't supposed to hear all that, and I don't want to get in the middle of—"

I shake my head, blush even harder. "No. It's not you, it's them. Well, my mom. She's just overbearing. It's whatever."

I shrug, but Grant sees right through me. Judging by the empathetic look on his face, he sees how much it bothers me.

Together, we ascend the stairs, both of us headed to our respective bedrooms. His is right beside mine; we share a wall.

I don't enter my bedroom yet. I linger in the hall awkwardly.

"For the record," Grant's soft voice begins, "I think you're doing amazing. I'm really proud of you. Am I allowed to say that? Because I am. You're doing so good, honey."

Honey. Grant Wilder just called me *honey.*

His words and the way they penetrate into the pores on my skin, filling me with a head-to-toe sensation of comfort and validation, drives my voice mute.

When I am still unable to reply, he softly whispers, "Goodnight, Ava."

CHAPTER TWENTY-TWO

GRANT

We've all made it to the beach after finishing up with lunch back at the house this afternoon.

This is where we spend the majority of our time when we're in Montauk. Here or the pool.

I can't help glancing at Ava when she undresses out of her denim shorts, revealing her petite frame in a yellow bikini. I watch her near bare body walk toward where I'm sitting. She stops when our toes nearly touch. I tip my head back to look at her.

"You're staring at me, Wilder," she teases, cocking an eyebrow. Ava crosses her arms.

"You're wearing my favorite shade of yellow," I explain, my voice coming out defensive.

She rolls her eyes and laughs. "I commend your save." With a bright smile, she then asks, "Hey, you wanna play volleyball with me?"

"Why are you so good at this?" I call out to Ava across the net, receiving a shrug in reply.

Ava and Ben teamed up against me for a game of beach volleyball. When it's her turn to serve the ball, it smacks me square in the face once it's flown over the net. Ben howls. In his attempt to hit the ball once I serve, Ben slips, falling on his ass. With my brother's ass planted deep into the sand, Ava loses it. I watch in amazement, listen in awe, as she laughs *her* laugh. Ava's laugh.

The one from the comedy club last year.

The one from that time we watched *Borat*.

The one from that pancake breakfast when she called me a grandpa because I didn't like all that syrup.

It's fucking *beautiful*.

I smile when I watch her. My chest squeezes, and my throat constricts, because I don't think I have ever felt more genuine happiness than I do right now. There is something about this new version of Ava being happy that strikes me in a whole different way. It's genuine happiness for her happiness.

My heart soars watching her. I want to experience this again.

I pull my phone out to film her, snap as many photos as I can while she laughs joyously that Ben ate shit. She gives a shy smile when she catches me with my phone aimed at her. I have this urge to squeeze her and throw her over my shoulder and spin her around.

I do something bold because I can't help it. It's Ava.

I crouch under the net and grab her hand, pull at her arm. I bring her flush against me and hug her so damn tight.

Ava doesn't flinch or freeze or pull away. She lets me hug her.

She's still laughing, but now it's muffled by my skin. "I get a hug for laughing at your brother?" she teases, smiling up at me. "That's a pretty good deal."

I stare at her lips. I want to kiss them. I want to nibble and lick and peck them. Ava bites the inside of her cheek when she notices where I'm looking. She swiftly averts her gaze when she whispers, "*Just friends*, Grant."

To ease the serious tone in her words, she pokes my cheeks with her two index fingers. When Ben tells us to get a room, Ava rushes to move out of my vicinity.

"Go to the other side of the net," she demands.

I jog to where the ball landed and run back over to the volleyball net.

"All right, I'm serving!" I call out.

Ava hits the ball back over to my side, but I miss it, distracted by her boobs in a bikini when she jumps to tap the ball. I cannot be blamed.

Ben misses the next shot. Ava rolls her eyes.

"You guys suck at this."

"Hey!" Ben cries out. "Maybe tall people are just bad at volleyball."

Ben is six foot three, like our father. Two inches shorter than I am.

"That makes no sense, Ben. You should be better at it."

"Whatever, Campbell. Let's go back, you guys. We gotta get ready for dinner." Ben grabs the volleyball and jogs forward, leaving Ava to walk back with me.

We're going to a seafood restaurant in town for dinner. We eat there often throughout the summers as a family.

On our walk back to the house, I hand Ava a water bottle and demand she drink to stay hydrated. She takes a long sip, then passes it to me. I bring up dinner.

"Hey. Do you maybe want to drive to dinner with me?"

"Sure!"

CHAPTER TWENTY-THREE
GRANT

I glance into Ava's opened bedroom when it's time to leave for dinner to find it empty.

"Grant!" Annie calls out from the bottom of the stairs. "Get your ass down here. We're leaving!"

"Language!" I hear Mom shout. That's her thing. She can hear one of us cussing from a mile away. I swear, the woman has bat ears.

My eyes scan for Ava amongst the sea of my family members when I run down the stairs. I halt a few steps short of the landing when I spot her because…*wow*. She's wearing a flowy, red dress; she's got her hair down and some sparkly eyeshadow, but the most beautiful thing about her is the giant smile plastered on her face when she carries Josh and tickles him to make him laugh. Annie notices that I've stopped descending the stairs and smirks at me.

"I did a thing," she murmurs, leaning her head close to me.

I chuckle quietly. "What's that, An?" I murmur back.

"I did her makeup, and she looks insane."

Ava finally spots me coming down the stairs, and her face gets shy with that small smile of hers. She waves at me and rolls her eyes, but she laughs at the goofy grin I give her back. I walk down the last few steps and stand beside my sister, watching that beautiful sunshine of a human hold my nephew.

"What's up between you two?" Annie asks under her breath. I can tell she's concerned. I get it.

I want Ava back. I want to marry the girl. Annie knows that.

"We're going to try being friends." Annie shakes her head like she knows I'm an idiot for subjugating myself to the friend-zone with all of these feelings. I shrug. "I have to start somewhere, An."

I walk over to Ava standing on the front porch. Her skin is so gorgeous and golden. Her Spanish roots are blossoming nicely.

"Hey."

"Hi!" She's glowing. *Actually* glowing. I tell her that she looks pretty. She assesses me from head to toe, then says, "Ditto. Well, handsome more than pretty."

When my rowdy family exits the beach house into the rounded driveway, I nod my head toward my car and ask, "Ready?"

Ava follows me to the Porsche. When I open the passenger door for her, she mockingly declares, "Wow! Such a gentleman!"

I tap her nose and round the sports car to sit beside her for our thirty-minute drive.

I LOOK UP to find a smiling, flushed Ava walking back toward me.

We've been seated at dinner for the last hour. Ava talked to my mom for the entirety of the meal until she excused herself to go to the restroom. I stand up and pull out her chair once she's made it to the table.

"You good?" I mutter by her ear before sitting down beside her.

"Mhmm," she hums contently.

Ava reaches over to snatch a green bean from my plate. She takes a bite out of it with her front teeth then rolls her eyes. "*Of course* you chose green beans as your side dish."

"You got the French fries, so I didn't have to," I explain.

Ava deadpans with those honey eyes. "The second-best option would have been mashed potatoes. Duh."

"Next time," I chuckle. I am so in love with her personality.

When the dessert menu lands on the table, I briefly browse through it. Ava leans over to read with me. She lifts her hand up to cover her lips when she speaks directly into my ear.

"Could you get me the chocolate lava cake?" she whispers. "I'm too shy to ask for it out loud, and I know *you're* not going to order it."

I smile, shake my head, and think to myself: *this girl.*

When the waiter takes my dessert order and walks off, Ava raises her palm up for a high-five and whispers, "Great spy work. Well done."

I look at her, amused. I'm positive I have hearts in my eyes. "You're so weird."

She waves her hand in the air. "Oh, please. You love it."

You have no idea how much.

Ava scrunches her nose, and I get this burst of glee in my center. Nostalgia, of the best kind, blooms in my chest. I always loved when she did that.

On our drive back to the beach house, Ava turns to me, smiling. I can barely see her face because it's dark out, but I can feel how happy she is, the buzz radiating from her body. I'm happy she enjoyed herself at dinner tonight. I'm really happy she feels more comfortable with my family.

"Hey, I like the idea of you being my friend," she perks up giddily.

"Good," I reply.

"It makes sense. Does that make sense? That it makes sense you're my friend now?"

I tell her she's weird again, and she replies the same way she did at the restaurant.

And although being friends is a good start, I want this weirdo to be *mine*. I want to be the one to get down on my knee before her one day because she's the only one I'd ever do it for. I want to be the one to slip a diamond ring on her finger, to have children with her, to grow old with her.

I want it to be her. *Only* her.

CHAPTER TWENTY-FOUR
AVA

He's not downstairs yet, and an anticipating itch to see him overtakes me. When I looked in the mirror this morning, I was glowing.

Julia is making pancakes. Ben is being an idiot. Layla and Annie are setting up the table outside for breakfast on the patio.

"What can I do? Put me to work," I say to Julia at the stove. She effortlessly flips a pancake on the griddle. Everything about her screams elegance.

She smiles at me. "Oh, I've got it! You just go sit and relax, sweetheart."

I turn my head to the kitchen entrance when I hear a booming voice.

"Good fucking morning, everybody!" Grant yells into the kitchen, strutting in half-naked with a giant grin on his face. Before Julia has a chance to chastise him, he points to her and says, "Language, Mom."

Suddenly, the natural chatter of Grant's family quiets down. Everyone seems to be frozen, staring at him. Not because he cursed, but because of how happy he seems, like this is unusual. Like this isn't the Grant they know. Like Grant being cheerful is foreign to them.

"Good morning, Miss Campbell," he says to me, breaking the silence. I can't help but blush madly and shake my head at him. He is bringing way too much attention to me right now.

"Go help your brother with the drinks, you brat!" Annie calls out into the kitchen from the opened patio doors. She studies her brother then looks at me with curiosity. I notice her murmur something to Layla beside her. Layla has that same curious look as her sister.

"Gladly, Annie dear. Ben, honey, where are ya!" On his way to the pantry, Grant shuffles my hair.

"Okay, everyone outside! Breakfast is ready! Maddy, baby, can you go get Grandpa from the couch?" Julia asks Madison.

We all watch as she skips into the living room and shouts, "Grandpa! The pancakes are ready!" in her sweet, high-pitched voice.

I walk over to the pantry where Grant idles, arguing with Ben about something sports related.

"...and Houston can suck it, Grant. What's up, Ava," Ben says with a giant smile, walking past Grant and me with an armful of drinks. Ben is the happy-go-lucky guy. He's always smiling.

Grant turns to me when we're alone. His face brightens tenfold when he's talking to me over Ben.

"Good morning again," he utters quietly, tapping the tip of my nose. I swat his hand away, and he laughs that deep, throaty laugh.

"This is not friend etiquette. *Stop*," I whisper.

"We decide that, Ava dear."

I bite the inside of my cheek to stop myself from grinning like a circus clown.

When we're seated at breakfast, the trays of delicious food getting passed around, Grant hands me the bottle of maple syrup, then pours himself a cup of coffee. He casually looks forward to say something to Layla across the table, leaving me with a lone bottle of maple syrup in my hand. I have zero pancakes on my plate. I shoot him a weird look.

"Oh, sorry. Do you want some pancakes with that?" He's got this hidden smirk on his annoyingly handsome face. It's ridiculous.

I can't help it. I snort in an attempt to hide my laughter, then he bursts into a cackle. The table quiets down to observe us, laughing in a small huddle and blocking out the rest of the world.

It's weird. It's *really* weird. Firstly, because we're friends now. Secondly, because this is the first time Grant is beaming since we got here. Apparently, he's made everyone question the way he's acting.

Grant cuts the table's silence, asks Jackson to pass the pancakes. He puts four pancakes on my plate and smiles knowingly at me when I pour a cup of syrup on top of my stack. I roll my eyes at him.

"Grandpa," I whisper beside me. He squeezes my bare leg under the table and takes a sip of his black coffee.

Okay, this is my formal ask—where is the line?

ONCE BREAKFAST IS over and we've all helped clear off the patio table, half of us end up at the swimming pool and the other half at the beach.

With blue-striped pool towels in our arms, Grant and I join the twins in the backyard where they've already made it into the water.

"Grant, I'll give you a hundred bucks if you throw Ava into the pool right now!" Ben calls out to us from the deep end where he's standing upright.

The tile on the inside of the pool reads 5.5 feet, so I'm not surprised he can stand effortlessly.

I whip my face to Grant's and warningly say, "Don't you dare."

Grant shrugs a naked shoulder, looking at me like it's obvious with his vivid, riant eyes. "Ava, it's a hundred bucks." He smirks at me, amused. I look at the twins in the pool. They watch Grant like hawks with the most stunned expressions.

Why is his happiness an anomaly to them? Why are they so confused?

"You do not need a hundred bucks and you know it." I inch away from him, but Grant follows me, preventing me from escaping.

I attempt to negotiate. "Fine. Throw me in, but I get the money."

He chuckles hoarsely, shakes his head. "Nope. Not how this works."

"Then no one gets the money!" I call out before cannonballing into the pool with a loud shriek. I hear an echoed splash while I'm underwater. When I reach the surface, Grant is in my face.

"You are a little communist," he teases. A loud laugh busts out of me, surprising even me. We glance at each other when Layla says, "Awww! You guys!"

"Isn't she the best?" Grant asks, eyes sparking with all the love in the world.

This is a man in love. He's still in love, but with *who*? The girl he tried fixing, someone who no longer exists, or the person I've become?

The discovery I've made while on that FaceTime call with Mom comes back to me, not that it's ever left. It's been living on the backburner of my brain for the last two days.

Sheer hope and anticipation that Grant notices I've changed frightens me.

That's my real issue. That's my real fear.

It's like my brain is hoping to show Grant that everything he did to break me didn't work. That I triumphed, even after he took a knife to my heart.

I stare at the water below me with all this muddled contemplation going on in my head. Grant's voice interrupts my thoughts. I glance up at him.

"Where'd you go just now?" he murmurs, so only I can hear him. He studies my face, worried. "You okay?"

"Uh…yeah," I croak quietly. "Just…thinking about some things."

CHAPTER TWENTY-FIVE
GRANT

Something has shifted between us in a matter of minutes. Since that brief moment in the pool where Ava mentally disappeared, she's been acting weird. She has been avoiding me.

When I walk into a room, she slips away. When I ask her a question, she replies with as little words and emotions as possible.

I know it's not me. I know I'm not making this up. I know that whatever thought she had while we were swimming was some sort of trigger. I'm hoping, *God*, I'm hoping it isn't retraction.

I can't handle it if she left me again. The thought of Ava ending this friendship scares me so much that I ask myself—was this a terrible idea? I am already anxious about losing the small piece of her that I have, and it's been a couple of days at best. I don't know if she's actually upset with me, and I'm already freaking out.

But she isn't someone you walk away from, give up on, no matter how much or how little she's willing to give. I'll take what I can get with her. I've known that since we met.

I have to clear my head. I have to take a breather before I see her again.

Ava and Annie took the kids to the park to kill some time. We'll start on dinner in about an hour, so she'll be back soon. Maybe then we could talk. I don't want this tension between us at the dinner table.

I slip on a pair of sweatpants and sneakers, chug a half-gallon bottle of water, then jog to the boardwalk for a much-needed run. Running always clears my head. It's this place where I can either think clearly or not think at all.

I have to start thinking clearly.

I know that if I'm going to survive this new friendship with Ava and keep my sanity intact, I cannot psych myself out without having a single reason for why she is acting withdrawn.

I have to have tougher skin if I'm going to do this. If I'm going to attempt a platonic relationship with someone I am desperately in love with.

Madison is in a pink, frilly bathing suit playing sudoku at the foot of the stairs when I return from my run, so I know Ava is back from the park. I ask my niece where she is.

"Your girlfriend is in her room," Madison replies, hunched over the tattered sudoku book, aggressively erasing a line of numbers.

I wish she was, Mads.

I knock on Ava's bedroom door beside my own. I'm so desperate to clear the air that I don't bother showering first. I'm covered in sweat.

"Come in!" Ava calls out.

I slowly open her bedroom door, poke my head in, and ask, "Hey. You got a minute?"

"Sure."

She hastily clears off her bed to make room for me, but I drag the desk chair over instead. I want to be able to see her, and if I'm beside her, I can't.

"You're here to ask me why I'm being weird," she says once we're both seated.

The *honesty*. I've never had this with her. She's never been this way.

"I feel like I did something. I want to apologize, but I just don't know what for."

She lifts her glossy lips up in a small smile and stares at her delicate hands in her lap. "You didn't do anything. I'm just being in my head. It's stupid."

I lean forward to catch her eye. "No, it's not. Nothing about you is stupid," I say with sincerity. "Do you want to talk about it? Because I'm here if you do."

She looks me in the eyes and nods. She believes me. I give her an encouraging smile. She reciprocates it.

"I'm having a hard time separating then and now," she mutters.

I knew this was coming.

I nod, look at her attentively. "I can imagine how confusing this must be. What can I do to help?"

When Ava finds it hard to form a reply, she groans and leans back to lay on the bed. I chuckle and squeeze her knee in support. She speaks to the ceiling.

"My mom said something the other night about how I have nothing to prove with this friendship. And then it's like, what if my subconscious is trying to prove that I'm okay by agreeing to be friends? Like, *hey, look at me! I'm so healthy that I could be friends with an ex-boyfriend!* Why is it so important to me to show you that I've changed?"

The thing is, Ava didn't only prevail over what I had done to her, but rather she prevailed over her old self. I had nothing to do with it. She set her sights on getting healthy and being happy, and she achieved it. She would have done so even if she never met me. *I had nothing to do with it.*

She leans her head forward to face me. She pouts.

"You have every reason to be proud of yourself, Ava. It's okay to flaunt that. You deserve to."

"It's not that," she counters, shaking her head. "I was proud of myself before all of this. This is about you specifically."

I don't expect the trajectory of this conversation to reveal how much of a hold I still have on Ava.

I hunch over, stare at the ground between my feet. I'm still shirtless from my run. And with the realizations of Ava's words, I feel sick to my stomach. I am so angry at myself.

I wanted her to hate me. I *needed* her to hate me. Believing that is the reason I was able to move on. It was the reason I could get engaged, get up in the morning, and shave.

I had a beard for months after our break up.

The thought that I had no chance with Ava ever again allowed me the luxury of trying my hardest to erase her from memory. It didn't successfully happen, but chanting something in your head enough times can make you act as if you believe it.

She hates you. You're never going to see her again. She'll never take you back.

Two lies and a truth.

Hence, the engagement. But now I'm learning that I've had a hold on Ava all this time and that makes my stomach sink. I lost the privilege to have any imprint on this girl when I broke her heart.

"Are you…" I gulp. "Are you only agreeing to this friendship so you could prove something? Because—"

Ava springs forward to look at me when she stresses so boldly, "*No.* I want to try to be friends. I mean, we already are friends. You're my friend, Grant."

I think I feel my heart murmur. "I can't tell you how happy that makes me."

A small, shy smile from Ava's beautiful mouth tugs at my heart. She takes a deep breath, readies herself to admit, "I felt validated when you told me you were proud of me the other night. It's like I've been craving your acknowledgment that I'm not her anymore. The girl you dated. Why?"

I take a deep breath, think for a minute. "You know what I think?" I finally ask her.

"What?"

"We are every version of ourselves. The girl I dated will always be a part of you, and that's something to be proud of. Be proud of yourself that you did her a service by pushing through, by ensuring your happiness. That you *did* change, but only because you were her once, and that's okay. She was amazing. I fell in love with that person, remember?"

Ava's breath hitches, my passionate and forthcoming words startling. It is not *just friends* etiquette, but I can't help it. She is my future. She is going to be more one day, I know it. I'm marrying her.

Ava cocks her head. "What about you? You're also different. Your family…did you notice that? Your family was so confused when you were acting all jolly, but that's the Grant I remember."

I take a deep breath. "You make me really happy," I admit quietly. I gulp. "I haven't been this happy since us."

CHAPTER TWENTY-SIX
AVA

Grant and Ben are wrestling on the beach this morning. The entire family is taking a side. Just for the hell of it, I'm on Team Ben.

Ben and Grant don't look the same. They don't even look related. While Grant's hair is nearly black, Ben's is a light brown. While Grant's eyes are piercingly green, Ben's are blue.

Ben's eyes are light-filled, even when Grant is clearly winning this wrestling match. His butt is pretty much glued to the sand by now. In retaliation, he lifts his hand for Grant to help him up but tugs hard to throw Grant off and bring him down. Grant's stronger than that, apparently.

Ben groans when his attempt at pulling Grant fails and leans back in the sand.

"Bro, you only have two inches on me! This isn't fair!"

"In my pants, too," Grant responds, a coy smile curling his lips. I hold in my laughter and continue to watch this free and glorious entertainment.

"I hear you're on Team Ben," Layla mutters beside me. I laugh and confirm, then ask Layla whose team she's on. She tells me she's on Team Grant, and I gasp.

"But Ben is your twin! You shared a womb!"

Ben somehow hears me amongst the loud cheering and shouts, "THAT'S RIGHT, LAYLA. A MOTHERFUCKING WOMB! BITCH."

"Language," Julia states sternly.

Annie glares at Ben and whisper-shouts, "Ben, think about the children!"

"What does motherfucking mean?" Josh wonders innocently.

It's suddenly silent. Then it's loud as we all cackle and shake our heads. Annie gives Josh some explanation that I can't make out, but I'm sure it's hilarious.

Grant seems confused that we're all busy laughing, still standing where he and Ben were wrestling. His palms face up.

"Is this a ploy to distract me, Benjamin? Cussing in front of Mom?"

Ben responds to Grant with a tackle. Grant lands on his bare back with an *oof* but gets up swiftly. He has more motivation to win this than necessary.

"Go, Ben, go!" I holler at the boys. I'm doing it to garner Grant's attention, which I have. He wags a finger at me, and it makes me laugh. I hear Julia laughing at us, too, so I look back and smile at her. She rolls her eyes at her handsome sons and lifts herself off of the sand to come sit beside me. I smile at her as we both continue to watch Ben and Grant, amused beyond words.

"He's different with you," Julia tells me softly. "He's a whole different person."

I tilt my head and ask, "What do you mean?"

"I've never seen him look so alive. Not once in the twenty-nine years he's been my son. It's like when you're around, a weight has been lifted off of his shoulders. He can finally be himself."

"He's not usually like this with you guys?" I ask Julia.

She shakes her head. "Not at all. He was always a happy kid like Ben, but that changed when he got older. I guess now I'm realizing that maybe he just needed you to keep him grounded. You're like his safety blanket. I think when he has you in his life, he feels like everything is going to be okay."

To me, Grant is being normal. This is the Grant from last year. This is the Grant I remember. When we were together, he *was* just like Ben.

Hearing Grant's mother imply that he's barely alive without me makes my stomach roll because one day, he'll have to figure out how to be happy without me. I won't be in his life forever. He can't marry me.

I swallow thickly and awkwardly tell Julia, "We're going to try to be friends."

She squeezes my hand and gifts me a sweet grin. "You're good for him. I don't care in what capacity, that's between you two, but thank you for bringing my son back to life by coming back into his."

Whoa.

I inhale a sharp breath of air. "Julia..."

"I am being truthful, Ava, dear. Callum would tell you the same. Ben would too. Look at them. I haven't seen Grant and Ben like this since they were kids."

We continue to watch these gorgeous giants tackle each other, dust themselves off, and continue on repeat. When they seem to have exhausted their abilities to beat each other up, Julia excuses herself from beside me when Grant heads in this direction. I unscrew the cap off of the water bottle between my legs and reach up to hand it to Grant.

"Did you win?"

I watch him take gulp after gulp of water, watch his neck bob and the sweat fall down his chest and…

Fucking hell.

Grant heaves loudly once he's polished off the water. His chest is disconcertingly hard not to stare at, so I force myself to focus elsewhere.

How many grains of sand can I count on the beach in Montauk?

"Of course I did," he says, plopping down beside me.

"LIES!!!!" Ben shouts toward us with his own water bottle in hand.

Grant flips him off, then turns to me. "I heard you were on his team," he teases. "Sucks for you."

I giggle. "I'm gonna go with Ben on this one. LIES!!!!"

Grant taps my nose. "What were you and my mom canoodling about?" he asks.

That you're only alive when I'm around you. That you're a whole different person with me. That I'm good for you.

"She told me about the time you wet the bed when you were fifteen."

His sweaty eyebrows pinch. "What? I never did that."

I put a hand to my chest and pout my lip in feigned sympathy. "Awww, you forgot? It's okay, Grant. Denial can sometimes do that to a person, but I'm here for you always, okay?"

He is so confused.

I snicker, giving myself away. Grant begins to tickle me in the sand until I'm thrashing and begging for mercy. When he hovers above me, his face is dangerously close to mine. We both stare at each other's lips. I hold my breath. Grant sucks the air when it gets too much, then backs up to sit next to me.

He clears his throat. "You having a good time?" he asks quietly.

"The best time ever."

CHAPTER TWENTY-SEVEN
AVA

I don't want to be told that he needs me or that I keep him grounded or that when I'm around he feels like everything is going to be okay.

It can't be true. It *isn't* true.

Grant seems to be modifying who he is for me, and I'm starting to think he always has. If his family sees him as this withdrawn, aloof guy, but I see him completely different, I feel gypped. Like I never really got to know him, the real him.

If we're going to be friends, I want him to be his authentic self. *Even* if that means he's grumpier. I just can't stand the idea of Grant faking who he is for my sake.

I never expected things to be the same as last year, that's pretty much impossible, so who is Grant when I'm not around if the Grant I've experienced *is* full of life?

I don't get it.

I want to get it.

We're eleven people in this house, so it's always pretty loud, but once the kids are in bed, the house stills automatically. When it finally does, I throw on a sweatshirt and flip flops and slip out of my bedroom. I knock on Grant's bedroom door.

When he opens it, he's happy to see me, like he's *finally* happy because he's seeing me.

Who is he? Seriously, who is he?

"Hi, you," he welcomes me warmly.

"Hello. I was wondering if you want to come on a walk with me."

"Fuck, yeah. Let's do it."

I follow him downstairs and across the beach to walk near the water. He holds my flip flops for me along with his.

"Can I ask you something?" If I hesitate any longer, I'm afraid I'll be too chicken to ask. I have to blurt it out so there's no taking it back. My voice is casual, but what I'm about to say isn't.

"Of course." His voice is so deep and masculine. "Go ahead."

"Why do I know a different Grant than your family does?"

Grant winces, seeming uncomfortable about my observation. "Oof," he mutters to himself. He rubs his shoulder while looking at the ground. I wait patiently for his reply. "Well, I've never really been this…I don't know, this enthusiastic guy before you happened. I knew our relationship had a timer on it, so I tried really hard to be the happiest person I could be for you, and I was. I was so happy."

"But they know someone different, and they're your family. All I'm hearing is that last year was fake. You modified your personality for me. I never really met you."

Instead of feeling flattered about the exclusivity I apparently have with Grant, it does the opposite. It's insulting that I've never been accurately included in his life. That everyone who knows him knows the real him while I get a phantom version. It feels like I'm being baby-talked to. Like, *she can't handle any roughness so we'll have to coddle her.*

I don't want to feel like a child. I don't want to be coddled.

What is it with him and my mom? Why can't I be a new person? *Dammit.*

Grant stops our walk and turns to face me. His eyebrows furrow in deep concern. "No way. What? No way, Ava."

"Then who are you? I want to know the real you," I admit quietly. "Don't be different with me. That's so wrong, Grant."

If I'm going to be myself beside someone who can't show much of the same, I don't want this. It'll make me insecure that every time he smiles at me, he's doing it for show.

It *does* make me insecure.

Grant takes a couple of minutes to think. He focuses on our bare feet embedded in the sand, then slowly looks up at me. "Lying to you and breaking your heart took a massive toll on me. It still weighs on me so hard, but I'm trying to be the best version of myself for you." He chuckles at the ground and takes his voice down a bit. "I feel like I'm on edge that you're going to…I…my hopes are up pretty high these days. I'm just trying to get a handle on it, to make the most of it."

"Why?" I stress.

"I think it's coming from a place of guilt and un-deservingness that we're in touch again. I'm really happy about this," he whispers. "I don't want to be too happy in case it all…in case you come to your senses, but I also really, really want to make the most of what you're willing to give me."

Fuck, if that's not the saddest thing I've ever heard.

"You think I'm going to run," I state, finally understanding.

"I wouldn't blame you if you did."

I'm trying to be different. The Ava from last year would run, but she also wouldn't be friends with Grant after what he did. I can't be both people to him. Either he believes that I've changed or he doesn't, and if he doesn't, we can't be friends. I should hate him. I know she would.

I wanted honesty, and because of it, I'm forced to ask myself if no matter what I do, I'll always be the damaged calamity in his mind that he tried fixing. That *still* needs fixing.

It makes me mad.

"You're upset," he says, studying my face.

I scoff. "Just trust me. It's not that hard."

"I do trust you."

I shake my head. "I'm not her anymore. I need you to believe that. If you can't, this can't work. It isn't fair for you put me in a box without giving me a chance to prove you differently. We're both different now, and if I'm going to be open to getting to know you, I want you to do that, too. I'm not changing myself for you. Don't do that for me. Be yourself, even if that person isn't happy-go-lucky like Ben. If you're naturally a grump, I don't care. As long as it's the real you, I don't care."

He softly touches my lower back and stops walking, encouraging me to do the same. I don't look at him. Instead, I cross my arms and dig my toes in the sand. I don't face him, even when he asks me to.

"I'm so sorry," he stresses quietly. "You're right. I'll give you my authentic self, and I'll trust the hell out of you. I promise."

I tamper the stupid, smitten smile that wants to paint my face and focus on the conversation at hand.

"I told you I would try being friends," I whisper. "The Ava you knew last year would never do that. You know that to be true, Grant. You told me you were proud of me. If you don't believe I'm different, what are you proud of?

"I don't like having to push this narrative. I want you to let me prove that I could handle this. Don't be like my mom. She doesn't let me move on because she's keeping me in a box. With you, I want…

Okay, maybe I *do* want to show you that I'm good now, but so what?"

"Exactly," he rasps roughly. "So what? Say it louder."

"So what?" He shakes his head, gesturing for me to try again. "SO WHAT?"

"Better. God, you're fucking perfect," he groans to the sky.

You are, too. You're perfect, even though you'd never believe me if I say it.

CHAPTER TWENTY-EIGHT
AVA

"Do you want to move in?"

Annie and I are sitting in the living room with Josh this morning. It's not yet 7:00, so we're the only ones awake. Madison and Jack are still asleep. Josh is sitting on top of me, and I've been poking him and clapping his hands. His giggles are the cutest. I'm in love with this kid.

When the sound of descending footsteps echoes throughout the room, our heads shoot up to the stairwell, but I don't have to see him to know that it's Grant. I know the sound of his walk.

My breath hitches when he comes into view. He's wearing a white sweatshirt with the hood on his head and a new pair of gray sweatpants. His feet are bare, his black hair is a rumpled mess, and his green eyes are still squinted from sleep. I want to groan in (sexual?) frustration when he speaks.

"Hey," he mutters deeply. His voice is hoarse with sleep. *Fucking kill me.* "Morning."

"What's up?" Annie says to her brother.

Josh is still sitting on my stomach while I'm still laying on my back. The top of my head faces Grant, so I look at him from upside down. I give him a backwards smile. He's all groggy and mopey having just woken up, his eyebrows drawn together, but the side of his lips lift in a smile back to me.

He points to the kitchen. "Coffee," he mumbles.

I watch his long strides to the kitchen, then face Annie. She swiftly darts her head away like she's been caught staring.

"What?" Annie tries brushing me off, but I nudge her. "Oh, come on. What were you staring at me like that for?"

She shrugs. "I was just curious what's going on between you guys, but please don't feel like you have to tell me. That's between the two of you only. I'm just being an annoying big sister."

"Leave her alone, An," Grant calls out from the kitchen, coaxing mine and Annie's laughter.

"Just friends," I whisper.

Annie nods, but no part of her expression is believing. *A really, really close just friends? Best friends?*

Josh crawls into Annie's lap and curls into her. I take this bout of freedom as an opportunity, jump up from my position on the floor, and pat down my staticky hair. Annie smirks.

"*Annie,*" I whisper warningly. I'm not trying to impress him. I'm really not! She waves me away.

"Hi." I talk to Grant's broad back when I reach the sunlit marble kitchen. "Can I help you with anything?"

"Hey. I got it, thanks," he mumbles.

Okay...?

This feels like tension. Grant is seemingly annoyed this morning, and now I'm self-conscious about how intense our conversations have been lately. I opened up to him more than I ever have. I split my chest and my brain open and let him have a look. I was upfront and spoke my mind, and I ask myself if it was to a fault.

Walking over to stand beside Grant at the wide counter, I look up at him and talk to his profile.

"Are we okay?" I ask him. I can hear the insecurity in my own voice. "Are you mad at me?"

He immediately stops what he's doing with the coffee grounds and wipes his big hands on the kitchen towel beside the French press. He lays a flat palm on my back and shakes his head. His green eyes are full of apology and concern.

"No way. This isn't you, Av. I just didn't sleep well, so I'm tired."

My heart dips at that nickname.

He called me Av.

Honey. Av. Both brand new.

The Grant and Ava Starting Over Starter Pack. New nicknames.

I have to think of a good one for him.

Grant continues to silently prepare his coffee while I idle beside him. I've convinced myself that I'm intruding on his personal space, so I turn away to exit the kitchen but hear him from behind me.

"Where are you going? Come back here."

I turn to face him. My face feels hot. I chuckle self-consciously. "I feel like I'm bothering you."

He looks at me like I'm crazy. "You are not bothering me. You're never bothering me. Come back here," he repeats in a stern tone.

I start to giggle when the realization hits about how I've essentially asked for this. Grant asks what's funny with furrowed brows.

"I think you're kind of a grump," I whisper. "You're just being the real you, and it's unusual for me."

He's suddenly anxious. "I—"

"No," I interrupt him, shaking my head. "This is what I wanted. The real you."

He squeezes my shoulder in appreciation before finishing

preparing his coffee. I sit with Grant at the kitchen island. It's quiet between us, but it's comfortable.

One by one, all of the Wilders join us in the kitchen. Ben saunters in first with a goofy smile on his face. The guy is a younger and wealthier version of Ted Lasso.

Layla is in a tan-colored workout set and has AirPods in. She just got back from a seven-mile run, because of course she did.

Eventually, Grant's parents and Annie's family crowd around. Julia is in a gorgeous silk robe that has lace detailing at the cuffs, and her long black hair is in a neat ponytail. Callum kisses the top of Layla's head, then hits Grant on the back.

After firing up the stove and whipping out the necessary ingredients, Julia starts on breakfast.

"All right!" she shouts, clapping her manicured hands together. "Who's ready for Sunday waffles?"

My eyes instantly shoot to Grant's when it dawns on me.

"What! That's where you get it from?" I exclaim eagerly.

Grant laughs. "Yup," he responds with a nod.

I'm laughing. I am so excited right now.

"Wait, what? What am I missing?" Layla asks us after witnessing this exchange. They are all looking at us at this point, so I scan the kitchen before landing back on Layla's face.

"Every time Grant and I ever went out to eat on a Sunday, he always ordered waffles. Now I know why."

"We've been doing it since the day I was born," he says to me, hunched over his mug of coffee. He smiles at me, his eyes squinted. We're sharing a memory from last year, and it doesn't feel like too much. It feels normal. It isn't scary. It doesn't feel like we're crossing a boundary.

I missed him so much.

"Since the day *I* was born," Annie interjects. "And in case you're wondering if we've gotten sick of it over the years, Mom always changes things up. She'll do flavored waffles, Belgian waffles, cinnamon roll waffles... Awww, Mommy! You're the best!"

Annie kisses her mother on the cheek. Julia chimes in then.

"I look forward to it. I love these big babies of mine." She ruffles Grant's hair. "But I didn't know you continue the tradition when I'm not cooking. How sweet of you, Granty."

He is his mother's twin. It's borderline scary.

"He looks so much like you, Julia, it's insane."

"My male clone. I know," she says. She winks at me with eyes identical to Grant's.

"Okay, next topic. What's on the agenda for today?" Ben calls out into the kitchen.

Grant chuckles deeply. It's really, really hot. He shakes his head. "Ben can't handle the attention being on anyone else. Me and Ava are going out."

We are?

I look at Grant, a silent question forming on my face. He nods with an assuring smile.

CHAPTER TWENTY-NINE
GRANT

"You brought me to an arcade?!" Ava screeches, the most excited I've seen her since she was my girlfriend.
Probably *ever*.
"Oh my god! Let's play something!"
She tugs at my hand and drags me further into the fluorescently-lit arcade. Within minutes, I have Ava doubled over in laughter as we're playing air hockey because I'm trying to beat her and the puck just flew across the room.

"You're supposed to let me win, you know," she sasses cutely. "That's the polite thing to do."

I click my tongue. "Nah, you're not that kind of girl. You like to win fair and square."

She smiles at me from across the neon air hockey machine and nods, wrinkling her nose and *holy shit*, I've missed that. I can't help it anymore. I walk toward her, wrap my arms around her gorgeous body, and squeeze. She doesn't seem to mind it.

This isn't fake. This is real. It's amazing how relaxed I feel about our friendship after last night's conversation. At first, it worried me, but by the end of it, I felt so reassured and thankful to Ava.

She wants me to act normal. The pressure that relieves is unreal.

When I've won a second game of air hockey, Ava slaps me a five before dragging me further into the noisy room.

"Oooooh!" she calls out over the natural ruckus. She points to a free-standing photo booth. "We've never done one of these!"

We enter the booth. It's so squishy in here that our sides press against each other. I squirm to hide my hard-on.

This is the part that makes me question my self-control because of how badly I want to make a move. It's the summer. I watch Ava in these short skirts and tiny dresses, and it's impossible not to imagine her tanned legs on either side of me. It's exhausting when I have to keep shoving my imagination aside.

I want her. I miss her. I miss doing that with her.

"Give me your wallet," Ava demands when we're settled in the photobooth. She slips a five-dollar bill into the machine and selects a Christmas theme for the border of our photo strip.

We pose four times, collect the photo strips that I will be holding onto forever, and shoot for the ticket games next.

While standing in line waiting to redeem our prizes after an hour of playing with greasy arcade machines, Ava stands so close to me, our sides lightly touch. I think the conversation we had last night was this weight that's been lifted off of the metaphorical shoulders of this blooming friendship for the both of us.

We got the insecurities out of the way, and I'm hoping I've reassured Ava that I'll be good to her. That I'll be real. That this friendship will be amazing.

I notice Ava looking to the side every so often. "What are you looking at?" I ask.

"I think someone is taking a picture of us," she whispers.

I follow her gaze to find that *Yes, Ava, someone is* definitely *taking a picture of us.*

"I see you, Taylor," I call out to the blonde girl holding up her sparkly iPhone aimed at Ava and I. "Put your phone away."

"Hi, Grant," Taylor teases. Her singsong voice is irritating.

Ava observes this juvenile exchange unfold without saying a word.

"Taylor," I say warningly. "*Go.*"

Taylor rolls her eyes at me and scurries off in a pair of giant sandals. I look straight ahead once she's out of sight, but I can feel Ava staring at my profile.

"Is that someone you hooked up with?" she questions with a light chuckle.

Ouch.

That's not fucking funny.

No more faking. No more armor.

I snap my head to face her. "Do you just assume that every girl I talk to is someone I hooked up with? Is that what you think of me?"

Ava's eyes widen when she sees that I'm offended. "*What? No!* I was just wondering why she was interested in snapping a photo of us together."

Ava reaches for my hand, but I slip them into my pockets to avoid her grip. It surprises her. "Grant, I'm sorry. It was stupid. I shouldn't have asked you that."

"Her name is Taylor Hamby. She's Hannah Butch's best friend." Ava freezes. Her tanned face is stunned. I have a feeling saying my ex-fiancée's name in front of Ava will affect her for a long, long time.

"Is she going to send that photo to Hannah?" Ava wonders.

I shrug and say, "Probably."

"Does that bother you?"

"No."

I don't want Hannah to hurt; I never have. I hope Taylor doesn't send the photo, but it wouldn't bother me if she does, not the way Ava is asking. I can't stop Taylor from sending that photo. I can't control whether or not I'm going to bump into Hannah when I'm with Ava. The fact is, Hannah knows exactly why I couldn't marry her. The idea that I'd be trying for a relationship with Ava again is surely expected, to Hannah especially, so it's Taylor's prerogative to be sensitive to her best friend's feelings if she thinks that photo will hurt her. There is nothing I can do.

Ava and I redeem our 877 tickets at the ticket counter. After much contemplation that I find endearing since these toys are worth less than a dime, Ava chooses two matching friendship bracelets and a few toys for Annie's kids. She gets Jackson these plastic toy soldiers, Madison a yo-yo, and a bouncy ball for Josh.

On our way back to my car, Ava secures one of the friendship bracelets to my wrist with full concentration. I open her car door once it's tied, but before she sits, Ava turns to look up at me.

"Can you tie this on me?" she asks, handing me the second bracelet.

At first, she gives me her left hand, but when she realizes that *my* bracelet sits on my left hand, she switches and gives me her right. I can only assume it's because when we eventually hold hands again, our wrists will match.

Assume or hope. It's a fine line.

I pay close attention when tying the bracelet around Ava's delicate wrist.

"Forgive me for earlier?" she whispers. I nod and stand straight once I've finished tying the bracelet. Before I can walk over to the driver's side, she grabs my arm and lays her wrist on top of my matching one. She looks up at me.

"Hey. Do you want to be my best friend?" she asks timidly.

Fuck, the things she does to me, to my heart, to the blood that streams through me.

I smirk. "Do I have to fight Bridget? Because I would."

She giggles then shakes her head. "Mm mm. Or Chloe. They'll have to fight *you*."

I put a large palm on Ava's bare shoulder and squeeze. "I would love that."

"'Kay," she squeaks. "So, best friends?"

"Best friends."

"Can I taste that?" Ava asks, leaning her body into mine.

After our hour at the arcade, we drove the thirty minutes and met my family at the Inn for an early dinner. When Ava asks her question, she has this shy smirk on her face. It makes me laugh. I push my plate toward her, and she beams when she forks a piece of steak and pops it in her mouth.

"Good?" When she nods, I swap our dishes and take her salmon.

"Thanks," she chuckles.

"You like stealing my food, huh?" I tease.

Ava shrugs. "It just tastes better. Should we go?"

Ben and Layla made plans to meet a group of friends at Muse, a popular nightclub in town, and ask Ava and me if we want to join them once dinner is finished. We decide to tag along with the twins on our last night here.

Ben, Layla, Ava, and I walk toward the driver waiting at the curb after we say our good nights to the rest of our family at the valet booth. I drape my jacket over Ava's bare shoulders.

I know that it's an intimate gesture. I know that it could be considered an act between two people who are more than friends, but I mean, we dated. We were in love, we made love, and we were obsessed with each other. Whether Ava feels it or not, I myself can sense that portion of love within this newfound friendship. So, I'll follow the rules and I'll hold back when I want to kiss her, but I won't hold back when it comes to these kinds of gestures. The small, touchy gestures that say *I care about you. You're my person. There isn't anything I wouldn't do for you.*

Ava looks up at me and smiles, scrunching that freckled nose of hers. It must be a summer thing because I don't remember Ava having freckles when we were together.

She pulls my jacket tighter around her body.

"You good?" I ask her quietly once we've ascended toward Muse in the back of this black Escalade.

"Yeah," she whispers. "I'm *so* good."

CHAPTER THIRTY
AVA

I've never seen him smile so big.

I mean, maybe I have. I probably have, but everything about Grant from this point forward is real to me. It's the truth. I'm getting to know him all over again.

So, I've never seen him smile so big. Drunk Grant is my new favorite Grant.

We've also never done this before — gone drinking, bar hopping, dancing. It isn't unusual for me—Chloe is a party animal that likes to drag me places—but it's foreign for me and Grant to do it *together*.

By the time the party dies down at the third bar we've found ourselves at and it's nearly three in the morning, the twins, Grant, and I huddle outside while Ben orders us an Uber, stating, "I am courteously ordering us bitches an Uber".

Grant turns to me with a cheeky smile.

"Let's go swimming when we get back to the house." I laugh at him but then realize he's being completely serious. I tell him that it's cold out, so he says, "Okay, we'll heat up the jacuzzi. I'll text Annie to do it now."

Dangerous. Territory.

Grant notices my nervous expression once he's sent Annie a text, so he chuckles and mumbles at me, "Don't look so terrified."

Terrified isn't the word. More like, circumstantially disappointed.

This man is sexy as hell. I'd sleep with him in a heartbeat if there wasn't a bigger picture at stake. I'd rather have him for a long time in the form of a best friend than have him for one night in the form of a lover. That's how it'll play out; we'll realize that we can't move on as just friends after hooking up.

We'll remember that we can't be together, either.

Sayonara.

Grant drank a lot more than me tonight, which is why he's still drunk by the time we're dipping into the hot jacuzzi. We sit across from one another once we're completely immersed. The bubbles foam up the water while the lights from inside the jacuzzi shine under Grant's face, basking him in this iridescent glow.

His eyes look insane right now. The water's reflection has turned them turquoise.

I reach across the concrete that borders the jacuzzi to grab my phone, so I can take a picture of him. He smiles for me.

"What are you taking a picture of? Do I have a booger?"

I can't help the burst of laughter that exits my throat. "Your eyes look blue," I explain.

"Oh. Cool," he says, shrugging.

He lays his head back on the concrete and closes his eyes. I study the dusting of wet and darkened hair across his somewhat tanned chest, the contoured lines of his long neck, the deep dips and protruding slants of his collarbones.

I want to bury my face in them. I want to kiss them.

Before I do something stupid and unjustifiable, I lean my head back like Grant is doing and pin my gaze on the sky. The Wilder's beach house [mansion] isn't in the heart of town, so when it gets dark outside, the stars are visible here. I love looking at them. I don't get this in the city.

"What are you thinking about?" Grant whispers. His voice is drained and tired, but he somehow makes it sound happy still.

"Your boogers." I love when we tease each other. That part I know has always been real.

A husky chuckle reverberates through his naked chest.

"What are *you* thinking about?" I ask.

"*Your* boogers."

I laugh. "I don't have boogers. I've never had a booger in my life."

"That doesn't sound healthy, Ava. You should get that checked out."

"You're probably right."

"Do you still go to Dr. Helstad?"

Whoop. That *was unexpected.*

When I tell him that I don't, I sit up to find that he's no longer laying down either.

"Really?" he asks.

"Yup."

His smile is lightning. He stretches an arm out to fist bump me. "That's really, super awesome."

He says it with such sincerity and pride that I feel lightheaded, and I don't think it's the alcohol or the steaming hot water. It is the pure emotion he's made me feel that has knocked the wind right out of me.

Grant is the only one who truly knows what this self-rehabilitation has meant for me. He is the only one I've shared my entire life with, and so he gets it. He gets *me*.

"I don't think I can share this with anyone else the way I can share it with you. Thank you for that. It means a lot to me."

He studies my grateful face, nods in understanding, and smiles.

"Of course, honey. That's what best friends are for."

CHAPTER THIRTY-ONE
AVA

Psychological or not, the moment Grant's car crosses the bridge into Manhattan, I begin to panic.

After the jacuzzi, we went inside to sleep for a few hours before driving back home. I was going to drive back with Annie and her family, but she encouraged me to go with Grant.

I look out the window at the familiar city streets.

This is it. This is the moment that our new friendship enters the real world.

We won't be in close proximity like we were in Montauk. We won't be in the confines of his glorious beach house surrounded by his family members. We won't be forced to engage. We won't be on vacation.

Now that we're in the city, we'll actively have to try at this thing. We'll have to put in substantial effort for this friendship to continue. We'll have to hang out and spend time with each other's friends and—

Oh God. Why am I panicking?

Naturally, Grant senses my psycho-analysis.

"It doesn't have to be complicated. It won't be. I give you my word."

"Yeah, but what about when one of us—" *Oh, God.* I didn't think about this part until this moment.

"When one of us what?" he inquires softly, glancing at me quickly before focusing back on the road.

I wince. "Dates?" I all but squeak.

"I'll be supportive. That's what best friends do."

He says *I'll* be supportive, not *We'll* be supportive. Like the idea of dating is the last thing on his mind, and that irks me more than it should. He told me that he walked away from his future *in pursuit of the one I really want*, but the fact is, he can't hold out for me. Not because I don't want to be with him. Not because he broke my heart or hurt me beyond measures. It's nothing he'll ever know.

I can't marry her, Hannah. She can't have children.

Grant finally looks over at me after parking in front of my apartment building. I can sense he's nervous to ask me what he's about to.

"Ava…" He gulps and swipes at his dried lips. "Fuck, I've avoided this question, but I have to just… Is there no hope for us as more than friends?"

I can't tell him the truth. I can't ever tell him what's holding me back from being with him again, but I can't leave him hanging either. I won't lead him on. I'd never torture him with false hope.

"No. There is no hope for us. We can't ever be together." Panic surges through me at this sudden desperation for him to really comprehend that we won't be together ever again. "And if I've sent the wrong message in Montauk, we can't be friends either."

"I…I," he stutters. He blinks a bunch and leans his head back in shock. "Wow."

I've hurt him. I've pissed him off and let him down, but I've also met his expectations. I can see it in his face. He was expecting this. I can hear it when he scoffs.

Grant knew that I would freak out. Grant expected me to run all along.

"I have to put some boundaries in place if we're going to try being friends," I whimper from the passenger seat. My voice is quiet, terrified that he can somehow see right through me. Scared that those nine words are tattooed on my forehead, that he's read them and he's prepared to convince me that he wants to be with me either way.

I won't do that to him. I won't let him suffer for me. If I don't put my foot down, he'll think we have a future and giving him false hope would be cruel.

"I'm going to go inside. Thank you for everything," I tell him, quickly exiting the car. He follows me out onto the sidewalk. His stance is aloof and rigid when he studies me, but he still cares.

"What am I missing here?" I shake my head at his question, silent. *"Ava,"* he pleads, bending to meet my eye. I don't look up. I busy myself with the house keys, with my phone, with the strap of my tote bag.

"Ava. Look at me."

I can't marry her, Hannah. She can't have children.

Do the right thing, Ava. Walk away.

"This isn't going to work," I whisper, swallowing. "I'm sorry for telling you that I would try being friends, but we can't."

"Don't do this," Grant whispers desperately. "Don't disappear on me."

My throat is on fire. *Fire.*

"Thank you for everything," I whisper before rushing into my building.

As soon as the door to my apartment closes behind me, I rush to the window and move the curtain to observe him, because I know he's still there.

I watch him stand by his car, staring at the front door of the building where I walked through a minute ago, like I'm going to come out at any moment.

He rubs his eyes, presses his huge palms on the back of his sports car. He leans forward, lets his head hang low, and when I watch him experience the clear anguish he feels, the lump in my throat gives. For the first time since I overheard those nine words, I finally let myself cry.

CHAPTER THIRTY-TWO
GRANT

I knew she'd run, but it doesn't hurt any less.

CHAPTER THIRTY-THREE
AVA

"God, you're so stubborn, I want to strangle you," Chloe mumbles around a slice of extra-cheese pizza.

It's Saturday night, and we're sharing a pie on the loveseat sofa in our tiny living room. We've spent all day in our pajamas with no plans to leave this apartment until we have work on Monday morning.

I turn to her and squint. "What did I do?" I say with my mouth full.

"He's not going to text you. He's not going to reach out when you essentially told him it was over without a reason."

I guess I've been perpetually staring at my phone if Chloe noticed.

I regretted it the moment I watched Grant drive down my street and away from view. I wanted to run after his car shouting, "Wait!" while flailing my arms to catch his attention in his rear-view mirror. I wanted him to slam on the breaks, and I wanted to run up to his window, huffing and puffing, and say, "I didn't mean any of that. I want to be friends with you. Let's get some pizza."

Everything doesn't have to change once we're back in the city, and I wish I could go back in time fix my panicky brain during that car ride. I freaked out for no reason. I acted like the Ava that once let fear dictate her life, and I want to take it all back.

If I had a time machine and someone said I could time travel just once, it wouldn't be to Pat or to the bathtub or to Rocco's. I'd time travel to two weeks ago.

We didn't cross any lines at the beach house. We figured out how to navigate this new friendship. Hell, I'm proud of us at how quickly we picked it up. I'm proud, but I'm not surprised. It's us. *We could do this.*

I could do this.

I can't let something I eavesdropped on dictate my friendship with Grant because at the end of the day, that's all he's really asking me for. He didn't outright tell me he wants to be with me, he just asked if there was hope. He never tried to kiss me. He didn't tell me that he still loves me.

Friends. That's what he asked for.

Best friends. That's what *I'm* asking for.

There is no excuse for what I did by running at the first chance I got. For the flame I put to this amazing friendship before it had a chance to flourish. And if Grant tells me I'm too late, I wouldn't blame him, but the thought that I've lost him for good terrifies me.

He hasn't been at Annie's once in the last two weeks. I haven't heard his name or seen his face or peeked at a FaceTime call he was having with his niece.

Nothing.

So, the next time Thibault picks me up from Annie's, I give him Grant's address instead of my own. I screwed up, and I owe him the biggest apology in the world. I'm also here to grovel.

I knock on Grant's door and feel a mixture of both relief and anxiety when I hear his footsteps grow louder. I'm scared to face him because I'm scared that he's going to tell me I'm too late. I squeeze my eyes shut. Embarrassed at the audacity I clearly have coming here after hurting him, after being spoiled at a beach house for a week and squashing it like it never happened, I wince as he opens the door.

He doesn't say anything. I can feel him watching me from a few feet away, but Grant doesn't say a single word. Neither do I. I can imagine how ridiculous this looks. How *weird* this looks.

He likes that word.

Eventually, the silence hurts my ears, so I squint out of one eye, open both, and straighten out. I look into his green eyes with apology and sincerity and shame. There is something neutral about the look he returns to me. I can't pinpoint it, but I know that it isn't relief. He doesn't trust me. He expected this shift, and he doesn't want to get his hopes up that I'm not going to do it again.

Don't do this. Don't disappear on me.

"Am I too late?" I whisper. Grant holds my gaze, but he doesn't reply. He examines me. It's so damn quiet, I'm getting nervous. "Because if I am, that's really humiliating, and for the sake of my gag reflex, please reject me nicely so I don't vomit."

I blink up at him to find Grant pursing his lips, trying hard not to laugh at me; not to react at all but apparently, I'm too entertaining for him to stay expressionless. He curls his pouty lips to hold in his amused snicker.

Ha! I've cracked him!

But he still doesn't react, so I try again. "Wanna hear a story? One time, I waited in line at a pizza shop because I saw people with ice cream until I realized that it was a child's birthday party and the line of people in front of me were the kid's friends waiting their turn."

He's the one who closes his eyes this time since he knows if he lets himself look at me, he'll react and he'll laugh, but I'm determined to win this. He continues to hold in his bright laughter. He's like a

Queen's guard in London.

"I order my Starbucks under the name Shi-theed because I think it's funny. It sounds like a real name, but when I spell it out, they end up writing 'shit head' on my cup."

Okay, we're getting somewhere! His eyes are opened, clearly charmed. He strains to curb a big belly laugh, but I *need* a laugh. It doesn't count as a win until he laughs.

"Ugh, I don't have that much ammo! Okay, let me think." I look up at the ceiling of Grant's hallway and remember another one. "When I was seven, I accidentally went home with another family after Cooper's baseball game. I was so tiny that they only realized I wasn't their kid halfway through their drive home. I have never seen a middle-aged white man drive a mini-van so fast."

I look between his eyes to gauge if I've finally got him. His eyes are full of wonder, but *it doesn't count as a win until he laughs.*

"More," he demands in his deep voice. *Ah! He speaks!*

I have to rack my brain, but I don't care. I'll do whatever he says.

"My roommate, Chloe, has a theory that her Chapstick can walk and that's why she can never find it. I've actually been playing a prolonged practical joke on her where I hide the Chapstick and then, because I feel guilty, I'll buy her a new one since she 'lost hers,'" I say with air quotes. "And I don't know why I don't just give her the one I was hiding instead of buying a brand new one, but if I do that, the prank isn't sufficient."

"When do you plan on telling her?"

Oh my goodness! My face must give way to the excitement that Grant just spoke more than a single word because he smirks knowingly at me.

"I hope her lips are *really* dry around Christmas."

Yes!!!!! A laugh! A husky, sexy, wholesome, perfect laugh! *I win!*

I tilt my head back, close my eyes, and take a deep breath. "Ahhhh," I sigh contently. "Sweet, sweet victory."

I bite my lip to keep from Cheshire-Catting when I face him.

CHAPTER THIRTY-FOUR
GRANT

She didn't have to act in a way that'd make me fall more in love with her, but everything about Ava does.

I love her more with every second that passes.

That's why it broke me when she told me that we were over before we really started. I was excited about the prospect of friendship. I was excited to see what that looked like back home in our every-day lives. She stole that from me, from *us,* because of scenarios she made up in her head.

It didn't surprise me, though. That's why I was trying to make the most of our friendship in Montauk. As soon as she started to freak out in the car ride home, I instantly knew. It was too good to be true that Ava would agree to any kind of relationship with me so soon after seeing each other again. I think a piece of me will always anticipate Ava running, but for now, I'll take the sweet, sweet victory.

She thinks she won by making me laugh. I won because she's in front of me.

I reach my hand out to pull her into my apartment. I casually ask, "Are you hungry?"

She follows me toward the living room. "Yeah, actually, I—wait."

Ava pulls my shoulder to twist me around. "That's it?" she asks. I shrug. "Do you forgive me?"

"Yes." Ava is utterly confused. She shakes her head and furrows her eyebrows.

"Wait. No. Don't let me get away with this. Be upset at me," she says frantically.

"I was," I reply.

"*And?*"

"And you literally stole ice cream from a little kid's birthday party, so…"

Ava cackles. I can't help myself from staring at her with every sound that exits her throat.

She is still uncertain, and I know that it's coming from a place of shame. I make sure that she's listening closely when I say, "As long as you're back, I want to move forward with you."

She nods hurriedly. "I am back. I want that, too."

"Good. Now, let me feed you."

CHAPTER THIRTY-FIVE
AVA

Grant was recommended this sushi place by a friend, says it got a Michelin star, whatever that means.

It's one of those restaurants where the appetizers are bite-sized and the mains are so tiny that even once dinner is done and Grant pays the bill, I'm still hungry. We exit the restaurant but before we head to Grant's car, he turns to me.

"I could use a fat steak right now," he declares, rubbing a large palm down his torso.

I sigh. I was going to microwave a freezer burrito when I got home. "Oh, thank God," I groan. "I'm starving." He chuckles at my reaction. I smirk at how weird he finds me to be.

"There's a place not far from here," he says. "We'll walk."

We walk in tandem down this New York City sidewalk. It's humid out but somehow, even after a sticky and muggy day, summer nights here come with the most refreshing breeze. I love this weather.

I'm wearing a dress tonight. I started doing that more ever since Chloe and I met. She's got me all fashioned up. I own *leather pants* now.

My dress is strapless, and I'm in sandals, so I halt our walk to quickly slip on my cardigan when the breeze blows. Out of the corner of my eye, I notice a very familiar building.

I turn my body to face the restaurant's front door and tilt my head to read the sign on the forest green awning. I'm standing in front of the steakhouse from our first date.

Grant follows my gaze. He blinks, then looks apprehensively at me once it registers.

"Of course this has to happen the first time we go to dinner back in the city," I joke, chuckling. I roll my eyes at Karma.

Grant nods his head to the other side of the street in response. "Come on."

"You said you wanted steak," I remind him.

Grant shakes his head. He clears his throat before replying, "There's a place not far from here."

"Grant, we're standing in front of a steakhouse. Let's just go inside."

"I can wait ten minutes, Ava. I don't want to put you in an uncomfortable position. I don't want to bring back memories you'd rather not revisit. I gave you my word that this wouldn't be complicated." He nods his head down the street and gives me an encouraging smile. "Come on, let's go. This other place is delicious. I know the owners, so I could introduce you."

I look up at him with what I am sure are doe eyes when we've walked in silence for a few minutes toward the new restaurant.

"Why are you so good to me?" I ask quietly.

His reply comes fast. "Because you're still it for me."

Oh my God, I've missed that.

Grant casually shrugs when he sees my overwhelmed expression at his heart-puncturing words. "You asked."

I guess I did, didn't I?

It's fun sitting at a restaurant when the owners know you.

I feel cool that we're getting all of this special treatment.

The servers have been coming over to our table all night, bringing dishes that Yannis, the owner, insists Grant tastes because *Mr. Grant knows food.*

Yannis drags a chair to sit at our table. In his thick, Grecian accent, he says, "Mr. Grant, why don't I see you here anymore? Whose steakhouse is better than this one, huh?"

"Yannis, how dare you ever *think* there is a better steakhouse than your own!" Grant is animated when he talks and teases Yannis. I'm just sitting here, laughing at their banter. "No better wagyu beef than here, my man. I promise to come more often."

"And bring this pretty girl again, yes?" Yannis teases, wiggling his thick, bushy eyebrows.

Grant replies, "Feed her well and we'll be back. I go where she goes."

My heart.

When Yannis excuses himself to go to the kitchen, I ask Grant, "How do you guys know each other?"

Grant swallows his food before facing me, smiling. "It's funny, actually. He dated Annie over ten years ago."

My eyes widen and my jaw drops. *Annie used to date him and Grant is still friends with the guy?*

He chuckles. "I know, but they're still friends, so it's cool."

I like what I hear. I *really* like what I hear.

"That's comforting," I tell Grant across from me. I smile, but he doesn't match mine. He pinches his eyebrows and tilts his head. He studies me but doesn't seem to translate my words and their meaning.

"What is?" he asks.

"That she's still friends with an ex, even though she's happily married with three kids."

Grant stiffly pauses to place his fork and knife down, presses his tongue into the inside of his cheek. Something about what I just said bothers him. I'm not sure why, but I instantly panic because it hurts me when he's hurt.

"Sorry. Sorry, I didn't mean that in a bad way. I—"

"No, you're right. It means we can be in each other's lives indefinitely." He lifts up his cutlery and cuts into his steak again. He smiles at me from across the table.

"Yeah. That's what I meant," I rasp in the small space between us.

Within a millisecond, his irritation dissipates. He acts unaffected, but I know he does not appreciate what I've said. I hate that he's pretending. I want Grant to be himself, and the fact that I was being insensitive, even if he doesn't want to show me, makes me want to cry.

Is that what having a best friend feels like? Or is this the effects of loving someone? Being mutually affected by their hurt.

I still love him. I look at him, I study his face, and I just want to tell him that I never stopped loving him. Instead, I ask, "Can I say something?"

"Always," he replies after swallowing a piece of meat and dabbing at his lips.

CHAPTER THIRTY-SIX
GRANT

"I do want to try being friends, and I don't want you to be scared that I'm going to... I know that you're expecting me to run again. I know that it didn't surprise you, what I said after Montauk, but the fact is... I'm scared, you know? You and me is just... It's scary. It always has been, so I'm trying to figure this out. I don't know what I'm doing, but I promise that I'm going to try really hard to be the best friend you've ever had."

She rants nervously. I've always loved when she did that.

"I know that we can't be *together* together, but it doesn't have to be a big deal. Being best friends is good enough for me; it's perfect actually. It's enough for you too, right?"

I take a deep breath before giving Ava the reassurance that she's giving me. I look at her pointedly and say, "*Of course it is.* Honey, I'm sorry that I expected that reaction from you. It was wrong, it wasn't okay for me to assume anything. And I get it. This is scary. I don't expect you to know everything because this is new territory for me, too. I love how brave you are that you're willing to be friends with your ex-boyfriend. And I want you to know that I have faith in you, okay? I believe in you. I am proud of you, *so* proud of you, Av."

As if a ray of sunshine hits her face, she beams at my words. I laugh.

"What?" I ask while playing footsie with her underneath the table. She kicks me back.

"I'm going to give you the biggest hug when we leave this restaurant that your lungs might collapse and you might die."

"Death by ordinary hug? Eh. Maybe. Death by an Ava hug?" I pause. "I'm in."

CHAPTER THIRTY-SEVEN

GRANT

Things are good. Thing are really fucking good.
I've seen Ava a couple of times in the last few weeks. We watched a movie at Annie's twice once the kids went to bed, and she met me for dinner on a random weeknight. We got burgers. I kept the receipt.

It's seven in the evening. I got home from work a little bit ago and lug my black gym bag toward the elevator to the weight gym upstairs when my phone sings Ava's designated ringtone. I still haven't gotten used to the flutter in my chest when she calls.

"Hey, you," I answer after one ring.

"Hiya!" she shouts into the receiver. I have to pull the phone away from my ear. I lower the volume, then try listening again. "How are you?"

"I'm great. What's up, honey?"

"Chloe and I are having some people over tomorrow night at eight. I was wondering if you wanted to come?" I'm flattered at her invite. I attempt to accept the invitation, but before I have a chance to reply, she interrupts me. "I mean, I want you to come," she corrects herself. "I really want you to be there. Can you come?"

I didn't think I could love her more. I always felt that I love Ava so much, that I'm at max capacity of how much a man can love a woman, but no. I also hadn't realized that having Ava as just a friend could have an impact on me like it does. That I could grow to love her more when she *isn't* mine.

If this is the case, I am so screwed.

"Of course," I reply. I have such a smile on my face. I wouldn't miss being hosted by Ava in her new apartment for the world. I am so eager to witness her growth, to experience this new version she developed into that she's so proud of. "I'll be there. What can I bring?"

"Just yourself. I'll see you tomorrow!" she exclaims. "Oh, wait! And beer!"

This.

Fucking.

Girl.

"AVA! RUTHIE!" A tall blonde girl shouts piercingly into the small apartment after she opens the door for me and takes the two six-packs from my hands.

She turns to face me and smiles. "Hi. I'm Chloe."

My eyes light up in recognition. "The roommate."

"That's me!"

I reach for Chloe's hand and shake it. "Grant Wilder. It's nice to finally meet you, Chloe."

`She leans her back against the door post, crosses her arms, and rolls her eyes. "Do you really think I don't know who you are?"

I chuckle. Ava talks about me? And if so, does Chloe know who I am in the form of Pat's lawyer or Ava's [best] friend?

Maybe both. Probably both.

I am completely but pleasantly startled when I've barely made it into the apartment and a petite body crashes into my chest, forcing me to take a stumbled step back.

Ava.

She squeezes my neck and hugs me tightly.

Is this really happening?

"You came!" she squeals. She leans back and smiles up at me with flushed cheeks.

Ah. This is the effects of Drunk Ava. I should have figured, but I'll take what I can get.

I smile widely at her. "Of course I did. Hi, you." I grin when I recognize the t-shirt Ava is wearing from last year. She's also wearing her dirty Converse and a flowy mini skirt that I've never seen before. I have to try hard to avoid looking at those long, tanned, shiny legs. It is not easy.

Ava's short hair is in a top bun, but she's got light brown chunks behind her head that have fallen out of the elastic. They sit messily on the back of her neck. I observe her from head to toe, and my chest explodes.

This is her. This is Ava.

"Hi!" she exclaims over the music. "Do you want to meet everyone? This is Chloe, by the way. My roommate." Ava nearly hangs off of her when she throws her arm around Chloe's neck. Chloe is a head taller than our little Ava.

"We just met," Chloe tells Ava. "He's practically my best friend now."

"No, he's *my* best friend." She beams when she says that. Then, she turns to me. "Hey, Grant, look! We're fighting over you! Okay, come meet everyone," she whines, tugs at my arm, and drags me into the apartment.

Chloe follows us into the small crowd of their friends. Ava introduces me to a few people, but she mentions she doesn't know everyone here because a lot of them are Chloe's mutuals. I meet Chloe's boyfriend, Gabe, and a guy named Derek.

Derek's clammy hand feels miniature in my palm when he leans in for a handshake. "Hi, Derek. It's nice to meet you."

This guy watches me intently. It's like he feels threatened by me, and when I notice a frozen Chloe observing Derek and I meet, it quickly dawns on me that Ava and this guy have history. Whether it's current or not, there seems to be something here. I study him and immediately know that this guy can't make Ava happy. He won't do it for her. He's not enough.

I chastise myself.

My speculation about Ava and Derek when I don't know if there is a substantial story between them is insane. It's ridiculous. I've nulled him as a potential candidate for Ava to date as if I have a choice in the matter.

Does this make me crazy?

I somehow end up talking about Wall Street with a kid in a vest when Ava continues her hosting duties around the noisy apartment. I would much rather hang out with her right now, but seeing her in this space, in her new element, is euphoria for me.

I watch her. I observe her. Every little detail.

She grew up. She transformed. She *bloomed.*

The girl is a dream.

She creates sunshine wherever she goes. Seeing Ava happy is *magic.*

CHAPTER THIRTY-EIGHT
AVA

"Derek is being so weird," I mumble to Chloe at our fridge. She's finally putting away the now warm beer that Grant brought to the party earlier, more like hiding it because *"that man looks expensive, and I'm not serving these people our newly acquired, expensive beer."*

If only she knew how *expensive he is.*

"He's been eyeing me and Grant the whole night," I continue.

Chloe scans the crowded room and witnesses Derek's gaze fixated on Grant. Grant is chatting with Chloe's boyfriend, Gabe, and unknowingly has a certain someone's beady eyes on his back.

"Oh, shit," Chloe murmurs. She widens her blue eyes when she looks at me. I widen mine back.

"I'm so weirded out," I whisper.

"The poor boy is jealous, Ava. He's curious what he's up against."

Up against? I scoff. I laugh. I want to howl so loudly with laughter that I get a six-pack of abs. I want to pee my pants.

Derek and Grant being put in the same caliber sounds ridiculous. Derek doesn't hold a candle to Grant. Not even a drop of wax.

"You're a comedian, Chloe Danes. Should I try getting you onto

Saturday Night Live?"

She's a theater major. She works on Broadway. I probably shouldn't have said that because she shouts into my face, "Yes!!! Can you *really*?"

We now have the whole room's attention.

Actually, who's *we*? Chloe, as per usual, has the entire apartment's attention.

"I'm standing right here. You don't have to shout." I turn my attention to the room and announce, "All's good! Chloe is just being Chloe. Carry on!"

Grant catches my eye when I face everyone, so I match his giant smile and wave at him across the room. He winks at me. He fucking *winks* at me.

I whip around.

"If I don't have sex with that man one more time, I think I might die. I'll get so horny and throbby that it'll be painful and I'll combust. It's going to happen, Chloe. Something is going to happen to my ovaries if I don't give them what they want."

"He looks like he's good in bed." She whispers this, thank *God*. "Why do rich guys automatically look like sex gods?"

I whine because she is not making this any easier. "You have no idea," I groan.

Chloe probes me to tell her everything and *Right this second, Ruthie*. I get on my tiptoes to speak directly into her ear since I will most definitely die if someone overheard what I'm about to say.

"My legs would shake so violently every single time. I'd come so hard, I saw stars. I could've woken up the entire city with how loud I moaned if he didn't live in a penthouse."

Just *talking* about it has my stomach rolling with *that* sensation. I feel the throbbing between my legs. I have to squeeze them tight when I begin feeling that wave of oncoming, but unsatisfactory, pleasure.

"You should get back with him for that reason alone," Chloe mumbles before steering her focus behind me. I don't have to turn around to know Grant is walking toward us. I feel his presence. I always have.

"What are you two whispering about?" he asks, chuckling that amazing, masculine chuckle.

"Not at all about how good you are in bed!" Chloe nonchalantly ousts us, shrugging. I close my eyes and deflate. I am going to kill her.

I haven't looked at Grant yet. He's still behind me.

"If Chloe Penelope Danes ends up dead, don't bother looking for a suspect. I did it. Will you pay my bail?" I ask Grant, finally turning around. He looks down at me, amusement in his green eyes. He's got this pursed, teasing smile, and his eyes are dancing, watching me. This is funny to him because *of course it is*. Meanwhile, I'm mortified and caught.

I close my eyes and anticipate his pleased reply.

"Bail for what? I have no idea what she said. Do you plan on ending up in jail for something?"

No.

He didn't.

God, he did.

Perfect. He's perfect.

My eyes shoot up to his, disbelief written all over my face. Grant had every opportunity to question why I'm thinking about him in bed when we're supposedly *just friends* with *no future*, but he didn't take it. He's being sensitive to me and my boundaries.

This is like the night he wouldn't go to the steakhouse from our first date. He's being cautious for me. He's doing all of this for me. He gave me his word that this friendship wouldn't be complicated, and he's doing everything in his power to make sure I'm at ease.

I'm so grateful, I feel like crying.
We stare at each other. I swallow, then exhale shakily.
"Thank you," I whisper. "*Really. Thank you.*"

CHAPTER THIRTY NINE
AVA

"Thanks for staying to help me," I call out into my small living room.

Grant stayed back to help clean up the apartment after the party since I forced Chloe to go to Gabe's house. If I have to be woken up from her headboard banging against my bedroom wall one more time, I'm pitching a tent outside.

Grant waves me off like it was obvious he'd stay.

"Of course," he says, lifting a tub of Red Vines from the makeshift coffee table.

Chloe and I painted about thirty wooden crates a pretty shade of yellow and secured them with wood glue.

"Where do you want these?"

"In my room," I reply.

He bites the inside of his cheek to stop himself from howling. Grant looks at me with pure amusement circling his eyes. I'm glad I'm entertainment for him.

"Do you have a junk stash in your bedroom, Ava?" He teases me.

I pout. "Chloe eats all of my stuff when she's drunk, so I have to hide it from her if I want it to see the light of day."

I stare at Grant's eye creases when he laughs like this. They're beautiful, his creased skin displaying an extra layer of happiness on his pretty boy face. He notices me watching him and states, "Show me this junk stash of yours."

"Okay, but my room is messy. You can't judge me." I walk toward my bedroom and nod my head so he'll follow me.

"I won't judge you. Not for the mess, at least," Grant jokes, winking.

I shove him playfully and whine, "Hey!"

I'm about to let Grant into my room. Grant Wilder is about to see my bedroom.

Holy shit, I'm so nervous.

I walk slower than necessary in anticipation of how it'll feel seeing him in there. Seeing him in my new life, *bringing him* into my new life in this intimate way.

It's where I sleep every night. Being in my bedroom isn't meaningless, at least it isn't for me. This is a big deal, so, hello, *nervous*.

Grant reads my body language and circles around my frame, planting himself in front of me.

"You don't have to show me your bedroom, Ava," he says sincerely. "There is zero pressure; you know that, right?"

I blush and shuffle my feet in a nervous tick. "No, no. I want you to see it. I'm just nervous." I softly laugh at myself.

He shakes his head. "It's just me. I don't want you to be nervous with me."

It's not just you. You're not a just to me. You're pretty much my everything. You're the person I cherish the most in this world. Sharing my new life with you is the best thing that's ever happened to me.

I grab Grant's hand and march over to my room. It's the same way I brought him into the apartment earlier. Feeling his hand in mine gives me such fullness that it's tragic he isn't my forever person.

Grant analyzes my bedroom with a large grin splitting his unmarred face. I stand at the doorway as I watch him make his way around my stuff.

It's bizarre seeing him in my room, but it also isn't.

He lifts a random Post-It note from my nightstand with his long fingers, reads whatever is on it, then puts it down. He skims the back of a book I have on my desk with eager eyes. He bends and squints to view the photos I have taped to the wall opposite my bed. He unsticks one of the prints and tucks it into the inside pocket of his jacket without saying a single word, without asking for permission.

I don't ask which photo he took. I'm sure he finds it lovely if he's willing to steal it.

"Junk drawer?" he asks, pointing to the bottom drawer of my white Ikea desk. I nod, so he opens it. While sorting through the candy and chocolate I've accumulated, Grant snickers. He grabs a green Hi-Chew, unwraps it, and pops it in his mouth. He widens his eyes and gasps before I have a chance to mock him at the fact that he's eating candy!

"*Gasp! How dare I!*"

"I'm telling your dentist. You probably never even get told to floss anymore."

"Weirdo." Grant glances at the alarm clock by my bed. "It's getting late. Let's finish cleaning up."

It takes us another fifteen minutes to finish cleaning, but by the time we're done, the apartment is sparkling. It's infinitely cleaner than it was before the party.

"You could sleep over if you want," I say when I notice Grant checking his pockets to make sure he has what he needs to head out. He peers at me, gauges what I'm implying with my offer like it's something more than how it sounds. I quickly explain, "Just so you don't have to travel back home so late."

He peers at me, shakes his head. "I don't think that would be appropriate," he says.

"Okay, yeah. Yes. Of course. I'm sorry," I babble. "Sorry. Whoa."

"It's all good. I'll see you, okay?" he tells me at the door. The smile he offers me is tight.

"Yeah," I croak quietly. "Night."

CHAPTER FORTY
AVA

During my senior year of college when Chloe and I were roommates, I became a yes girl.

I said yes to everything because of her encouragement, her suggestion that in order to stay present and move forward from the pain I went through losing Grant, I would need to get out more, distract myself, meet new people.

Meet new people.

When I was so far down the deep end of my depression, I hated meeting new people. I felt like I was obligated to explain to them why I looked the way I looked.

Despondent. Dead inside.

That I had an excuse.

I was less than thrilled when Chloe had a million friends who she wanted me to meet. She'd bring me to parties with hundreds of people, and it always came with a little bit of anxiety that they would wonder about what caused me to look the way that I did—*what fucked* you *up?*

Retrospectively, I know I didn't owe anybody an explanation, and in the long run, Chloe's persistence was really good for me. I *did* meet people, and I made friends. Now, we have this group of ten of us that do everything together. Derek is included in that group as well as Gabe, Chloe's boyfriend. When his cousin, Sadie, got to New York a couple of weeks ago, Chloe took her under her wing.

It's Sadie's twenty-first birthday today, and because Chloe is kind of like a big sister to her, she organized a girls' brunch to celebrate how Sadie no longer has to use her fake ID. Later tonight, we're all meeting for dinner and drinks.

Chloe and I have our arms hooked around each other after brunch, supporting each other's weight. Bottomless mimosas are dangerous.

"I'm too drunk to subway back home," Chloe groans, plopping onto a nearby bench. "And too cheap to Uber."

Dinner tonight isn't until eight. We don't have to be home for another four hours. I look around to see if I recognize where we are, shrug, then pull my phone out. I may have left things awkwardly the night of my party, but Drunk Ava and Drunk Chloe need a safe haven right now. I push the cringey moment aside and call him. Grant answers immediately.

"Hello!" I shout into the receiver. My voice is overly chipper. He chuckles at me and says the same. "So, I have a question."

"What's up?" *God, I love his deep voice.*

"Can me and Chloe swing by your place? We're in your neighborhood, we're both a little drunk, and we don't have anything to do until—"

"Of course. Come on over."

GRANT SHOVES A water bottle in both of our faces when we show up wobbling down his apartment hallway still drunk from brunch.

Chloe and I look at each other and burst out laughing when we take the water from his big hands.

Once inside, Chloe sits with Grant at his kitchen island. I lie on the hardwood floor beside the sofa. If I turn my head a certain way, I can see them both.

My two best friends banter a few feet away about who I like more.

"I like you both the same, losers! Stop fighting!" I shout toward the kitchen. They're arguing like an old married couple.

"Hey, look, Ava! We're fighting over you!" Grant calls out.

"HA HA." He's making fun of what I said the night of my party. "You're the funniest person I've ever met," I say sarcastically.

He flicks a blue bottle cap at me. It lands in the center of my forehead.

Chloe proceeds to divulge embarrassing stories about me in an attempt to show Grant who knows me better. And because I drank too many mimosas and I'm still a little bit tipsy, I can't help laughing uncontrollably from the living room floor.

"CHLOE!" I shout across the room, trying to stop her. Grant is not having it.

"This one's mine, Ava! Don't even think about it!" He nods at Chloe to keep going, so she does. He hangs on to her every word like an excited puppy.

"We were out in the city one night, and Ava had a little too many. It was probably one of the first times I ever saw her drunk. Anyway, we're walking down the street toward our Uber when this older guy, like probably forty years old or something, heads in our direction with outstretched arms.

"Ava, for whatever reason, thought she knew him so she ran into his arms and hugged him so tight. He froze, but Ava just kept hugging him. She's like, 'You're so warm, mister,' and he asked, 'I'm sorry, do

I know you?' Anyway, his wife was right behind us looking so damn confused. I had to explain that Ava was drunk. When I pulled her off of him, she was yelling, 'But he was so warm! His belly was so warm!'"

I am choking. I am belly laughing. I am laughing so hard that my stomach hurts. Grant is laughing really hard, too, his deep voice echoing around his massive apartment. His emerald eyes squint, his head is thrown back, and he palms his stomach.

When Chloe has concluded this incriminating story, he asks for more. He isn't done yet. Chloe groans.

"Okay, I have to think of something!" She complains that it isn't easy because she's drunk. Grant looks at her sitting across from him with anticipation in his eyes. He smiles fondly.

"Anything," he tells Chloe. "It doesn't matter. Tell me everything about her. Tell me everything that I missed."

Gah, my heart.

Chloe proceeds with another two stories she manages to dig up out of that drunken brain of hers. One about the time I fainted while presenting in front of our Communications class and another about the time I couldn't kiss Derek the night of my birthday.

She's drunk. She doesn't realize who she's talking about and who she's talking to.

"She just, like, couldn't kiss him because he wasn't you. Isn't that crazy? I mean, I love Gabe and all, but I doubt I'd choke if another guy came so close to me."

My breath hitches. I begin to sweat uncomfortably and wave her off, chuckle through a choked throat. "Chlo, he doesn't want to hear about that. Come on, stop."

She continues as if she hasn't heard me. "She'll take you back one day, I guarantee it. Don't you worry. It's just a matter of—"

I stand abruptly from my stance on the floor. With furrowed

eyebrows, avoiding Grant's eye, I face Chloe and angrily retort, "No, I won't. Why would you give him false hope like that? Chloe, you have to stop. Stop talking. You're drunk."

I walk over to Chloe, continue to avoid Grant's eye when I profusely apologize for the lines she's crossed, then grip her wrist and scurry to the door.

With a shaky voice and an incredible amount of shame, my hand gripping the door knob to Grant's front door, I awkwardly call out, "Sorry. She's just… Sorry. I'll see you, okay?"

Out of the corner of my eye, I watch his slow nod, his frustrated expression as he observes me panic. The lump in my throat grows heavy. I swallow it the entire way home.

CHAPTER FORTY-ONE
GRANT

My phone pings with a text message from Ava.

We haven't seen each other since the last two times; once at her place and once at mine. Both times left me with questions impossible to answer.

I don't want to confront her. I swore that I'd keep this platonic friendship simple, and I very much intend to do that. I gave Ava my word on our drive home from Montauk that it wouldn't be complicated, but that feeling of hope that one day I'll get her back, especially with the signs she's been unintentionally giving me, will always simmer in my chest. I hate that it's a false hope, as she called it. I don't know if Ava is giving it to me or if I've construed it on my own.

I'm pretty sure it's the former. But how do I even try to understand that? *Why* is she talking about me in bed? *Why* did she invite me to sleep over? *Why* couldn't she kiss someone else? Is it really because it wasn't me? Is it because…

Like I said. Questions that are impossible to answer.

I check the text.

>Ava Ruth: I have a lawyer question. It's for work.

Oof. I didn't see this coming.

> Me: All right. Hit me.
>
> Ava Ruth: Is dispute resolution the same thing as settling?

God, she's cute.

> Me: Yes.
>
> Ava Ruth: Thanks
>
> Ava Ruth: Also, can you explain deposition to me?
>
> Ava Ruth: Just kidding
>
> Ava Ruth: That was a joke

I belt out a loud laugh. It's incredible how solid she is now.

> Me: You are unexpected, Campbell.
>
> Ava Ruth: It's part of my charm.

You don't say. Another ping sounds.

> Ava Ruth: Are you still a lawyer?
>
> Me: Technically, yes.
>
> Ava Ruth: Cool. I'll call you esquire from now on.
>
> Me: Please don't.
>
> Ava Ruth: CALLUM GRANT WILDER III ESQUIRE!!!
>
> Me: Get back to work, weirdo.

Ava Ruth: Ok byeeeeee.

THE NEXT DAY, Ava texts again.

It's eleven at night. I imagine her the same way I am: in bed, showered, comfortable. I love that she's texting me before she goes to sleep. Work has been insane, and I miss her.

Ava Ruth: Are we still friends?

As if I could ever walk away from this friendship.
I'm enjoying this. I'll enjoy it for however long she lets me.

I must have made Ava feel like I'm distancing myself from her because of everything that's happened; what she said the night of her party, what Chloe said that same night, what Chloe told me at my place. I've honestly just been busy with work. I haven't had a second to focus.

I text Ava back.

Me: We are definitely still friends.

Ava Ruth: Promise?

Me: Swear. We are BFFS 4ever.

Ava Ruth: HAHAHAHAH

Ava Ruth: Yay

Ava Ruth: I like that

Ava Ruth: Yayyyyy

I'm about to head into a big meeting when my phone vibrates. I slip away to check it in case it's Ava. Sure enough, it is.

> Ava Ruth: Hi
>
> Ava Ruth: Do you want to get dinner with me tonight?

Damn. I'm disappointed that I have to decline, but this meeting is important. If it wasn't, I'd leave. I hope she knows that. I hope she knows that I still love her. I hope she knows that I want her back. *Does she know that I want her back?*

> Me: I'm so sorry, but I can't. I have a meeting. Rain check?
>
> Ava Ruth: Yeah, okay
>
> Ava Ruth: Good luck on the meeting

Four hours later, yes *four hours later,* I close up shop and leave the office to head home. I check my phone while waiting for the elevator to reach my floor and find an unread text from Ava.

She sent it five minutes after her last text, but because of the meeting, I'm only seeing it now. That breaks my heart.

> Ava Ruth: What about Thursday? I have a work thing. Do u want to come with me?
>
> Me: I'm sorry, I'm only seeing this now. I'd love to go to a work thing with you.

Ava responds within a matter of seconds. The typing bubble appears before I can read my text back to myself.

Ava Ruth: Really?

Me: Of course. Why not?

Ava Ruth: Idk. I didn't think you'd say yes

Ava Ruth: But I'm happy you did

Ava Ruth: It's in Tribeca at 6:00 on Thursday

Me: I'll be there.

CHAPTER FORTY-TWO
AVA

"Hi!" I exclaim at the sight of him.

My heart is pounding. I swallow. *Don't scare him off.* I tone it down. "Sorry. Hi," I repeat quieter.

I haven't seen Grant in what feels like months, hence the loud greeting, but tonight he's randomly showed up at Annie's house.

If only I hadn't suggested he sleep over the night of my party, I wouldn't have pushed him away. If only Chloe hadn't told him we were discussing how good he is in bed. If only she kept her mouth shut about my aversion to Derek's lips. Now, I've given Grant a level of confusion he doesn't deserve. This was supposed to be, and only ever will be, friendship. Platonic, through and through, but it feels like Grant is coming to terms with the fact that I'm really not taking him back and has decided to distance himself from this friendship. Like he was only in this for the potential relationship we'd have again and is uninterested in being anything less.

After Montauk, I told Grant that I would try my best to make this friendship work, and I have. The moment I noticed a rift between us, specifically after Chloe's ramble at his apartment, I've been trying really, really hard. I've texted him a million times, but he's only replied passively, took his time. I would have even called him, but if I'd heard his voice, I'd have choked. I wasn't prepared to hear his less than excited tone because I know I'd be all bubbles and unicorns.

That makes me want to never show my face again. I feel so dumb.

I blush hard, embarrassed with myself at how happy I still am to see him, and attempt to walk away toward the kitchen, but Grant pulls at my arm.

"Wait. Don't go. Hi back," he says, looking into my eyes. He smiles that pretty smile I long to see, and it creates a lump in my throat. I avert my gaze.

"Um, I'm leaving now. It's 8:00, so…"

"I know. That's why I'm here," he says. "I sent Thibault home. I'm driving you tonight."

I blink up at him, disoriented. "Really?" My voice is small. I want to punch myself. I seem desperate because I am.

When Grant hugs me tightly, I stiffen. He can sense it. There is guilt in his eyes when he finally leans back to look at me. "I'm sorry I've been M.I.A. Work is just insane right now, but I promise I'll make it up to you."

I shrug nonchalantly, but I'm not convinced that's all this was. "You have nothing to be sorry for," I say, my tone casual. "You don't owe me anything. I'm good."

I am not good. I am on the verge of crying.

Annie's voice has us both swinging our heads in her direction. She suddenly slows her typically rapid descent down the stairs and watches us, looking back and forth between her brother and me.

Her eyes are on mine when she asks, "You good, babe?"

I vented to her about this. She knows I feel abandoned by him. She knows how idiotic I feel for the texting and the trying and the receiving barely any reciprocation. She knows how stupid and naïve

I feel at how excited the prospect of a platonic friendship made me.

I nod with a tight smile.

"Do you want to go home with him? I could tell Thibault to come back."

Grant looks between Annie and me, genuinely baffled at what she's implying. He is so taken aback. Grant is *offended*.

"What…I… Okay, *what*? What's going on? Why wouldn't you want to drive home with me?"

I don't have an answer for him, but I don't have to. Annie takes matters into her own hands. "I don't know, maybe because you ghosted her for the past two weeks?"

His head inches forward. His eyes spring wide. "*Ghosted? What?*"

This isn't a thing, this isn't a thing, this isn't a thing.

I'm not doing this, I'm not doing this, I'm not doing this.

"She's exaggerating. We're all good. Shall we?" I head for the door but stop to walk back over to hug Annie goodbye. *Then*, I head for the door, fist the door knob, and step out onto the front porch of Annie's brownstone.

Grant stops me mid-power walk toward his car once I've made it to the sidewalk. The expression on his face reads *shattered*.

"I swear to God, I've been busy with work. Ask Dina. Ask Adam. Look at my email. I'm not lying to you."

I keep my expression even. I keep my voice steady when I reply, "Okay. I believe you."

He doesn't like my tone of voice. He scoffs at me.

How was *I* wronged, and *he's* the one who's upset?

"Let's just—"

"I'm still in love with you. You know that, right?" he states strongly.

I freeze. I shake, itch to walk away because *holy shit*, I don't want to do this right now.

No, no, no. I'm not doing this. No.

When I fail to respond, Grant continues. "Tell me why I've been friends with other girls before, yet this feels different? And not just because I still love you, but because of the way you've been acting toward me."

Because I want as much as I can get from you before this all ends when you find your future person. Which can't be me, as you so eloquently told your fiancée.

He continues. "Offering for me to sleep over and talking about me in bed and—"

I'm going to die if he keeps going. *I'm going to fucking die.*

I interrupt him. "I'm not having this conversation. This doesn't have to be a thing. You were busy with work. It's fine. Just take me home, okay?"

Grant looks down at me from three stories high. He mimics my tone of voice from earlier and steadily says, "I thought you didn't want complicated."

"I didn't," I retort. "I don't."

"Ghosted sounds complicated to me," he says monotonously.

"I didn't use that word, your sister did. I didn't say shit."

"Then why are you all depressed when I've just been busy with work?" he spits, annoyed at my obvious wish to end this conversation.

Okay. Hear me out. Once you've been diagnosed with a chemical imbalance in your brain that ruins your life, that word no longer poses as a loose adjective. I deflate at that word. That word isn't allowed anywhere near me. That word doesn't belong in my vocabulary or the vocabulary of my best friend.

Ha. Best friend. *As if.*

It hurts when he calls me depressed. It hurts. "Fuck you," I whisper. My throat is knotted. I feel like I've been knocked out.

Shock must be written all over my face. I take a step back.

"Ava—"

"Don't you dare ever use that word with me again."

"Ava—" Grant tries again. He's frantic, eyes wired.

I walk away from him. I march down the street, but no, I'm not done here. I'm not done yelling. But the moment I turn around to shove him as hard as I can, his palms are on my cheeks. My face is cradled in his hands. His lips are an inch away from mine.

I freeze.

Please kiss me.

Please don't kiss me.

"I'm really sorry. I'll never say that word again. But please stop giving me false hope," he rumbles into my mouth. "And it isn't Chloe, it's you that's doing it. Now, get in the car."

I stare at his back when he walks to his Porsche, but I don't move an inch. He's the only person I want comfort from, a big warm hug, but he's why I need comfort. His distance hurt me. He could have texted me to let me know he's busy with work. I'm still pressed about that.

Grant slips into the driver's seat and watches my every move, or lack thereof, through the windshield. Eventually, he takes a deep breath, exits the car, and walks back over to me. He stands a foot away.

"Do you want to pretend that the last ten minutes didn't happen, or do you want to talk about it?"

"I want to punch you," I respond dryly.

"So, punch me." I roll my eyes at him. "I'm serious. Punch me."

"Go away. I'm ordering an Uber."

When he follows my direction and walks away, I have to mentally glue myself to the sidewalk to keep myself from running after him like I want to. I won't. I need some self-preservation and dignity after the last couple of weeks.

However, he doesn't head for the driver's seat. Instead, he opens the trunk of his car and walks back over to me carrying two things under his arm.

"Give me your right hand," he demands roughly.

"Why?"

Grant exhales in frustration and takes my right hand himself. He pulls a roll of fabric out from under his arm and begins wrapping my hand in a distinct and intricate way.

"What is this?" He doesn't answer me. "What are you doing?" He remains silent, but it slowly comes to me when he pulls out a boxing glove that his elbow has been supporting against his waist and slides it onto my hand.

He securely fastens it then takes a step back. "Punch me."

"Grant—"

"I'm giving you what you want," he interrupts. "You said you want to punch me, so punch me."

With lifeless eyes, I deadpan when I look up at him. "You have issues," I say.

"Lots of them," he agrees with a nod.

"I don't like you very much."

"I don't like me very much either."

With the desire to tease him because that is my favorite part about us, I ask, "Where can I punch you?"

His eyes finally come back to life. I bite my lip to keep from smiling. I think my eyes are coming back to life, too.

"Anywhere," he says.

"You don't mean that."

"I do." Grant takes my arm and securely positions my gloved hand. "Come on, punch me."

"Do you have a pain kink?"

"I have an Ava kink. Now, punch me."

That's interesting because what do you know, I have a Grant kink!

"I'm going to do it," I say stiffly.

"Good."

"I really will."

"Then, do it."

Both mine and Grant's phones ping at the same time, distracting us from this stupid banter. It's not easy, but I manage to shuffle around to grab my phone with my left hand since I'm currently immobile in my right.

We check the message; we look at each other, then at Annie's house. She stands at the floor-to-ceiling window with her phone out. She sent us a picture of us in real time. We look ridiculous.

"You guys look ridiculous!" she yells out of her living room window.

I look back at the photo, then back at Grant. Instantly, we erupt in a loud cackle. It takes us a few moments to catch our breaths.

"Fuck, Av. I missed you," Grant groans toward the sky. "That's not us. *This* is us."

I missed you, too. More than anything. "I know," I rasp.

"I'd do anything to hug you right now."

He doesn't have to do a single damn thing because as soon as he finishes speaking, I throw myself at him. I hug him so tightly that his neck might snap.

I really missed this stupid boy.

"I can't tell if you're trying to hug me or kill me," he grunts out jokingly. I chuckle and ease my tight grip.

He buries his lips in my hair. After a few seconds, he whispers, "I'll try harder, okay? I swear to you that I'll try harder."

CHAPTER FORTY-THREE
AVA

I wake up to an unread text from Grant.

Somehow, I knew I would after last night. I believe him when he says he'll try harder. I know he wasn't ghosting me. My stupid insecure brain was just telling me that I want this friendship more than he does, but I know it's not true. It can't be true. He was busy with work. If I'm naïve for believing that, so be it.

> CALLUM GRANT WILDER III ESQUIRE: Hey, you! Good morning! How did you sleep?
>
> Me: Hey, G Wagon
>
> Me: I slept good. What about you?
>
> CALLUM GRANT WILDER III ESQUIRE: New nickname?
>
> Me: I get honey and Av. It's only fair.
>
> CALLUM GRANT WILDER III ESQUIRE: Noted. I slept well. Thank you for asking.
>
> Me: I would, too, if I had your ginormous bed

CALLUM GRANT WILDER III ESQUIRE: Ha ha. Can I call you?

I roll my eyes at his formality and pull my phone out to call him. He's excited when he exclaims, "Hey! I was just about to call you."

I giggle. "I know. What's up?"

Grant asks if we're still on for that work thing on Thursday night that I mentioned. I tell him that I'll be going, but he doesn't have to come.

"If you're going, I'm going." How *resolute*. "Are you busy Friday?" he asks.

I'm not working, but I don't think the office is opened because of the party on Thursday night. Mr. Homer made partner, so the firm is throwing him a little soiree at a hotel cocktail bar. I was invited because I'm his assistant. I don't have many work friends, but I can't not go which is why I asked Grant to join me. I mean, I want him at my side at all times, but I wouldn't ask him to forfeit his evening for a law firm party unless I was desperate.

I realize that he'll be surrounded by a bunch of lawyers and wonder if this is a big ask.

"No, but…," I start slowly. "You know I work for a law firm, right?"

"Yes."

"Are you still comfortable coming with me?" He tells me I'm sweet for the warning, but that he'll be totally fine.

"More than fine, actually. I'll be hanging out with you." *Gah.* Then he says, "So… My parents are hosting a fundraiser at their house on Friday morning, and my grandparents flew in for it. I wouldn't be going otherwise, but I'm wondering if you wanted to come?"

His *grandparents*. I've never met his grandparents.

Did Hannah? *Gulp.*

"The Texas ones?" I wonder.

Grant hums an affirmative sound. "Yeah, my dad's parents. They're coming out here from Houston."

If anything, to meet your grandparents. To meet everyone in your life before you're not mine anymore.

Well, not that you're mine now, but…

Enough, Ava.

"I'd love to come!" I reply, getting more excited the more I think about it. "Thanks for inviting me."

Shortly after we conclude the conversation with plans for Grant to pick me up before Mr. Homer's party, he calls me back.

"Wait. Talk to me. What are you up to today?"

Trying.

"You're going in that?"

I study Grant head to toe from the front step of my apartment building. He stands opposite me with his back against his car. He's still wearing his work suit. The whole thing.

Grant opens the door for me, then glances down at his outfit. Once I'm seated, he asks, "Why? Should I not?"

I frown. He doesn't look like himself.

When he closes my door then slides into the driver's seat beside me, I admit, "You look uptight and grumpy." He releases a low chuckle and shakes his head at me like I've charmed him.

"Okay," he states. "Help me look down loose and happy then."

I am pleasantly stupefied. "*Down. Loose.*" I groan at the dad joke.

He shrugs. "It's the opposite of uptight."

I reach my arm over the console and flick Grant's five o'clock shadowed cheek. He grabs my hand before I can take it back and kisses it.

He kissed my hand. I gasp quietly, then clear my throat.

"Who's the weirdo now, Wilder? The fuck?"

"You going to help me or not, *Campbell*?"

He parks around the block from the hotel once we've made the twenty-minute drive to Lower Manhattan. I stand before him to assess how I could make him look *down loose* once we slip out of his car.

I tap my index finger on my lower lip and take more time than necessary to study every inch of Grant Wilder. He seems amused, anticipating my suggestion when he studies me studying him.

"Lose the tie," I say finally. "Unbutton the top two buttons of your shirt, and…" I scruff his hair to make it a little messy. I do it twice because his hair is soft.

"There. You're welcome."

I wait for him to make the necessary adjustments, then walk toward the hotel beside him.

When he looks down at me, there is light in his eyes. There is admiration in his eyes.

"What?" I ask. When he shakes his head endearingly, I whine, "What?"

"We're headed to a work thing. *Your* work thing. Do you know how fucking proud I am of you?"

It will never not make me feel like a trillion dollars when Grant tells me he's proud of me.

His palm grazes my back when he leads me into the hotel bar. I haven't managed to finish my first glass of champagne before the questions about Grant and I come.

How long have you two been together?

How did you meet?

You two are the most attractive couple I've ever seen.

"He's my husband," I explain casually to an older woman I've never met. She is draped in pearls and a tweed skirt suit. Her wispy white hair is blown out like she had it done on the drive over here.

I'm hoping she isn't a client or an employee at our firm as I continue my fib.

"We've been married *ten* years. How crazy!"

The woman looks perturbed. She turns to Grant for confirmation. He nods. "It's true," he replies deeply. "Eleven in January. Just had our first grandchild."

I snort into my drink, then cough to mask it. "Sorry. The bubbles. Haven't had a glass of champagne since the baby was born."

I look up at Grant with a tender smile as a display of affection for Edith (an uneducated guess). I'm pretty sure we've scared her away because when the tall bearded server approaches us with more champagne, she quickly scurries off.

When the server asks if I'd like another glass, I exclaim, "Ah! Yes! Fill me up!"

I can feel Grant lean into my ear from behind me. He waits for the server to walk away before mumbling, "That's what she said."

I slap a palm over my mouth when an obnoxious cackle bursts out of it. Then, I turn around and beam up at him. "You're twelve."

He takes a sip of champagne and shrugs. "You laughed, didn't you?"

"Is that your only goal? To make me laugh?"

"Quite literally, yes," he replies deeply.

I poke his hard belly. Then, I fist bump it because there is no give.

After introducing Grant to Mr. Homer (not as my husband), I've decided we've been here for an appropriate amount of time and can officially tap out of the party. There are signs for a rooftop lounge in the lobby of this hotel, so I ask Grant to take me. Naturally, he does.

My nose scrunches the moment we step onto the skyscraper-lined rooftop. I lean my head back in disgust. "What is that smell? That is *putrid*."

"Marijuana," Grant replies factually.

No way.

Hell yes.

Yes, yes, yes!

I gasp excitedly and mischievously narrow my eyes at Grant. He slips both hands in his suit pants pockets and shakes his head. "No," he refuses curtly.

"Why not!" I whine.

"No chance, Ava. You're not going to win this one." I pout and flutter my eyelashes. He watches me with one eyebrow raised. "You really think that's going to work?" He sounds bored.

"I *know* it's going to work," I sass.

"It won't." But after a bit more of my puppy whining, it does. He caves. "Fine, but only if we do it at home, and I source it."

"Deal."

Oh my God, we're getting high together.

I'm so excited, I could die.

CHAPTER FORTY-FOUR
AVA

"I'm not sure about this, Ava."

We're on Grant's upstairs balcony standing across from each other. He pinches the weed between his index finger and thumb and looks at me guiltily.

"Grant, I'm going to smoke at least once in my lifetime, and when I eventually do, I want you there because I trust you. If I start to have a panic attack or whatever, I know you'll take care of me. There's no one else I have faith in like I do you."

I smile cheekily after my spiel. I haven't seemed to ease his nerves, though.

"You really want to do this?" I nod to assure him. "Swear to me," he demands.

"I swear."

He clicks his tongue. "No, say the full thing." I roll my eyes at Mr. Professor over here and recite, "I swear I want to smoke this joint and get high right now."

Grant shakes his head at me, takes a deep breath, and mutters, "Anything for this one."

He puts the joint in his mouth, lights the tip of it with an orange

BIC lighter, and inhales. He holds it out for me, but when I take it, I don't put it in my mouth. I look down at it in my fingers, then up at him wearily.

"Could you tell me what will happen?" I ask.

He nods. "Everyone's different," he begins explaining. "Your body could feel super relaxed, your brain can run a mile a minute, you could find everything funny, and you'll likely get the munchies."

"I'll be hungry?" I wonder.

"It's more so that you'll want to eat, not get hungry. Does that make sense?"

What's Grant like when he's high? Does he find everything funny? Does he finally eat junk food?

I love experiencing all the different sides of this man. As a brother, an uncle, a son.

Drunk, happy, grumpy.

And now, high. *Ah!*

I briefly weigh the pros and cons of getting high in my head just to say that I thought this through, but I already know I want to do this more than anything. I want my first time to be with him.

Frankly, I'm glad I haven't done this yet, so Grant could be my first.

He'll always be my first.

My first everything. My life started again when I met him.

I look up at him. His eyebrows have been perpetually knitted since my work party. The reluctant look hasn't vanished, even after I swore to him that I want to do this.

I reach up and rub the creased space between his thick eyebrows with my thumb.

"Why are you so hesitant?" I ask tenderly.

"Because I feel responsible for you, and I've supplied you with drugs." I ask Grant if he made sure that whatever we're about to smoke is clean. "Of course. It's the cleanest out there. This shit is straight from a farm in Connecticut."

As soon as he caved on the rooftop earlier, he sent someone a quick text. By the time we got to his apartment, Bobby, Grant's doorman, had the sealed, black pouch waiting for us behind the front desk.

I snicker and sarcastically say, "Whoa! I'm about to smoke rich people weed? I'm the coolest person ever!"

He sticks a finger up my nose. *There he is.* I shove him away and giggle.

"Hey, you better do this with me," I tell him sternly. He assures me that he will. I hand the joint back to him and say, "Then you go first."

I watch his every move with bright eyes and a giddy smile. I can't properly articulate how stoked and excited I am to meet High Grant. After taking a few puffs, he passes it to me.

"Inhale it slowly. Don't let the smoke sit in your mouth."

I inch the joint toward my mouth, but before I can do anything, he quickly stops me.

"Wait, wait. Let me get you some water. You might cough a lot since it's your first time."

Grant steps back onto the balcony a couple of minutes later and hands me a blue plastic cup that has junk food motifs all over it. I laugh when he says, "I forgot that I got you this."

"I love it. When?"

"Like last week? It reminded me of you."

I beam at him. He's the sun.

"I wish I was there to witness you placing this cup on a conveyor belt looking the way you do," I tease. He asks what I mean. I reply, "Stoic, intimidating, and untouchable."

The chuckle Grant releases is sultry and deep. "Are those the three words you'd use to describe me?" he asks.

"Objectively, yeah."

"And subjectively?"

There are about a bajillion other words I'd use to describe the person you are to me and what I think of you.

Grant stands a foot away from me. When I don't give him his subjective words, he swallows before quietly saying, "Sunshine, vigor, and compassion. Those are your three. Subjective and objective. That's just who you are."

Mr. Wilder, would you stop making me fall more in love with you, please?

I mean, don't, but do.

Kiss me, but also don't kiss me.

"Are you trying to distract me with nice words, Wilder?"

He chuckles and reaches for the joint in my hand. "Nah. Here, let me light it for you."

Grant places the skinny end of the joint between his wine-red lips and pulls the lighter out again. He focuses on his movements when he places flame to joint and inhales. Then, he gives it to me, but not in my hand. He puts it in my mouth.

"Inhale slowly."

Naturally, I take too sharp of a drag and launch into a violent coughing fit. Grant quickly hands me the water and rests his warm palm on my back until I've settled down.

When I give him the go ahead, he relights the joint. "Try again. Slowly, hon. Use your lungs, not your mouth."

I close my eyes to focus on following his very specific direction.

"Exactly like that. Good girl," he mutters deeply.

Oh, he did not *just "Good girl" me!*

After two successful hits of the joint, I attempt a third, but he stops me. "Start with two. You could always do more."

"Okay! So, now what?"

"Now, we wait," he explains like he's talking to a nine-year-old.

"How long does it take? Are you high yet?"

There's that deep throaty chuckle I love so much.

Oh God, everything he does tonight is going to make me swoon, isn't it?

"Getting there," he mutters. He watches me with every ounce of love in this world accompanied by reluctant anticipation.

"Really?!" I squeak. I flap my hands in the air. "Okay, okay. Quick. Say something funny."

I can hear the echo of Grant's loud bellow across the balcony into the night sky. I want to record it and save it for forever because it's my most perfect, favorite sound in the world.

"It doesn't work like that, clown." He shuffles my hair and looks at me the same way I'm looking at him.

We watch each other with such admiration, and the best part is that even if this is intense and somehow already emotional, I don't feel like running or distancing myself from what could never be. Tonight, I feel like savoring the love I have from him and enjoying it and throwing myself into it with resolve.

"I'm bored," I finally say into the silence. I slump my shoulders. "Can we get some food and go to the park or something?"

Grant's lips purse, but not in a strait-laced way. More like he's holding in his laughter.

"What?" He doesn't say anything. "What!" I whine.

He inches his head slightly forward and opens his eyes wide. They're so red, it's scary against the flickers of a dozen shades of green.

"It hit you?" I guess. Grant shrugs. "Say something! What do you feel? What do you want to do or say or eat? Are you remembering something funny?"

Grant sighs with humor in his eyes. He doesn't know what to do with me. "Don't wait for something to happen, honey. Relax and ride the wave, okay? I want you to enjoy it." He nods to his front door. After asking if I'm okay walking, he says, "Let's get food. Central Park is waiting for us."

I skip to the door like Dorothy and Toto.

I put my palm into Grant's palm when he reaches it out to me once we've made it to the sidewalk. It feels different. We've held hands before, and I'm not only referring to when we were together last year. Tonight is different because it's initiated by Grant, not by me. That makes it feel real. That makes me feel like he's pretending I'm his, too.

Within the first few steps of our journey to find food, he laces his long fingers with my small ones and lightly squeezes. I squeeze his hand back. He never does boyfriend stuff with me, so I'm reeling. If we decide tomorrow that whatever happened tonight is too much, we'll blame it on the high.

"What do you want to eat?" he asks.

"You choose."

"No, no," he tsks, clicking his tongue. "You know how this goes, Ava Ruth."

"It's Opposite Day because we're high," I whisper loudly into his chest.

After repeatedly assuring him that I'm good and I'm not anxious and my heart is beating fine and I don't have a headache, he untenses his shoulders. When he knows I'm doing well, he can finally relax. How crazy is that?

"What about you? Are you okay?" I ask him.

"I'm great. I'm glad you pushed for this. This is fucking amazing," he admits. He mumbles the words because I've officially secured myself an *I told you so* moment.

"I'm always right, you know."

He giggles at me. Grant Wilder *giggles*.

I skitter ahead to stand in front of him and halt his step, placing my palm in the middle of his hard chest.

"Do that again," I demand. I am a no-nonsense woman right now.

"What?"

"You just giggled. Do it again."

"I have no idea what you're talking about." He says it in a joking way but also shyly. To change the subject, he asks, "What do you think of Chinese?"

"Like the people? What do I think about them?"

"The food, Ava. Chinese food. For dinner."

I laugh so loudly at myself. Grant looks at me, amused. I am his greatest source of entertainment. He should pay me double what he pays his cable network.

"Are we acting weird?" I whisper into him. "Am I being crazy?"

"No. You're acting like yourself, only a little…ditsier." Grant smiles at me. He is absolutely smitten with High Ava right now. "It's really cute. Adorable actually."

I scrunch my nose in response. He groans up at the sky. "Fuck, I love that face."

Eleven minutes later, I follow Grant into a fancy Chinese restaurant. He sits us in the corner of the room away from most of the other patrons. He's quick to skim the menu and call the waiter over. There is no reason for him to order eight things off the menu, but he does. When I tell him he ordered too much food, he sighs and groans, "I'm fucking starving."

"Babadadum! Behold! The munchies! Gimme your phone." I make a *come here* motion with my hand. He hands it to me immediately.

"0-5-2-2," he says. His password.

Is that a freaking joke?!

"You're insane," I tell him pointedly.

"Hm?" he wonders. His lips are puckered at the end of a straw. He peels his mouth away from the plastic and asks, "Why?"

"That's my birthday," I state plainly.

He waves me off like he thought I'd say something a little more riveting and what I've said is nothing to fuss about.

"That's been my password for two years, Ava."

I study him. He looks at me like I'm overreacting, like it isn't a big deal that every time Hannah opened his phone, she typed in her fiancé's ex-girlfriend's birthday. *Dear God, I'd hate to be her.*

I type in Grant's password, pull up the camera app, and set it to selfie mode. I lean the phone against the glass bottle of water on our table and look at the screen together with him.

It's just our two hazy and loopy and goofy faces. I hit record.

"You're documenting this?" he asks.

"Yup."

"Don't let your parents see it. They might kill me," he mutters quietly so the mic doesn't pick up on what he says. I roll my eyes at him then turn back to the screen.

"Hello. I am Ava Ruth Campbell. My date of birthday is May 22, 1997, and my social security number is 118-30—"

Grant slaps his palm over my mouth before I could recite all nine digits. "You are an identity thief's greatest treasure."

"Your turn," I mumble into the skin of his palm.

He turns to face the camera and begins his introduction. "Hello. I am Callum Grant Wilder—"

"The third!" I chime in.

He nods once. "The third. My date of *birth* is—"

"December 16, 1989!" I interrupt again.

Grant looks straight at the camera. "I have a spokesperson. Anyway, we're at Liu Sin's in the Upper East Side. We might be a little inebriated—"

"We're high as fuuuuuck." I use a deep bro dude voice, and it makes Grant laugh. "Hey, guess what! Grant giggled tonight!"

"I did no such thing." He says it in a teacher voice.

While we're still recording this silly video, our server walks over to our table with three plates of food. Grant thanks him and maneuvers the plates to fit on our table. I lean into his phone, so my mouth is close to the mic and whisper, "Our appetizers are here."

Grant feeds me before he feeds himself. I have chipmunk cheeks because he's shoving food in my face.

I love him so much. He takes such good care of me. Grant catches me watching him and sends me a sheepish smile.

"What?" My mouth is full, so I shrug my shoulder in response.

I love you, I love you, I love you.

That's what.

That is what I think every time I look at you, pretty boy.

I AM BEING carried via piggy back ride toward Central Park. This muscular back holds me up, firm hands keep me close.

We snuck into an alleyway to smoke more once Grant paid for our food and we left the restaurant. He helped me inhale the weed then, too.

When we finally reach Central Park and Grant finds a spot that's quiet and he deems safe, he stands tall, so I can slide off his back. We plop onto the lush grass and both groan in unison, leaning back to lie down.

My stomach hurts from all the food we ate tonight, so lying down is uncomfortable. Turning on my side, I use my hand as a headrest and face Grant. He turns onto his stomach and rests his head in the crook of his folded arms, so he can see me better. He smiles so vividly and brightly, even if he isn't showing any teeth. He's doing whatever grinning without teeth is called.

His eyes are… I don't think I have to describe it. I'm not sure I adequately can, but imagine a kid staring directly into a tub of candy.

Even clams aren't as happy as Grant is right now.

"Hi." His voice is calm and raspy. My two favorite combinations.

"Hi," I whisper back. I bite my bottom lip to keep from painting my cheeks with the biggest smile in the world, but he knows. I know he knows because he feels it, too.

"How are you feeling?"

"Great. What about you?"

"I've never felt happier in my life." His voice is hoarse and nervy, but it's real. His love for me is so fucking *real*.

"Me too," I rasp nervously. To lighten the mood, I joke, "Can we get high every day?"

"It's not the weed," he mutters, watching me. "It's you. It's us."

I lay my stomach on the ground and change positions to match Grant's, so we're both pressing our cheeks into our folded forearms, looking at each other.

I'm not sure how long it is that we look at one another like this, but man, it's glorious. It's golden. It's perfection, every meaning of the word. My heart feels full. My heart doesn't think about our broken future. My heart is here in Central Park with Grant Wilder. My heart is his. This time, I don't say it in a bad way. My heart is his, and he's taking perfect care of it.

He's loving it. He's loving every millimeter of my heart.

Grant removes one of his long arms from under his scruffy cheek and reaches for my head. He plays with my hair, intently watching what he's doing. I see him following the movements of his hand.

He's so perfect. He's the best person to ever exist.

"I'm happy I met you," I tell him quietly.

"Yeah?" He tucks my hair behind my ear and lays his palm on my back. When I nod, he says, "You sure about that?" in a teasing tone.

"I've never been more sure about anything. Except..." I try to think of something silly to say but blank. "Yeah, no. Can't think of anything."

"Junk food," he jokes.

"You're ranked slightly higher than junk food."

"Ice cream," he tries again.

"Third place," I tell him.

"Kraft mac and cheese."

"Whoop!" I shout. "You got me there! You've been bumped down to second place, and you have nobody to blame but yourself."

"And the Kraft family..."

I giggle. Laughing in this state is wonderful.

"I actually know a Kraft," Grant recalls.

I snort. Of course he does. "Of course you do."

"He smells like cheese."

I close my eyes and brace myself for the laughter that comes on stronger with every second. I'm near losing it, and his comment was not a ten out of ten funny.

"That's my favorite sound in the world." Grant gulps. He's back to being in love with me.

Quietly, I ask, "Why do you care about me so much?"

The word *much* doesn't fully leave my mouth before Grant replies,

"Because you're perfect. You're a beautiful person. Sometimes, it feels like you were made for me. Like God handed you to me and said, 'This one is yours now. Take care of her.'"

Dear God.

"Grant," I sigh. He's about to apologize for the intimacy, but that's not why I sigh. I sigh because the burst of emotion I feel in my chest at his words needs companionship.

"Tell me more," I whisper. "Tell me everything."

We're high. We have the perfect excuse, even if we'll remember it all tomorrow.

Grant takes a deep breath. He says this next part with his eyes glued to mine. "I didn't know what love was until I had you to protect."

It's too much, his gaze on mine, so I close my eyes and anticipate more from his heart. He manages to somehow deepen his already deep voice.

It's his Ava voice.

"All of the good in my life is because you're in it. You're my soulmate. It sounds cliché, but if soulmates are real, you're mine."

"You know how I know this is real?" I rasp with my eyes still closed because of how intense this conversation is between two people who can't be together.

"How?" he whispers softly.

"Because you still act like we're in the honeymoon stage."

When Grant and I are happy together, it's like we've started dating for the first time. Like a new relationship, giddy anticipation that happens every time we see each other. Like that puppy love is big and bright, like our eyes have bouncing hearts in them. We look at each other like the other could do no wrong.

"When we're good," Grant starts, "We're always in the honeymoon stage. Look at me."

"I don't know if I can," I admit quietly. *It's too much.*

"Just do it. I need to see your eyes." So, I do. I open my eyes and slowly meet his green ones. "Do you know why I call you honey?" he asks.

"Because I'm sweet?" I'm being witty, but it's the wrong answer.

"Your eyes. Your eyes are the color of honey. They're my favorite color in the world."

I look at him with a dead stare. This man has the eyes of a god, and he's telling me mine are nice. That's funny.

"It's what's behind your eyes that make me love them so much," he explains.

"And what's that?" I ask.

"Honesty. Innocence. Kindness. I could say a hundred more."

I'm not innocent. I'm also not honest, Grant. At least not with you.

"That reminds me. I never gave you your three subjective words."

He smiles with his eyes. His beautiful green eyes. I already know what I'm going to say. "Generous. Determined. Perfect."

"I'm not sure perfect counts," he counters jokingly.

"It covers everything, though. Three isn't enough." He pinches my cheek. "Hardworking. Completion. Necessity," I continue.

"Ava." He laughs, a soft blush blooms on his light skin. "I got it. You could stop now."

"I don't want to stop. Committed. Devoted. Patient. Generous."

"You said that one already."

I shrug. "I'm saying it again."

"You done yet?"

"No way. Handsome. Pretty. Grumpy. Smart. *God*, you're *so* smart."

"My turn," he tries, but I shake my head.

"Nope. Thoughtful. Reliable." I gulp. I say this next one quietly.

"*Mine.*"

Grant watches me, watches my eyes tear up, and studies me for a few quiet minutes. He takes a deep breath. After deep contemplation, he nods knowingly a few times. His gaze swings to mine, and it hardens with a tangible intensity.

"Always," he mouths finally.

"Promise?" I mouth back.

"Pinky," he grunts, holding up his pinky. "Swear. You're my girl. I love you more than anything."

"Will you always love me? Even if I'm not around?"

My throat swells. I can hear the emotion in my own voice, the way my question ends in a tight octave. I know he does, too.

He returns to playing with my hair. I think he's doing it to avoid looking at me.

"In my imagination, you're always going to be around. You'll always be in my line of sight."

When his eyes find mine within our shared, heavy silence, he quickly darts them away. It's like he's scared that I might be upset that he's saying all of this, but I need this. I need this conversation to look back on. I'll never get any of this emotion from him ever again, so I have to savor every second. I hope I remember it tomorrow, even if I'm going to pretend I don't.

"Please don't look away from me," I beg quietly. "I need to see you when you say this stuff to me. I need to savor it."

"You don't have to savor it," he says dismissively.

"What do you mean? I want to be able to…I don't ever want to forget everything you're saying to me."

When he explains what he means, I die a little inside. "You don't need to savor this because it'll happen again and again and again until the day I die. I'll say it to you when you finally come back to me.

I'll say it to you when I propose. I'll say it to you at the altar of our wedding."

The tears. There are so many tears.

"I'm going to marry you one day," he whispers roughly. Grant swallows hard. "You're going to be my wife. We're going to have babies. We're going to give Annie's kids cousins. We're going to make your parents grandparents. We're going to make your brothers uncles. We're going to grow old together. You're the one I see in the rocking chair beside me in 60 years, Ava. *You.*"

Retched sobs.

Sobs that I have never ever heard come out of me, that I didn't know were possible.

I pin my forehead to my forearms and cry into the grass. My body shakes, my back especially from the force of all of this crying.

I don't let myself counter what he's saying, to him or in my head. I don't want to ruin these memories with the truth. I want to live in the clouds and act as if painful realities don't exist and that the world is perfect. I want to be gullible and foolish and clueless and innocent tonight.

I don't care if that makes me stupid or dumb. I don't care if I'm the biggest idiot on the planet because right now, in this moment, everything feels perfect. When I let myself feel and believe Grant's words of our non-existent future, nothing else matters. Not my tubes or graduation night or his desire for fatherhood.

I can feel Grant shuffle beside me until he's in a seated position. With two strong hands, he lifts my body off the ground and into his lap.

This change of scenery does nothing to stop me from crying. My face is Niagara Falls, and I don't think I'll ever be done.

He encases me and rubs my back hard, both bringing me closer and comforting me at the same time.

"Shhh," he whispers into my hair. "Just dream with me for a little bit, okay?"

Grant kisses my temple when I nod. He presses his lips into my skin and keeps them there.

Maybe in another lifetime. Maybe we'll die in sixty years and come back as two different people who will fall in love and get married and have babies.

"Tell me more," I beg in a quiet croak. "Dream more."

He is resolute in his body language like he's telling me, *Say no more.* "I'm going to take you on the best honeymoon. I'm going to buy you the house of your dreams. I'm going to cook for you in our kitchen. I'm going to watch you sleep beside me, and I'm going to know that I'm the luckiest man alive."

"Tell me more about the kids," I whisper, torturing myself. But ironically, this dreaming is the best I've felt about my situation in a long time. Hearing all of this, imagining it to be true, feels like a dream you want to go back to sleep to experience again.

You know it isn't real, but it still feels damn good.

His deep voice is soothing, it could put me to sleep, but I don't ever want to go to sleep tonight because tomorrow will come and tomorrow means that we have to go back to being…friends. *Just* friends.

"They're going to be the kindest, most beautiful human beings on the planet," Grant says. He swallows. "They're going to be just like their mother."

That word. That word and the pain of my necessary, but dreadful detachment to it.

I tuck my face into his soft neck and sob.

"I can't be a mother," I whisper tightly, painfully. "You already know that."

This is the closest I've been to telling Grant what my adamancy about our impossible future is about, and I feel like I'm going to vomit. When I hear what he says next, I do.

"I'll make it happen. For you, I would do anything. You already know that."

I slap my hand over my mouth, jump out of Grant's lap, and run into a corner of bushes. It's projecting violently out of my mouth. I have never vomited so much in my life. The worst part? I'm crying as I'm doing it.

Grant rushes over to where I've run to and comforts me with encouraging words and his large palm rubbing up and down my heaving back.

"I'm so sorry," I whimper, panting. I'm bent over, hands gripping my knees, gauging if my body has any more vomit to release.

"Don't ever be sorry, baby." *Baby.* "Come on. Let's get you something to drink."

CHAPTER FORTY-FIVE
AVA

G atorade.
That's my beverage of choice.

Grant carries me like a bride to a 24-hour bodega near Central Park. He calls me a sugar fiend when I choose the Gatorade that he bought over the water bottle.

We slip into an Uber, high and drowsy, back toward Grant's place. We're headed to Scarsdale tomorrow to his parents' house, so I'm sleeping over tonight.

Guest room.

I fold into myself once I'm in bed and clutch the blanket tightly. I think it's the moment when he sees the melancholy look on my face that he lowers himself to sit on the corner of my bed, watching me closely.

He sighs. "Let me guess," he mumbles roughly. "In the morning, we pretend this never happened?"

I feel a sting cross my chest that he knows exactly what I'm thinking and views me poorly because of it, but if I want him to have all the amazing things he mentioned tonight, I need to free him. I need to free him from whatever this is because he can't get that perfection of a future with me. If I want this to work, I can't act as if we are possible. I need him to adopt a mindset of moving forward, holding on to the desire for a wife and a family and searching for the woman who could give him that life.

"Just trust me. It has to be this way," I whisper.

Grant's shoulders fall. "You're killing me." His voice is strained, pleading.

I'm not trying to. I don't want to burden this perfect man. I want to make his life easier, not harder.

"Grant... You said we were dreaming. You know that everything we said wasn't real, so why are you saying that I'm killing you?"

"You want it to be real." His voice is rough and almost...accusatory. "You want a life with me."

Yes, I do. More than anything.

He can see the obvious torment in my eyes. How I'm so close, so fucking close to erasing grad night from my memory and pretending like we saw each other for the first time after the break up at Annie's house. That I'm so close to rewinding the last few months, relive that conversation we had on the beach and telling him that I want him back instead of telling him we can't be together.

I feel stuck. Words are lodged in my throat.

"Baby," he whispers. His green eyes glance at all corners of my face. He looks into my eyes, fixates on my lips, observes every inch of me with eyes full of desire. "Be with me. Be mine."

"I am yours. I'm your best friend." I smile at him to ease the finality of my words.

He shakes his head. He clicks his tongue. "Why won't you let me love you, Ava?"

It's so goddamn tempting. Tempting to say yes.

Yes, Grant. I'll be yours.

I would be so happy, I'd cry every day because of it. I'd move in. I'd wake up with him every morning. That sounds like a literal dream, but there's that word again.

Dream.

"Why'd you call it dreaming earlier?" I ask, avoiding his pressing question.

"I didn't want the conversation to end. It felt really good to imagine all of that with you." He lowers his voice. "To say it out loud for the first time."

I shuffle onto my back and stare at the ceiling. I can feel Grant's observant eyes on me.

"I want answers," he says quietly, a confused undertone laced within his words. "I need you to tell me why this isn't more."

"Please, Grant," I breathe, begging. "*Please.*"

"What?" he asks.

I swallow hard. "Please let me have this. Just let me have you without the questions and talks of the future. Just live in the now with me. It's really, really good this way."

"I cannot stand that you're lying to yourself, Ava." He grits his teeth. He closes his eyes.

"Fine. I'm lying to myself," I admit. "But if we can't have a future, I'm not going to waste my time imagining one. You shouldn't either."

Grant takes a deep breath, puffs his cheeks. He blows it out slowly. "*Just friends* is proving to be really hard for me."

With his words, I panic. I fully freaking panic. I sit up in bed and frantically pat down my hair, curling the loose pieces behind my ears three times before I have the courage to finally speak.

"You…you want to stop being friends?" He doesn't answer. Grant studies his shoes, deep in thought like the answers of our impending doom are stitched into this million-dollar carpet.

I'm still in a panic; sweat beads under my boobs.

"Let's just be happy being best friends. Let's stop talking about the future and focus on the now. I need you in my life, and I… This is our time slot. I'm asking you to enjoy it with me instead of jumping to the next step. We're wasting time talking about something that's out of our control. Our friendship *is* in our control, and I'm asking you to focus on it instead of the relationship that we can't have."

When he watches me ramble, he cocks his head. His eyes are finally bright again. He enjoys everything that I'm saying and the way I'm saying them.

I blush because I've given myself away. I *need* him.

"I'm not going anywhere. I don't ever want you to worry about that, honey," he tells me.

I take Grant's hand in mine and squeeze. "No more questions, okay?"

"This is what you want?" His voice rumbles between us. I nod. "Then this is what I'll give you."

Good God.

"So, tomorrow…" My sentence fades. I feel bad saying it, so I wait for him to.

"Tomorrow, we pretend this never happened. Tomorrow, we go back to normal."

CHAPTER FORTY-SIX

GRANT

Pretend it never happened. Pretend it never fucking happened, Wilder.

"You okay meeting my grandfather?" I ask Ava beside me.

"Yeah," Ava laughs. "Why wouldn't I be?"

My mother is hosting an elaborate fundraising event at the Scarsdale house today. They're collecting money for some charity organization that my parents started when we were living in Houston, so my grandparents flew in to New York for the event. I asked Ava to come because I want to be with her at every goddamn waking moment. And I vowed to try.

With Ava, trying isn't hard.

I scan the wealthy crowd of people and find my burly grandfather huddled up with Ben. *How important can it be if he's huddled up with Ben?*

"Grandpa!" I call out to my namesake. When he doesn't turn around, I howl, "Hey, G-Cal!"

"Like Google Calendar?" Ava is puzzled.

I chuckle softly and roll my eyes. "Ben came up with that. Grandpa Cal. G-Cal. It stuck."

Just then, my grandfather saunters over to where Ava and I are mingling, clad in his cowboy boots and hat. Ava's jaw drops when she gets a good look at him, but it's not his outfit she's surprised by.

"You. Are. Ben. Oh my goodness! Genetics!" she exclaims excitedly. She marches over to Ben, tugs at his arm, then places him to stand beside my grandfather. She squeals. She pulls her phone out to take a bunch of photos, then finally composes herself with zero shame.

"Okay. I'm good now." I laugh at this endearing human that I get to call a best friend.

"Grandpa, this is Ava. This is Callum Wilder the First." I wink at Ava. She called me Callum Grant Wilder the Third when we first met.

Ava turns to Grandpa Cal and smiles sweetly. She's got that kind energy that instantly puts a smile on G-Cal's face, on anyone's face. I mean it when I say she's sunshine.

"Howdy, Ava." His Texan accent is thick as ever. New York really washed Dad's out. "Hmm. Ava. Why do I recognize that name?"

My grandfather turns to face me, staring into my eyes, so I give him a slight nod at his telepathic question, confirming what he already knows.

Yes, Grandpa. This is the one. This is the woman I ended my engagement for. This is the girl I'd do anything for.

This is the love of my life.

Ava blushes when she observes our silent dialogue. She has to know what's happening in my head.

Grandpa nods at me in mutual understanding, then brings his attention back to Ava. "Well, it's nice to finally meet you, Miss Ava."

"Ditto! I've always wanted to meet Grant's namesake! Howdy!"

I close my eyes and smile, feeling at ease with Ava in my life. At ease and at peace with her happiness and her growth. I step around to stand behind her, place my hands on her shoulders, and knead into them. I kiss the top of her head softly.

I can't not. She's being amazing right now. My family is intimidating, and she just…she's herself. Friendly, fun, kind. It helps that she doesn't seem to mind it. Ava places her hand on top of one of mine and squeezes it in reassurance.

"Tell me about yourself, Miss Ava. And while you're at it, why don't we filler up?" Grandpa reaches his thick arm out for Ava to hook her delicate one into.

"Grandpa, leave her alone," I interject and roll my eyes for Ava's sake.

"No!" she exclaims. "This is my best opportunity to hear embarrassing stories about you!"

Ava looks up at Grandpa with raised eyebrows. "Do we have a deal?"

Grandpa bellows a loud, manly laugh. "You bet, darlin'."

I watch them saunter away, Ava talking with passion, and my heart squeezes with all the love in the world.

CHAPTER FORTY-SEVEN
AVA

I'm actually giddy in my search for Grant after my interrogation with G-Cal.

I made him tell me all of the embarrassing stories about Grant, so I'd have something to tease him with.

Hearing that laugh, watching his head tilt back exposing his long neck, his Adam's apple. He's just so pretty when he laughs. Knowing I can do that for him is the best feeling, and I just...

God, I love *it.*

The party today is located across the giant backyard of Grant's parents' house. I've only been in this backyard once before for his twenty-eighth birthday party. If I were to speak in front of all of these people about Grant again right now, I'd smile, and I'd crack jokes. It'd be eons different than it was two years ago.

Maybe for his thirtieth birthday. I should probably start planning that.

I'm not widely familiar with the estate, so I have to find my way around without Grant. I wander upstairs, downstairs, the *other* downstairs. I halt when I hear muffled speaking.

I quietly inch closer and hide myself but keep my ears peeled.

I should have learned my lesson about eavesdropping the night of my graduation, but this is too tempting. It's tempting because it's Annie berating Grant.

"I don't understand what the fuck you're doing." Annie is shouting at him in a hushed tone. "Are you stupid? No, really, Grant. Are you dumb?"

"Yeah. I am," he responds dryly. "With her, I'm dumb, Annie."

I freeze. I hold my breath because I want to hear more. I need to hear more. Who is *her*? I wait what feels like a full minute before Grant speaks again.

"I want her. I know that Ava doesn't want me, but…I'm not going to forfeit this. She's letting me in her life, An. After everything I did, she *wants* me in her life. Do you understand how huge that is?"

Of course I do. Of course I want him in my life. He's the best part of my life, the best part of my days spent with him, without him, on the phone with him. Even those random texts of a single heart emoji he's been sending lately is the best part of my day.

He's trying. He's trying so hard for me.

"She's playing games with you," Annie tells him.

Wait, *what*? Is that how it seems? Like I'm playing *games*? Annie knows me better than that. I'd never intentionally hurt her brother. I love him.

Well, if you loved her brother, you wouldn't beg him to be your best friend.

"She's not." Grant defends me. "She's just…" He sighs heavily without finishing his sentence.

"I'm trying to protect you, Grant. You know what happened last time. I'm not losing you again."

What happened last time? Losing him? What? What does that even mean? Say more, say more, say more!

She does.

"Grant, I love Ava. You know I do, and I'd never accuse her of doing this on purpose. I know she isn't trying to hurt you, but if she says there's no hope—"

"I don't care what she says." A pause. "I'm waiting, An," he finally grunts. "I'm waiting for her. I'll wait as long as forever."

My breath hitches. I hold it when I tiptoe away from Annie and Grant.

You won't wait as long as forever, G Wagon, because I won't let you.

CHAPTER FORTY-EIGHT
AVA

Nothing is wrong with me.

Dr. Helstad is sure of it, so I believe him. Painful periods happen. It is what it is.

I come home early from work due to said period cramps to the best surprise ever. A sweatshirt and a card sitting on my bed. I lift the sweatshirt.

Kraft. The company. For whatever reason, it makes me cry, a burst of love and appreciation shaping in my chest.

I slip the sweatshirt on and rip open the card. The front has a sketch of a bowl of mac and cheese and it says, *You're the mac to my cheese.*

Inside, he wrote:

> What the front said.
> The sunshine to my day, too.
> G Wagon

Seeing Grant's handwriting releases more tears from my already soaking eyes.

His *handwriting*.

I flip my phone camera into selfie mode, reach my arm above my head and position myself in the screen, so the sweatshirt is clear in the frame. I smile hugely and give a thumbs up for the photo. My obvious tears are in there, too.

With the photo attachment, I write: I bump you up to first place

> Me: Mr. Kraft can suck it
>
> Me: Never taking this off
>
> Me: Best surprise ever
>
> Me: Smiling mucho!!!

Grant calls me immediately once the photo shows delivered. "Are you okay?"

More tears. I sniffle. "Yeah," I squeak. "You just made my day."

"Why are you crying? What's wrong? What happened?"

He's frantic. This man is frantic because I'm crying and he thinks I'm sad.

"No, no. Nothing happened," I assure him. "I got my period last night and… Okay, you don't want to hear that. I—"

His deep voice interrupts me. "You got your period last night and?"

He does want to hear it. God, he's such a *man*.

"I'm in pain, and I was already PMSing when I saw the sweatshirt and card and started crying for no reason." I laugh at myself. I groan. "Mother Nature can suck it alongside Mr. Kraft."

"You're home?" he asks with that same worried tone.

"Yeah, but you don't have to come. I'm really okay."

"You'll be home for a while?"

It's like he picks and chooses what he wants to listen to me say and what he doesn't. If it's anything along the lines of declining his care for me, he's not having it. I love that about him.

I love everything about him.

I love him.

"Yeah, I'm staying home today, but you really don't have to come, Grant. I'm really okay. I do this monthly." I chuckle. I don't want him to go out of his way because of a period. His panic is unnecessary.

"Okay. All right. But do me a favor, yeah? Go to bed. You need rest. Text me when you wake up."

My eyes are still blurry and half-closed when I exit my bedroom and see color.

Like, lots and lots of color.

I rub the sleep out of my eyes, and when my vision clears, I have to hold in my laughter. I smile, but it's a little lopsided. Grant's eyebrows scrunch.

He stands in my doorway holding a bouquet of balloons and a bouquet of flowers. Chloe is beside him holding four shopping bags.

Oh God.

"Is it my birthday?" I tease. I work hard to curb my laughter.

"I was thinking the same thing," Chloe says next. "When he asked me to come downstairs to help him carry this stuff up, I checked the calendar on my phone. It's not your birthday."

"Oh. Thanks, Chloe, for the confirmation."

When we both start laughing, Grant studies us back and forth. His face blooms red. The poor guy has never done this before. I never told him when I was on my period last year. I was insecure as if I had a reason to be.

"Oh, uh…" His voice is raspy. He clears his throat. "Too much?"

"For a period? Yeah. But I love it. When have you not been too much?" I smile at him for reassurance.

I want to run into his arms and squeeze him until he passes out, but Chloe is here. I know she'll make an annoying comment, and I'm not in the mood for this to get awkward.

She starts for my bedroom with the bags in tow. "I'm going to put these in your room!" she calls out. "Don't bang the headboard too hard!"

And there she goes. Making the comment anyway.

I groan. Grant's face is still full of concern when I look back at him. He's not laughing.

"Sorry. She's—"

"Did you take something for the pain? You're pale. Did you eat? What can I get you? Tell me what you need right now."

"A hug." I spread my arms out and wait. He places the balloons on the ground and the white roses on the couch before putting himself where I wish he'd stay forever.

I hug him.

"You're my best friend," I mutter into his chest.

"And you're my best friend."

"I'm so lucky."

Grant chuckles deeply. "I'm a hell of a lot luckier."

I look up at him and smile. "Can I open my presents now?"

CHAPTER FORTY-NINE

GRANT

I panicked.
I frantically collected my stuff at Annie's house when Ava called me crying. When we hung up the phone, Annie stopped me at the door.

Before she had a chance to say anything, I held up my hand. "I know what you're going to say, and I don't care. Let me be, Annie."

"But—"

"She is my priority. I don't give a shit about anything else, my own feelings included. She needs someone, and I'm lucky that there's a chance she might let me be that someone, so I'm taking it."

"But, Grant—"

My sister really wanted to warn me, but I don't want to hear any of that stuff. If I was going to listen to a warning, it would have been in Montauk before everything became so…real. True. Significant.

"Like I said, An. I don't care what you're going to say."

It's the middle of a work day. I drove over to Annie's for a quick lunch. We started this hang out idea when Ava and I broke up last year. I think Annie had to see for herself that I wasn't going to lose it, so she'd demand I come over in the middle of the day, pretend she had something important to tell me or to have me fix. Then, she simply fed me and watched me eat with hawk eyes.

I called Dina in a panic from the backseat of Lenny's car once I left Annie's house. She told me to chill out and to breathe.

"It's just a period, Grant. Holy shit, relax. I thought she was dying."

"Don't let those words exit your mouth *ever*, Dina," I spat. My words were curt and angry, but I knew Dina would understand.

"Oh, you smitten, little piece of shit. What do you need me to do?"

I texted her a list of things to buy after Googling **Things to Get a Girl on Her Period.** I had a couple of hours to get everything in order, hoping Ava was taking a nap. She sounded drained over the phone, and it pulled at my chest.

Following Ava into her room, I note that I shouldn't bang the headboard too loud.

She heads straight for the bags Chloe set on her bed.

Her eyes widen when she sees the La Perla one.

I intervene quickly. "It's not lingerie."

She blushes instantly. I think I do, too. Ava puts both her hands on her warm cheeks and giggles when she looks up at me. "We're so awkward. You're blushing. We're both blushing."

"Nah, this is a sunburn, Campbell." I nod my head to the nicely wrapped box. "Open it."

I got her a few pairs of those silky pajama sets. Number six on the list I Googled was pajama sets. Apparently, *girls love that shit.*

Ava laughs when she sees them. She holds up the first one, a blue shorts set, and smirks. She looks back at me.

"I'm going to be the fanciest person in the world. I'm going to be fancier than you. Fancier than your mom."

I chuckle at her. "Nobody is fancier than my mom."

"I'm about to be. You'll see. Just call me Ava Kennedy."

I want to call you Ava Wilder. That's the best name in the world.

The other gift was for movies. Ava rummages through the second bag and squeals.

"You got me an iPad?! Are you insane?!"

My favorite reaction of hers is the one when she sees the third bag. Her jaw drops as she shuffles through the mounds of junk and sugar.

"This is my favorite one of all of them," she tells me.

I laugh. "I know it is."

The fourth bag has about three different boxes of pads and three different boxes of tampons. I didn't know which to buy. And to my surprise, I felt nothing but pride asking the lady at Duane Reade to help me choose the right stuff for Ava.

When she sees the last of the lot, she takes a deep breath. "Thank you so much. Really. You didn't have to do all of this. It's so crazy. It's like—"

"Did you take anything for the pain?" I interrupt her. "Are you hungry? What do you think of takeout?"

I don't want the thank yous. I don't want her to tell me I didn't have to do all of this. If I was her boyfriend or fiancé or husband, I *would* have to, and her words remind me that I'm not.

Ava looks into my eyes, right to left. She slowly nods.

"Yeah. I'd love takeout," she says quietly. Ava bites her lip nervously.

I place an order on a food delivery app then climb onto her bed. I stand on it. "Come here."

"What are you doing?"

I look at her with mischief. "We're going to screw with Chloe a little bit."

My (*I know, I know*) girl's gorgeous face splits into a massive grin. She places all four bags on her desk and climbs onto the bed.

"Jump," I whisper loudly. I have to duck because these aren't high ceilings, so I look absolutely ridiculous. I look like I'm imitating a monkey on purpose. Ava throws a hand over her mouth and tears up, holds in her laughter.

If we want to mess with Chloe, she can't out us by laughing.

When Ava's phone begins to buzz violently with a string of texts from Chloe after our jumping successfully bangs the headboard into their shared wall, Ava allows herself to laugh. I don't even want to know what Ava's best friend wrote to her. All I want to do right now is admire *my* best friend as she laughs so joyously, so beautifully, my favorite sound in the world.

I smile at her while she cackles.

I sit on my knees and spread my arms wide, inviting her in. She throws herself at me and hugs my neck like she always does. Like she's trying to suffocate me.

"You trying to kill me with these hugs, Campbell?"

"No," she whispers. Her voice is sincere. "I'm just making sure you're really here. That this is really my life."

"I'm here." I rub her back. "I'm always going to be here." Ava rests her cheek on my shoulder. She slumps against me like she needs me to hold her up.

"You want to know something?" she asks tenderly.

"I want to know everything," I reply.

"This is my favorite place in the entire world."

CHAPTER FIFTY
AVA

I let him lay on my bed.
　　Well, more like he accepts my offer to lay on my bed. He's the one feeling led on. I just can't help myself.

Grant helped me get the iPad (*what the hell!*) set up. We brought the burgers he ordered for us into my room and set up a stack of books at the end of the bed for the iPad to lean against. We sat cross-legged and ate while watching *Inside Out*.

That cartoon movie about emotions. It had me crying.

"I'm on my period!" I cried out in my defense when Grant teased me for getting emotional over a cartoon.

We clean my bed up, but we're both not ready to say goodbye for the night. We sit beside each other and lean our backs against my headboard. To tease Chloe again, we shove our bodies into it repeatedly.

"I'D MUCH RATHER HEAR THE BANGING IF YOU GUYS WERE ACTUALLY BANGING EACH OTHER," she shouts from her bedroom.

I'm going to kill her.

"Remind me to kill her," I tell Grant, throwing my thumb toward the wall Chloe and I share.

"Are you happy?" he asks abruptly. I smile awkwardly but quickly realize he's asking this because of the movie.

I nod. "Yeah, I'm really happy."

"Good," he rasps. He nods in contemplation. "Good." I squeeze his hand.

"Are *you* happy?" I ask. Grant doesn't respond. In fact, my question has silenced him. I fear the reason is because he's not and, in this moment, I recognize that I am in love with this man more than I've ever been. The idea of Grant being unhappy destroys me inside.

I love him so much.

I want to be with him so bad.

I wish he didn't tell Hannah why he can't marry me because I want him to be mine.

"Please tell me you're happy," I whisper shakily. "I couldn't handle it if you're not."

After long moments of dragged-out silence, Grant finally speaks. "Aw shit," he groans hoarsely.

"What?"

"You. You're what makes me happy. The only thing."

Toxic.

Everything about that sentence is toxic.

I know because it's exactly how I was with him. When we were together, I was so distracted by the love Grant gave me that I had no motivation to learn how to give it to myself. Until things ended and I felt so lost. I had relied on him so much for my happiness that I had to relearn how to be happy with myself when I could no longer rely on him anymore.

I don't want to be for him what he was for me last year. It'll only leave him in the crosshairs of pain and loss when this inevitably ends.

When we have to say goodbye and I can no longer fulfill that happy void within him.

"Grant?"

"Hmm?"

I face him. I tell him how I felt when things ended, when I relied on him for happiness, but I don't mention the fact that this will never last. I tell him that he can't rely on my presence for his happiness because it isn't healthy, not because it isn't permanent.

"It's more than just having you in my life. It's knowing and seeing that despite what I did, you flourished. You're incredible, and that's what makes me happy. Your self-sufficiency is what makes me feel more content than I ever have."

I swallow before asking this next question. A part of me wants to while another part of me really doesn't.

"What were you like after the breakup?" I ask reluctantly.

Grant shakes his head, clicks his tongue. "I'm still the way that I am. I just have this added sense of happiness seeing you like this."

"What does that mean? What is the way you are?" When he doesn't answer, I push. "Tell me."

He takes a deep breath, fills his lungs with air and emotion and love and feeling, and quietly tells me, "Guilt can eat you up inside, Ava. It doesn't ever disappear."

My heart. My heart for his heart.

"But it can dissipate," I counter. "It has for me."

"Ava, you had nothing to feel guilty for. You had nothing to hate yourself for. I, on the other hand, do. It's not the kind of guilt that you can rid yourself of. It's guilt involving another person. A..." He clears his throat and lowers his voice. "A really, really good person."

My heart hurts. My chest constricts. His pain causes mine. "What are you talking about?" I ask. "I blamed myself for that abortion. I hated myself for being so fucked up."

"And then?" he asks.

I shrug. "And then I didn't."

"How?" he rasps.

Grant is twenty-nine, I'm twenty-two, and this is somehow the most beautiful conversation we've ever had. The most beautiful moment. Little old me preparing this successful, handsome man to rid himself of the guilt I know he has been carrying since we met.

"Chloe?" I chuckle. "I wish I could say I did it on my own, but she helped me a lot. She's the reason I am the way I am. Healthy."

"*No*," he disagrees strongly, his voice deeper than normal. Grant shakes his head. "Maybe she helped guide you, but you did all the work."

"What about you?" I whisper. I am so over the Pat shit that Grant still holding onto guilt because of it hurts *me*. "I don't want you to feel guilty about that stuff anymore. Promise me."

"I can't ever promise you that. I'm sorry." His voice is resolute, *too* resolute.

I hate this.

"Please?" What I say next is manipulative because of how much he cares about me, but it's for his sake, so I say it anyway. "Do it for me?"

He swallows hard. I reach over to hold his hand tightly and clutch our clasped hands to my chest. "I'm going to help you. We're going to do it together, okay?"

Grant grips the back of my neck in an intimate gesture. He squeezes it lightly. "Why does this mean so much to you?" he asks.

"Because I care about you. You carrying unnecessary guilt around for my sake is so counterintuitive, and I don't want you to feel this way anymore. I'm good. I've grown. I'm past it, and you should be, too."

Thinking deeply, he hums, directs his gaze to his lap. I wish I could be in his brain and read his thoughts. I wish I could somehow help him discover how amazing he is. How perfect he is.

"Say 'I'm amazing'," I demand. Grant chuckles but this is important. "I'm serious. Say it."

"Ava, I'm not saying that." He thinks I'm kidding, so he shakes his head, but I'm not.

"Fine," I whine. "Then, say… Say 'I'm a good person.'"

Grant exhales shakily, looks down, hair shuffling in all the right places, making him look both put together and loose.

"Say it, Grant," I demand again.

He gulps. He looks me deep in the eyes, and with purpose and resolve, states a firm, "No."

When I thought I was the literal devil over what happened with me three years ago, I carried myself like I was shameful. I hunched over a lot, I crossed my arms, I hated putting my hair up.

That's part of the reason I cut my hair. I used my long hair as a shield. I chopped it off when I was ready to get healthy again. I didn't have anything to hide behind anymore because I had no reason to hide at all. Grant, however, carries himself the exact opposite.

"You know what's interesting about you?" I start. "You have so much self-hatred, yet you're still confident. You still hold yourself so solidly. You aren't insecure, and I don't get it."

"Of course I'm insecure, but only with you. I hate myself for what I did to you. It's all about you. Everything in my life, Ava, since the moment we met, has been about you.

"I…Damn, I can't believe I'm going to say this, but I wish every day that you and me never met. Not at Rocco's, not even at the deposition. I don't wish I hadn't looked into you, but I do wish it stopped there. I know I should be out here wishing Pat never called me, but then I'd never even hear your name. I'd never know you exist. I'd never see your picture or know your birthday. I let myself have that little piece of you, but I wish I hadn't been so inclined to meet you because I wish *you* never met *me*."

My throat closes up, my chest aches, and it's both from a mixture of being offended and feeling sorry for him. This time, it's not from my period.

He's the best thing that's ever happened to me, and Grant wishes we never met? *How?* How is that a thought that crosses his mind? It not only makes me sad, but it hurts.

"You're the best thing that's ever happened to me, and—"

"I'm not," he interrupts curtly.

"You are," I counter. "You showed me what love is. Okay? You showed me the love I deserve to have. Not all of it. You fucked up royally, but the parts of our past that have nothing to do with Pat or my past or the case are moments that'll level my standards for how a man should treat me.

"You tried. The point is that you tried, and you wanted to try. That's the beauty. You wanted to try for me, and you worked really hard to be the best boyfriend you could be. You're my standard. Don't you get that? So, how can you say you're not a good person?"

With a quiet voice, he gives a meaningless excuse. "I think we're both a little stupid when it comes to one another."

"I'm not. Grant…" I blow out a heavy breath. "Am I biased? Sure. Are you the only guy who's ever loved me? Yes. But I know in my heart that you wish you didn't do what you did. I know that it ate you alive. We were in the same relationship, Grant. We were both there.

"Everything happened the way it was supposed to happen. If even one thing was tweaked, we wouldn't be here. I'm happy it happened. I learned a lot in the last two years. You gave me what I needed at the time. You're a good person. You try. I once watched you hand a homeless man a hundred dollars like it was pocket change. You tip so generously, and—"

"Ava, that's because I have money."

I cry. That's it, that's what happens. I surrender and I cry. I cry for him. That's how much I love him. I cry for this man. He's good. He's good, I know he is.

Bad men don't feel guilty. Bad men aren't charitable. Bad men don't fund an apartment and tuition and lawyer fees and hospital bills for a girl they barely know. Bad men don't kiss their sisters on the head. Bad men don't take care of a girl they could never marry. Bad men don't spoil a girl they could never marry.

Bad men don't buy tampons!

The fact that Grant is so inclined to feel like an asshole hurts me. He has so much potential. He's good. Grant Wilder is a good person.

"Okay," he grunts. "I'll say whatever you want me to say. I can't watch you cry, Ava."

"Bad men don't care if a girl cries!" I wail. "Just say it!" I swipe at the tears on my cheeks.

This has nothing to do with my period.

"Okay, okay," he finally surrenders. "I'm a good person."

"I'll help you. I want to help you. We'll do it together. Trust me. I'll give to you what Chloe gave to me."

He grabs my hand, laces our fingers together and squeezes tightly. He doesn't let up like he's keeping me here, keeping me from floating away.

"I'm not going anywhere," I tease. "You could stop blocking off the circulation in my hand."

Grant releases his tight grip on my hand, but he doesn't laugh. He doesn't look at me either. He still holds my hand, though. I watch him closely. Grant's eyes seem to water. When the silence drags on, he clears his throat and says, "I'll be right back, okay?"

I nod at him. He kisses my head before exiting my room. His eyes are bloodshot when he's made it back to me, but he finally smiles.

He went to cry. He didn't want me to see him cry.

I study him. I look at his beautiful eyes, now slightly pink and veined.

"Chloe texted me because you weren't answering," he says hoarsely. "She said that a few of your friends are going to a rooftop bar if we wanted to come, but I figure you're not feeling up for it. What should I text back?"

If I get to have more time with Grant tonight and it doesn't require us to be in the confines of this tight and emotionally provoking bedroom, I'm in.

"I'm feeling fine. I'll just take more Midol. That sounds fun."

"Are you sure?" he asks. "We don't have to go. We can go another time."

We. We're a *we.*

"We'll go tonight, but first… Tell me why you didn't want me to see you crying."

He sighs. When I sense him about to object, I say, "Tell me."

He swallows. Quietly, he says, "I don't ever want to make it about me. I don't want to ever mitigate your feelings."

My feelings? He means the feeling of pain I experience knowing he deals with all of this self-hatred? He didn't want to mitigate my pain for his pain?

He holds his hand out for me, dismissing the fact that he's cried. He offers a small smile and says, "Ready?"

The emotion in my chest from tonight and him and all he's done for me is unmatched.

The Midol he tucked into his pocket before we left my apartment, the way he opened the passenger door for me, the constant question of *You okay?* that he's been asking me all night.

I counted. He's asked me a variation of that question four times since we got to this bar only thirty minutes ago.

We've been glued to each other's sides. And I don't care that we look like a couple tonight. I don't care that Derek is looking at us weirdly. I don't care that he told Hannah he can't marry me.

Tonight, I indulge. More than I should, less than I want to.

Grant leans his long back against the rooftop ledge. I lean my back against his front. He hugs me from behind, rests his forearms on either side of my bare shoulders. Thanks to my strapless top, I can feel his warmth, the hair on his arms brushing my skin. I smile when I look to my side at his arm against my shoulder. Dark and light.

Our fingers are intertwined with all four hands resting against my belly. Grant's right thumb strokes the back of my hand.

We both just don't care tonight.

Chloe watches us. She smiles with her pretty blue eyes from across the rooftop, but it's slightly melancholy. She knows I can't take him back. Not the why, but the what.

I smile back at her. *Isn't he the best?* I want to say. I lean my head far back, so I can catch Grant's eye.

"Hi," I whisper.

"Hi, honey," he rasps. Cold lips kiss my upside-down forehead. "You feeling okay? How are your cramps?"

I nod to assure him that I'm fine. "Can I get you anything?" he asks.

I squeeze his hands. "No, thank you. I'm good, G." He kisses my forehead again, squeezes my hands in affirmation.

Chloe is still watching us when I straighten out.

"I love him so much," I mouth, my lips lifting in a sad smile.

"I know," she mouths back. Of course she knows. Hell, everyone at this damn bar knows. "Tell him."

I shake my head. I can't. That'll feel manipulative.

Grant, I love you. I'm telling you I love you, even when I know you can't marry me one day.

I mean, that's just wrong. He said what he said the night of my graduation. That was his truth.

Chloe's gaze is slightly above mine now, as she watches Grant. He's talking to one of Gabe's roommates. He's always so handsome when he's in deep conversation with someone.

When Chloe's eyes meet mine again, she mouths, "He already knows that you love him."

"I know," I reply. *I know he does. I know he's onto me. I know I'm leading him on.*

God, I need alcohol. I dismiss myself from Grant's arms and head toward the bar.

CHAPTER FIFTY-ONE
GRANT

"Who's coming to get tattoos!" Ava shouts, wiggling her eyebrows at our group once we've made it out onto the street.

She's fairly drunk. Well, no, like *really* drunk.

I shrug. "I'm in," I state casually.

Ava's eyes widen. Her jaw drops, revealing the inside of her pouty mouth. I am not sober right now. Seeing the inside of her wet mouth, her tongue and her throat, pulses a desire in me that I've been trying not to feel. Except tonight, I don't have much control because Ava hasn't kept her hands off of me since we got to this bar. We couldn't keep our hands off *each other*.

I want her so goddamn badly. I want her to be mine.

"You'd do that?" she squeals. "You'd get a tattoo? *You?!*"

"For you, I would," I reply like it's obvious.

"Oh my God, I'm so excited right now." Ava looks around at her friends, then inches closer to me. "Okay, everyone else can suck it. Let's go, just me and you."

I grip the hand that Ava reaches out for me and follow this human rainbow down the streets of Chinatown. After casing the place, I'm not convinced the tattoo parlor Ava brought us to is hygienic, but we're doing things Ava's way tonight.

"Hello!" Ava exclaims when she walks up to the check-in counter, leaving a dinging door in her wake. "I'd like a tattoo please. Two actually. One for me and one for him." Ava points to me.

A man with a name tag that reads **Bradley** hands Ava and me a stack of forms to fill out.

"Ugh, I hate official form stuff. Could you fill mine out for me?" she whines.

I take Ava's form and begin to fill it out before I fill out my own.

"Do you know what you're getting?" she asks, jumpy in her seat beside me.

"Mhmm," I hum casually, writing out Ava's date of birth and home address.

"What?" Ava is giddy. She's literally bouncing in her chair.

"Surprise," I mutter.

"Could you hold my hand when I do it? Needles suck."

How could I say no to those pretty eyes? "Of course, honey."

We're led into a room with two identical, red leather reclining beds. My arm is long enough for Ava to squeeze if I stretch it out to the bed beside mine. The first tattoo artist aims for Ava's bed first. She discreetly shows him a picture on her phone of what she wants to have tattooed and decides to put it on the back of her forearm. I'm getting my tattoo needled above my left pec. Precisely where my heart is.

Ava most definitely squeezes my hand, hers clammy in mine, almost slipping out of my grasp from the moisture of her sweat. Her eyes are squeezed shut, and her face is flushed a light shade of pink, but even under the fluorescent lighting, Ava still looks so beautiful.

I pull my phone out to take a picture of her. Then, after a quick Google Images search, I hand the second tattoo artist my phone with a picture of what I want. I unbutton my shirt and only remove my left arm out of it. Ava watches, amused.

"You don't want people to see it?" she wonders.

"I want only the right people to see it," I reply.

Ava squints, attempts to gather the meaning of my words, but she fails. She will once the tattoo is finished, which is approximately twenty minutes after Ava is done with hers. For the final reveal, since they know we're surprising each other, the two artists exit the room and agree to bandage us up once our moment is over.

"Ladies first," I say once the door closes, leaving us in an anticipatory silence. Ava itches to show me. She removes her arm out from behind her and displays the tattoo for me to see. It's a sketch of a pot of honey.

Honey.

I grin like a mad man.

"Because you always call me that!" she exclaims. Her laugh is amazing.

"I gathered that. I love it so much. It looks perfect on you."

Ava scrunches her nose at my compliment. Then, she nods her head to my chest. "Okay, now you go."

I reveal the tattoo. Ava's face holds question. "I don't get it," she says.

I didn't think she would, not right away. I wanted it to be personal but inconspicuous. I'll explain it to her in a second.

Above my left pec, there is now a tattooed circle on my skin. But the circle isn't an ordinary circle because in the top left curvature of the sphere, the tattoo's ink changes from black to red for that small portion, that small curve. It's a math thing. It's an arc.

"What is it? It's a circle with a red curve. I don't get it," Ava repeats.

"You don't?" She shakes her head. "It's math," I explain.

Ava snickers at me with an eye roll. "Of course it is. Is there any significance to it?"

"So much. So, so much significance to it," I tell her.

"Care to share? I mean, only if you want to. If you'd rather—"

"The red part," I interrupt. "It's an arc."

"An arc," she repeats. Her eyes narrow in confusion. I nod. "An arc. An arc. Oh... Wait. Arc."

"Mhmm." I hum affirmatively.

Her jaw drops. "You're kidding me."

"I am very much not kidding you, Ava Ruth, no."

"Those are my initials. A-R-C." *Finally, she gets it.*

"I know, Campbell," I tease. "Like I said. So much significance."

"How are you going to explain that to your wife one day?"

You're *going to be my wife one day*, I want to say.

"I won't," I tell Ava instead. "This is just for me and you. It's our little secret."

Ava hops off her tattoo bed to stand closer to me. She steadies herself between my legs and leans forward to look at the fresh tattoo closely. Her eyes meet mine, and a small smile paints her shy face. "I like it," she whispers. "I like our little secret. And to everyone else, mine just looks like a honey pot, but it's also our little secret. I got it for you."

I watch this perfection of a girl below me. I watch how her eyes skim my skin with an awestruck expression. I notice how she bites her lower lip to keep from smiling too much because she's not sure she should be this happy about my tattoo. About both of our tattoos and our little secrets.

I brace myself for the words that will come out of Ava's mouth next because suddenly, her breaths turn heavy. I know, I just know what she's thinking.

"Grant?" she whispers.

"Hm?"

"Can we pretend?" Ava's voice is a hidden sound. She swallows. "Just for one night?"

"Pretend what?" *I know exactly what.*

"That we're together. That…" She lets her words drift away.

I breathe deeply before saying, "It's not easy suppressing how I feel for you as is. If I have you for a night…" I shake my head. "It's over for me."

"What if…" Ava gulps nervously. "What if we… What if it isn't just one night? What if we…what if we do it all the time? But still be friends."

Ava reads my pained expression at her question. How my eyes plead with her to stop asking because of how hard it is to say no. Because of how badly I want to say yes.

There are things Ava has done to put up her boundaries. For one, labeling this friendship as just that—a friendship. If Ava and I were to start something like she's suggesting while still being the best friends that we've been the last few months, how is that not a relationship? It is the exact definition of what a relationship entails.

Emotional connection. Physical connection. Being in love with your best friend.

"This is the hardest part. Not being able to—" Ava is interrupted. *Saved by the bell?*

Not being able to what, Ava? To fuck? Because the hardest part for me is not being able to love you the way that I want to. Not being able to call you my girlfriend, my fiancée, my wife.

The mother of my children.

Ava's tattoo artist knocks and enters our now tension-filled room, acts as the buffer I didn't know we needed. He bandages Ava's honey pot and my arc, then leads us to the checkout counter to pay. Ava seems shaken up. She walks as if there is a wall in front of her that she's pushing forward. It's a heavy walk.

I pull my credit card out to pay for our tattoos, but Ava uncharacteristically insists on paying for hers. I wonder if it's a control thing—Ava actively taking control of her role in my life since she feels a sense of rejection. Ava no longer trusting that I could take care of her because I'm saying no to something she wants when up until now, I've given her whatever she wanted. It's an uncomfortable feeling that settles in my chest when I come to this conclusion.

The moment we walk out onto the quiet midnight sidewalk, Ava speaks. "I'm sorry. I shouldn't have asked you for that. It just…the whole first tattoo experience felt really intimate. I mean, the whole night has. I guess I was in my head a little. I know that it's not what you want from this friendship. Please don't be mad at me."

I shake my head. "I'm not mad at you. I don't want anything to change, Av. I want to be best friends the way we've been since Montauk."

"But I've been confusing you," she whispers. "Why do you still want to be my friend? Why are you still here? Why haven't you left yet?" The insecurity in Ava's voice breaks my heart; her words even more. I shake my head.

"I'm not even going to answer that," I reply. "Hey, I have a question. Why didn't you let me pay for the tattoo?"

Ava looks up at me, her eyebrows pinched. "Because I got the honey pot for you, and it wouldn't have felt personal if I let you pay. It wouldn't have felt like a present, you know?"

Oh.

"I thought you were mad that I was somehow rejecting you."

Ava shakes her head hurriedly. She stops walking, so I do, too.

"I'm not mad. I don't feel rejected."

"So, how *do* you feel?"

"Honestly…" Ava faces the ground, hides her face from me. "I feel ashamed. I don't know why I'm…I'm confused. I'm always confused with you, and—" I take Ava's face in my hands when I notice that she's crying. She squeezes her eyes shut. "Ignore me. I'm drunk," she explains. "I always act crazy when I'm drunk."

"You're not acting crazy. What's going on?" I ask quietly. "Talk to me."

She swallows thickly. Quietly, she admits, "When you're not around me, it feels weird. It feels like something is missing."

CHAPTER FIFTY-TWO

AVA

"That's just because I'm tall," he teases.

I ignore his comment; I have more important things to say.

I'm afraid you'll leave. I'm afraid of the day your significant other makes you drop me.

"I can't lose this and I'm scared that you'll drop me. And I really, really can't handle that, okay? I can't lose you again, even if it's in a different way, and—"

He grabs me, hugs me into him. His giant palm sweeps down the length of my short hair. He tucks my head under his chin, and with the hand that isn't playing with my hair, he's got this locked grip around my waist. He sighs heavily.

I cover my mouth with my hand, squeeze my eyes shut, and somehow, he knows I'm holding it in. He says, "Let it out, honey. I'm here."

I shake my head. I don't want to break in front of him. I can't present all of my cards. I have to keep some dignity for myself for when I'll need it. For when I'll have to stay strong and watch him fall in love with a beautiful woman who could have kids, who will give him the future he wants.

Grant's voice interrupts the gut-wrenching scenario I've created in my head, but I don't hear what he says. As soon as he speaks and I feel his arms around me, the arms of that beautiful woman's future husband, I take a step back out of his embrace.

I'm stealing him away from her. I'm stealing him away from every woman out there who he could love, but it also kills me to think of seeing him with someone else.

I just need answers. I need to know what to do.

Telling him the truth isn't an option. Call it miscommunication, but no one understands that he. will. choose. me. over. himself.

"Stop, stop. This isn't about me," I say. He shouldn't be comforting me after what I've done to repeatedly confuse him.

His voice is deep. It's strained, almost a whisper. "It's always about you, Ava Ruth. Don't you get it?"

"You…you can't do that. Comfort me. I'm not…you're not…we're not together, and…"

He watches me unravel, panic. It's *embarrassing*. "What's up?" he asks softly.

Unable to meet his eyes, I gnaw at my lips. "You're going to meet somebody one day, and she's not going to like the way you are with me."

Grant takes a deep breath. He nods to the ground, then faces me. He doesn't even need to ask what I mean because he knows exactly how he acts with me. Like I could do no wrong.

Oh, Grant.

"If she can't handle the way I am with you, she's not the one for me." He sounds so resolute. So confident in his words.

"Really?" I whisper

"Do you doubt that?" I remain silent. "Ava… As much as I wish it had, nothing changed. I can see that. You're asking me to trust you, and I don't want to be pushy or manipulative like I was last year. I'm dying to know; I'm dying to be with you, but you're asking for my trust. I have to honor that.

"When you're ready to tell me what this is about, I'm sure you will, but…but until then, I get you like this—this friendship. It's the best thing in my life, too. I *do* appreciate what we have, and I'm sorry that I haven't been clear about that. I love every part of life with you. I'm not going to drop you, ever. You're my checkmark. You're at the top of my list, and I would never not want you in my life. It feels shitty to think I let you believe I could ever drop you."

You're my checkmark. You're at the top of my list.

"I don't deserve you," I say quietly. "I don't deserve everything that you're giving me. You take care of me and spoil me, and I don't deserve it after I've confused you a bunch." I hate the reality of my words, but it's true. Grant chuckles it away.

"Oh, Ava. It's me who doesn't deserve you."

CHAPTER FIFTY-THREE
AVA

It's one of the worst hangovers of my entire life.

I don't know who let me drink so much. Probably Chloe. She's been drinking since high school, stealing liquor from her parents at the ripe age of fifteen. I only started drinking, *really* drinking, since I met her. For whatever reason, I try to keep up with her like we're the same.

We are not the same.

Grant and I followed the group out of the bar. Then, we got tattoos together. Then, I unraveled.

Something I wouldn't wish on my own worst enemy? Limbo. Limbo is bound to make a person go mad. In my case, I panic and unravel at the sheer unknown of it all. I have so many questions.

What happens when he moves on? Do I get to keep him as a best friend? Do I have to say goodbye? Does he disappear from my life completely?

All things I couldn't handle. All things I tell myself to ignore, to stop thinking about, to shove into the crevices of my mind and live every day as if tomorrow, Grant will meet his wife.

My phone's *ding* alerting me of a text message makes me want to pull my head off of my body, it's so loud. I feel like there's a shopping mall in my brain. My sore arm isn't helping the hangover situation whatsoever.

> CALLUM GRANT WILDER III ESQUIRE: Last night was fun. Adore you always.

His text comes with an attachment. I tap on it and watch the video. My face immediately splits into a giant grin.

It's of Grant and I drunk on the dance floor. I can hear Chloe's laugh from behind the camera, so I gather she was being an instigator and filmed us. I could kiss her feet because this is the best video in the entire world. I'll need it for when he's no longer in my life and memories are all I have.

We both laugh really hard, the intoxication apparent. We jump and dance to the song that's playing. He reaches his hand out for mine, and my smile in that moment—I have to pause the video. I screenshot the frame. I've never seen a happier smile on me. I have never seen myself look as happy as I look in this video.

Grant spins me around, over and over, under his long arm. He turns his arm airborne so fast that I stumble as I'm twirling in front of him. He does this on purpose to tease me, to make me laugh, and keeps going until I can't handle how hard I'm laughing and have to stop. The best part of the video is the long kiss he plants on my head once I've managed to compose my laughter.

It is clear as day that the two people in this video should be together. It is clear as day that they are in love. But they say you never know what someone is going through; what doesn't show on this incredible video is the fact that the girl in the video cannot have children. That the man in the video wants children. That the girl is making the biggest sacrifice of her life for her best friend forever.

CHAPTER FIFTY-FOUR
AVA

I love his voice.

That deep baritone, the throaty sound, certain voices that he only uses with me.

I shouldn't be squealing and giddy at eleven on a Monday, but I am when Grant calls me while I'm at work. My cramps have lessened significantly, so I came into the office.

When Grant saw my sad expression as he was dropping me off by my apartment door the night we got tattoos, he nodded. Quietly, he said, "I know. Pretend this never happened."

"Except the tattoos," I joked to lighten the mood. "They're kind of permanent." He nodded seriously. It gave me the chills, that feeling of shame at what I'm doing to him.

We're being stupid. I'm being stupid. We're acting like a couple; I make believe like he's mine, and then I act as if it's a one-time thing when we say goodbye for the night. Then, the next day, I do it all over again.

I'm leading him on. It's only a matter of time before Grant can't take this anymore.

"Hi," I answer my phone.

"Hey, you. How's your tattoo feeling?"

"Good, and yours?"

"Good. Thanks for asking, honey." Then, he says, "Come to lunch with me after work today."

My ovaries.

A man who's assured is a *man*. Rich men are another breed entirely. Grant is a catch, and if anything, I'm glad he has so much going for him. He'll need it when he starts to move on.

I agree to lunch with much enthusiasm. I am eagerly jumpy for the next few hours, excited that I get to see Grant again today. Every minute away from him feels like days.

After overhearing his conversation with Annie at the party the other day, I feel like time is slipping away from me. Like I have to start preparing for goodbye because I know that this can't go on. It's not sufficient. It's a pretend relationship. It's like we're fake dating, for nobody but ourselves.

He picks me up from outside of my office building at 1:00 sharp. A pressed white dress shirt is folded up to his elbows, the top two buttons opened to allow me a peak of his sharp collarbones. He's tucked into his creaseless pants, donning a navy-blue tie; he must have left his matching suit jacket at work. This man really left his office in the middle of the day to take me out for lunch.

I have a blinding smile on my face when I see him. Grant greets me with a warm hug and pecks the top of my head quickly. I look around, noticing that he's standing alone on the sidewalk.

"Where's your car?" I wonder.

"We're walking," he answers.

"How'd you get here?"

"Cab." Grant shuffles away from me and starts down the busy pavement calling out for me to join him. I have to run because a single step of Grant's is about four of mine. I'm breathless when I make it to his long self and fall into difficult step beside him.

I look up at him, confused. "You took a cab for me?"

"There's nothing I wouldn't do for you, Av. Sushi, pizza or Mexican. Your choice."

Gulp.

"I love when you let me choose. Pizza."

I sit beside Grant in the leather booth near the front door of this unnecessarily fancy Italian restaurant. It's a Monday afternoon. *Oh, how the other half lives.*

In between bites of white truffle pizza, Grant casually asks, "Is it too forward of me to ask you to come with me to my high school reunion?"

"No." Grant's surprised expression reads pleased. *I just have one question first.* "But will…" I gulp. "Will Hannah be there?"

Grant isn't fazed by my mention of his ex. He replies with a nod and a simple, "Yes."

"She'll probably throw eggs at me." I laugh awkwardly. "I don't think I should come with you."

"I'll protect you," he teases. "I'll bring you a hazmat suit. A blue one."

When he looks at me, his eyes squint like I'm the sun.

Everyone loves him.

Everyone is excited to talk to him.

Mr. Popular over here introduces me to his former classmates as his best friend.

I watch Grant in awe when he talks to a blonde guy in a pair of leather loafers and a suit. Blondie's hair is slicked back, and he looks as poised as ever.

They're talking about Grant's business, the only thing about Grant I have no interest in having a lengthy conversation about.

I let Grant know that I'm going to use the restroom. And just my luck, Hannah stops me on the way out.

"Hey, can I talk to you for a second?"

I'm a frozen walking snowman as I follow Hannah Butch to a corner of this noisy bar. The Masters Class of 2008 rented out this venue for the night. Hannah and Grant went to school together.

As soon as she brings us to a spot where we can speak privately and turns to face me, I blurt, "We're not together!"

This whole situation is intimidating enough, but her height and her heels aren't helping. I feel like I'm being microscopically picked at.

Hannah's perfectly waxed and gelled eyebrows pinch, so I continue to babble an explanation. "Grant and me. We're not together. Like, he's single and I'm single. He's not back with me, I swear."

Hannah tilts her head, a strand of wispy blonde hair falling over her face. She blows at it, then asks, "Why not?"

"Oh, um... Wait, what? You want us to be together?" My voice does not lack surprise.

"Of course I do. Why aren't you?" I tell her that it's complicated because I can't think of any other words to describe what we are.

You know the line that's crossed when friends become lovers? So, we've thinned out that line so drastically, we barely even see it. It makes no sense, I know.

Hannah shrugs nonchalantly at my reply. "Fair enough. Anyway, I wanted to clear the air between us and apologize for how I've treated you. You're a sweet girl. You're in Grant's life, and we're going to see each other often. I want to be friends, if you'll have me."

Whoa.

Like, WHOA.

"Oh," I croak nervously. I clear my throat and continue. "Of course. I'd like that, too."

"Good."

"Does this mean you're not mad at me? I thought you hated me. I told Grant that you were probably going to throw eggs at me tonight." I chuckle awkwardly. I press my lips into a tight line because *Ava, you goddamn idiot.*

Luckily, Hannah chuckles alongside me. "I'm not mad at you. I never have been. When we first met, I was jealous of you. I saw the way he looked at you, and I wanted that, but…but I realized that I didn't love him, I lusted him, you know? And he could never love me. He loves you too much. He adores you. He's so, so different when he's with you, it's insane."

My Grant.

"Julia tells me that, too."

Hannah looks at me expressively. "It's true. Take it from the people who know Grant pre-Ava. It always plays out that way, doesn't it? When a playboy changes for one specific girl? Anyway, I'm crossing my fingers that things uncomplicate themselves, but I don't have to. Granty will wait as long as it takes for you to take him back." She winks.

Most girls want to hear that the love of their life will wait as long as it takes, but not me. And I believe her because she knows him in a way that I don't. Her words form a twisty wave in my stomach and not the good kind.

The one that gives me the shudders and makes my stomach hurt.

"He shouldn't. I mean, I won't let him…" My voice is small and breathy.

"I'm not sure you could stop him if you tried," she chuckles.

Speak of the angel (*because he isn't a devil*), Grant clears his throat from above us.

"Is everything okay over here?" he asks deeply.

When I give Grant an assuring nod and Hannah excuses herself to head back into the rowdy crowd, I feel those piercing, green eyes study me. I hear Hannah's words over and over in my head. *Granty will wait as long as it takes for you to take him back.* That's what has me so shell shocked.

"You okay?" he asks. It's just us two in this quiet corner. The blaring of the surrounding music hits my skin from the sudden hyper awareness at Hannah's confirmatory words.

He's going to wait for me. I'm going to be adamant that I can't be his future because I want him to have children more than anything, but he'll still wait. He won't date somebody else.

"Yeah," I croak quietly. I clear my throat, then aim for the party, but Grant grips a warm hand on my forearm. It instantly provokes goosebumps across my skin. He stops me, then walks forward so he can quietly speak into the tight space between us.

"What did she say?" His voice is apprehensive. It's this deep rasp that has pleading and desire and love laced within it. It's that voice he reserves only for me. It's protection.

I attempt to shrug him off. "Nothing important. She was nice."

"Then, what has you so shaken up?" he mutters, concerned.

Grant must assume that I'm covering for her, that Hannah said something mean, but he doesn't realize that the only person being mean to me is myself.

"She said that she's rooting for us, and that feels really weird. I'm good. It's fine, I'm totally fine. I'm going to get myself a drink and say hi to Elizabeth."

I quickly skitter away, leaving Grant in that little corner before I have a chance to see what my fake explanation looks like on his face.

Elizabeth pulls me in for a giant hug when I walk over to say hi after grabbing a drink for myself at the bar. Her big belly smacks right into me. *Karma.*

"You're pregnant!" I squeal, palming her belly. She's wearing a silky pink dress with her perfect midsection protruding through it. She looks like an angel.

"I'm having a boy!"

I lean into Elizabeth and squeeze even tighter. "I'm so happy for you. This is amazing. How are you feeling?"

It isn't easy. It isn't easy, but I'm happy for Elizabeth. I'm not faking it; I just feel the wring in my chest when I remember that I'll never look like that.

I've always loved pregnant bellies. Ever since I was a kid, I've been obsessed with feeling the baby kick. I practically lived at Bridget's side throughout her three pregnancies.

Elizabeth tells me she's feeling great. She skims her eyes across the room, then faces me with a daring smile.

I roll my eyes at her. "What?"

"I didn't know you guys were…" She circles a manicured finger in the air. "I'm happy this is a thing again."

I have a feeling I'll be explaining mine and Grant's friendship to everyone we encounter who ever knew we dated at one point

"Oh! I mean, not like that. We're just friends."

Elizabeth bumps her hip to mine. "That's not Grant's idea. Why are you friend-zoning him, cutie?"

I've got to come up with an answer for this question. I told Hannah that it's complicated. I use that same excuse with Elizabeth, but she doesn't let it pass.

"Is it because of what he did?" she asks conspiratorially.

Her question catches me by surprise. Are there people in this room that know Grant was my ex-boyfriend's lawyer, unbeknownst to me? "You know? He told people?"

"Just Freddy and I. Maybe Hannah." Elizabeth looks me in the eyes. "He's always been really private when it comes to you. He never talked about you after the breakup."

He was ashamed. He didn't talk about me because of the shame. I didn't talk much about him either because, for the most part, I chose to grieve alone. Well, I was grieving with Grant. We were grieving the same thing. Only *we* knew what the other was feeling.

"It's all water under the bridge now," I tell Elizabeth with a hand wave. I bring the cold tumbler to my mouth to take a much-awaited sip of alcohol. Tonight turned out to be heavier than I thought, and the liquid relaxant in my hand is exactly what I need to take this weird edge off.

Screw high school reunions, man. And it's not even mine!

Naturally, the bar we're in is loud, but because I'm so in-tuned with him, I immediately feel Grant behind me, walking over to us. He says hello to Elizabeth, kisses her cheek, then hugs her. He palms her belly, and that—that visual… I don't expect tears to bubble inside my throat, but they do. I blink to push them away.

I'll never have that. He'll never palm my pregnant belly like that. No one will, but especially him. Especially his palm.

"How many more weeks?" he asks with a soft smile. The true happiness he feels for Elizabeth and Freddy being parents soon shows in the calmness of his eyes. He's so good.

Elizabeth drops her jaw. *"Nine.* You down to be his godfather?"

"Is this your official ask?" I'm beaming for Grant. *A godfather!*

Elizabeth waves her hand airborne. "Nah, Freddy wanted to ask you when he's born. Pretend you didn't hear a thing."

"Noted." Grant smiles at Elizabeth, then looks at me at his side. "Hi, you."

"Hey."

"You good?" There's that voice again. *Protection.*

"Yeah. You?"

"Dance with me."

Elizabeth groans. We look at her in unison.

"Fuck, you guys are so hot together. Make! Babies!" she jokingly yells in my face before hugging us both and leaving our small huddle.

Unsurprisingly, when hearing those words, I'm stuck in place. It's like there's glue under my sandals, like the tiled floor is pulling at me. I can't move, not when Grant talks to me, not when he tugs my arm a little. The voices and sounds surrounding me are echoed and play in slow-motion. Everything is distorted.

"Ava. Hey. Look at me." I shake my head, then nod to the dance floor.

When Grant pushes again, I swallow and say, "It's nothing. It was nothing. I'm good."

"Just ignore her," he pleads. "No one understands us. No one has to."

Grant telling me to ignore Elizabeth somehow brings on this feeling of rage inside my chest. It brings me back to grad night.

I should ignore her, shouldn't I? Because you *could never marry me! You told Hannah you can't, so what is this?!*

God, sometimes I want to scream at the tipping scale in my brain. I've construed two separate emotions of how I feel toward that sentence I overheard Grant say to Hannah. Both of them come flying at me with no warning, all the time. I understand why he said what he said, why having children is so important to him. I get that wholeheartedly, but I'm also hurt and angry by his words. But then again, he said what I eavesdropped on to protect his future, just like I am by "friend-zoning" him.

If I was in his shoes, I'd do everything I could to protect my future as a mother, too. I'd take whatever he'd be willing to give, take as much as I could without ensuring permanence.

"I know," I tell him. I smile as if Elizabeth's words didn't shatter me moments ago. I tease Grant because that's what I'm good at. "I'm *so* honored that the Prom King wants to dance with me."

He winces and rolls his eyes. "You saw that?"

We chuckle together. "And took about 400 photos of it," I admit.

Off to the side of the entrance to the bar, a poster of Grant's senior prom is displayed on a metal stand. He's standing with who I'm positive is Hannah, because of course she was the Prom Queen.

I look back at him. We watch each other ease back into our normal selves, our brains align, chests find that solid equilibrium we're familiar with.

"You good?" His voice is raw. "Are we okay?"

"Yeah. Of course we are. Dance with me, Prom King?"

CHAPTER FIFTY-FIVE

GRANT

"...And if we don't go all out, I'm afraid I'll end up in the Hudson," Ava whispers.

She is discreet telling me about Chloe's upcoming birthday celebration. We're on her couch. Gabe and a few other friends came for a game night. I stopped by a little late, so I only observed their game, slapped Ava high-five for beating everyone at Uno, and now, we're on the couch chomping on pretzel sticks. Ava keeps darting her eyes around the room, then slowly inches closer to me.

"There's this nightclub that she loves. She likes the DJ who plays there, and there's a lot of dancing. Help me plan it? It has to be perfect. We have to plan a whole night worth of fun, but Gabe is a boring stockbroker whose idea of fun is watching the NASDAQ, and no one else loves her as much as me."

"I have a limo," I tell Ava. "Does that help?"

I jump from Ava's voice squealing. "Um, YES!" She takes it a million octaves lower and whispers, "A limo? That's *perfect*."

I snicker at Ava's shy expression when she leaves her bedroom all done-up for Chloe's birthday tonight.

She's in a silky strapless top and a pair of leather pants. She's wearing heels.

Ava Campbell is in a pair of heels.

"What?" she whines, unable to meet my eye. She's blushing so hard that it looks like she has a sunburn. "Is it because I'm showing too much cleavage?" she asks quietly.

I love torturing her like this. I get a kick out of Ava being shy about something mundane that the other girls I've been with wouldn't have thought twice about.

"No," I tell her.

"Then why are you smiling? Graaaant," she whines again. "You're going to make me sweat from embarrassment, and then I'm going to smell, and no one will want to be near me all night. Tell me why you're smiling, or I'm just going to change."

That, I won't let her do.

"It's just cute that you do cleavage now," I finally say, focusing on her brown eyes and not her soft, tanned chest. She's fucking glowing. *That skin.*

Ava looks down her body, then up at me. "Real Cute or Slutty Cute?"

"Ava Cute." She rolls her eyes, but I see the little smirk she hides when she thinks her head is completely turned away from me.

Chloe struts through the living room with one shoe on and half of her blonde hair curled.

"You need a necklace with that top, Ruthie," she demands, points at Ava's chest, then walks back to her bedroom.

"Ruthie?" I whisper to Ava.

"Chloe calls me Ruthie," she explains. Then, she turns to shout into Chloe's room, "I don't own a single necklace!"

Yes, she does.

Ava whips her head to me when the words fall out of her mouth. I smirk at her wide eyes.

"Wait, yes, I do. I still have it," she informs me. "I didn't get rid of it, just so you know."

"Okay," I say, nodding.

Ava's eyes dart between her room and me. "Should I…? Is that weird?"

I let her speak her mind, let her figure out what she wants and what she's comfortable with on her own. "I mean, I could, right? We're friends now."

"*Best* friends," I correct her.

Ava studies me. Finally, she decides, "'Kay. I'm going to do it. I'm going to wear it. Be right back."

When Ava exits her room a minute later, her head is hunched forward as she clasps the necklace at the back of her neck. My stomach does this flutter, vibration, when I see it on her again.

Christmas. Two years ago.

She was mine. My girl. *My everything.*

Once she straightens out her neck, Ava maneuvers the necklace, so it's sitting perfectly in the middle of her chest. She looks down at it. Ava stares at the diamond heart. She puts it between her two fingers, closes her eyes and breathes deeply, exhales slowly. When her eyes open, she smiles softly at me.

"I missed this thing. I'm going to help Chloe finish getting ready."

CHAPTER FIFTY-SIX
GRANT

Ava didn't give Lenny a hug when she saw him standing straight by the limousine.

No, she threw herself at him and climbed him like a spider monkey. Lenny didn't know what to do with himself. He hesitantly tapped Ava's back a few times and said, "It's very nice to see you again, Miss Campbell."

She jumped off of him and emphasized, "*Lenny!* Ava! A-V-A."

"Ava. Yes. It's good to see you."

Ava declares that before we pick up Gabe, Derek, and the others, she's going to take advantage that the seats are unoccupied and lays her body across them. She stretches her arms up and wiggles her legs in the air.

"This is the life. Grant, I hope you know that this is the life. Do you have snacks in here?"

I shuffle through the mini fridge and the little pantry. I offer Ava a few options, but she doesn't take anything for now. She does request, however, that I save a granola bar for her for later when she's blackout drunk and needs a pick-me-up.

"Are you getting blackout drunk tonight?" I laugh.

She bends her chin into her neck to look at me from her position across the seats. "Duh. It's Chloe's birthday bash. You better drink, too, G-Wagon."

Once we've filled the limousine with Chloe's birthday attendees, we head toward the nightclub Ava mentioned Chloe loving. We get into the back of the line to wait for the bouncers to check our I.D.s and let us in. I don't do the name thing that I usually do to avoid lines and wait with the rest of our group. I like observing them. I like seeing Ava's dynamic within her group of friends and how she acts amongst everyone, individually and together.

"My feet are killing me," she groans, shifting from one leg to the other ten minutes into our wait. She blames Chloe on lending her *this* specific pair of shoes, then drops down to the dirty, New York sidewalk, so she doesn't have to stand. I pull at her arm, but she whines.

"You are not sitting on the ground, Ava," I chuckle, shaking my head at her. "That is revolting. I'll carry you. Come on, get up. On my back, you go."

Ava springs up from the concrete with excited eyes. *All of a sudden, her feet are better, huh?*

Once she's scaled herself up my back, Ava cranes her neck to glance up and down the street and above the heads of everyone in line.

"We're all just miniature people to you, aren't we?" She tightly clasps her legs around my waist, her arms around my neck, and puts her lips on my pulse. She settles into me.

"Is this okay?" she whispers. "Please tell me this is okay because I am in literal heaven right now. *Actual* heaven."

I squeeze her soft thighs and nod, but it's not okay. None of this shit is okay. She isn't mine but she's acting like it.

What the hell am I doing to myself?

Here's the thing they don't tell you about being friends with an ex.

They never *actually* feel like they're your ex.

We've been dancing with our sides pressed together all night. We've been downing cocktail after fruity cocktail, choking from laughter at absolutely nothing. Well, not nothing. I choke on laughter at Ava's terrible voice belting out every lyric to one of the songs playing.

I want this.

A ring. A house. A future.

But she's my ex. She *isn't* actually mine, and reality hits me head-on when we're at the dark V.I.P. booth that Ava and Gabe secured for the night and Derek offers her his denim jacket. I overhear the exchange.

"I'm not cold yet, but thanks, Derek!" I look over both Derek and Ava's heads at Chloe because Chloe is also listening in. She catches my eye. We look at each other. I shrug when her expression reads *Do something!*

But what can I do? I can't claim her as mine. She doesn't want me like that.

Just friends.

"Hey, you guys!" Ava shouts to our booth, waves her skinny arms to catch everybody's attention. "I'm going to the bar. Does anyone want anything?"

They all seem to be okay beverage wise, but Derek says, "I'm good, but I'll come with you."

Ava shrugs and replies with a laidback, "Okay!"

She doesn't realize she's getting hit on. That she's being, for lack of a better word, courted.

Once Ava and Derek walk off and are no longer in ear shot, Chloe and I glance at each other and immediately howl. We laugh so damn loudly that the rest of the group wonders what the hell just happened. Chloe walks the few steps to stand beside me.

"She's a little bit of an airhead, isn't she?" I joke.

Chloe cackles, shakes her head. "Oh my God, *yes*. She's the smartest airhead I've ever met."

CHAPTER FIFTY-SEVEN
AVA

Derek got a little touchy when we walked to the bar together. It had me thinking bad, bad thoughts about him and me and how easy and simple it would be. I had to physically shake my head to stop thinking like that.

When I make my way through the dancing clubgoers back to our booth after peeing for the fourth time tonight, blonde hair catches my eye. For a second, I think it's Hannah, and because I'm drunk and unwanted thoughts force their way into my mind, I remember our conversation and what she said to me at the high school reunion.

I then completely sober up. Well, not exactly.

Grant will really wait for me, won't he? He'll wait. He will waste his life away waiting for me. Girls will want to get to know him, but he won't bother trying. He will smile at them in passing with only me on his mind.

God, that is so fucked up.

I can't marry her, Hannah. She can't have children.

I need to take a step back. I need to start facing reality and recognizing that we're not permanent. I have to do something to change the trajectory of his future. I have to give him that little push that he needs after inserting myself in his life and begging him to be my best friend.

I sift through the crowd of people and tap a beautiful redhead on the shoulder. I have whiplash when she turns to face me because I have never seen someone more beautiful in my life.

She's perfect.

"Wow."

Her eyes squint, but she still smiles at me. Her auburn brows pinch. They're full and lush and natural. "Hi. Did you tap me?" she asks so super politely.

I'm both satisfied and angry at how motherly her voice sounds to me. I'm projecting, I know. But still.

"Are you single?" I ask.

Redhead smiles sweetly and says, "I'm sorry, but I'm not into girls."

"No, no, no! Not for me! For my friend!"

She rolls her eyes and chuckles, then asks who my friend is. I point Grant out to her, and she faces me, raises her eyebrows. She has green eyes like Grant. They'll make perfect feline babies.

They'll *make* babies. Babies. They. Both of them, together.

I swallow down the lump. Now is not the time for self-pity.

"Okay, I'm listening." How could she not be interested? Look at him!

I tell this gorgeous girl all about my best friend in the whole world. I tell her about his close-knit family, his self-made job, his Ivy League education. She stops me when I mention UPenn.

"I don't need to hear any more. My dad went to UPenn. He's going to love this guy, and my dad is hard to please. Introduce me."

I put on a brave face. The bravest I can. I grab her toned arm, then drag her over to our booth. I tap Grant's shoulder. When he turns and sees me, his grin is blinding. He doesn't even notice the girl whose arm I'm gripping because he's so focused on me, me, me.

"Grant," I begin evenly. "This is... Wait, I didn't catch your name."

"Molly," she states.

"Molly," I repeat. "This is Molly. Her dad went to UPenn."

Grant looks at me like I'm insane. Like I'm wearing one of those glasses with the plastic noses attached. Actually, if I were really doing that, he'd smile and laugh and shake his head endearingly at me. But he's polite to Molly. He turns to smile at her and offers his large hand for a handshake.

"Grant. Hello. Nice to meet you."

"You too," Molly teases. "I've heard such great things."

She's flirting. *I am watching this beautiful woman flirt with Grant.*

"So, how old are you, Grant?" she asks.

"He's twenty-nine!" I chime in. "His birthday is…"

Molly looks at me like I'm in the way. That's my cue.

I scurry away because I don't care to eavesdrop on their perfect-people conversation. I move in the direction of the bathrooms to vomit. Quite literally. Within minutes, Chloe holds my hair, and I'm puking into the nightclub bathroom after I text her, HHV.

It stands for *hold hair, vomiting*. We coined it together.

Luckily, the cover charge at this club was pricey for a reason, so the bathroom is clean. I can't recall how many gross bathrooms we've encountered that somehow seemed cleaner *after* I threw up.

Once I'm done, I'm happy as a clam. I put Molly's perfect, stunning face in the backburner of my brain. I grab Chloe to dance with me, but she refuses. Instead, she drags me to an empty corner of the club.

"Are you okay?" Concern is written all over my best friend's beautiful face. I nod, but she doesn't buy it. "Who is that girl?"

"I have no idea." I chuckle but it's fake.

"Then, please explain to me why you introduced her to Grant."

I swallow. "Because he has to stop waiting for me."

Chloe pulls me in for a hug, and I have to will myself not to cry. She pulls back, grips my shoulders, and faces me. "Why does Grant have to stop waiting for you? Why won't you take him back? You love him so much, Ruthie. So, so much."

I look away. I shake my head. I don't want to go there. I don't want to reply. I don't tell Chloe what I overheard the night of my graduation.

"I'm not doing this tonight. It's your birthday, and I love *you*. Let's get tequila shots!" I exclaim.

I attempt to pull Chloe out of this corner and back into the party, but she nudges me back to my position across from her. I give her a sad smile. "Chlo, come on. I'm fine. Let's go."

Chloe's back faces the wall behind us, so she has a view of the rest of the room. I watch her gaze stop somewhere behind my shoulder. I don't want to do it, I wish I had no inclination to, but I ask, "Is the girl still there?"

"No."

Did they leave together? "Oh...," I mutter.

"*She* left," Chloe interjects quickly. "Grant's standing there, watching us talking." Chloe waves, then looks back at me.

I plead with her to play it cool, to pretend we're just doing girl things. "I'll tell him you were giving me a tampon. Just don't say that we were talking about him, okay?"

She agrees to keep quiet if I agree to come back to the booth with her. Taking a deep breath, I plaster a dazzling smile on my face and follow Chloe across the vibrating club's dancefloor toward our friends. I smile at Grant, then focus on something Gabe is saying.

I feel Grant observe my every move. His huge body hovers above me, around me, and I can feel his hard, studying gaze on my face. I can feel his judgment. I cannot have him ask me questions, and I also can't have him mention perfect, beautiful, fertile Molly. I close my eyes.

Please don't say anything about what I just did. Please pretend that never happened because I know you're good at that. We both are.

"Ava, what about you!" Gabe shouts over the piercing rap music.

I blink up at him. "What?" I say, startled.

"Body count," he boasts with a big laugh. I scoff because *Misogyny, much?* And what would I even reply? *Two? One and a half?*

"Oh my God, Gabe! What the hell is wrong with you?" Chloe shrieks, pulling at his ear like she's his scolding mother. He has the audacity to be confused at our scorning looks.

"What? We're all saying them! Fine. Wilder, you go. Body count."

Gabe, I am going to fucking kill you.

And because I can't bear to hear Grant reply to his question, I swivel, but before I have a chance to saunter away, no *run* away, a giant hand grips my forearm. I know whose it is, but because of all the emotions that swirl in my body from tonight, I pull my arm back spitefully.

"I think I would rather die than hear you answer that question," I say to Grant's broad chest. I make it ten steps before Grant spins me around by the shoulder. His eyebrows are drawn, green eyes squinted.

"I wasn't going to answer him," he retorts, frustrated. "You really thought I would?"

"You probably don't even know your body count," I mumble. I don't know where this is coming from. I want to blame the alcohol, but it's not that at all.

I blame my circumstances. I blame *Pat*.

Grant deflates at my comment. He tries to meet my eye, but I don't let him. I'm ashamed about what happened tonight. I brought this feeling onto myself. If I was so stressed about another woman being good for him, why did I introduce Grant to Molly?

"What did I do?" his deep voice rasps in a beg. "What's going on?"

He's your best friend, Ava. You love him. You want him to be happy. Stop being cruel.

"Nothing," I whisper. It's taking everything in me not to cry. "I'm… I don't know. I'm sorry."

"Who was that girl?"

"I don't know."

Grant studies me in the corner of this club. I bite the inside of my mouth in a nervous tick to keep me from sobbing. I do not want to be this person right now, but I also can't do the smiley thing. I can't fake it. Not tonight. I have no energy. Grant reads that.

"Let me take you home," he says resolutely.

I shake my head. "No, it's Chloe's birthday. I can't—"

"Chloe and Gabe just left. Come on."

CHAPTER FIFTY-EIGHT
GRANT

I'm seated at Ava's white Ikea desk, my body turned so I can face her.

I brought her home in a cab and let the rest of our group take the limo back to their places. Lenny was happy to do it. He asked me to check in when we got to Ava's.

When we did, she crawled into her bed in everything but her heels. Now, she lays on her belly and has her arms crossed in front of her like she did the night we went to Central Park. She lays her head in the crook of her arms and faces me with a timid expression.

"Do you hate me?" she whispers.

I shake my head. With an even tone, I reply, "No way."

"Do I make your life stressful?"

Breathe in, breathe out.

I think about her question.

"Not stressful, no…" I inhale deeply when I watch her, watch the mutual thought processes that go through both of our heads when we look at each other.

Molly? Really?

She can tell that it bothered me. If there's anyone who should set me up with another woman, Ava is not it.

"I didn't mean to upset you, and I hate that I have."

Her voice shakes with emotion, and every word coming out of Ava right now is pouring out of her heart, straight into the air between us. It's intense.

With a guilty conscience and the love that I have that burns for this woman, I reach my arm over the bed to rub her back softly. "What's going on? What was that earlier?"

"You can't wait for me, Grant." Her voice is soft and pleading. My heart splits in two, and my body freezes in place.

That's why Ava introduced me to Molly tonight? Because she's pushing me to date? To find someone else since she's adamant that we can't be together?

Yeah, that's exactly what she's doing. I just don't understand why. *Fuck.*

Is it what I did last year?

Could it be the Hannah thing? But I broke it off, and she knows I did it for her. It's not the Hannah thing.

Then, what could it be?

With Ava, I'm usually spot on. For the most part, I know what she's thinking and how she's feeling and I get her, but *this*? I haven't a single clue.

"I am so confused, Ava." *We got* tattoos *together. Does that mean nothing? Does that prove nothing?*

"I'm confused, too. If I push you to date, I lose you. If I don't, I'm holding you back. I can't lose this. I can't," she chokes quietly. Her voice is strained like she's holding in tears. She continues. "I know that you're holding out for me, Grant, and you can't."

I have no idea what's happening right now. Ava is speaking full-on cryptically.

"You're not going to lose me. I'm not going anywhere," I declare, each syllable puncturing the air, floating, the devotion in my voice authentic and true. I want the meaning of my words to penetrate within her every inch of skin. I want her to *know*.

"One day, you will. You'll have to. You'll meet someone, and you'll have to drop me."

An ache in my chest passes through when I fathom that she's serious. She believes this. She believes there's a girl out there that will one day be more important to me than her.

"That's never going to happen." I say it again. "That's never going to happen, Ava."

"You can't wait for me," she repeats. "We can't be together. I know you're waiting, but you need to stop."

My heart squeezes at her finite words. "Why can't we be together? You never did give me a reason," I tell her desperately.

Her eyes immediately cast down, away from my gaze. It's like she's guilty, like she's caught. Or like *I'm* guilty. Maybe all along, it *has* been the McCall thing. Maybe Ava can't get past it, even if she says she could. Maybe she would think of herself as weak if she took me back after everything that I did to her.

Her reply to my big question, "You just have to trust me." I scoff. "What?" she probes timidly.

I clench my jaw. Evenly, I tell her, "I think it's finally time you explain it to me."

CHAPTER FIFTY-NINE

AVA

But how could I explain it?

How could I explain it when I know what his reply will be? When I know he'll choose me over his future; future wife, future family, future kids. I love him more than anything, and I could never live with myself if I were the reason Grant Wilder never had children.

Maybe it's the tradition embedded in me, but this is a big deal. It's important. More so because of what he said to Hannah.

I can't marry her, Hannah. She can't have children.

If we got married, I'd watch it unfold bit by bit throughout the years; Annie's kids' birthday parties, Madison's Sweet Sixteen, Ben and Layla having their own babies. He'll watch them, he'll be happy for them, but I'm not convinced he wouldn't resent me if he committed to me with my circumstances. I don't want to be a regret. I don't want him to regret choosing me when Freddy and Elizabeth have their third kid and Grant and me are still just Grant and me.

"You just have to trust me," I tell him again. I'm almost pleading when I tell Grant, "Trust me. Have faith that I'm doing right by you."

He exhales sharply, annoyed. "That's blind faith, Ava. I need to know what I'm dealing with before letting this go."

Of course. He's an engineer. He needs to know the mechanics of my decision, each part in its own sense before putting this conversation behind him. He'll hypothesize and will never stop until he knows what my persistent reluctance is all about, but I have to stand my ground.

I can't let him know that I overheard what he told his fiancée. I can't let him know that I'm making a sacrifice, so that he can have the future he deserves. I know he'll tell me he wants me either way. I won't stop until I know Grant is getting the future that he's always dreamed of having.

I'll go to his wedding because I'm his best friend, or was once. And from the front row, because Annie will insist that I sit with her, I'll smile at him and tell him how happy I am with my eyes.

I'll mouth, "You got this."

He'll wink at me. And then the music will play. His future wife will walk down the aisle toward him, on her father's arm.

I'll stand. I'll watch his mesmerized face as he watches his future walk toward him, the love of his life, and I'll be so incredibly happy for him.

I'll also always know what I'm missing out on. But that's okay because at least he's getting what he always wanted.

"Yes," I tell Grant. I swallow. "Yes, it is blind faith. And if you love me like you claim, you'd trust that I'm asking for your blind faith in good faith."

He stands up from the chair beside my desk. Black locks fall to his forehead when he looks to his side. His stunning eyes are hooded, but I'm hoping it's the effects of alcohol and exhaustion and not the stress I probably cause him.

Grant sucks his teeth, shakes his head. "You think I don't love you if I ask questions? If I don't want to have blind faith, it means I don't love you?"

Somehow, he still looks at me like I'm the loveliest person, but he's finally letting his guard down. He's showing me that he thinks I'm being unreasonable. He's letting go.

"I want you to be happy. Do you believe that to be true?" I ask.

"This is what I think is true. I think you want to remove yourself from me because even though you say you're over it, you're not. What happened last year. I think a part of you is still upset at me for being McCall's lawyer, and it's making it hard for you to take me back."

I sit up on my knees, so I can face him better. I watch his eyes glance quickly at my arm, then my chest, then back at my face.

The tattoo. The necklace. Me.

I make sure he's really listening when I say, "That's not it. I don't lie."

How can I get him to believe me? How can I make him understand without telling him the truth that I really am doing what's best for him? That the choice I am making allows him the future he wants and not the future that *I* want. Because when I wasn't an option, he came to his senses. When he was no longer blinded by the love he had for me, he was in his right mind, he knew that me being barren won't work for him long-term.

"This is not about what I want. I hope you know that. I hope you know that everything I'm doing is for you," I say.

Grant scoffs. He is so upset with me. "You can't do that, Ava!" he stresses.

He hates that I'm being cryptic. He hates when I'm not upfront, when I won't be straight-up with him. I can imagine how frustrated he is. I know that I'm being confusing, and I hate that I'm stressing him out, but I've also asked for him to let it go like he said he would.

I want our short time together to be as fun as possible. I don't like these conversations. I don't want even a second spent together worrying about things that are out of our hands. I want to utilize every moment I have with Grant as my best friend in the best atmosphere.

I need him. I want him to let the questions go, so we can go back to having a fun time together. Permanently let them go.

"Please let it go," I beg quietly. "It's good like this."

His piercing eyes shoot up to mine. He squints. "For who? For you?! Because I'm the one left in the fucking dust when you leave me one day!"

I'm not going to leave you. You're *going to leave* me. *You're going to move on. You're going to be a father.*

I swallow thickly but remain silent. He's so angry. This is the most frustration he's shown since he put that stupid boxing glove on me.

I still have it. I kept it for the memories.

Grant takes a deep breath. He lowers his voice and asks, "At what point, Ava, do we realize that this isn't sustainable?"

My heart drops.

He's right. I'm asking for too much.

My voice is small when I mutter, "We said it wouldn't be complicated."

Grant sucks his teeth. He brushes his long fingers through his hair. "We said that after Montauk, Ava. If things between us stayed the way they were at the beach house, then fine. Fucking *fine*. It would never have been complicated. It got complicated when you crossed boundaries."

No.

Please.

Don't.

Don't say it. Don't shed light to it.

"You took this too far, Ava," he whispers tightly. "You're leading me on. You're giving me false hope. You're acting like you're mine."

"You're acting the same way. It's not one sided," I say softly, the fear that he'll stop reciprocating filling my voice. I could never handle that, but I know I have to prepare myself for it. One day, he'll make all of this effort for someone else.

With furrowed eyebrows, brokenness in his expression, Grant admits, "You're right. I am matching the way you act when you make as if you're mine, but the difference is that I want you in my future."

"Want." I laugh humorlessly. "Want," I say again.

"I don't..." He clicks his tongue and scoffs quietly in a way that's self-loathing. "I don't know what my role in all this is. I am trying to navigate this friendship by taking everything into account, but it's not adding up. Your actions aren't adding up, Ava. Help me understand. Just make sense of it for me."

My throat constricts, tightens because he's right. And that feeling—the feeling of knowing I've created this game of cat and mouse—makes the guilt within me rise to the surface of my every emotion. I'm encompassed by a feeling of guilt so fierce that it pulls at the tears until they're displayed in surrender.

My chest heaves when I look at him with the pain that runs through my blood. I wipe angrily at my tears that give me away. Everything in my face gives me away when it comes to Grant because he knows me so painfully well.

That's why he's not fighting me. That's why he isn't running away. He's just...confused.

He must understand from just looking at me that this feeling of being unsure clings to me so tightly, but now, with the guilt that ferments within me more and more, it feels like I'm finally going to crack.

It's on the tip of my tongue. I ready myself to tell him because I am so tired. I'm tired of keeping this pain inside me. I'm tired of being unable to confide in my best friend about something that's on my mind 24/7, especially since he's the reason for it. He's the reason I can't tell him. His unconditional love to me. His devotion over anything else. Over his future children.

"This is breaking you," he says quietly, studying my eyes with a deep frown. "You're victim to this secret. This mysterious thing that you can't tell me more about. Why are you doing this to yourself?"

I shake my head, close my eyes, and smile painfully. "It's much more than that. I'm victim to the feelings I have for you."

"Then, explain what this is. Explain why—"

"I have a question for you, all right?" I interrupt. He nods. "Do you think this is easy for me? Do you think I don't hate this as much as you do? Because I do, okay? So, you can stop pretending that this is one sided. You can stop pretending like I'm doing this willingly. Like I *want* this. Like I *want* to confuse you."

His leveled expression causes fury to fester in my chest, a desperate need for him to match my tone, but he doesn't. His level of calm is eerie.

Before he has a chance to talk, I interrupt him again. "I hate this. I don't want to answer to you anymore."

"You don't have to answer to me. You never have to answer to me, but you do have to start respecting my feelings. Respecting that I'm being pushed in so many directions by you, I feel like I'm looking at some optical fucking illusion.

"It's all I ask, Ava. For you to take my feelings into consideration when you act on yours. Drunk or not. If you say there's no future, act like there's no future. I'm fine with that as long as you live by your words."

"Just leave it alone. Why do you have to question this so much?

You said you wouldn't." My words exit my mouth in a strained voice. I'm giving him every reason to question it, that's why.

"Because every time you touch me and you hold my hand and you hug me like our chests are glued together, I breathe this mental sigh of relief that you're finally coming back to me. That you've finally realized that you and I are meant to be together, but then you say some shit like 'Let's pretend that didn't happen' or 'Let's go back to normal.' Then, I break. I fucking break, Ava."

"Please stop," I beg quietly. "Please don't tell me that."

I slip under the duvet cover on my bed, avoiding Grant's eye. It's a way of hiding. Somehow, having cotton draped over me feels like I grant myself space from his aura. Being around him makes me feel so much that I become blinded to common sense, and I'm scared I'll crack like I almost just did. When I'm around Grant, he's the only thing that matters to me. He's the only thing I think about.

Well, my love for him, rather. If I really thought about what's best for him, I wouldn't lead him on.

His gaze locks on me from the desk chair, catches what must be my broken eyes. Honey eyes; that's what he calls them.

He makes a *come here* motion with his hand when his chest deflates. Seeing me in this state, sad and terrified, is hard for him.

I don't walk over to him. I remain cuddled into myself and shake my head.

"I hate that you're crying. I hate that I made you cry. I just… I don't know, Ava. You have such a hold on me that it's unhealthy, you know, and I can acknowledge that. I know that this…this feeling I have for you exists nowhere else, but this is who I am. I am the guy who is in love with you. That's become my identity, and it's terrifying that I'm not really allowed to love you. Not the way I want. Not forever."

I have to gnaw at the inside of my cheek when I listen to his confession, the passion flowing out of his mouth because this is easy for him. He doesn't hide that he loves me. *I, on the other hand…*

"I don't want to have a hold on you like this. That's why Molly happened. If you move on, you'll… You admit that it's unhealthy, how you feel about me. Do something about it."

Grant pinches the corners of his eyes, releases a heavy sigh, causing embarrassment to bloom within me. The guilt is too much for me to bear that I'm suddenly encompassed by heat and sweat; moisture forms behind my neck, on my chest.

I'm complicated. Me, as a person. Relationships with me are complicated, so, as selfish as I am, I close my eyes and when I open them, I ask, "Grant, could you please leave?"

CHAPTER SIXTY
GRANT

It's Ava.
 She's worth it. There's nothing I can do but wait.

CHAPTER SIXTY-ONE
AVA

It's causing me to hallucinate, knowing I'm torturing Grant with my friendship.

Knowing that I'm leading him on, making him feel like we have hope for a future, when I know I'd be a terrible person if I let him be with me, a barren woman.

God, that word. *Barren.* So finite.

A piercing pain sears through me every time I think about how he's better off without me. Better off letting go of this friendship, moving on from the pain and confusion I bring him by dating a woman who wouldn't. Who would never hurt such a good, good man.

Because he is. He's good. He's my good. He's my version of the best man on the planet, and the intrusive thoughts that swim in my brain wreck me.

If only he couldn't have kids either.

God, *I know.* I know it's terrible. I hate myself and my brain for concocting such a thought, but I can't help it. I love him too much. I want him too much. But I want him to be happy more.

Chloe is at Gabe's *again*, but I need her right now. I feel like I'm reeling, panicking, to a frightening level. It's the worst it's been in years. It's bad because I'm the problem. I hate knowing that I'm the problem. I hate acknowledging it.

If I was a good friend, I'd remove myself from Grant's life. I'd understand that since we can't be together, cutting off ties would be the healthier option. Not being best friends. Not having a little bit of him. Having none of him would be in his best interest because I'm giving him false hope. I just can't help it. How do you put a lid on the kind of love that bursts out of you? That makes you so happy, it feels like your blood bubbles like a pot of water?

It's impossible to tame it. It's impossible to say goodbye, too.

I don't fully recognize where I've gone until I see Bobby. He stops to ask if I'm okay. I tell him, "Grant deserves better from me, Bobby." Amidst my panic attack, I tell his doorman that he deserves better.

This is a bad one. A really freaking bad one.

I knock and swallow the lump down because what I can't do is show up with teary eyes. Not to him. He'd break, seeing me that way. That's how much he loves me.

I'm surprised when Layla answers the door and she's the one with teary eyes. I gasp because the thoughts that run through my mind when seeing her are instant and irrational. Thoughts that something must have happened to him if his sister who lives in Boston is answering his apartment door with wet eyes.

"Oh no. Is he okay?" I ask frantically. "Is he okay?"

When she doesn't reply fast enough, I begin to cry. With a tight voice and gushing eyes, I choke out, "Please tell me he's okay, Layla. Please tell me nothing happened."

Layla pulls me in for a hug and chuckles. "He's totally fine, babe. He's just on a work call."

This time, my crying comes from relief.

This is so chaotic. I'm so messy tonight. It's embarrassing.

"I'm so sorry for intruding. I...I'm going to go home. Don't tell him I came, okay? Just... I want to ask how you're doing, but he's going to leave the office soon, so I'll text you. Is that okay?"

Layla shakes her head. "If Grant knew I let you leave, he'd kill me."

She looks at me, knowing that she isn't wrong. He'll be pissed, but I don't care. Let him be. I'm not in my right mind. I just assumed something bad happened to him because his sister is crying. I can't face him with this toxic mayhem I exude.

But our conversation spans for too long of a minute. Apparently, the call is over. I hear his footsteps.

"Who's there, Lay?" I hear him call out. The sound of his voice twists a knot in my chest. *I love you, Grant Wilder.*

"Your favorite!" she calls out once I've given her a nod when she asks the silent question: *Can I?*

"Who? Ava? Ava's here?"

Layla stands to the side to make room for me. I walk in and face him in the kitchen. The way his eyes, his face, his entire being lights up when he sees me makes me want to vomit.

"Ava's here," he sighs contently.

After everything I've done, am doing to him; after Grant finally told me off with good reason, he still reacts this way to me. He's so blinded, this stupid man.

"Hey," I croak quietly, lift a hand up. Layla and I stand side by side. When Grant takes a moment to read me, then looks over at his sister, his movements turn slow mo.

The way he studies us while he wipes his hands on the kitchen towel. The way he looks when lowering it down to the marble island. Finally, his deep voice turns hoarse as he asks, "What happened? Who...who?"

Oh goodness. He thinks someone died.

Layla identifies his thought process because she hurriedly explains, "Nothing! No one! Nothing happened." She puts her long arm around me. "We're just both being crybabies today. Are you on your period?" She turns her head to ask me. "Because I am."

"I'm about to be," I chuckle awkwardly.

"Ah. PMS. The culprit."

"So, you're both okay? Everybody is okay?" he asks us slowly.

"Yes, brother," Layla replies.

"Av? Honey?"

"Hm?"

"Are you okay?" he asks, smiling small.

No, I'm not okay. I'm torturing you, and it's torturing me. "Mhmm," I hum.

"You want some candy? I think my girls need some candy," he chuckles.

Layla mentions she hasn't had a piece of candy in four years. I salivate and take him up on his offer. Grant leads the way to the kitchen, opens a drawer that used to have Tupperware in it from what I remember last year, but it is now filled with piles of colorful bags of sugar. I look up at him in question. He laughs at himself and shrugs.

"It's my Ava drawer."

Oh, my heart. An Ava drawer. I want to cry again.

I'm not surprised that it feels comfortable hanging out with Grant and Layla together. They've always treated me like family. And if I didn't think it would hurt his feelings, I'd leave when Layla does, but I'm not mean enough for that. Apparently, I am for bigger things, though.

"You're not okay," Grant states once she hugs us both, he kisses Layla on the side of her head, and the door shuts behind her.

"I am," I object casually. "I just…had a headache."

"You came here with tears in those sad eyes of yours because of a headache?"

I can hear how ridiculous it sounds. I shrug.

"Honey, what is it? It's me. You could tell me anything," he says softly.

The way he says it.

The endearing pet name he calls me by.

The fact that his sister seemed to be having a bad day and came here. *To* him. *To her supportive brother.*

The panic creeps up on me again until I'm a loose cannon. "I can see what I'm doing to you. And I'm the worst friend. I can't handle knowing that. I want to be a better friend, but that means letting you go. But letting you go is the most painful option for me, and I just can't… I know that I'm torturing you. I'm bad for you. But I'm not strong enough to let you go completely. I'm not. I wish I had the courage to do the right thing and remove myself from your life, but I don't. Not when it comes to you."

I exhale heavily. When Grant begins to come in for a hug, I take a step back and shake my head.

He nods once, slips his hands into his trouser pockets, then lifts his eyes to mine. With thick emotion in his voice, he states, "I'm really glad you're not strong enough for that, then, because I'm not strong enough to lose you either. I'll never be strong enough for that, Ava. Not again. Never again."

Yes, you will be. You have to be.

I look up at him; at the sincerity in his eyes and the nervousness on his lips. My chin quivers, but when I see him ready himself to approach me again, I take another step back. He winces then quietly scoffs at himself.

"You're mad at me," I whimper and gulp. "You have every right to be."

"Ava, honey, no way. I'm not mad at you. I'm not mad at anyone but myself."

My eyes shoot up to his with question. He rakes long fingers through his unruly hair, licks his lips, then begins to berate himself. "Look at how…I bleed you fucking dry. I'm complicating this thing between us. I've caused this…this shift after the night of Chloe's party. I'd like to blame it on the alcohol I consumed that night, but that isn't fair to you. You deserve more.

"I'm sorry I lost it. I'm sorry, Ava. I…I was caught off guard by what you did trying to set me up, and I really hated the way Derek was hitting on you." My eyebrows furrow because *since when has Grant observed Derek's crush on me?*

Grant observes my surprise. "Yeah, I know. He likes you. Then, Gabe's body count comment made me spiral. I'm sorry, honey. Okay? You did nothing wrong. Nothing. It was all me. And I hate myself for acting the way I did because look at you, my little weirdo. You're devastated. Come here. Come hug me, so I can squeeze the sadness out of you."

Leave it to Grant to take responsibility for my own wrongdoings. To turn the trajectory of this conversation where he's at fault when I'm begging him to see that I am.

I shake my head, even if his outstretched arms are exactly where I want to be. Cuddled. Cradled.

"I can't walk away from this. I don't know how to lose you. I don't know how to walk away, even when I know it's the right thing to do. What kind of friend am I? And a best friend at that."

"Ava—"

"You were right. Everything you said that night. This isn't

sustainable. I'm leading you on. I am because of how bad…"

I can't say it. Then, it'll turn into a conversation where the answer to his impending question is an explanation of what I heard him say the night of my graduation, and I'm not willing to give that to him. I never will be.

"I'm so angry at myself, Grant. You don't deserve this. You don't."

He puffs up his cheeks and releases a hefty breath. "Oof. A lot to unpack here. A: I probably deserve it. I mean, of course I do. I broke your heart when you needed me. And B: sometimes being best friends with the person you're in love with blurs the lines. I get it. We're on the same page."

I begin to cry when he utters, with confidence pouring out of him, the words *being best friends with the person you're in love with*, so he hugs me. He doesn't let me say no, he just holds me while I cry to him.

"I hate what I'm doing to you," I cry, choking out the words with a burning pain in my throat. "But this is the way it has to be."

I can hear him thinking. I can hear him telling himself not to ask again why we can't be together. I can hear him question my irrationality.

But because of his nature toward me, he doesn't say anything other than, "What you're doing to me, Ava Ruth, is giving me everything that you could give me right now. Which is enough. It's more than enough." He grips my shoulders and leans back to look me in the eyes. "You know that, right? Because I need you to know that, although I want you back and I love you and it's hard for me to understand where your reluctance is really coming from, the piece where you're my best friend is amazing. I love this. This isn't something we could have if we were together. This is its own genre, you know?"

I nod quickly. That's exactly what it is. Its own genre.

"Just don't try to set me up. That's a hard one. I hear you when you say we don't have a future, but I would prefer you didn't make it so real. Let me live in a bubble. It hurts either way, so I'd rather enjoy the time I have with you without the blatant reminder of how you're adamant that you're not going to be my wife one day."

Wife.

I bring a shaking hand to my lips, cup my mouth, and squeeze my eyes closed, causing a fountain of tears to escape my eyes.

My heart is breaking. My heart is broken. Look what I've done to him.

He's willing to put himself in pain to be my friend. I am, too. We're both doing this for each other.

And then there's Derek. He has to watch Derek flirt with me and buy me drinks. He has a constant reminder that I'm not his every time we go out together. I'm spared unless I commit myself to the self-infliction like I did with Molly. Breaking my own heart by trying to mend his.

I sniffle and wipe my tears from my soaked face. I take a deep breath and attempt an explanation. "I just want you to find your forever person. I need you to find her, so I can feel at peace."

"I found her." My eyes shoot up to his. He watches me like a hawk from his tall stance. He looks between both my eyes and swallows nervously. "I found her," he repeats.

I attempt to retort back to him, but he holds up a hand. Finally, a sense of anger bestows him; his jaw twitches from grinding teeth.

"You can ask me to enjoy the now. You can ask me to stop asking questions. You can ask me to accept your decision, but you *cannot* ask me not to love you. That's not okay. That's not fair."

"So, leave. Leave me. We both know it's what's best. You leave, so I don't have to, because I can't. I don't know how."

"Stop it," he begs quietly. "Please. Just stop it, Ava. It's enough already."

I turn red. My head spins as I take a few steps away from him. I'm embarrassed. I'm so embarrassed.

"Why? Why do you stay? Why do you stick around, despite all the stress I cause you?"

"I'm not answering that like there are two options for me," he scoffs.

"Answer it," I demand.

He rubs up his face. I'm suddenly afraid of his hold on my heart. Without knowing what he's going to say next, I anticipate it. And then he melts my heart with, "If you saw you the way I see you, you'd understand. I... You're... I don't know. You're my Ava. You're the best thing that's happened in my entire life. You're all I see. You're it for me. Ava, I stay because I love you," he breathes, tired. "It's not that complicated."

I gulp. "My head tells me I should let you go, but my heart would never let me do that. You own me. You're like the puppeteer of my heart," I admit, my voice small and shaky.

"So, *be with me*. Be *mine*," he pleads. His voice is full of yearning and passion, and *You're all I see. You're it for me.*

I dart my eyes away from his desperate ones, that shade of jade piercing not only my heart but my skin, a warmth coming over me. A heated sensation that I relate to embarrassment. Shame. I'm ashamed.

I do my best to lighten the mood, something I'm good at, curious if it's a running tactic but fully aware that it undoubtedly is. I take a couple of steps toward Grant's long body, then reach my arm out for a handshake. "Hi. I'm Ava. It's nice to meet you."

When it registers to Grant that I'm running, because I seem to be good at that, too, he sighs. "Ava..."

"*Please*," I whisper. I swallow hard. "Just play along. Let's move on. I can't do any more of this. Please, Grant."

Grant's eyes blink slowly when he concedes to me. His hand meets mine in surrender, his grip firm and assertive. I could've guessed he has a solid handshake. God, everything about him is hot.

"I'm Grant," he grunts quietly.

"Hello, Grant. Do you want to be my best friend?"

Grant remains quiet, watching me. I dart my eyes away from his knowing gaze, that heat making its way to my cheeks again.

"Well?" I try a second time. I'm desperate. "Do you?"

"But we've only just met," he finally teases back.

A sense of obsession for this man that I've never felt before comes over me. He deserves so much more than I can give him. I'm not only happy, but frankly, I'm proud of myself that I have the grit and the love for this man to ensure he gets all the incredible things life has to offer. If I didn't think this was the right thing to do, I would never do it. Never.

I reply with, "I've already asked Gabe. I'll take the risk. I'm a really good investor."

I smirk when I've cracked Grant, make him laugh. I wait for him to compose himself. Finally, our eyes meet, and we absorb each other in this silence of acceptance, lay it all out flat in our brains, recognizing that this is all we'll ever have and we just gotta make the most of it.

"Best friends?" I repeat in a timid whimper.

Nothing about the expression he gives me is real. He fakes it for me, pretends to accept this conclusion, and it just cracks open my heart deeper and deeper.

Grant nods. With kind eyes, and a crushed chest, he states, "Of course, Ava. I'd love to be your best friend."

CHAPTER SIXTY-TWO
GRANT

It doesn't make any sense.
I convey that to Freddy and Elizabeth while sitting at their dining room table. The more I talk about the situation Ava and I are in, the more I recognize that the words coming out of my mouth don't add up. Just like her actions don't.

Make it make sense.

I space out with my gaze on Liz's very pregnant belly, and all I see, *all I fucking see*, is this life with Ava. Ava's belly like that. My kid inside of her. Our kid, our life, our future.

I told her we were going to have babies. Why does it feel, even after all of Ava's retraction, that it'll still happen? Us making children together. Does that make me crazy?

"Does that make me crazy?" I mutter. "To keep wanting her, even after she's made herself clear?"

"It makes you in love. Hopelessly, Grant. That's the key word here. Zero hope."

I'm not looking for Liz's reasoning. I want someone to tell me to keep fighting, but what kind of advice would that be?

See, I don't need convincing. I just need someone to tell me what the hell is going on in those honey eyes I love so much, in that confused brain of my girl's.

I hug my friends goodbye once we've come to an unsatisfactory conclusion, promise to keep in touch, and not retract into a shell like I've done previously, but as long as Ava is around in any capacity, there isn't a chance of that happening. I want to be present in her life, in any way she'll have me. I know that. So does she. She knows I'll never walk away. Ava knows she has me in such a chokehold, I'd do anything for her regardless of the possible detrimental affect it'd have on me.

It *has* on me.

When I slip into the front seat of my car with a deep inclination to drive over to Ava's current apartment, I instead head toward her old one. We haven't spoken in several days, something that's become unusual for us, but I'm not mad. Last week was a lot, for her and for me, so I'm giving her space. I'm letting her breathe, regulate herself, because I know Ava. I know that her vulnerability now is harder on her than it was back then.

She needs some sort of recuperation. She needs to remind herself how to go back to pretending.

It's weird being back here. I've only been a few times since the breakup, but this apartment, the location where it all started, will always hold a place in my heart. I remember everything, detail by detail, and that's the problem, isn't it? My brain or heart or rationality refuses to forget. She's it for me. She'll always be it for me. Ava has been on the forefront of my mind for the last three years. She's a constant.

I hold in this tsunami of emotion as best I can when I gather the evidence of our past relationship and tuck them into a notebook alongside the pen that she bought me for my birthday. God, what that pen put me through.

It was a random Friday night. Hannah and I were getting ready to go out to dinner when I frantically patted myself down, searching for the linear piece of metal that's lived on me since I was given the gift. I couldn't find it.

I could hear the shakiness in my voice when I peeked my head into the bathroom where Hannah was getting done up. "Have you seen my pen?"

"What pen?" she asked, inches away from the mirror, leaning over the sink to put on her perfect face. And I do mean that. Hannah is a pretty girl; luckily, I'm mature enough to admit that.

A little dignity goes a long way.

"It's silver, skinny. It's just a pen, but I can't find it anywhere," I muttered.

I pushed off the doorway and began my second search of the night for the stupid ink stick. I was digging into the couch cushions when I heard two consecutive clicks behind me. I whipped around at the sound of it.

"This pen?" Hannah asked, her eyes glued, and I mean *glued*, to mine. Ava had engraved it. Hannah knew exactly where it came from and why I was frantic because of what it meant to me.

Means to me.

I walked over to her like I was approaching a lioness and took the pen from her pinched fingers. Safe to say, we didn't make it to dinner that night. I put Hannah through hell. I left and came here, to Ava's old apartment, when my fiancée begged me to explain my situation with Ava and I couldn't.

I didn't want to admit it was over. I got mad that Hannah tried to get me to.

Now, I hold the clunky notebook in my hand and crouch down

to sit at Ava's desk. So much guilt swims in my stomach, streams through my blood that I have no idea how to handle it anymore.

Guilt for Ava. Guilt for Hannah.

I call my ex. And not Ava, because I am an absolute crazy person that I refuse to categorize her as just an ex.

Before Hannah has a chance to finish her hesitant, "Hello?", I lay myself bare.

"I never wanted to hurt you. I don't want this. I don't want to love her like this, I just do. And shit, Hannah, I'm sorry. No, sorry doesn't cut it. I put you through hell. You must hate me. You should hate me; I hope you do. I hope you despise me because I hate myself for what I did to you."

I take a deep breath, and when I reel it all in, force myself to be mindful of what I'm doing, ready to hear a spew of hatred, almost *wanting* it, Hannah surprises me.

"I don't hate you, Grant." A pause. "I tried to wiggle myself back into your life when I saw how vulnerable you were about Ava. That was my mistake. It was obvious you weren't over her. It was always obvious, Grant, I just pushed it away."

And yet, I can't have her back. Even when Ava assures me that it isn't something I did, it's only natural for me to believe that I'm the reason Ava doesn't want to be with me. She'll never admit it out loud, but somehow, I just know it's not as deep as she's making it out to be.

I lied to her for six months. I represented her piece of shit exboyfriend. I almost married someone else.

"What's going on?" Hannah asks sincerely. I attempt to brush her off because how awful would it be for me to vent about the woman I've loved this whole time, but Hannah pushes. "I'm dating someone. I'm really over it. You can talk to me."

"Hannah, you're not—"

"Talk to me, Grant," she insists.

I exhale, surrendering because of the desperate need to talk about it. The confusion is blinding. "She...she's doing a lot of pretending, and it's making me crazy. I feel like I'm going to lose my mind." I pause, gather the words, the rough explanation I have about what's going on. "She's really touchy, and... Hannah, I'm not talking to you about this. I care a lot about you to put you through my Ava shit again. I'm going to go, okay?"

Hannah mumbles something to someone away from the receiver. She takes a deep breath when a door shutting sounds.

"I'm a girl who knows you, and I'm a girl who understands what wanting you is all about. I care about you, too. She's touchy and what?"

This isn't right. Yes, it'd be liberating to have any and all opinions about what Ava is doing, but it doesn't feel right. Hannah assures me with my silence. "Talk to me. I'm being a friend here. I swear, I'm fine with it. Ava and I cleared the air at the reunion. I'm neutral here, Grant."

I surrender. I have no other choice. "She's just acting like we're back together, but when I call her out on it, about the touchiness and the things she says, she'll come back at me with something like, 'We're just friends, Grant.' Her actions and her words don't add up, and I'm getting nowhere with my questions. She's giving me not a single clear answer, and it's killing me."

Softly, Hannah says, "I think you guys feel the same way about each other. Maybe she's mad about you and me and can't get over it." Hannah reads my mind. I tell her that I've been thinking the same. "Do you want me to talk to her? Tell her how detached you were?"

God, my heart sinks at Hannah's recollection. The guilt eats at me.

"No!" I call out nervously. "Shit, no, Hannah. She'd be hurt if she knew I was talking about her to you. Listen, I don't have many options and I know that. I'm going to go, all right? Thank you for talking to me, and… and I'm so, so sorry."

In my manic state, I hang up the phone abruptly. Then, I stare down at Ava's old desk, put my face in my hands, and cry.

CHAPTER SIXTY-THREE
AVA

I was eleven-years-old the first time I lashed out at my mom.

I can't recall the exact events of what happened, but once I said something along the lines of, *I wish I had a different mom!*, I threw up. The guilt consumed me so deeply, the knowledge that I made a terrible mistake, that my body couldn't handle it.

In the following days, I hid. I'd come home from school and bolt to my bedroom, stayed there until dinnertime. I'd purposefully spend more time with my brothers, watched whatever movies they wanted, so I could avoid my mom.

I couldn't face her because I couldn't face myself.

Retrospectively, I'm realizing I haven't changed. I've been avoiding Grant.

The shame that the tension between us is my fault entirely is unbearable. When I see him, I see the bad parts of myself. I can see in his green eyes exactly what I'm doing to him.

I want to take a comb to his perfect hair and check for grays because I'm sure he's grown a few since our reunion.

Those nine, life-changing words have such a hold on me that I'm bursting. Bursting with the need to let it out. To tell someone, anyone;

to ask for advice, to have somebody reason with me, to validate my resolution in hiding what I overheard Grant say from him.

At my desk today at work, the deep inclination to say it out loud wins over the shame I feel, so I text Chloe.

> Me: Hey bb, are u home tonight?
>
> Chloe: Yes!!!!!! Missed you!

She's been spending too much time at Gabe's. I've missed her, too.

When she gets home from Broadway, I give her time to settle in before spewing all of my drama onto her. I peak my head through her door after it's been an hour. "Chlo?"

She faces me and smiles warmly. "Hey, babe." Whatever she sees in me must be plastered all over my demeanor, my face, because immediately, after studying me for a millisecond, she asks, "You okay, Ruthie?"

I am so drained and guilty that being asked that question, if I'm okay, deflates me. I am drained from the feelings I have for a man who deserves so much more than what I could give him. Drained from the yearning for a future with the only guy I'll ever love. My first love. My one true love.

"Not so much," I chuckle, a lump lodged thick in my throat. "You have a minute?"

Chloe nods. She scoots over on her white, fluffy comforter to make space for me. I sit beside her, lean my head on her shoulder, and take a deep breath. I swallow the tightness in my throat, but eventually, I can't take it anymore. I choke out a sob. Chloe's eyes widen.

"Ava? Oh no." Chloe's long arms encase me. She tightens her hold on me and strokes my hair as I continue to cry into her neck.

"Sweetie," she whispers lovingly. "Talk to me."

I hate Pat so much tonight. I usually don't bother thinking about him anymore, but tonight, I have burning hot, red anger toward him, and I just want him to die.

He's the reason. He's the reason I can't have Grant.

Yes, I'm aware it was a medical malfunction that left me without tubes. I blame him anyway.

I want to confront that asshole. With the strength I now have, I want to slap his face and give him a piece of my mind, but Grant would never let me. He'd say something about how it isn't worth affecting my mental health. It'd be the truth, but it would be unsatisfactory.

"It's not fair." My voice is pained, excruciatingly pained. "It's just not fair."

"What isn't fair?" Chloe asks tenderly.

So, I tell her. I tell Chloe what I overheard Grant say to Hannah. I tell her that I'd be doing him a disservice if I accepted him back. That I'd be holding him back from the future he wants. That it's so hard not to want everything. That I'm leading him on by wanting everything.

The first thing she says is, "You're amazing." I shake my head. Chloe squeezes my shoulders. "Look at me, sweetie. You are so selfless and pure. You're good, Ava. You are so, so good."

"I'm not good. I just want to be with him," I cry. "I wish I didn't overhear what he told her." I swipe at my cheeks and lean over to Chloe's bedside to grab a tissue. I blow my nose, then turn to Chloe. "Am I being irrational by keeping what I heard from him? By making this decision behind his back, by not telling him why we can't be together?"

Chloe takes a deep breath in contemplation. She turns to me and with kind eyes, asks, "You're sure he'll tell you he wants you either way?"

"Chloe, he got a tattoo for me. I'm positive."

"And you're sure he'd choose you over having kids?"

"A hundred percent."

"Okay. Do you want my advice?" Chloe offers gently. I nod. "Move on. Keep him in your life, but move on."

"How?" I whisper, like it's an irrational thought.

"Derek?" she asks reluctantly, wincing when the name leaves her mouth.

I groan. I rub my eyes with the heels of my hand. I crawl under the covers of Chloe's bed and curl into a ball. She follows after me and holds my hand in the space between us.

"He likes me, doesn't he?" I ask. Chloe deadpans, and it makes me giggle. I sigh. "He's a good guy. He's just not Grant."

"But you've made up your mind. Grant isn't an option." She squeezes my shoulder.

I swallow thickly at her finite words. "I know. I just want him to have everything, and he can't with me. His kids are going to be perfect. They're going to look like him. They'll probably have their eyebrows perpetually furrowed. I just know they're going to be perfect, but they won't be mine."

"This means a lot to you? More than letting him choose you?" Chloe asks softly.

"Yeah. It means the world to me," I whisper. I let the tears fall again. Knowing that it's no use wiping them away, I don't. "Grant being a father means more than anything to me."

I think about Chloe's proposal. *Derek.* Derek is a sweet boy. If Grant wasn't in the picture, I'd be with Derek. I know I would be because I liked him back until Grant came into the picture. And I can't blame Derek one bit for being threatened by Grant because Grant has it all. He's everything. He's the whole package.

But the shitty reality is that I have to walk away. I have to stop leading Grant on and put some space between us, so I decide to finally reach out to Derek with the intention of giving him a chance.

Chloe gives me a warm goodnight hug before I leave her room for mine. I slip into my bed and pull my phone out to text him.

Me: Hey

Derek: Hey, Ava, what's up

Me: Do u want to go to dinner tomorrow night?

Derek: Hell ya

We meet for dinner the next night, somewhere cheap where I know there isn't a chance of Grant showing up. Not that we've spoken much because I'm a better runner than Usain Bolt, but still. I don't want him to know about this. I don't want him to feel hurt or betrayed by me when I can't give him the answers he's asking for. Begging for.

But I won't let him choose me. I just won't. Not when I know he's going to be the best dad on the planet.

Derek makes me laugh at dinner, doing impressions of everyone in our friend group. I howl when he nails his impersonation of Chloe. When he leans in for a kiss once we exit the restaurant, I shove Grant's face out of my head, swallow thickly, and kiss him back. I'm surprised at how easy it is, considering that when he tried to kiss me the last time, I freaked out. I'm surprised that I don't hate it.

I kind of even like it?

"That was nice," he says. His eyes glimmer. "Thanks for not running away."

When I blush, Derek leans over to squeeze my shoulder. "I'm only kidding. I'm glad we're finally doing this. And Wilder…"

"He's just a friend," I say. "I swear."

Derek gauges my honesty, I think. I smile at him with confidence and assurance because that isn't a lie. Grant *is* just a friend.

When Derek asks if I want to come back to his place after dinner, I freeze for a quick second but think about it logically. I haven't been with anyone since Grant. It always felt like cheating, but this somehow feels right. It feels like a good next step.

Derek isn't a stranger; I've known him for over a year, and we *did* like each other before graduation. If it gets to that point, it's okay. I'm twenty-two. This is what I'm supposed to be doing, so I follow Derek to his apartment.

Cue the gasps.

CHAPTER SIXTY-FOUR
GRANT

It takes Ava a little longer than I expect to regulate her emotions and recuperate from our very heavy conversations post-Chloe's-party, which is why my breath hitches when more than ten days since we last spoke, her contact photo lights up my screen with a phone call.

I shut my office door then answer with a questioning, "Hello?" I clear the anxiety out of my throat.

"Hi," Ava says quietly. Her voice is a little raspy, nervous. "Um, it's me. It's Ava."

My chest squeezes. The formality is killing me. This isn't us. "I know," I reply. "How are you? How have you been?"

"I'm fine. Um, I'm just in a little bit of a situation, and I..." Her sentence falls short. She starts over. "I don't mean to—I know we haven't talked in a while, and if this wasn't important, I wouldn't have called."

Again. The formality is killing me.

I haven't seen you in two weeks. I'm losing my mind, and I miss you like crazy. If doing you a favor means I get to see you, I'll do it. Whatever that may be. "Sure," I tell her. "I'll do whatever it is."

"Wait." She gives an awkward chuckle. "I didn't tell you what it entails yet."

"Doesn't matter. What is it? What do you need me to do?"

She takes a deep breath, then proceeds to ramble. Her signature nervous response. I love it so much when she does that. "I have a meeting for work, but I'm just an assistant, and Homer, that's my boss, he called in sick this morning. There's this huge client, and he's going to Europe soon, so Homer wanted me to go alone. I don't really know lawyer jargon all that well. I'm going to sound so dumb. If you could come with me and pretend to be my coworker, I would really, really appreciate it. I have no one else to call."

There is *no one else to call. Don't ever stop calling me. Don't ever stop needing me,* please. "When is it?" I ask.

Ava sighs. "Like, right now."

I'm about to see Ava within the next few minutes? *Oh. No warning, huh.*

I check the time, type out a quick message to Dina via our company's servers, and slip on my suit jacket. "All right. Text me the address. What time is the meeting?"

"It's in twenty minutes. I can stall if I have to."

The address she sends me via text is down the street from my office. "I'll see you in five."

I CHUCKLE THAT Ava doesn't wait until we're off of the client's floor before reaching up for a high-five.

I had about ten minutes to look over the files before we headed into the meeting. Homer's client had to sign a contract after having the terms read to him. I guess that's the lawyer jargon she was afraid of.

We idle opposite each other once we exit one of many skyscrapers on this New York City sidewalk. Ava's demeanor is fidgety. She can't seem to look me in the eyes.

"Ava," I say evenly.

Her cheeks heat instantly. She gulps, then tells me, "Thank you so much. You're like the smartest person I know."

"Of course." I'm not ready to say goodbye, so I ask, "What are you doing now? Can I take you out?"

Her eyes shoot up to mine, surprise hidden in them. "You...you don't hate me?"

I deflate at her question. A lump even forms in my throat. Quietly, I take a step toward her and say, "Of course not. Why would I hate you?"

"You know why." Her voice is tight. "I disappeared on you. I should... I'll leave you alone. Have a good day, okay?"

When Ava begins to walk away from me, I grab her arm and step as close as possible to her. "Please don't go. I can't take another day of this. Be my best friend. Let's go back to normal. Please smile for me, Ava. Don't run away again."

Ava doesn't smile. Instead, she curls her hair behind her ears, crosses her arms, then looks down at her shoes. "You don't mean any of that," she whispers.

"I swear, I do," I plead. "I need you. Seeing you like this is killing me. Smile. Give me that smile."

She shakes her head, not believing what I'm saying. "I ruined everything. I know I did." When her voice wavers, a sob clearly lodged in her throat, she laughs at herself. "*God*, I..."

"You what?" I rasp.

"I missed you," she cries quietly. "I know I have no right to your friendship anymore, but you still mean a lot to me. I really care about you. I need you to know that."

"Ice cream."

Ava looks up at me. "What?"

"You need ice cream. I'm not letting you leave until I feed you some ice cream. Let's go."

It's a hot day today, but I don't think that's why she obliges. Knowing I won't take no for an answer is why she hesitantly follows me to Lenny's car. Only a few minutes later, we've made it to a small gelato place. I tell her to choose whatever she wants, and naturally, Ava goes for the ice cream flavor with the most food dye in it.

Standing side by side at the pick-up counter, she catches me smirking at her. We're both handed our respective flavors, and before I have a chance to point it out, she looks up at me and in a mimicking voice, says, *"Why am I not surprised you chose the flavor with the most food dye in it?"*

She's mocking me. *Fuck, I missed her.*

I smile at her when we sit together on a bench outside the shop. "There you are, Av."

Her lips curve slightly upward. "I don't think I have it in me not to tease you when I have the chance."

Good. At least there's something *you can't walk away from.*

To tease Ava back, I take my spoon filled with coffee ice cream and rub her nose with it. She is not remotely fazed.

"I have more ammo than you, so I suggest you stop," she mumbles around a big bite of ice cream. I laugh and ask her what she means. "I have food dye ice cream in my arsenal, and yours is" —she leans over to look into my cup— "*beige.*"

I chuckle and shake my head. I missed her so painfully. "Fair enough."

"Also, you're in a white shirt. I'm in dark blue. I am untouchable today."

"I'm not worried, Campbell. I'll get you eventually," I tease.

She tsks and clicks her tongue. "When will you learn? *Untouchable*," she says condescendingly, turning her eyes beady.

"I missed you so much," I tell her quietly. I take my last bite of ice cream. "Don't ever stop being you."

I don't wait for a reaction. Instead, I lead Ava to Lenny's car again and ask her what she's doing after this.

"Working at Annie's," she says.

I shake my head. "Nope. I already texted her that you're not coming."

"In that case, looking for a new job." There she goes, teasing me again. She really can't resist.

I tap her nose, then ask, "Do you want to go swimming with me?"

CHAPTER SIXTY-FIVE
AVA

I should be sorry for the way I'm choosing to grieve the relationship that can't happen between Grant and I.

Sleeping with Derek shouldn't consume me with the guilt that it does but somehow, I still live with a heavy guilty conscience every time I'm with him. I know Grant and I are not together but I still feel like I'm cheating on him by sleeping with Derek because I'm cheating on my feelings for him.

And now, it hurts even more when I look at Grant knowing what I'm doing, knowing that I haven't spoken to him in weeks because I've found myself a distraction.

I love him so much that it physically hurts me to be near him because of what he said. Because he told Hannah that he can't marry me. Even if he loves me.

The last two weeks have been hell. Yes, Derek was a distraction but can I really say that I haven't thought about Grant? No. Of course not. I thought about him at every waking moment and I just wish we could have a platonic friendship without this ginormous chest of baggage between us; passion and love and loyalty. Well, loyalty is a funny word right now, isn't it?

I missed him so much.

If my lack of answers comes up again, I'm going to lie, so I can keep this intact. I'm going to give him some bullshit answer, so he can stop asking questions and accept that we'll only ever be best friends. It's going to work.

My plan is going to work.

CHAPTER SIXTY-SIX

GRANT

Rule number one of being friends with your ex: don't offer her your *other* ex's clothes.

Dumbass.

Ava offers to swim in just my Harvard t-shirt that I handed her, but I want her to be comfortable. And because of the irrelevance of my prior engagement, I don't think twice before handing her a bathing suit that Hannah left here, almost excited that I have something to give Ava to swim in.

Ava takes the bathing suit from my hand, but when it registers whose it is, her face flushes. She fidgets with her bag when she says, "Oh. Okay, yeah, no. I'm not going to wear that. I'll just go home. We'll go swimming another time, okay?"

Ava rushes to pack up her bag. She doesn't answer me when I say her name. She's desperate to get the hell out of here, but I can't let that happen. Not again. I won't let her run anymore. This was a miscommunication.

"Ava. Ava, wait. Stop packing up. I'll give you something else."

"I'm not wearing your ex-almost-wife's clothing. That's so twisted. That's so insane. Why would you even…" Ava rubs her face. "Okay, this is…I don't want to argue with you. I don't want to lose you again, so let's just call it a day, okay? Thanks for…today. For the meeting and the ice cream and… Yeah. I'm gonna go."

No fucking chance. No way. No fucking way is she running from me again.

"Ava. Ava, look at me." I am begging. I am *pleading*.

She clenches her jaw tightly when she finally twists around to face me. I study her flushed face, and it's like every ounce of anger has made it into her blood stream in the last ten seconds. Her chest heaves, her hands ball into fists.

I look into her eyes and say, "You're upset."

"You just…we were…you said you loved me, and then you got engaged. We were…" She swallows thickly. "We were in love. It felt like you…"

She shakes her head. She doesn't want to continue.

"Ava. Ava, I'm sorry I offered the bathing suit, okay?" I'm frenzied. "It was stupid. I shouldn't have. I don't know why I thought you wouldn't care."

I bend to meet her eye, but she looks away. I need to fix this. I can't do the love triangle thing because there isn't one. Genuinely. Ava is it for me. Even *Hannah* knows that.

"It's not about the bathing suit. You *know* that," she stresses, passion and rage sounding in her tight voice.

Holy hell. Holy shit. That's what this has all been about?

"You're angry at me for the engagement?" I wonder in complete and utter shock.

"I'm angry that you made our relationship disposable!" she shouts. "You weren't even thirty yet. I thought I had time!"

And it seems like everything Ava has felt and thought about my engagement to Hannah seeps out unexpectedly. There is a fire in this woman that is about to explode, and there is no hope of reeling it in. But I'm ready. I'm ready because *finally*, I'm getting answers.

You weren't even thirty yet. She's referring to that dumb pact.

Ava continues, preventing me from defending myself. "It fucked with me so bad, you have no idea. I felt like an experiment, like I was a practice round, so you could be a good boyfriend—no—*husband* to her.

"It felt like I was a project you took on to prove to yourself that you could be a decent boyfriend for the first time in your life and that you're not the asshole you were to every other girl in New York. That you could look at someone like Hannah while you were with me and actually pass up on the offer, despite her looking like a supermodel, and say, 'Wow, kudos to me because I chose Ava instead! Meek, average Ava!' How noble of you, Grant!" Her sarcasm comes with such deep hurt.

Ava felt like our relationship was *practice*? *What the fuck?*

My face pales. My chest caves in. *No.* "Ava…" I say.

She doesn't let me speak. She continues shouting at me. "That isn't true, though, is it, Grant? You *couldn't* pass up on the offer. You flew right back into her arms when I ended things. How do you think that made me feel?"

"*Ava,*" I plead anxiously.

It's not true. None of this is true. Ava isn't taking me back because of a lie. "You know I ended it with her for you. Don't tell me that's what this has all been about. My engagement."

She stares into my eyes, right to left, like she's weighing her options. Like she's coming to some sort of decision. Evidently, it's to admit the truth. To give me answers. "Maybe it is. Maybe I just can't seem to get over the fact that you got engaged."

"Maybe?"

She shakes her head. "No. I mean, it is. That's what this has been about. Feeling secondary."

I close my eyes. This can't be true.

I attempt to deny every single thing Ava says. "You were *always* who I wanted. *You* just didn't want *me* anymore, and I don't blame you, but what was I supposed to do? You left."

"You were supposed to wait!" she yells through a choked throat. "Wait until you were thirty! Wait more than *nine months*!"

Ava surges. The truth displays itself. A truth I had no idea was effective.

How can you be friends with someone when you feel like they used you? How is she so committed to being my best friend if this is what she believes I did?

Ava telling me I should have waited for her when she's been adamant, over and over, that I'm not allowed to wait for her now is… It's going to make me crazy. It's completely senseless.

"Why should I have waited?" I test her. "It's not like you would've taken me back."

"I would have," she admits in a low voice. "If you didn't get engaged, I would have."

So, this really is *the fucking Hannah thing. That's what this has all been about.*

"Then, take me back now. It's in your hands. What, I should have waited until I was thirty before, but now, you can't take me back?" I refute. "I've shown you that you're it for me, Ava. I've proven that to you, so maybe it's time to be honest with yourself. You know you're mine. You know I didn't want her, and you know this is about stubbornness. It's time to make a decision. If you want to be with me, be with me."

Ava looks to the ground. She avoids my eye because I'm right, but there's also this insecurity there. I can't pinpoint where it's coming from. I've made it clear to Ava since day one that she's the one I've always wanted. What could she still be insecure about? I want no one else. She knows that.

"You don't even want me anymore," she whispers.

"What are you *talking* about?" I almost yell. I am a desperate mess from all of this irrationality. I can't take it anymore, *goddamn it!*

Ava responds with a quiet, "You want someone who you could marry."

"I could marry you. I'd marry you tomorrow. I'd marry you right fucking now."

"That's…no, that's not…" Her voice is timid. She shakes her head, dejected.

"What do you want? Tell me what you want, Ava," I beg.

She laughs humorlessly. "You can't ever, ever give me what I want, Grant."

"Try me."

"You could never marry me." *She wants to* marry me*?!*

"What makes you think that? You're implying that you want to marry me, but that I am the one who doesn't want to marry you. I'd propose to you in a second if you gave me the go ahead. Or at least the *hope* that we could be more than friends. You're not even letting me have *hope*."

I rub my hands up my face. I say this next thing, *my* biggest insecurity, with such fear laced in my voice. "You want me to get down on one knee in front of you, only for you to tell me no? Is that what you want? My *dignity?!*"

Ava aims for the door without responding, but I can't do this. She needs to stop running.

"PLEASE STOP RUNNING AWAY FROM ME!" I shout.

The levels of emotions in my body tonight are sporadic and unsettled, and it makes me feel utterly hopeless. I hate that I just yelled at her, but my confusion, and my panic at my confusion, is freaking me out.

My unexpected shouting catches Ava's attention. She turns around, displays her disheartened face. How she's clearly crying. How her eyes are bloodshot, and she's sniffling, and her face is all wet.

I immediately feel like an asshole. After everything that I did to this girl, I can't hurt her anymore. In *any* capacity. Yelling hurts.

My stomach drops, my heart squeezes, and I force myself to put everything I'm feeling aside for the wellbeing of this beautiful, hurting girl.

"Ava, no…" I whisper. Her tears are the last thing I can handle. I can't know I'm making her cry in addition to the message I've apparently sent when I got engaged to Hannah. It's too much heartache to put on her. "Why are you…I'm sorry. Come here."

She shakes her head. She stays by the door. I want to hug her, but she won't let me.

None of us say anything. We both stare at the ground because facing each other is too much.

"I don't even know why I'm crying," she chokes nervously. "I'm sorry. We're good. Nothing's changed. We're best friends, and everything's fine. I'm gonna go home, okay?"

"Let me at least drive you."

"No, I can—"

"If nothing's changed, let me drive you," I spit.

She swipes at her eyes. "You…you hurt me," she whispers. "You hurt me by moving on. I know that's not allowed to hurt. I know that was the point, but…I don't know," she cries. "I just thought you'd wait for me."

"I'll wait for you now. I will. For as long as you need."

She shakes her head fast before I finish my sentence. "I don't want you to. Not anymore. But I thought maybe…maybe I'd see you again, we could talk things through, and I could get closure before you moved on. I wish I could say that I didn't care about you being with her, but it lived with me for a long time."

"I'm so sorry, Ava. I thought you hated my guts, and—"

"I never hated you." She takes a step forward. "You're putting words in my mouth. I never, ever hated you!" she cries frantically.

"I don't know how," I rasp, shaking my head.

"I wish I did. It would have been easier if I hated you. But I didn't. I don't, okay? You're my person. You've been my person for two years, and I just…" She sniffs and swallows thickly. With heartache in her voice, she whispers, "I thought I was your person, too."

I take a step toward her. She looks into my eyes with her bloodshot ones. "You *are* my person. You're my person, Ava."

"You almost got married."

Is it possible Ava will ever let me live this down? Will she stay hung up on my engagement that I was almost completely detached from, even after knowing I ended it for her?

"I didn't marry her."

Ava shakes her head. "You would have. If I didn't come over on grad night, you would have married her."

Then, I decide, fuck it. I'll take her there. I'll show her just how unwilling I was to move on, even when it seems like I did because my heart never, ever healed from losing Ava.

"Let me drive you home. I want to show you something."

CHAPTER SIXTY-SEVEN
AVA

Nausea stirs in me at the fact that I've been lying to Grant all night, but at least I'm giving him answers.

It's easier this way. I almost wish I'd have lied months ago to avoid all of our terrifying and sometimes unbearable conversations. One after another, nonstop, since Montauk.

I'm mad that you got engaged. I can't get over that fact, no matter how bad you want to be with me.

It's so easy. It's so *simple*. The fact that it comes from a little bit of truth makes it even more so.

We quietly slip into Grant's sports car after a silent elevator ride to the parking garage. My breath hitches the moment I recognize the driving route he takes because I've driven it with him a million times.

He takes a deep breath, remains in the driver's seat once he parks outside of the building.

"Why are we here?" I ask quietly. I look out of the passenger window, remember myself in this space. Walking through those doors; walking up the block.

"I want to show you something." His voice is so heavy with emotion, raw with exhaustion.

It's a still, silent moment, a frozen moment. It's like I don't hear any background noise, just the echo of our descent. I hear Grant's shoes on the pavement. I hear my heart beating in my chest. I hear the squeak of the front door to the building when Grant opens it.

I feel robotic walking up the three flights of stairs behind him.

Naturally, the memories emerge back into my brain, but not the good ones; our breakup ruined this apartment for me. The fact that he owns it did, too. I don't know what he was thinking bringing me here.

I gasp when he opens the door and nods for me to go ahead in front of him. It's exactly the same as the day I left it. The linen wasn't mine; the furniture wasn't either. None of this was mine, it was his, so I left it and ran.

The bed is unmade. A half-empty water bottle sits beside my old bed. A crumbled receipt and a bookmark lay on the side table. Post-It notes are stuck to the walls with psychology terminology written on them. I guess I hadn't removed them after I took whatever exam these were for.

I survey the apartment, and when the good memories seep into my heart, I shove them away. I force myself to think of the bad memories instead because of the hurt in my heart from tonight's conversation. Because yeah, Grant's engagement hurt me. It isn't *the* reason we can't be together, but I'd be lying if I said that what I told him tonight isn't the truth. The only lie I told tonight was when I said, *That's what this has all been about.*

I *did* feel like he made our relationship disposable, I *did* feel like a practice round. Grant getting engaged genuinely broke me. I'm not ashamed to say it because I have every right to say it. I've moved on, but that doesn't mean I forgot.

I continue to look around, then face Grant.

"It's so clean." My voice is shaky. "How is it clean but messy?"

"A cleaning crew comes to clean it once a week. They have strict instructions not to move anything. I don't let them change the linen either," he explains with that deep voice of his.

He is planted opposite the front door with hands in his pockets, watching me process whatever this is.

"Why? Why is it still like this?"

He shakes his head, closes his eyes. When he opens them, he speaks directly into my heart. "I didn't have much of you left when things ended. This was all I had, and I couldn't erase you. I didn't want to. I never wanted to pretend that you didn't exist."

I stare him in the eyes. I have not a single clue what to say.

Grant points a long finger toward the kitchen. A thick notebook catches my eye because it isn't mine. It's placed in the center of the granite counter. I walk over to see what it is.

I pick it up. I do it super slowly, waiting for him to stop me, but he doesn't. Instead, he encourages me to keep going. I open the bulging flap of the leather notebook. My heart claws as soon as I do.

The pen. The pen I got him for his twenty-eighth birthday. That's why the flap wasn't closing all the way. Then, I see my picture. I pick up everything beneath it.

A Polaroid photo of us in his bed. Two movie ticket stubs from a movie we saw together. Another Polaroid, this one a photo of me sleeping. There's even a grocery receipt from Whole Foods. I hold it up.

"What's this one?" I whisper. My voice is hoarse from the tears I cried and the ones I'm currently holding in. Knowing he saved all of this breaks my heart.

"When I bought you water bottles for your apartment." His voice is quiet, too.

I resume sifting through this pile of memorabilia.

A card I wrote him. Our boarding passes from our flight back to New York on New Year's. A hot cup sleeve from Rocco's.

I sort through all of these memories and several other things from our life together. I close my eyes; I sigh and put my face in my hands.

"Why?" I whisper, muffled.

"I couldn't get rid of it. It felt like I'd be ripping my soul out of my chest." His voice is so resolute, but it's also drained. Like he's still so confident in his love for me, but he's also tired of having to convince me how loyal he is.

"But you got *engaged*."

I freeze at his next sentence. "I never proposed to her. I never got down on one knee. I had her send the link of the ring she wanted to Dina."

Just like that, my attention is caught. I remove my face from my hands, so I can look at Grant's green eyes that hold every ounce of truth within them. I believe him. *He didn't propose to her.* That means that the visual of a heart-eyed Grant Wilder looking up at Hannah Butch from the ground with a giant diamond in his hand has no basis to it.

"Why?" I rasp.

Grant takes a hefty breath, readies himself to answer all of my questions. His certainty comes pouring out of those perfect lips. "I only wanted to do that if it was *you*. I only wanted to put in effort if it was for *you*." He pauses. "The engagement was…arranged. Literally. I didn't want to marry her. I just wanted to escape. I just needed a distraction, something to make me forget about you."

"But you didn't. You didn't forget about me because you came here."

He laughs at himself, shakes his head. "I didn't forget about you for a lot of reasons, but if I got rid of this apartment, somehow that'd mean *erasing* you. I couldn't do that."

I don't say anything. I idle in the middle of the room, wait for him to spill and spill, to talk and say everything that's in his broken heart.

His voice lowers, deepens. "You were never practice. You were my end game. You were my last stop. I wish I didn't have to say that in past tense."

Then, why did you tell Hannah you can't marry me? If I'm your last stop or your stupid fucking end game, why'd you tell her that? You're lying to me right now!

"Why are you telling me all of this? What's the point?" I ask.

"To show you that you're still it for me. That you've been my girl for the last two years. That I never got over you, that I never wanted to. That I felt like I still had you whenever I'd come here. You were so much more than a girlfriend to me, Ava. You were my future."

"I'm not your future. I'll never be your future," I remind him.

He swallows hard. He looks to his side. "Okay," he rasps.

"I'm sorry."

He nods in a solemn manner. "I understand."

"These are our circumstances. This is our only time slot."

"Okay."

"Why aren't you talking?"

Grant faces me, exhales deeply. "What do you want me to say?" he sighs.

"I don't know. Your answers are annoying me."

He ponders, nods to the ground. "You know what's funny about all of this? That some days I don't even want you to take me back because of what I did to you. Because I want you to have everything, and I know I don't deserve you. But I also want to fight for you and for us because I love you, and I think you love me, too. Then, there's the piece of me that doesn't want to cross the boundaries you're trying to set because I'm also really happy being your best friend."

...and I think you love me, too.

Damn, you!

"So, just...be happy being my best friend," I beg. "Let that be enough."

"I'm trying." *You're making it impossible,* I'm sure he wants to say next.

I glance around again. It almost feels uncomfortable being back, like I don't want to get too close to the walls or the furniture; like I can't connect to this space the way I should because the girl who lived here is so far from who I am today. The Ava who lived in this apartment let her past own her. Ironically, I'm letting the future own me now, but it's his, not my own.

"There are so many memories from this place," I whisper.

"I know," Grant whispers back.

Bad memories, Ava. Think about the bad ones. This man cannot be yours. Remind him.

"You could have just showed me the notebook. I don't understand why you brought me here." My voice is shaky. I'm not quite crying but almost.

"I thought it'd be nice to see it again with you. I thought this place would remind you of how good it once was." He is so assured. He is still so confident that he wants me forever.

It does, but I wish it didn't. It reminds me of the best memories of my entire life. I'm dying inside.

Then, the reason in my brain: *He can never be yours, Ava. Stop thinking about the best part of your life, the parts that you're eventually going to lose. Think, Ava! Think! Bad, bad, bad.*

Bad memories.

I walk over to the opened bathroom door, point a long arm toward the sink. "That's the medicine cabinet where you found my pills."

He nods his head at the small sofa by the bed. "That's the spot we stood in when you told me you wanted to be intimate with me." He is so ready for this. His voice is strong. It's assured.

I stand in the general vicinity of the apartment. "The place I told you I couldn't have kids." *That one hurts.*

He still isn't fazed. He's poised when he points somewhere near my feet. "The place I told you I loved you for the first time."

I point at the front door. "The door you slammed when you told me why I have to be medicated." *Wow. I'm digging deep.*

Grant doesn't surrender. He walks over to the kitchen, plants himself in front of the fridge. "The freezer we stocked up with ice cream after our first date."

"It wasn't a date," I mumble.

"Fine." He opens one of the cabinets and pulls out a Brita pitcher, places it onto the granite counter. "The Brita you used as a makeshift vase for the roses I bought you from our *real* first date."

That one claws at my chest, the randomness of it and the fact that he remembers.

I walk over to the bed. I lift my arm and point downward to the rumpled linen. "The bed I sobbed myself to sleep in after finding out you were Pat's lawyer."

Still nothing. He has something good to counter even *that*.

He puts his hands in his pockets. His eyes hold mine when he says, "The bed we made love in. The bed you gave me a key in. The bed we spent so many happy fucking nights in."

"Stop it," I whimper.

His eyebrows pinch, he tilts his head. "Why? Why all of the bad ones?" I shrug flippantly. "Tell me why, Ava."

"Because I'm still upset." *That I can't have children.*

He scoffs bitterly. "Even after tonight? You're still upset after everything I told you? *Showed* you?"

I wish our story could be resolved and put back together in the matter of one night. I wish, Grant.

"It doesn't work like that," I say.

"It should. It could if you let it. I don't know what this stubbornness is all about. I'm trying to understand, but I just don't."

Don't try to understand. Just stop asking questions, and be my friend. Fucking stop it already.

"This isn't me being stubborn," I counter. "This is me being adamant. There's a difference."

"What's the difference?" he spits.

"Because one is out of spite, and one is…" I choke on the tears in my throat. I cough and say, "One is sacrifice."

"What are you sacrificing?"

"My happiness," I whisper.

Grant's hand sweeps down his face. He pinches the corners of his eyes and shakes his head. "I am so done with all of this ambiguity. I want an explanation."

I told him there wasn't any hope for us, and he's still here fighting me. He could put it behind him and continue our amazing friendship, but no. Not Grant. Not Mr. Persistent.

I want as much as I can from you before I have to let you go. Please let me have this. Please.

"I've been asking the same thing of you for months, Grant, and you're still here fighting me. Let it be. Stop asking questions. We're *best friends*. You're basically getting me back. I'm giving you everything I have," I stress boldly.

"But I want to be with you." He faces me with a pointed look. "I want you to be mine."

I look away from his piercing gaze. "I am yours." I laugh humorlessly. "You'll always fucking own me."

"Ava—"

"Take me home. I'm done talking. I'm exhausted. This was the longest day of my life, and I just want to get into my bed and fall asleep and forget about all of this…all of this stupid bullshit."

"Ouch," he mutters. I quickly look away from his solemn face. "What part is stupid bullshit?"

"The fact that we're even having these conversations. I didn't want this friendship to be complicated. You gave me your word that it wouldn't be. I wanted it to be normal and civil and smooth sailing, but of course, Grant, you have to make everything so…so intense! For no reason!" I shout.

"My love for you is really intense, Ava. I couldn't agree more. You want me to stop talking about it, about us altogether?"

"Yeah. Yeah, that's exactly what I want you to do. I'm so… Goddammit, just take what I'm willing to give you and appreciate it for two goddamn seconds! You keep thinking about what you want in the future when you're not even spending the time enjoying the friendship you have with me now. If you can't be grateful for what we currently have, why am I wasting my time with you?"

I can't see what my words do to Grant. I bolt out of that stupid apartment as fast as I can and hail a cab a couple of blocks down.

CHAPTER SIXTY-EIGHT
GRANT

She's running away, but no matter what, I'm running toward her.

I was added to the group chat with Ava's friends sometime after Chloe's birthday party. I've never been active. I've only ever looked at it when I saw that Ava had sent a message. I've seen her latest messages about dinner tonight, but she hasn't spoken a word to me since the night I took her to her old apartment.

I gave her space. I stayed away, but I can't anymore. I'll let her ruin me, over and over and over, and I'll still come back. I swore that I'd do whatever it takes to make up for what I did to Ava. This is a part of it: fighting for her.

Nothing can stop me. If Ava is going to this dinner tonight, I am, too. I text the group chat that I'll be there and change out of my work suit.

When I arrive at the table of the Mexican restaurant Gabe suggested for tonight, I scan each face for Ava's, but she isn't here. Every time I see a figure, any figure, walking toward our table, I quickly look up hoping it's Ava, but she still isn't here. And I just have this feeling that when I said I was in for dinner, it meant she was out.

My phone buzzes in my pocket, so I lean back to slip it out. It's a text from Chloe.

> Chloe Danes: Don't worry. She's coming. She just had to stay a little late at your sister's.

I look up to Chloe across from me and nod once. I then text Annie to make sure that Ava is okay and safe.

> Me: Is everything okay?
>
> Annie: Yeah, Thibault just left with Ava. She's on her way to this infamous dinner. Are you having fun?
>
> Me: No.
>
> Annie: Cheer up. She's really nervous to see you. Don't let her down.

The table erupts in loud cheering while I'm reading Annie's text. A sense of guilt presses down on me that Ava is anxious about seeing me tonight, anxious enough to vent to Annie about it.

"AVA!!!!"

"RUTHIEEEE!!"

"Over here, Campbell!"

"Oh shit, I didn't know you owned Gucci!"

Ava has her skinny finger pressed against her lips. She shushes her friends, quickly skitters toward the table. Her face blushes, and she laughs quietly.

"You guys are crazy! Shh!"

Ava hugs the few friends that sit at the edge of the table that she's standing next to. I'm on the far end, so she'd have to walk around to be near me.

I watch her, watch how she interacts with her friends, how she makes everyone feel like they are the most important person in the room. How she asks specific questions to show that she listens to her friends. Asking about one guy's promotion and a girl's visit from her parents. Hugging Chloe from behind, kissing her cheek and saying, "Hey, sister. How was the event planning today?"

"Hi, sexy. It was exhausting, but what about you? You look amazing. Did Annie lend you these clothes?"

Ava's face blushes when she nods. Annie likes designer clothing. Ava is decked out, and it's fucking adorable. "I didn't have a choice. She wanted to use me as her mannequin. Madison sat in the closet, too. I cannot be judged for my overpriced outfit."

She avoids looking here, even when she talks about my sister and my niece. At this point, Ava has said hi or waved or hugged every person at this table but me. I even notice when Derek offers Ava an extra flirty smile that she rolls her eyes at. I wonder what that's about.

I continue to watch Ava, wait for her to notice me. Finally, she looks for a place to sit. There's an empty chair to my left that was intended for her to sit in. When everyone directs her to that seat, she finally has the courage to lift her eyes up to mine.

Shame. That's all I see in them.

I stand when she makes it to my corner. I spread my arms out for a hug before saying hi or greeting her at all. Before she says anything, too.

Ava slowly inches into me bit by bit until her arms lightly encase my waist. I pat her hair down with one hand and rub her back with the other. I guess it's the moment she realizes that I've missed her that she finally gives me the hug I've been looking for. She squeezes tight. She changes positions to lock her arms around my neck, stands on her tiptoes, and squeezes again.

"Does this mean you're not mad at me?" she whispers into my

neck. "Because I didn't mean it, it wasn't stupid bullshit, but I got scared and—"

I squeeze tighter. "Shhh. It's okay. I just really missed my best friend and am very happy to see you right now."

When Ava sighs in relief, it's like the muscles in her chest fit themselves between the muscles in mine.

I rest my arm on the back of Ava's chair when we both sit down at the table. She quietly asks me to order her something that I think she'd like. When the dish comes, she rolls her eyes at how good it is. At how well I apparently know her, but that isn't a secret.

I put effort into knowing her. I love how well I know her.

I smile at Ava's adorable laugh at something Chloe says to her. I wasn't paying attention because I have nowhere else to look but at the sunshine girl beside me.

The glass that housed Ava's *second* margarita is empty. Two cocktails should do it for her. She looks at me to her side with a bright shine. Her face is flushed.

Drunk Ava.

"Hello," she says, smiling cheekily. When she burps and I poke fun at her, she elbows me. "Not everyone can be as fancy as you, Callum."

I chuckle. She's never called me that before.

I'm not surprised when Drunk Ava plays games with me. When Drunk Ava rubs the hand that I have resting on the table; leans her back against my front. At one point she puts her hand on my thigh under the table and squeezes.

"How do you guys know each other?" a girl I've never met asks, distracting me from the warmth of Ava's hand seeping through my pants. She sits across from Ava and has been studying us for a while.

Ava giggles, unsure how to answer. I don't either, so I wait for her to take the reins. When she looks at me, I nod and say, "Go ahead."

"Wellllll, we may have seen each other naked a time or two!" her bubbly self explains.

I tilt my head to the ceiling and groan. Ava laughs at my reaction. "Oh, so you slept together." *It was a lot more than that, blondie.*

When I notice Ava's shy expression, I intervene. "We dated."

"And now?" *We have a nosy Nelly over here, don't we?*

Ava interjects before I have a chance to reply. "Now, we're single and ready to mingle! Do you know anyone for him? Six five, black hair, green eyes, the coolest family ever, and he drives a Porsche! Oh, and his family has a beach house in Montauk! Well, actually, it's more like a beach *mansion*!"

I want you. I don't want anyone else but you.

I told you I don't want you to set me up. Let me live in a bubble.

Blondie looks at me with a flirty smile. "I'm Lana. Single, too."

"I'm not looking for anything, but it was nice to meet you," I respond coolly.

Ava then interjects, "That's not true! He is totally looking for something! Don't worry, I'll give you his number," she whisper-shouts and winks at Lana.

I grit my teeth, press my nails into the inside of my palm, but remain silent. I clear my throat, then take a sip of water.

She's torturing me. This girl is fucking torturing me.

I'm so angry. Irrationally but positively *angry*.

You know what, *no*. This is completely rational. For once, it's my turn to get angry.

The apron-clad waiter comes over to our table at the end of dinner and informs Chloe that the bill has been taken care of when she asks for the check. Even though she's drunk, Ava figures it was me that covered dinner, so when we gather outside of the restaurant, she stands dangerously close to me, away from everybody else and quietly says, "You didn't have to do that."

I wave her off, tell her it's no big deal.

"It *is* a big deal. That was really nice of you."

When Ava smiles up at me, she sweeps back a lock of my hair that hangs off my forehead. I swallow, pierce her with pain in my eyes, beg her to notice that she's killing me. She doesn't seem to notice the torture she's putting me through though because Drunk Ava rakes her fingers through my hair, and with the palm of her hand, cups my neck and continues down to my shoulder and my pec. She stops in the middle of my chest, rests her delicate palm against me, directly on top of my tattoo.

I look at her with a question in my eyes, but she doesn't deny what she's doing, nor does she defend it. Instead, she *explains*.

"Sorry. I shouldn't touch you like that. I'm just making sure you're really here, that I'm not dreaming."

"I'm standing right here, Ava," I tell her.

"I really missed you," she whispers. Ava swallows nervously. "I was such a bitch to you, and the relief I feel that you aren't mad at me is…

"You're my best friend," Ava continues. She takes a step closer to me with barely any room. Our chests graze against each other's. "I just really missed having you near me. It feels like it's been years. Hi."

I remain silent. I have no idea what to say.

When Ava proceeds to holds my gaze, her eyes flame. She's dying for this. She's dying for me to touch her the same way, but I can't. I cannot do it. I respond to her physicality with a small step backward.

Changing the subject entirely, I tell her, "Tell me more about Chloe's event."

CHAPTER SIXTY-NINE
GRANT

I came to Chloe's rescue.

She's become like a little sister to me.

Chloe is fundraising for a production she wants to direct off Broadway. She planned an extravagant event that she had saved up for because she really believes in the play. I was at her and Ava's apartment when she got the call that the venue flooded. That it was cancelled. She was sobbing.

I interjected when Ava jumped up from her spot beside me on the couch to console Chloe. I offered my apartment, said it was a great space for an event like the one she had planned because of the open concept and the big kitchen. Chloe climbed my body for a massive hug, then got to work calling all of the vendors with a change of address.

Nothing's changed between Ava and me, and I mean it in a negative way. I have been driving her home from Annie's some nights, so we can spend a little bit of time together. Between helping Chloe with the event and Annie with the kids, Ava has been swamped.

Our friendship has been on eggshells since I took her to her old apartment. I'm trying to get us back on track, but we can't seem to have much of a good time together unless one of us is drunk. Apparently, we require alcohol to go back to normal.

We're falling apart.

When I park in front of her building tonight and begin to exit the car to walk her up, Ava's voice halts me mid step. "Do you…um, do you not want me to come to Chloe's event at your apartment?"

My eyebrows shoot up. I have to ask myself if I heard correctly. "Did I say something to make you feel like I don't want you there?" She shakes her head. "Then, why on Earth would you ask me that?"

Ava's voice is soft, but she chuckles self-deprecatingly. She shrugs her shoulder. "I don't know. Because the last time I came over, we fought about…your engagement."

Ava's question fills me with palpable anger. I have never given her an inkling of an idea that I'd ever want her anywhere other than right fucking next to me. Not once.

"What's up with you? This isn't you, Ava," I state strongly.

Ava pinches her bottom lip with her fingers. She's nervous. "I'm just insecure," she barely whispers. "Stop attacking me."

"Insecure about *what*? What am I doing to you? Tell me, so I can fix it!" I practically plead.

It feels like in this moment, everything is slowly crashing all around us. Ava agreed to this friendship with the adamancy that she was over what happened between us, but it's all going downhill now that she's essentially admitted she's still angry at me; when she had no mercy telling me how my engagement made her feel. That all her nonchalant *I forgive you*s and *I'm over it*s were forced and fake and a means to convince herself what she so badly wished could be real. What she wishes she could get over.

That when we go to dinner and get tattoos together, that's just Ava pretending to forget about her anger toward me for those small moments, so she can prove that she isn't the Ava from last year.

It's all tied together. She proves that she isn't weak by pretending she isn't angry.

Fuck.

It doesn't surprise me that I'm willing to lose my dignity for her, all so I can keep *something* between us. I'm willing to give her anything she wants, but I need her to give a little bit. I'm not asking for much.

"Are you still insecure about the Hannah thing? Because I swear to God, Ava, she is so irrelevant to me, it's pathetic that we're still saying her name."

"Okay," she replies.

That's all she says. Just, *Okay.* Then, Ava exits the car. I rush out of my seat, so I can walk her up to her apartment. At the front door, she smiles at me like *nothing is wrong* and hugs me goodnight. She flips that switch. She becomes the Ava that she thinks I want. What she doesn't understand is that this feigned strength is the Ava *she* wants to be. I want her either way. I'll always want her either way, and she has to know that.

She's worth it. She's worth it. She's worth it.

CHAPTER SEVENTY

GRANT

I'm talking with Chloe when Ava walks in to her event. Chloe tries to ask me a question, possibly kitchen related, but I stutter like a middle schooler.

"Uh…I…what was that?" My eyes dart to the door every few seconds, unable to take my eyes off of her for more than a few moments.

White.

It's my favorite color. I told her that on our first date.

"Just fuck each other already," Chloe murmurs, annoyed, when I can't recollect her question. She rolls her eyes at me. There is someone else she should direct that gesture to, though.

When out of my peripheral vision I notice Ava walking toward me, I freeze. I'm not sure why. She hugs Chloe before Chloe heads into the crowd to continue her hosting duties.

Ava looks up at me. "Hello," she coos.

I still have to look below me, even though she's in a pair of heels. I respond to Ava's greeting with a tight smile.

"Fancy seeing you here," she jokes lightly.

I chuckle dryly, unable to get this irritation out of my head.

Why can't I have her?

Why is she being fake, even with me?
Why won't she let me fucking have her?
What can I do to persuade this woman to be mine?

Just be mine, Ava. You aren't weak if you take me back. I'll continue to make up for what I did last year for the rest of our lives. Hannah meant nothing to me. It could be simple if you let it be.

"Grant?" she nudges me when the awkward silence gets to be too much. Her big and bright smile wavers as she reads my body language; stiff, aloof.

I don't know what it is. Something about seeing her in white, in fucking *white*, has me reeling.

I am frustrated. I am angry. I am upset at how hopeless she's letting me feel.

"What did I do?" she whispers.

"You came here," I spit.

"I thought…I thought you wanted me to come. I'm sorry. I can go." Ava shakes her head. She has a confused look painted on her face that claws at my chest.

This is all wrong, so I push past my ridiculous grumpiness, grow a pair, and stop her from walking away by facing her like a man. "I did want you to come. That was a miscommunication. You…" I clear my throat into my fist. "You look very pretty tonight, Ava."

Ava's cheekbones redden. She looks down to study her frame, the white silky fabric that hugs her tiny waist, her perfect legs. "You think?" she asks, squinting. "Is it too much? Do I look like a bride?"

My bride. And that aloofness squeezes its way back into my chest when I realize how Ava will never allow that to happen. She'll never be my bride, no matter how hard I beg.

I don't respond to her question. Instead, I nod my head to the bar that's been stocked up for the event tonight.

With my continued neglect, Ava dismisses herself to say hello to a friend. Sulky and miserable, I spend most of my time drinking alone. I stand near the bar having just grabbed a drink when I notice two guys speaking in a hushed huddle. One I recognize as Derek and another I've never seen before. I'm close enough where I can hear their conversation, but far enough to go unnoticed. They whisper among themselves, then the guy I don't know pokes Derek and points across the room.

"Yo. Who is that?"

There is only one woman in this room who can garner that kind of attention. I follow his finger, and I'm right. They're watching Ava. They're watching her like how I watch her: in awe. And every part of me is saying to walk away, that whatever they're going to say about her won't sit well with me, but I can't. I'm planted here. I need to hear what Derek is about to say.

I have one hand in my suit pants pocket, and I'm holding my cocktail with the other. I look into my drink, but my ears are peeled.

"Oh. The one in white?" Derek's friend must've nodded because he continues. "That's Ava."

"Oh shit." And there it is. That fucking reaction. Hearing it come out of another guy's mouth has me seething.

"What?" I overhear.

"You tell me, bro. She's fucking gorgeous. Is she seeing anyone?" asks the first guy.

Derek chuckles. "You could say that."

I feel a sense of pride with his words. I feel territorial. *That's fucking right, prick. You could say that because she's* mine. I guess people finally realize what even she won't. But then I overhear Derek tell his friend, "It's complicated, but I'm kind of seeing her. Well, we're sleeping together. It's only been a few weeks."

I freeze. The heart in my chest stops beating. The glass I'm holding is paused midway to my mouth. I feel the blood rush to my ears, I feel vomit climbing up my throat. My stomach clenches. I feel like I can't breathe.

It's not true. It can't be true. Ava would never do that. Ava wouldn't…

I owe her the chance to explain. I need to hear it from Ava before becoming full-on livid. I have to wait for this dumb party to be over to ask the love of my life if she's been fucking this guy for weeks like I just overheard.

White fabric swishes in my peripheral vision, so I look up, ready to fake it until I have a chance to ask her. She looks toward this side of the room and gazes at me. I give her a blank stare. She scrunches her nose, and when she waves excitedly, I don't give her anything more than a curt nod. Her expression falters when I don't match her utter delight.

She's been sleeping with Derek for weeks. *What the fuck is happening?*

I need to take a breath. I head to the roof.

CHAPTER SEVENTY-ONE

AVA

I catch his eye from across the room to give him a big smile.

The expression he returns to me, however, is distant and tight.

Grant offers a single nod before he ducks out of the party. It gnaws at me, the way he glances across the room like I've upset him. And because the thought of that scares me, I go into fight or flight mode and set out to find him, but he's nowhere to be found.

I stay behind to help Chloe, Gabe, and the waiters clean up the main area of Grant's apartment. Derek stays to help, too. It's nearly one in the morning when we finally finish. Derek lets me know that he'll wait for me outside. I guess I'm taking him home with me tonight. I've been doing that a lot recently.

Poor decision making. I'm spiraling, and I can't stop it.

Everything is falling apart.

When I'm the only one left in the apartment, I begin my search for Grant. I finally find him standing in the corner of his upstairs balcony.

"Hey," I say softly. I walk onto the porch toward him, but he doesn't look up at me. "Grant?"

"What, Ava?" he spits, teeth gritted.

Whoa. If that isn't a hint that I should get the fuck out of his face, I don't know what is. When I turn to leave, I stop at the words Grant calls out to bring me back. "You and me need to talk."

I swivel to face him. I keep my poker face on. "Okay, sure. Let's talk."

Grant scoffs angrily. He shakes his head. "Not tonight. I cannot handle another fucking thing from you tonight."

What the hell is happening? What did I do? Where is this coming from?

I gulp but stay strong in my stance and in my leveled expression. "Okay. That's fine. It's late anyway. We could talk tomorrow."

Grant nods, clenching his jaw.

"Brunch?" I continue. "At eleven? My treat. I just got paid. We'll get waffles. It'll be fun."

His stoic expression remains. "I'll pick you up tomorrow at eleven," he says curtly.

"Perfect. Um… Goodnight?"

It stings when he doesn't give me anything more than a mumbled, "You too."

I SMILE AT Grant as soon as I see him waiting in my living room for our brunch date this morning, but he doesn't smile back. His eyes fixate on my chest since, for whatever reason, he can't look me in the eyes.

Chloe's back is pressed against the refrigerator door with her blue eyes popping cartoonishly, so I glance at Grant again, try to figure out this dramatic riddle moments after waking up.

He tightens his fists and clenches his jaw so hard that his teeth might snap. *Men.*

I announce to Grant that I'm going to get dressed and head for my room. His deep voice and what he says next gives me whiplash. "How long have you been fucking Derek?"

No.

No, he can't know.

How does he know?

I am an iceberg. I'm trembling. I don't turn around.

"Fucking look at me. Look me in the eyes and tell me," he begs like he's in physical pain.

I'm about to lose him. This is it; it's done. He's ending this. I can feel it.

I must've lost all color in my face because when I turn around to face him, Grant shrinks.

It is way too quiet. I stutter awkwardly. "Okay…I—I'm sorry for not telling you, but how exactly was I supposed to bring that up?"

I'm not going to let him ruin us because of this. I am going to play it off like it's nothing because it is. Derek means *nothing* when it comes to Grant.

Grant pinches the corners of his eyes. His nostrils flare, but his voice is eerily calm when he speaks. "I'm going to head out. I'll see you around, Ava."

He spins to leave. He is so determined to get to my front door, but I'm not letting him ruin this. I am not going to let him do this to us.

"You're not leaving!" I shout. My voice is assertive. I channel every ounce of strength I have within me to keep this friendship together. "We're going to talk about this like mature adults."

Grant refuses to look at me. He laughs at the front door. "Talk about this? I can barely look at you right now."

He pulls the front door at lightning speed. I jump from the crash of wood smacking the wall. I run after Grant in a desperation I've never felt before. I'm not wearing pants, but I don't care.

"Go back inside," he calls out once we've both exited the building. "You're not dressed."

I lunge forward to pull at his arm, but he pulls it back out of spite. Tears flood my eyes, and my throat swells instantly.

"Grant," I whisper. "Please. Don't do this."

He caves at my pleading voice and stops running away from me. He turns, so he can face me. I know I've lost him for good when I see his eyes. He's a few feet away but mentally, emotionally, he's miles gone. Those eyes are looking at mine like I'm sure mine looked at his when I found out he was Pat's lawyer. Betrayal. Deep fucking betrayal.

"I…how am I…I thought I—fuck, Ava!" he shouts.

Calmly, I tell him, "I'm sorry. We'll work through this. I'll end it."

He roughly sweeps his fingers across his lips. When I watch the way Grant's expression slowly takes on this acceptance, I begin to panic. He's done. He's going to end it with me, but I can't let that happen.

"Don't just leave. If you want me to stop, I'll stop. I'd do anything for you. I'll stop, okay? I'll stop."

"I'm not going to ask you to do that for me," he says.

I laugh humorlessly. I shake my head.

I can't marry her, Hannah. She can't have children.

I have questioned the veracity of his comment to Hannah for over six months now. I want to know how true his words are, so I say, "Of course you won't. It's not like *you* want me!" I begin to raise my voice. "You want someone you could marry, don't you, Grant?"

His face contorts in disgust. "I am so sick and tired of you telling me what I do and don't want. What I do and don't need. What's best for me and what isn't. Fuck, Ava, let me be me. *My God!*"

He's just upset. This is about pride. This is a competitive guy thing, it'll blow over. He'll get over it in a few days and everything will go back to normal.

"How long has this been going on for?" He sighs like asking me this question is the last thing he wants to do, but he's asking it anyway.

"Grant—"

"How many times?" The question makes me want to slap him.

"How many times did you fuck Hannah?" I spit. I cross my arms and squint at him.

His jaw drops. "You weren't in my life then. I was *engaged to her*!"

I laugh, rake my fingers through my hair. "Yeah. I know. You don't have to remind me."

I know I've been using the engagement as a guise. I'm angry about my infertility, and I've been letting it out vicariously through this feigned resentment about Grant and Hannah. I'm not actually mad at Grant. I'm mad at my circumstances.

"You know what, here's the deal," I start, ready to be proactive. "I'll end it with him. I'll text him right now. You go wallow for however long you need to, but just promise me you'll come back."

When he's silent, I say it again. "Promise me."

When he still hasn't given me what I'm begging for, my voice rises in a panic. "Why aren't you promising me?"

"Ava…"

"You're not going to come back?" I whimper.

"*You fucked him in my t-shirt, Ava.*" His voice is strained. It's like he's in pain talking to me.

Huh?

"What're you…what…" My voice vibrates, teeth chatter.

Grant sneers at me. "Look down. Fucking look down, Ava."

I'm wearing his Harvard Law t-shirt. I never gave it back to him the night we were supposed to go swimming since his clothes are my favorite. I'm wearing it right now because he's the one I love, he's the one I want to be with, but I can't. Life isn't fair. I'm losing him because I'm protecting his future.

I stammer nervously. "I…I didn't intentionally tell myself, 'Hey, I should wear Grant's shirt when I sleep with someone else.'"

"I don't care if it was intentional or not," he states curtly.

"So, you're going to drop me because I chose your t-shirt over a different one?"

Grant rubs up his face with two large palms. With intertwined fingers, he clasps his hands at the back of his neck and leans his head back. He tries to calm himself so he doesn't lose it on me, but I know that's exactly what he wants to do.

"What was I supposed to do? Be single forever?" My voice is timid. I am terrified that Grant has a fist around my heart and he's slowly squeezing it with every heated word he throws at me.

"No," he spits. "Be with *me* forever."

"We can't be together."

"Good," he offers apathetically. "We're finally on the same page."

Fuck, that hurts.

"You're really dropping me over this. You're actually…wow," I scoff.

He closes his eyes to take a deep breath. When opening them, Grant looks at me with despondent eyes, eyes that are usually bright and lively and optimistic.

I did that. I ruined him.

"You've always been worth it, Ava, but this is my limit. This whole situation. I just…I get it. I don't deserve you. I hurt you last year, and you can't take me back. *Fine*. But you're my best friend, and you know that I never would have done this to you. Never. You completely disrespected me, and that, I can't get over."

He isn't done yet. He continues on his rant, and with every sound exiting his mouth, the lump in my throat swells bigger and bigger because he's right.

"Do you remember Molly?" he asks, his voice pleading. "How tortured you seemed at the prospect of us going out? It's enough to watch you get hit on, but knowing you're sleeping with him? Do you have any inkling of an idea what that does to me?

"You want from me what you're not willing to give back, and I'm tired. I'm just fucking tired. I can't handle being in a friendship knowing you're sleeping with someone else." Grant sucks his teeth. "I can't stand around and pretend I'm okay with it."

It's funny how two people could have completely different perceptions of the same relationship. He must think I'm being selfish; that I'm shallow and horny and careless about his heart and his feelings, but it's everything I'm doing for him behind the scenes that negates that entirely.

He has no idea. He doesn't know how selfless I'm being for him, but I have to bite my tongue if I want this to work. If I want him to have a family, a future. He'll choose a relationship with me over children, and I'm not going to let that happen. Ever.

I have had to hold in my truth and pretend like I will be okay watching him move on, but I have a meaningless hookup with a guy that will never be anything more, that I explicitly said I'd end things with, and *I'm* getting rejected?

This time, I'm the one who's angry. I want from him what *he's* not willing to give me back. I want from him in this moment what I've given him until now.

Unconditionality.

My heart has been on the line for months, and I let it be. I care for his future more than anything. He can't be my friend anymore because I hooked up with someone else. Past tense. Because like I said, I'd end it in a heartbeat. I'll probably end it anyway.

But I don't say anything of the sort. He's choosing to drop me, he's making this choice. Although it's the hardest thing of my life, I'm going to let him. I know what I'm worth. I finally have a strong sense of self-worth, and if he can't value our friendship enough to keep it intact, he doesn't deserve me. If he can't love me as hard as I love him, he doesn't deserve me.

I have fought tooth and nail to be in his life, and he's telling me with this gesture that I'm not worth fighting for. He is worth any and all pain to me, but that doesn't apply vice versa.

Noted.

"So, this is goodbye, isn't it?" I ask him monotonously. I won't react how I want to. I won't break in front of him.

Grant stands before me, giant and still. He slips his hands in his pockets and nods to the ground. Finally, he replies, "I...I think so. Yeah."

"Okay." My chest tightens. I know my self-worth, but it doesn't mean this doesn't burn my insides. "I understand."

"It's just...it's too hard."

Nothing was *too* hard for me. *Nothing*. I'd weather any *hard* storm, just so I could be in his life.

You want from me what you're not willing to give back. The sheer irony.

"Okay," I reply.

Grant must see the torment in my eyes, what I refuse to display on my face, because his face is pained knowingly. We both know with the way we're looking at each other that this is hell. That this is pure hell.

Both of our biggest nightmares coming to life.

"I wish things were different," he whispers. There's a tightness in his voice. He's trying hard not to cry like I am. I've been gnawing at the inside of my cheeks for the last twenty minutes.

"Me too," I whisper back.

He faces me, but he doesn't look at me. He can't look at me when he says, with finality that breaks me, "Goodbye, Ava."

I don't reply. I simply nod. If I open my mouth after hearing those two words, I'll start crying, and I don't want to manipulate Grant into changing his mind about this goodbye by crying to him. I'm not going to beg him to stay.

Grant turns to leave. I torment myself and watch his short and painfully slow walk to his car.

I wonder if he's rethinking this break up. I wonder if he wants to take it all back. But then he opens his car door and slips into the driver's seat, and when he closes the door on himself, I wince.

I watch his every move. I stand outside, half-naked, but I don't move an inch from my stance. I'm going to watch him leave. I'm going to stay here until he drives away, until his car is out of sight. It doesn't happen quickly, though.

If it were me, I'd bolt. I'd drive away so fast, but Grant isn't leaving. He sits in the driver's seat, staring at nothing. He leans his head back on the headrest and presses the heels of his hands to his eyes. His shoulders shake.

Grant is crying. Grant is sobbing. It's a gateway to my own tears. I finally let them come into existence. I wipe them away, but it's pointless. I'm not fast enough for how quick they're gushing out of my eyes.

I want to comfort him; I want to hug him and cry together. I want him to stay.

I catch Grant's eye from the front of my building. His eyes are bloodshot. I shake my head no.

Don't leave. We're better than this. Fight for me. Stay.

"I'm sorry," he mouths in response. That's the moment I watch him drive away.

I press my back against the front door when I step back into my apartment and let everything that happened outside wash over me. I want to be numb. I look down and focus my attention on my blue-painted toes. Grant complimented them once.

"What happened?" Chloe asks, slowly walking over to me. I forgot that she overheard the beginning of our fight.

"It's over," I explain. "He said goodbye."

"No. I'm sure this is just a little—"

"It's not. He's done," I croak. "I lost him."

My best friend. The love of my life.

I lost him.

That's when I slide to the ground and shatter.

CHAPTER SEVENTY-TWO
GRANT

It's worse than when I lost her last year.
Way worse.

I couldn't sleep the night of Chloe's party after I heard Derek and his friend talking about Ava, mentioning that she's been hooking up with him for weeks. I was tossing and turning until it was 6:00 in the morning. I got out of bed and went for a fifteen-mile run. This time, I used it to clear my head completely.

I killed as much time as I could before it was unbearable. I needed to know, and I needed to confront Ava. We had brunch plans for eleven. I didn't think it'd hurt to head over to her place a little early.

I turned to stone when I bumped into Derek at the front door to Ava's apartment. He was straightening out his shirt. It looked like he had just rolled out of bed.

Ava's bed.

I stood in the doorway minutes after Derek had left. My chest wasn't beating. I was sure I had died.

A part of me wanted to disappear from Ava's life, block her number, and never see her again. A bigger part of me, however, was too fucking curious.

Chloe tried to defend her best friend within a stuttering sentence. I told her that I didn't want to hear it.

I waited five, ten minutes for Ava to come out of her bedroom. Finally, after twenty, she did.

Harvard Law.

No pants.

Sex hair.

She was rubbing the sleep out of her eyes when she entered the living area. I'm not sure she knew when Derek left because it hadn't crossed her mind that I may have witnessed him leaving. I assume she was still asleep when he left her bed.

The smile she gave me, as if she hasn't been hiding this from me for *weeks*, made me want to punch something.

It was time. We had to end things. I know that this is the way it has to be.

I am so miserable, but despite what she did, I'm dying to call her, to take it all back. However, every time I think I'm ready to forgive Ava, the visual of Derek leaving her apartment all disheveled burns in my brain.

I feel empty without her, but I'd feel worse maintaining a friendship while knowing she's someone else's. Knowing she sleeps in someone else's bed and another man touches her naked body.

Two weeks. It's been two whole weeks, and every aspect of my life feels bare. Mundane occurrences unrelated to Ava suddenly feel empty. My good mornings to Lenny feel empty. My drives and meetings and gym time feel empty. My conversations with my sister feel empty.

That's how full she made my life.

I'm reminded of the weeks following the deposition last year. I was desperate to be numb back then, and I find myself begging for that same lack of sensation now because of the pain; the pain of losing Ava, of hurting Ava, of erasing Ava from my life.

Of course I want her back. *Of course* I want to forgive and forget. I miss her like hell. I love her so much, and the guilt is killing me.

She didn't fight me. I thought the moment I told Ava that this was goodbye, she'd explode. I thought she'd scream and yell, but she didn't. She was so calm, it terrified me. Her acceptance scared me. Like losing this isn't as hard for her as it is for me.

I can't get her face out of my mind; the shake of her head when she looked at me from the sidewalk while I cried in my car. It took everything in me not to run back toward her. With every step I took away from Ava, I regretted it more and more. Then, Derek's face found its way into my mind, and I was angry all over again.

I understand that I can't be upset if Ava is hooking up with someone. She isn't my girlfriend; she is young and beautiful and single, but I am angry she did it behind my back. I won't lie and say that it'd feel good if she consulted me before sleeping with Derek since I know that would break my heart either way, but the feeling of disrespect and betrayal wouldn't exist. It would simply be jealousy.

Jealousy, I could do. This other shit…it's too much.

The loss of our friendship feels more final when Ava's name lights up my screen, and I don't have the urge to answer it immediately. I look at the contact picture I have of her, and it makes me mad. It's a photo of Ava smiling, holding up her arm to show off her tattoo.

Honey.

I watch the call ring until it goes to voicemail. It rings a second time. I decline that call, too. Then, my phone pings with a text from her.

> Ava Ruth: Please call me

But I don't. I can't hear her voice; I can't do this cat and mouse shit anymore.

For the twenty minutes after Ava's unanswered phone call, I grip my phone tightly, pace my living room, asking myself if I should call her back. But just like I want to call her back, I also want to throw this phone, block her number, and scream.

I don't throw the phone, though, because Chloe's contact photo lights up my screen soon after. This one is of her and Ava hugging. *I can't seem to catch a break.*

When I answer the phone, Chloe cries hysterically.

"Grant, oh God. Ava is… She's burning up. She's not responding, and I have no idea what to do. I really need help, Grant!" she shouts.

My heart plummets. I move like lightning, grab my keys and wallet, and bolt out the door.

I shout into the receiver, "Chloe, slow down! Breathe. What happened?"

"I got home from Gabe's, and I found her on the floor. Her skin, Grant, it's yellow, and she's… her lips are blue and—"

I can't believe I'm about to ask this next question, that I'm about to ask Chloe if Ava is still *alive*. "Is…Chloe, is she…" I can't finish it. "Check her pulse."

"It's there. It's really weak, but she's alive," Chloe tells me.

I don't get the relief I thought I would with Chloe's confirmation. Hearing that Ava's pulse is weak is just as bad.

"How long ago did you find her like this?" I ask.

"Ten minutes ago. The ambulance is on their way."

Chloe found Ava passed out ten minutes ago. That was ten minutes after…

When the realization hits, I nearly hurl.

That's why she called me. It was an emergency; it wasn't cat and mouse. She was feeling ill, she needed someone, and she called me. My fucking pride got in the way, and I ignored her. I wanted to *block* her.

Holy shit. Holy fuck.

"Tell me which hospital they take her to. I'll meet you there."

I rush over to Chloe sitting in the waiting room of Mount Sinai hospital as soon as I arrive. The entire drive over here, I just prayed. Prayed that Ava is fine, that she'll live, that if someone has to die for whatever reason, it should be me and not her.

Please, God. Not her. Not my Ava.

Chloe stands and throws herself at me. She hugs me tightly then begins to shake; to convulse. She sobs. Then, I start to cry, holding on to the closest thing to Ava that I have.

"She loves you so much. You have no idea how much she loves you," Chloe rambles. "You don't know what she's…please, just…forgive her."

"Okay," I whisper into Chloe's hair. "I will. I do. I forgive her."

"I want to tell you everything, but I can't and…"

I grip Chloe by the shoulders and pull back to face her. "Chloe. Ava's health is the only thing that we should be focusing on right now. Everything else is bullshit." Chloe nods. "Now, tell me what happened when you got here. Where did they take her?"

"Grant, they took her to the ICU." Chloe's voice is so quiet, it's like she's hiding this harsh reality from me.

"*WHAT!*" I bellow.

"You know how her periods have been crazy painful lately?" I nod. "They think she went into septic shock because of it."

"*No*," I breathe. "No, Chloe. *No.* The last thing I said to her was… *Oh god. Oh fuck.*"

"The last thing you said to her doesn't matter. She's not going to die. *She's not dying.* She *cannot* die," Chloe shouts, crying. She stomps her foot on the tiled floor. "She's going to be okay. She can't not be."

I cover my mouth in shock and shame and fear. I don't blink away the continuous tears flowing out of me. I let them come. I pace in front of Chloe, and the idea of *permanently* losing the love of my life settles in my chest until I begin to shake. I rake my fingers through my hair and head to the automatic doors for a breath of fresh air before I punch something or scream.

Ava.

My Ava.

She's in the ICU. The fucking *ICU*.

Chloe follows me outside and clutches my forearm.

"We have to do something. We have to do something." I'm crying, frantic, because I'm scared.

I am so scared right now.

Chloe squeezes my shoulder in reassurance. "They're taking care of her. We'll hear more soon."

"It's not enough!" I shout, shoving Chloe off of me. "It's *Ava*, Chloe! *Our* Ava! *My* Ava!"

I have to do something.

I compose myself on my march up to the front desk of the hospital. In an assertive voice, I state, "I'm here for Ava Ruth Campbell. She's in the ICU. I'd like an update please."

Dorothea (name tag) types on her keyboard, glances at the computer screen, then faces me. "Is she a wife?" I shake my head. "Is she a sister?" I shake my head again. "Come on, help me out here. Girlfriend?" Dorothea asks impatiently.

My chest constricts. Quietly, I say, "She's not my girlfriend. She's the love of my life. Please give me an update."

Dorothea does some sort of vibe check when she looks at me, then nods. "As of now, she's staying in the ICU overnight," she informs me.

"What happens after that?" I ask, my voice shaky.

"If the doctors feel she's okay to get sent to recovery, she'll be put in a room in our patient recovery ward for however long is needed."

"What kind of room is it? Is it nice? Is it big?" Dorothea deadpans. "I want her in a private room," I demand.

"Sir, insurance doesn't cover that."

"That's not an issue," I say, my teeth gritted.

Dorothea raises an eyebrow at me, and with a clenched jaw, I nod. She types on her computer again. "Okay. We have a few rooms available in the premium patient accommodations."

I pull my wallet out, slap my plastic credit card on the clunky booth separating us, and with a forced, steady voice, I tell the older woman, "The best one. I don't care how much it is."

CHAPTER SEVENTY-THREE

GRANT

I've been tasked with getting Ava a bag of her clothing for when she wakes up.

Chloe and I don't know when that will be, but we want to be prepared.

She gives me the key to their apartment. When I have the nurses' confirmation that Ava won't wake up any time soon, I drive over there. I call Annie and my father from the car to inform them of what's going on. They demand I let them know the moment Ava is released from the ICU.

I want to erase those three letters from existence.

I let out a shaky exhale once the door shuts behind me and I'm in Ava's apartment. It's insane that the feeling of emptiness I've had for the last two weeks disappears when I'm in her space again.

I feel fuller being surrounded by her things. Her shoes, her coat, her tote bag that she carries everything in.

Back to the task at hand: I am quite literally here on a mission. I pull my phone out to follow the instructions Chloe texted me.

> Chloe Danes: Get the blue backpack from the closet. Pack two sweatshirts, four pairs of leggings, a bunch of underwear, a bunch of socks, and her cell phone.
>
> Chloe Danes: FaceTime me if you need help finding anything. Thank you

I dart sporadically within Ava's room, stuff this backpack to the brim. I am finally down to the last item on the list. I find Ava's phone charging on her desk. I unplug it, pocket it, and nearly turn to head back to the hospital when something catches my eye, forcing me to stick around.

An envelope.

Grant.

Only a single word written on it.

Whatever is in this envelope came from Ava. The Ava who I love, the Ava who I haven't seen in two weeks, the Ava who is laying in a hospital bed right now. I stare down at it. I battle within myself on whether I should open it or not, but the decision is made for me when I fixate on her handwriting.

I lower Ava's backpack to the floor beside the desk chair, slowly sit myself down, and rip open the letter.

Dear Grant,

If you were to ask me what the worst thing that's ever happened to me was, I wouldn't say the bathtub. I wouldn't say our breakup. I wouldn't even say Pat. The worst thing that has ever happened to me was losing the ability to have children. To give you children.

You probably got sick of me telling you that we can't be together, that we don't have a future. I know I've owed you an explanation for a long time, so here it is.

The night of my graduation, after frantically knocking on your door and finding you and Hannah, I wanted to do nothing but get the hell out of there. Seeing you two together was hard for me, but for whatever reason, when you closed the door behind you, I decided to stay. Frankly, I was being nosy. I was drunk and curious what affect I had on your relationship. I planted myself outside of your apartment door and listened closely. I heard everything that was said between you and Hannah that night.

"I can't marry her, Hannah. She can't have children."

You said this to her. Hannah told you that you wanted to be with me, that you'd marry me if you had the choice, and this was your response.

I was embarrassed. I remember rushing out of your building and vomiting into the first trash can I found. Hearing what you said filled me with so much mortification, I wanted to disappear.

I don't have tubes. I can't have children, and you want children more than anything. You want to be a father. I want to be a mother, too. I think I let that idea slip a bit when I kept focusing on your future. This isn't easy for me. I wish I could be a mom. I wish I could give you children. I wish I could have a family with you.

I believe that the ultimate display of love is the sacrificial kind of love. That's the love I have for you, Grant. I am sacrificing my own happiness that I *know* I'd have with you, so that you can have your perfect future. And I will be happy for you. I am already happy for you. I've always wanted the world for you.

Grant, it has *always* been about you - your future, your fatherhood, your happiness. I wanted to be your friend so bad, to have you in my life in some capacity, that I was willing to torture myself with the prospect of seeing you with someone else. I was willing to watch you get married and smile on the sidelines knowing that whoever gets to marry you gets the best man on the planet. Knowing that she'll get treated like an absolute queen. Knowing that she'll never be me.

It's only been two weeks since we said goodbye, and I feel empty without you.

My life, that space in my chest that pumps for you, that beats for you, is stilled. It's hollow and desolate. Days where you're the first thing I think about when I wake up every morning. Days where I replay our best memories before I go to bed every night.

Days where every time I see a photo of you as a child at Annie's house, it sucks the life out of me because all of this boils down to the fact that we'll never make one of those together - a Grant/Julia cloned baby. Shocking green eyes, shiny black hair.

And someone will. Which makes it the best and worst part of this situation. Someone, someone else will give you a baby. Someone else will make you a father.

I miss you so much. And I hope that one day, in the far future where the wound of losing you has scabbed over, I'll bump into you. I'll see that clone of yours, that green-eyed boy on his daddy's broad shoulders. I'll meet him, and he'll tell me his name is Callum Wilder, but he goes by his middle name. He'll look ten, but he'll be six—I mean, his dad is 6'5".

Your wife will smile from her stance beside the love of her life, and she'll be beautiful and polite and say hello to me. Her pretty hands will grip the handle of the stroller where a mini-Madison sits. And when your wife reaches over to shake my hand with a ring the size of the world on her finger (obviously), her big pregnant belly will bump the stroller, and she'll laugh and say, "I'm a bowling ball these days! I knock over everything!"

And then, I'll look over at you. I'll look into your eyes, and I will tell you with mine

> that I'm happy you got what you deserve. That I'm happy you got what you always wanted. That I'm happy your future looks as beautiful as the one around us. That I'm happy I made the choice that would ensure you this full, wholesome life.
>
> That I'm so incredibly happy that you're happy.
>
> Love always,
> Ava Ruth

I CAN'T STOP crying.

I hunch forward, hold the letter in my tight grip. There were already ink smudges from when Ava cried while writing this letter, and I've only added more when reading it.

It was all for me.

Every time I got angry with her for leading me on or confusing me, she let it happen. She let me get angry with her, she took the flack. She let me say goodbye to her because she wasn't going to budge.

All the fights, all the conversations, all the misunderstanding and my pleading for a proper answer—she let it happen, let it hurt, for *me*.

I always knew Ava loves me, but not like this. She loves me more than I could possibly comprehend. She sacrificed her happiness for mine. She wants to be a mother, wants to have children, *my* children, but because of her circumstances, she let me go because she believes what I implied the night of her graduation. That wanting to be a father is more important to me than being with her. She was ready to lose our friendship because of it, and I know what our friendship meant to her.

Instead of telling me the truth when I confronted her about Derek and said goodbye, she let me go because she knows what I'd answer. *I want you either way.* And she's right. But Ava wants me to have kids. She let go of her best friend in the name of loyalty. Protection. Preservation.

Unwavering fucking devotion.

I'm a mess. I feel furious with myself for getting angry at Ava's constant hesitation. At Ava's cryptic responses.

She asked me to trust her, *begged* me to trust her, but I kept demanding answers. Meanwhile, Ava bared herself, opened up her chest, and gave me everything she could, even if she believed she'd have to say goodbye one day. She wanted to seize the time she had with me because in her eyes, I was going to end up with someone else.

Those kids she mentioned in the letter—the green-eyed boy named Callum and the mini-Madison—they're going to be her kids, too. I will find a way. I'll make her a mother. I'll give her whatever she wants because nothing, *nothing*, matters more to me than this girl's happiness.

I am going to do everything in my power to find proof that Ava and me *can* be together. I am going to stall my life and put every bit of strength into this. I'll meet with every doctor in the country, I'll pay for research, I'll do whatever it takes to show Ava that I'd only be forfeiting my happiness if I don't get her back. Not if I don't have kids.

Ava was willing to sacrifice her happily ever after for mine. I am going to show her that we're both going to have one. That us *together* will have one.

I place the blue backpack two chairs over from Chloe's in the Mount Sinai waiting room after the hazed drive back to the hospital. I sit next to Ava's best friend and hand her what is Ava's entire heart on a single piece of paper.

Chloe gasps. "Oh my God. She was going to tell you."

"I feel like an asshole," I choke out.

Chloe sighs. "She wanted you to make the most of it. She just wanted you to love being her best friend as much as she loved being yours."

I did. I *do*.

After reading the letter and discovering that this has all been for me, I feel so fucking *selfish*. I have to apologize a million times over for ever mentioning our future and getting mad at the lack of it. I'm going to fix it.

I'm going to do whatever it takes.

CHAPTER SEVENTY-FOUR

GRANT

Three days. They don't release Ava from the ICU for three days. I've sat in this waiting room since Chloe called me hysterical. I only went home to shower twice. I've been sleeping in the waiting room chairs that after this whole thing is over and Ava is healthy, because *Ava will get healthy*, I'll need a three-hour long neck massage.

Evelyn and David had to sign off that I can be notified and updated about Ava's situation. I've been in constant contact with them for the last seventy-two hours. Once Ava is released from the ICU, I'm getting them on a plane.

It *was* sepsis that landed Ava in intensive care. It isn't a common condition as is, but there was a higher likelihood of Ava getting it again than for someone to get it at all. They have good reason to suspect that Ava's body went into septic shock from a tampon. I don't know if she's aware right now that that's what happened to her.

I jump up from my seat in the waiting room of Mount Sinai when Ava's last name is called, and I'm glad when I see that Dorothea's on shift. She knows how special Ava is. She could tell by the number of friends willing to sit in a sterile waiting room to show their support.

Everyone stopped by in the last three days. Gabe, Derek, Sadie… Even that Lana girl. They wanted to be there for her because she always is for them.

I place two palms on the waiting room nurse's station and lean into the marble.

"Ava was put in recovery about an hour ago if you want to visit," Dorothea says.

If? Of course I want to rush over there, but I can't be the first person she sees when she wakes up. Not after what I did. I am unworthy of being able to see her at all, so I give Chloe a call. She drops everything, along with Gabe and Derek, to visit Ava. Chloe promises to text me from her hospital room about how she's doing and to make sure my money is going to proper use. They said premium patient accommodations. It better be premium.

> Chloe Danes: The room is really nice. It's huge. She's comfortable.
>
> Me: How does she seem?
>
> Chloe Danes: Weak and terrified.

My heart sinks. I hate this for her. I want to switch places with her.

> Me: Please hold her. Get her whatever she needs.
>
> Chloe Danes: Why don't you?
>
> Me: I guarantee she doesn't want to see me.
>
> Chloe Danes: You don't know that. I'm leaving with the guys shortly, but I'll be back later. Come upstairs. Room 1118.

I nervously brace myself before knocking on the heavy door to Ava's room. She inhales sharply when she sees me, like it was unexpected that I'd be here.

I fucked up so bad. She thought I wouldn't show up because I said goodbye.

I despise the awkward silence that fills the room the moment I walk in. It's annoyingly quiet.

I clench my jaw and tighten my fists when during Derek's goodbye, he kisses Ava on the head. That's *our* thing. That's what I have always done with her, and now…

Apparently, she's fucking him. There's nothing I can do.

I hug Chloe and Gabe goodbye, nod at Derek tersely, and turn to face Ava once the door closes behind her friends.

"Was this you? This doesn't look like a standard room." Her whimpering voice tugs at my already broken heart. She's lost and scared and *embarrassed*. She's always hated being the broken one, and now, she feels the same way she did three years ago. I know her well. I know how her brain works.

"I didn't want you in a standard room. You're not a standard person." I gulp. "Can I get you anything? Are you hungry?"

Among Ava's silence, the air in the room intensifies. It's heavy and tension-filled. We both know that I don't deserve to ask her a casual question about whether she's hungry or not.

I broke us. I said goodbye.

She looks up at me with those beautiful honey eyes, but they're not how I love them. They're bloodshot and wet, and the more she looks at me, the wetter they get.

We read each other because we've always been able to do that.

Ava needed me in a moment where she was terrified and in duress. I was a prick, bitter and pissed off, because she was sleeping with somebody else. She didn't actively do anything to hurt my feelings, I was just butthurt and mopey, so I didn't answer her call.

"I called you," Ava cries tightly. I can't help her tears from creating mine.

With my own wet eyes and an infinite amount of shame, I look back at her and say, "I know."

"You ignored me."

"Ava," I nearly whisper. "I don't even know what to say."

She sniffles, sweeps at the tears clustering on her cheek. "You…I needed you. You just…you dropped me. You left me. You did to me what you said you never would."

I rub my hand up my face, shake my head with that same paralyzing shame.

Ava loses her breath from the energy it takes for her to say these few words to me. Ava is also tense and anxious. She needs to focus on getting better, not the asshole who broke her heart twice now.

"Ava, we'll have this conversation. We will, I swear. But not while you're here. Not while you're sick."

"Then leave. If you're not here to talk or to say you're sorry, you shouldn't be here at all," she cries. "Go away and don't come back."

I will give her whatever she wants, whatever she asks for, even if it isn't me.

"Okay. I'll go. I'm sorry for coming. Feel better, Ava." I turn to leave. When I have one leg in the hallway, I stop when I hear her call out, "I saw you!"

I pull my foot back into the room, let the door shut behind me, and turn to face Ava again. She's still crying.

"The only thing I remember right before I passed out was seeing you in my head. Your face. I was so sick, and I didn't know why. It felt like I would never see you again. I remember feeling so scared. I wanted you to be there with me. I missed you. You were supposed to be my best friend. Best friends don't ignore calls. They don't…they don't drop each other, no matter the circumstances."

My eyes mist over until the tears cascade down my cheeks. "I shouldn't have said goodbye. You're everything to me, and I… I'm sorry, Ava. For everything. I don't deserve you. I've always known that."

Ava's tears continue to gather on her pale cheeks. "I understand how the Derek thing made you feel, but ending this because of it? It hurt. Your stupid pride really hurt me. It broke me."

What I say next is the truest statement I've ever made. "It was never about pride. It was about pain."

"Pain?!" she cries out. Ava sneers, tears choking her next words. "Sometimes, you go through the pain for the people you love because they're worth it. I had to live with the knowledge of you settling down with someone who isn't me one day, but I didn't care about the pain because I wanted you in my life. You were worth it to me. You have no idea how much I was willing to put myself through for you. You have no idea."

But I do have an idea. After reading her letter, I know exactly what her words mean now. The ambiguous explanations aren't ambiguous anymore. I can finally connect the dots.

She was willing to put herself through the pain of watching me have children with someone else because of how much she loved being my best friend.

"You're right, Ava. You're right." It's all I can say.

She heaves, shakes her head, licks a tear that's landed at the corner of her mouth. "What about me? You're all pissed about Derek when you got engaged to Hannah. I stayed around your family when I thought you were still getting married."

"I got engaged because I didn't think I'd ever see you again," I reply.

"You didn't even try!" she bawls. Ava doesn't want just one conversation right now; she wants all of them. She doesn't want to wait until she's feeling better to talk, she wants to hash it all out now, and the sense of finality that renders breaks me.

It breaks me because I was the one who said goodbye, and Ava is essentially doing what I asked for. But after reading her letter, that goodbye is moot. Everything about our relationship until now, or lack thereof, is senseless. I now have a concrete reason why we couldn't be together, and I can't accept that she's doing all of this for me. I won't let her.

Swallowing about a hundred times to keep the sob in my throat, I take a deep breath, so I can answer her.

"I did try. I called you every single day from the deposition until your graduation, Ava."

"No, you didn't," she spits back.

"I did. You had my number blocked. It went straight to voicemail every time, so I just kept trying. I wanted to give you a proper apology." Ava silently processes what she's now learned; what I haven't admitted to anybody; what I've never said out loud.

If keeping the apartment didn't shock her, this does. I've rendered her speechless. I continue. "It doesn't matter now. What matters is you, and I want you to be happy. That's all I want, that's all I have ever wanted. You've always been worth it to me, and I'm sorry my actions haven't reflected that. I'm sorry I acted selfish." Ava blinks down, plays with her fingers nervously. "Again," I mumble.

"Yeah," she rasps. "Me too. Seeing you happy will make me happy."

"And that's not with you." I confirm what I have about a hundred times by now.

"I…" She scoffs. "I can't believe I'm saying this because of how much you hurt me, but I wish it could be with me. I know I would be happy if we were together. I wish it could happen, but it can't. We can't be together. It's not up for debate."

My little martyr.

I want to hug her. I want to tell her that I read her letter and I know why she's saying what she's saying. I want to tell her that I want her either way, with or without kids. I want to tell her that she's more important to me than having children, but I'm done with the words. I'm done betting on my relationship with Ava based on words and words and more words.

Performance.

I've always been good at it, and this next step will be no different. There is nothing expected of me but action. Until I have tangible, solid proof in my hands to show Ava that I could give her whatever she wants in life, I can't ask for a single thing. I can't ask her to blindly believe me because I haven't given her any reason to.

I want to make her proud. I want to give her hope. I want to make her a mother.

"It's not fair that I have to go through this goodbye a second time," she mutters.

"I'm sorry for coming. I just had to make sure you were okay."

"I'm not okay. I'm not. Without you in my life, I'll never be okay. I care about you more than anything. I would have put myself through *anything* just so I could have even a little bit of you, but you couldn't honor the same loyalty when it was the other way around, when Derek doesn't even mean anything to me. I hate you for that."

I would have put myself through anything just so I could have even a little bit of you.

It's exactly what she wrote in the letter. She's saying it without actually saying it.

"But I also love you," she whispers. My heart stops beating when hearing those words exit her mouth again. Once isn't enough. "I love you. You always came first for me."

Holy shit, *twice*. *Twice*.

I want to say it back, but I don't have a single right. I haven't given her a single reason to believe that I love her because love, *real* love, is what Ava has given me all this time. It's unconditional.

I promise Ava, "I'm going to figure out a way for us to be together, and I'll come back for you when I do."

"There's no way," she rasps, shakes her head. She doesn't know I read the letter. She doesn't know that I have a plan.

"There is," I tell her. "I'll find it. I'll do anything I can to make you the happiest person in the world, so don't worry. We don't have to say goodbye again because this isn't goodbye. This is… This is 'see you soon,' okay?"

Ava crosses her arms, and with teary eyes, looks out the window across her hospital room. Her lips turn downward, chin quivers. She hates me and loves me and doesn't know what to say.

"Tell me you hear me," I whisper. Ava slowly nods at the window.

I walk over to the love of my life and stop at the side of her bed. From above her, I palm her head and bring it to my lips before turning to exit Ava's room.

I'm coming back for you. I'm going to give you whatever your heart desires.

You have my word.

CHAPTER SEVENTY-FIVE

AVA

Grant flew my parents to New York. They showed up a few hours after he left my hospital room. When he did leave, I spent the next two hours crying. There was so much I wished I could say to him.

I want the world for you.
You're going to be the best father in the world.
I love you so much more than you think.

I love him. I told him that I love him. Alongside the anger and hurt, that love remains. It always will.

I am so angry that he made our relationship disposable again, but then, I put myself in his shoes. I get it. I've been acting like there's hope for us because of how badly I wished that were true. I *have* been leading him on due to that tiny spark of hope in my chest wishing that we could be together one day. I've given Grant every sign that I want to be with him, and then, I slept with Derek. If he did that to me, I'd say sayonara, too.

He made a promise to me. I nodded like I believed him, but he doesn't know that his promise is impossible.

My mother sits in a chair beside my bed. Her hand has been

gripping mine so tight for the last hour that it feels cold. Dad is on the couch sorting through the medical records and hospital bills from the last few days. The balance is zero.

All three of our heads turn toward the door when rowdiness sounds. Tears immediately pool in my eyes when it opens, but I swallow really, really hard to keep from crying.

The Wilders came. Julia, Callum, Ben, Annie, Layla and Madison are all here.

Madison runs over to me first. She climbs onto my bed and gives me the tightest hug.

"Hi, Maddy baby," I whisper, kissing the side of her head. "Thank you for coming."

Madison leans back to face me. Sternly, she says, "I'll kill you if you die." It's the first time I've laughed in weeks.

Annie shoos her away and kisses my cheek. She takes my hand in hers and looks at me. "You're not going to die, but…what she said," she mutters. Annie's eyes are wet. I tell her not to cry.

"You're my sister," she tells me. "Of course I'm going to cry."

God, now I'm crying.

I notice my parents hugging, shaking hands with, and talking to Grant's parents in the corner of my room. If he and I had a future, this would be everything.

Layla hugs me next. Then, Callum and Ben. The moment I look at Julia, I cough into my hand. A sudden burst of sadness explodes in my chest when I see her. When she hugs me, she whispers, "Sweetheart, I'm so sorry this happened. You must be terrified, but we're going to take care of you. Everything is going to be okay."

My face flushes pink when we face each other. "Sorry." I laugh at myself, embarrassed. "You just…you look so much like him. I mean, he looks so much like you. Sorry. We ended things, and I—I miss him, so seeing you is—"

Julia grips my upper arms and squeezes. "My son is in love with you, Ava. He is coming back for you."

Dad is in the car waiting for Mom and I to come down once we're done packing up some of my clothing for the next few days.

We're staying with Devon and Sarah for a couple of nights because the only thing that can truly heal my heart right now is being with my family. Dad's taking the couch. Mama and I are taking the guest room.

My mother neatly packs up the clothes and underwear that I've placed on my bed in a small blue carry-on. She has me lay it out in piles, doesn't trust me to pack efficiently. She loves Tetris.

She tells me to pack up my personal bag while she takes care of the suitcase, so we can make it to Brooklyn before rush hour. When I reach my desk, I don't see the envelope that *I know* was here before I passed out. I panic.

"CHLOE!" I call out into the hallway. "CHLO?"

Chloe comes rushing over, wide-eyed. "I'm here. What? Is everything okay?" she breathes.

"There was a letter," I explain. She sighs, glad it isn't another medical emergency. I can't imagine the trauma she has from the night I got sick. "Chloe, there was a letter on the desk."

"I know. He came to get your clothes, so you'd have your stuff when you woke up."

He.

Grant.

No.

My entire heart, my entire truth is in that letter, and Grant has it. I put his name on it, but I never, not once, intended on giving it to him. I wrote it for myself. What I wish I could say to him. Apparently, I have.

I gulp. "He read it?" Chloe nods at me with a knowing glint in her eyes. She must have read it, too. "He knows?"

"He knows."

My stomach clenches. I feel like I'm about to hurl. "He didn't say anything. At the hospital, he didn't say anything about it."

Chloe walks over to me, takes both my hands in hers, and bends to meet my gaze. She squeezes my fingers. "He wants to say something in a different way."

"What does that mean?" I cry. Talking about him pains me.

"That actions speak louder than words. That the man is so head over heels in love with you and he's determined to find a way for you two to be together." Chloe hugs me tightly when she sees my eyes begin to water.

"I miss him so much," I whisper into her neck.

"He misses you more." Chloe keeps me in her arms. With my silence, she whispers, "Don't worry. He's coming back for you."

CHAPTER SEVENTY-SIX
AVA

I'm not a zombie like I was last time.

I'm proud of myself for it.

The first month without Grant, I had a plethora of mixed emotions. I was hurt and still recovering from the sepsis, so I wasn't dying to see him or anybody else. I had ended things with Derek the day Grant dropped me, but I didn't care to tell him. He made his bed. I was going to let him sleep in it.

Then, there was (and still is) a voice in the back of my head telling me to reach out, at least to make sure he's doing okay. But that's not really why; I just miss him. I feel like a piece of me is gone, and I hope to God this feeling goes away soon. One month has turned into two, which turned into three, and now, it's been four months since I last saw Grant. The pain of losing him is still fresh.

It's been four whole months, and the emptiness still lives in my chest. It isn't fair.

There should be a time limit on grief.

Every time I look at the honey pot tattoo, I'm forced to swallow the lump in my throat down, down, down. I don't think I would've gotten it if I had known how this would all end.

Gabe's cousin, Sadie, took over my job at Annie's. It was too hard. Even seeing Grant's photo was hard, and especially knowing when Annie was on the phone with him. I was a mess. I found myself asking Annie how he was doing more than I'd like to admit. Her answer was the same every time.

He's coming back for you.

I didn't believe it, even after hearing it so many times. Not until I walk into my apartment on a random Friday afternoon and find Grant standing in the middle of my living room. I freeze. My chest leaps and chills cover me from head to toe. I take a step forward but keep myself at the door post. A subconscious part of me is scared about what will happen next, so I ensure an escape plan.

It's so jarringly quiet that I can hear Grant's Adam's apple bobbing.

I look around to find that Chloe is here. That's probably how he got in. She walks over to me, gives me a tight hug, and whispers, "I love you so much. Hear him out. I'll be at Gabe's if you need me."

I nod and watch her leave, jerk at the abnormally loud sound of the door shutting behind her. I hug myself before looking up at him. He looks at me right back, that perpetual intensity still in his beautiful eyes.

Four months. I haven't seen this man in four months.

"Hi," he whispers finally. I can't bring myself to enunciate anything. No sound exits my blocked off throat. I feel like tar on pavement. "How are you feeling?"

I hug myself tighter, shuffle my feet. "What are you doing here?" I manage to choke out.

"Can I hug you? Will you let me give you a hug?" I don't want to reply too quickly out of desperation, so I don't respond at all. "Okay," he says, nodding. "Okay."

Grant misinterprets my lack of an answer to mean no, that he can't hug me. Meanwhile, I'm dying for him to mold every part of his skin to mine.

We stand in silence. We look inside of each other's brains. We feel numb, but we also feel everything. *Say something!* my brain yells. So, he does.

"I read your letter," he tells me.

My voice is small when I reply, "I know."

"I love you," he breathes.

My chest aches at hearing those words from Grant's lips after four months, *four months*, without him. Somehow, it takes me over the edge. "Why would you say that? I haven't seen you in four months. Why are you here? Why now?"

"I bought a plane."

If I let myself feel what's happening right now, I'll cry hysterically, so I toughen up my skin until it's rubber and retort crossly. "What does that have to do with me? Why are you here?"

He pulls a brochure-looking thing out of his back pocket and throws it for me to catch. When I do, I carefully open it, revealing a map of the United States.

It's a fucking map.

"Pick a place with a red dot." His voice is strong.

I study the dotted map, shake my head unsure at what I'm looking at. "What is this? Tell me why you're here," I rasp, confused.

"I'm here to grovel. I'm here because I promised I'd come back for you. I'm here to make you mine, if you'll have me."

I hadn't noticed the giant box on my coffee table until Grant rounds the couch to lift the lid. "This is one of three boxes," he starts. "Red, blue, and yellow. The other two are at my apartment. This box starts at A and stops at H. The red dots on the map correlate to the contents of this box. Arizona, California, Colorado, Connecticut,

Florida, Georgia, or Hawaii. Pick one." I stay quiet. "Pick one," he repeats.

"Hawaii," I croak.

Grant pulls out a file. He opens the folder and starts to read out loud. "Dr. Louis Hammer. Thirty-seven successful cases of In Vitro Fertilization. A fertility treatment called IVF."

He slips the file back in the box and faces me. "Choose another one."

"Connecticut," I whisper.

Grant pulls out the file for Connecticut. "Dr. Gemma Stone. Sixty-six successful IVF cases."

He slips it back in. "Choose another one."

"California."

Grant pulls out three files next. "Dr. Peter Manne. Dr. George Jessen. Dr. Penelope Slate. Eighty-one. Thirty-nine. Fifty-four. I wanted you to have more options close to home. Choose another one."

"Arizona."

"Dr. Florence Trantin. Twenty-nine." He slips that file back in the box and pierces my eyes with his. "There are three more states in this box. Choose again."

I can't say what's preventing me from running into his arms; I can only explain the waterfall of tears streaming down my face and the tight lump that has settled in my throat since he mentioned the first doctor. So, I just stare. I don't choose again. I wait.

"Four months," he begins. "Twenty-two states. About a hundred doctors' offices." Grant takes a deep breath but steadies his fierce gaze on my soaking wet face. He resumes speaking. "Ones that specialize in pregnancy after a salpingectomy. That's what the surgery of tubal removal is called. I learned a new word. I practically hear it in my sleep."

I hang on to his every syllable. I stare until he's blurry. He continues on a mission.

"I had your medical history from the case last year. I vetted every single one of those doctors. That's why I bought the plane. Nearly every week since we said goodbye, I visited two new fertility clinics in dozens of different cities. I researched every phase of the required treatments. I spoke to the doctors with the most experience. I showed them your files. It's yours if you want it."

I don't know what to say. Is there anything to say? I mean, how can I put my feelings into words? He did all of this for me. He knew the word "treatments" wouldn't have changed my mind.

Proof. He knew I'd demand proof, so he traveled across the country and got it for me.

It's too much. The way he's looking at me, his tired but hopeful eyes waiting eagerly for me to say something.

Swiveling to give him my back, I cup my hand over my mouth and squeeze my eyes tightly shut, feeling the tears yield to gravity and free fall to the floor. Then, my legs turn wobbly, so I drop to my knees, hunch over, and sob.

I hold my breath when I can feel him walk over to me. He's so slow, so anticipatory. I want nothing more than to be in his embrace right now. He gets down on the floor behind me. Grant slowly and gently wraps his long arms around my body, rests his warm forearms across the front of my waist. He places his forehead against my temple. I can hear his thick swallow with how close he is to my ear. His body is so close to mine that I can feel the banging in his chest. He's nervous. He's literally shaking.

"How?" I whisper.

"Whatever it takes," he whispers back, his warm lips moving against my head when he speaks. "I told you I'd come back for you."

"When did you start this?" I quietly wail. "Where did you go first?"

"I left the day you were released from the hospital. I didn't want to leave New York until I knew you were better. My first stop was Connecticut. Yale." He is so assured. He is so *determined*.

"Did you really buy a plane?" I whimper. "A whole airplane?"

Grant chuckles. "Yes. I'll show it to you."

I finally turn in Grant's solid embrace. I throw my arms around his neck and hold on as if my life depends on it. I don't look at him. Instead, I shove my face into his neck and cry these wretched, heavy sobs.

It's the relief. It's the feeling of the word *Finally*. It's happiness and guilt and *I can't believe you love me this much*.

My body convulses with every cry I allow myself to release. After all, I finally have an anchor. I finally have someone to hold me again.

Grant grips my side with one hand and has a large palm pressed to my back with the other. He brings my body flush against him, lets me take solace in his love, in his strength.

"Grant," I choke, my voice muffled by his soft skin.

"Yes, honey?"

"I don't know what's happening. I can't…I just…Grant, how did you—a plane?!" I cry out.

He chuckles again and my heart bursts from the gorgeous sound of his laughter. "It wasn't a big deal," he tells me. "It was actually pretty simple."

I lean back to finally face him. "Simple?" I cry. "You visited twenty-two states. Didn't you have work to do? Where did you stay? What did you eat? Did you sleep okay?"

Grant squeezes me once. "It's easy to do difficult things in life when you're doing it for the person you love. You showed me that in your letter." He releases his strong hold on me to reach into his pocket. He pulls out his black leather wallet, opens it, and pulls out a square of paper. When he unfolds it, I see my handwriting.

"I take it everywhere with me. I read my favorite part of this letter every single day," he says.

"Why not the whole thing?" I whisper.

He makes sure he's looking at me in the eyes when he says this next part. "Because the end of that letter will never ever, *ever* happen. Anything that mentions someone else is completely irrelevant and moot. *I believe that the ultimate display of love is the sacrificial kind of love.* That's the part that I read."

He memorized it. He doesn't read from the paper; his eyes are staring directly into mine when he recites that line word for word.

My wet face is cradled in Grant's shaking hands as I look up at him. He swipes two thumbs underneath my misty eyes, then curls my hair behind both ears. His voice is quiet when he finally speaks, his words that are only for me.

"You seem to think that there are conditions when it comes to you, but there never were. You overheard something that made sense in the relationship I was in back then. Between her and me, it didn't make sense that I'd be with someone who couldn't have kids, so I said that as an explanation. It made sense; it was an excuse that worked. But between me and you, Ava Ruth, it doesn't make sense to be with anyone *except* you.

"I love *you*. You're what I want. You are who I've always wanted, and if the last four months told me anything, it's that I could barely breathe without you near me."

"Me neither. I could barely breathe, too," I choke out in a whisper. I shake my head over and over. "Grant, this is crazy."

His lips lift in a soft, knowing smile. "You make me crazy."

I turn my head slightly to the left and press my face into the palm of his big hand. I shake my head again and again because I can't fathom all of this. It's insane.

"It's not easy, but we're going to do it," Grant continues. "Whenever you're ready. Whenever you want. Today or next year or in ten or never. But I give you my word that whatever happens, we will do it together. You're my person. I'll *show you* that you're my person."

I cough out a sob. "You're my person, too. You've always been my person." Grant does my favorite thing in the world next and kisses my head.

I nod frantically, almost snapping my neck, when he asks, "You with me, Ava Ruth?"

WE SPEND THE rest of the day on Grant's living room floor.

Everything comes back full circle, doesn't it?

Our relationship ended because of files on this living room floor. Our future is beginning again because of files on this living room floor.

When I composed myself enough to take a proper deep breath back at my apartment, Grant asked me what I needed. I told him I wanted to see the rest of the boxes. I spent the drive over here studying the last three states' files from the red labeled box. So many doctors. So many states. He bought a fucking plane.

Grant spent the entire drive to his apartment with his giant hand gripping my thigh. I was still as a deer. He's mine now, but we haven't even kissed yet. The prospect of having so much freedom with his body is frightening because it's everything that I've ever wanted. Now that I have it, I have no idea what to do with it.

I sit in Grant's lap on the wooden floor of his apartment with all three boxes placed opposite me. I'm almost through the blue box. **I-M.**

Grant rests his chin on my shoulder, looking over to the files in my hands as I go through each and every paper. Illinois. Indiana. Louisiana. Maine. Massachusetts. Michigan. Minnesota. Missouri.

Now, on to the next. Yellow.

I turn around in Grant's lap once I flip through the last folders in the yellow box, the Washington ones. Both D.C. and State. When I come face-to-face with him, I dissect the little specks of emerald and jade and sage in his eyes. I'm speechless. I have been since I walked through my apartment door a couple hours ago.

He sweeps a strand of my hair that's come loose. He gulps, a shaky breath seeps out of his mouth. "I…I want to kiss you."

"I'm scared."

"Me too," he rasps deeply.

I inch forward, he does too, but we're both too nervous to take the plunge and connect our mouths to each other's.

"You have to be the one to do it," I tell him. He cups the side of my head, strokes my cheekbone with his thick thumb, and inches close enough where his breaths make it into my mouth.

"That's not a threat," he whispers onto my lips. Our lips are barely touching. His thumb continues to softly sweep down my cheek, under my jaw, circles my temple. I hold my breath in anticipation. He's taking too long.

"If you don't kiss me already, I'm going to die," I blurt out. I'm not hiding my desperation for this man anymore.

My body shudders the moment his lips finally press against mine.

Feeling his warm mouth again, two long years later is... *God*, it's surreal. It feels like the first time all over again.

I kiss him urgently, press my forehead to his to catch my hectic breath, and rasp, "Take me to bed, Grant."

CHAPTER SEVENTY-SEVEN
GRANT

I thought I'd pass out when I finally had her legs on either side of me again.

I grip Ava's ankles and wrap her tanned legs around my hips. I lift us off the floor and keep my mouth on hers on our stroll to my bedroom. I can honestly say I have never felt happier in my entire life, but the energy between us is too intense. We finally got each other back. Now's the fun part.

I sit at the edge of my bed, reluctantly unglue my lips from Ava's, and smile at her. She looks between my eyes and blinks about a hundred times. I really did render her speechless.

"Hi, you," I utter in the nonexistent space between us. "You okay?"

"I love you, too!" she exclaims hurriedly. "I didn't say it earlier when you told me you love me, but I love you, too. More, probably."

"Doubt it."

"I'll prove it to you. Tell me how," Ava pushes. She's serious. She waits for a real answer from me.

Marry me. Be my past, present, and future.

"Move in with me," I say instead. Ava shrugs and answers, "Okay!" I pause, lean back to study her face. I ask if she's serious.

She nods once. "I'm serious."

"So, this is *our* house now. Not my house, *our* house. Not my room, *our* room."

"Sweet. Can I put this address on my driver's license?" she jokes.

I throw my head back laughing. She smirks because she loves to tease me. I bury my face in her neck, feel the drumming of her pulse against my cheek. "Are you finally mine?" I whisper gruffly against her skin.

She nods. "Yeah," she whispers. "And you're finally mine."

God, my heart.

I'm unsure what comes next because of how long it's been. I think Ava is equally unsure. It's endearing, really.

I keep my palms on Ava's thighs in my lap and wait for her to say something or make the next move. I don't want to come on too strong. I want to savor every second of this, as if I'm dreaming.

"I'm so nervous, I could die," Ava admits. Her voice trembles.

I offer a small smile. "Don't die, Ava Ruth. We have a whole life to live together."

Ava lifts her fingers and touches the top button of my shirt. Her breaths are shaky, but she carries on undressing me. Before fully unbuttoning my shirt, she tugs it over to the right to reveal my tattoo. She softly brushes her finger over it and hums. When she inches forward to kiss it, my body erupts in goosebumps.

I fist the hem of her sweatshirt once my shirt is taken off completely. When my breath hitches at the sight of her exposed chest, Ava giggles.

"My boobs are small. I never wear a bra."

I have her bare body in my face, and I didn't have to do a single thing. "This feels like cheating the system."

"If being naked for you is cheating the system, I want to break the system," she pushes softly, pressing her chest into me. "I want you so bad, you have no idea."

Well, that's about the funniest thing I've ever heard. I've had a perpetual hard on for Ava since I saw her in a bikini in Montauk.

I cup her breast with one hand and pull at her neck with the other. I suck on her collarbones, graze my teeth across her shoulder. A small moan escapes from her mouth.

I tilt my head back to face the ceiling. "That sound," I groan. "Do it again."

"Do something to coerce it out of me," Ava challenges.

I maneuver our bodies, so her back is in the center of my bed, and I hover above her. Her eyes flame as she gazes down my chest, then lifts her hands to feel up my skin.

"Please," she begs quietly. She bites her lip when I slip her pants off, cheeks flushing a deep shade of pink. I kiss her navel, nip at her chest. She squirms beneath me, moans, only louder now. I chuckle into her baby soft skin.

"What?" she whines. "Don't laugh at me."

"No, no," I mutter into her mouth, kissing her. I bite her lip. "I'm just in awe of your body. It's unreal."

"It's nothing you haven't seen before," she mutters. Her eyes find mine, face full of admiration.

I stare at her swollen lips when I admit, "Everything about you is new to me. I couldn't look at you back then and think of all of the filthy things I want to do to you."

"So, do them now," she whimpers beneath me. "Do all of them."

I palm a large hand over her breast and lightly tease the other with my tongue. Her back arches when I put her nipple in my mouth. I smooth my hand down the side of her body, fist the fabric of her panties, and tug.

"I want you out of these," I demand huskily. "I want you completely bare for me."

"Take them off." She's practically begging. I snicker at her after she's finally completely naked beneath me.

"Fuck. You're so hot."

"Grant, please," she breathes. "I need you."

I bury my face in her pretty hair. No matter how close I am to her, it's never enough. "How wet am I about to find you?" I ask hoarsely.

"Have you ever heard of the ocean?" she asks.

I laugh joyously into Ava's golden skin. "You can't resist the jokes, huh?"

"Never." I pull her bottom lip between my teeth and tug. She swallows, squirms for the hundredth time. "Touch me," she pleads quietly.

I keep our position the same but snake my hand between her legs. I groan when I finally feel how badly she wants this. Ava thrusts into my hand when I touch her because it's not enough. She wants more.

"I want a taste," I tell her. I'm the one who's begging now. "Let me taste you."

"Take whatever you want," she assures me. "I'm yours. All of me. Take."

My eyebrows lift in surprise. "Anything?" I ask, stunned.

"I swear." Ava hooks her legs around my waist and squeezes. She buries her face in my neck and whispers, *"Anything."*

I keep my eyes on her honey ones when I slowly inch down the length of her body. Fisting her ankle, I push her leg up. I do it to the other leg, too, then look down. I nearly salivate.

"Holy fuck," I mutter quietly. "Wow." I look back up at her. "That's mine." Ava nods at me.

The closer my mouth inches to her middle, the wider her mouth opens. She throws her head back before I've even done anything to her.

"No, no," I rasp inches from her skin. "I want your eyes on me when I taste you."

"Grant," she chokes, clawing at my arms until they bruise. "*Grant*."

"Eyes on me, baby."

She obeys. I look into those beautiful eyes and feel satisfied when I see that wave of pleasure cross her face. It only takes about thirty seconds of working my tongue until she arches off the bed, shoves her face in the pillow, and screams. I don't let up, though. I'm just getting started.

I slide two fingers inside of her, push myself up so we're face to face, and thrust into her.

"I want you in me so bad," she manages to choke out while I pleasure her. Her eyes flutter closed, despite her fighting hard to look at me with the happy expression she feels. I smile mischievously at her. I love knowing what I can do to her. She chuckles, then takes matters into her own hands.

Ava sits on her knees and rapidly unbuttons my pants, fists the waistband along with my briefs and tugs. She sits me down, then climbs on top of me. My eyes widen at her newfound sexuality. Well, new for me.

Her hand grips my sex before lowering herself onto me. If she keeps bouncing like this, I'm going to pass out. If she stops bouncing like this, I'm going to pass out.

"Who are you?" I groan in pleasure. "Holy shit, Ava. Look at you go."

She continues her thrusting movements but brings her wet lips to my ear. "I've wanted this for so long. I think about you when I touch myself. I have since we met. I've thought about this every single day for the last two years, and this is so much better than I expected it to be."

She breathes heavily, releases a guttural moan when I clutch her hips and take over our rhythm.

"Ava. Baby," I rasp. She whimpers louder with every second that passes; her legs begin to shake. "You like that, honey?"

Ava nods hurriedly. She looks into my eyes with an unexpected expression on her face when I press my thumb between her legs. Her eyes pop. Every nerve ending in her body goes haywire.

She shakes her head in refusal.

"Grant—"

"You can do it." I smack a kiss to her lips and urge her to, "Give me another one."

Unsurprisingly, Ava takes it all the way through. She presses her sweaty forehead to mine when she's on the edge for the second time tonight. I'm not far behind.

"Babe, I'm so close," she pants. "Come with me, okay?"

That scream.

That motherfucking scream.

CHAPTER SEVENTY-EIGHT
AVA

I grab Grant's face, and he grabs my face, and after a few moments of shared astonishment, we both burst out laughing.

It's that kind of laugh that hurts my stomach, that has Grant squinting his beautiful, green eyes. The echo of his laughter fills the room. The sound is like a cloud brushing against my soft skin, cocooning me, hugging me. When we manage to stop laughing for more than three seconds, he hovers over me in the middle of his huge, soft bed. He leans on his elbow and rests his head in his hand. With the other hand, he tenderly sweeps the sweaty sex hair out of my face, following the movement with his strong gaze.

"Why are you laughing?" he asks deeply. I love his voice so much.

"Why are *you* laughing?" I mock.

His eyes dance when he looks at every inch of my face with great adoration. He blushes shyly and asks, "You feel it, right?"

I have never wanted to reassure Grant like I do right now, about how big and huge my feelings are alongside his. I grab his face, kiss him strongly. "Of course I do," I say into his mouth. "How could I not? You're my person, Grant Wilder. My other half."

"My other half," he repeats quietly. Grant smiles at me

appreciatively. He kisses my forehead, then places his on mine. He takes a deep, satisfied breath. "You're a part of me. You always have been," he whispers. He slowly gazes down the length of my body then looks me in the eyes. "I am so fucking lucky that this is my life right now."

I bite my lip, curl my toes. I don't think I've ever felt giddier in my life. "I love you," I tell Grant, because I finally can. I say it another time, then another time, then another time. "I love you. I love you. I love you."

CHAPTER SEVENTY-NINE
AVA

I've been slowly packing up my apartment to bring everything over to Grant's place.

Well, to *our* place. He corrects me every time I talk about his apartment as if it's still just his.

I text him to let him know I'll be ready soon. We're going out for drinks with Annie and Jackson later tonight.

> Me: Hi, boyfriend!!!!!!
>
> Boyfriend ESQ: Hi, girlfriend!

I changed his name in my phone. I think it's funny.

> Boyfriend ESQ: How's it going over there? You sure you don't need help packing?
>
> Boyfriend ESQ: Love you, by the way.

I've rubbed off on him. Grant is a double texter now. Well, more like a quadruple texter. He text-bombs me all day long, but I don't ever want him to stop. I smile every time I look down at my phone and see an unread text message from him, anticipating what it'll say.

Sometimes, it's a declaration of love. Sometimes, it's a knock,

knock joke. Sometimes, it's a new acronym he learned, or more accurately, made up. The other day he texted me YIFM. After he explained what it meant to combat my utter confusion, I told him that 'You're it for me' isn't an acronym. He said, "It is now."

> Me: I'm sure. I'll be ready in an hour. So excited to see u!!!!!!!!
>
> Me: Love you, too, by the way

Grant shows up in twenty, standing proudly at my door. His grin is massive. "My love. My Ava."

"Hi, boyfriend." I beam up at him.

He taps my nose. "Hi, you. You ready to go?"

"No, I still have a few things to pack. I told you an hour!"

He waves his hand in the air. "I'll help you pack it all up later." He reaches his hand out for me to take. "Come on, I want to take you somewhere before drinks."

I shrug, then follow my boyfriend out to his car. I squeal when we arrive at our destination. Grant laughs out loud at my reaction.

It's nearly an identical setting to two years ago. I put on the extra coat that Grant keeps in his trunk. I sit in his lap on the cold sand at Rockaway Beach. His arms wind around me, tightening my back to his front. I put a hand over each one of his and lace my skinny fingers through his long ones.

"I love you, you know," he whispers into my neck. I lean my head all the way back until I can see him and smile. I stick my tongue out at him. He bites it, then sucks it into his mouth. I can't help the quiet moan that escapes my throat.

Don't even get me started. I couldn't describe the sex this time around if I tried. I am an unhinged woman. Anyone would be if they could be naked with my man because it's unlike anything I could have possibly imagined.

It's making love to the person you know you're finally going to spend the rest of your life with. It's the great unknown instead of the terrifying unknown. It's completion.

I wasn't confident in our relationship last year. I often feared the unknown, so letting go like I can now was impossible. But being able to finally let go both mentally and physically is something I hadn't realized I was lacking.

I find myself spacing out, remembering something Grant told me while we were in bed together. Missing his hands on me, daydreaming about things he does with my body on a loop. The things he says.

You are mine.

Let me spoil you.

That's my gorgeous girl.

Gorgeous. That's his bedroom name for me.

When Grant buries his face in my hair, his breaths are deep and slow and heavy. I turn to face him, concern on my face.

"You all right?" His face remains in my hair when he nods. "Okay. I love you."

One of Grant's arms disappears from my waist for a moment. He steadies me with his hand on my shoulder, then leans back to stand up. I feel like I'm looking up at a skyscraper when he rounds my body and places himself in front of me.

"Stretching?" I ask him. He shakes his head no. "Do you want to leave?" He shakes his head again. I chuckle. "Why aren't you talking?"

Oh.

Oh.

My breath hitches when I grasp what's happening. He lowers himself on one knee in front of me. He takes my hand. His breath is shaky when he exhales.

"I'm so nervous, I might throw up." It's so endearing, *I* might throw up.

"Don't be," I assure him. "It's just me."

"It's you, but not just. Never just." He shakes his head when he looks at me like he still can't fathom this is his life. I feel that way every second of every day. "Ava Ruth, you are the most incredible and extraordinary person in this world. You were made for me and I don't know what I did to deserve it. Fuck, I *don't* deserve it, but I got lucky. I got really lucky with you. Finding you, loving you, pleasing you.

"Everyone that meets you adores you because you are fairy dust, Ava. You are magic. And *I* get to love you. *Me.* You are sunshine and bloom, and you're *mine.*"

My voice is terribly choked and shaky. "If I'm sunshine, you're moonlight," I tell him.

Grant shakes his head, looks at me in awe. "That means we're on opposing schedules. Can you be a star instead? So, I can have you around me? You'll twinkle. You're a twinkler."

I giggle amidst my happy tears. "A twinkler, huh?"

We look inside of each other and smirk. He takes a deep breath to start again because he's not done. I don't think he ever will be. But something sparks in my brain, so I interrupt him before he continues *proposing to me.*

"Grant, wait. All of the files and the boxes… It isn't proof. I get that you vetted the doctors and you traveled…" I choke up. "And you traveled across the country to find specialists, but you still don't know if it'll work. You're proposing to me based on something that's still up in the air. It's an option, but it's not guaranteed. It isn't proof," I repeat.

"I never needed proof, Ava, love. *You* did." I look at his eyes, right to left to right to left. "I didn't do it for me. I didn't look for proof for me. I want you regardless. That's why you were adamant, isn't it? Because you knew I want you either way."

I nod; tears gather in my eyes.

"I have always wanted you no matter what, but we've spent the last year at the mercy of those nine words you heard me say the night of your graduation. I needed you to know that having children isn't a deciding factor for me. *You* are the deciding factor for me. Your happiness."

Grant swipes my tears away; a loving smile paints his face. "I did the research because it's something that you want, and I want you to have whatever that is, not because having children is a contingency to being with you. *You're* what I want. Nothing else; no one else. I love you. I need you. I want you and only you."

Grant pulls out a ring with not one, but two bajillion karat diamonds. I panic.

"Wait, Grant," I squeak hesitantly. I stare at it and fidget nervously thinking about how much this must have cost him. *Not me being financially conservative during my proposal.*

"Okay, it's…I mean, of course it's huge, but it's *huge*. *Too* huge, Grant."

"That's what she said," he teases. I burst out laughing. He smiles proudly.

"You're twelve," I whisper, leaning into him.

"You laughed, didn't you?" I pout at how cute he's being. When he adjusts himself to sit comfortably on one knee, I remember that he's *proposing to me*. With *two* rocks.

He holds up his palm when he senses that I'm about to resist this thing. "Before you say anything, I'm a billionaire. My mother is the granddaughter of the Harrison mogul. There is a six-billion-dollar estate that Annie, Ben, Layla and I are a part of."

My jaw drops. "Okay, *what?*"

"Yup."

"You're a billionaire?" He nods. "Harrison? Like, *the* Harrison, the oil tycoon?"

"Yes, ma'am."

Then, I begin to howl. Just lots and lots of laughing. Grant joins me but fairly wonders, "Why are you laughing so hard, clown?"

"I've known you for two years. I've been around your family, and I'm only finding out about this *now?*"

He shakes his head endearingly, taps my nose. "All it takes is a proper Google search, babe. And also, are we really doing this during my marriage proposal?"

"Nothing about us has ever been traditional, G-Wagon."

He shrugs. "That's fair."

"Six billion. So, what, you all get one and a half?" I am in awe. I am floored. *How! How do people live like this!*

"Ben and I each get two. The girls get one. Old school mentality. You can have one of mine. Actually, both."

"Did you just offer me two billion dollars?"

"Indeed." His eyes glimmer.

I take a minute or two to process all of this. I look up at him with wide eyes and shout, "You're a *BILLIONAIRE? With a B?!*"

Grant tickles me until I thrash under him, begging for mercy. He hovers above me when he stops and asks, "Hey, could I propose to you?"

I laugh. He pulls the ring out, thrusts it in my face. "Put it on. Marry me."

"You know, you didn't have to get me two rocks. I would have said yes with a paper ring. You know that song?"

Grant chuckles at me like I'm utter perfection. Finally, he says,

"No, I don't. Play it for me later. But for now, ask me what it means. The two diamonds. Ask me why two."

I study him narrowly. I smirk and ask, "Okay. Why two, Grant?"

"It's a toi and moi ring. It means you and me in French. Forever. What do you say?"

I nod, finally giving him the answer that he's looking for.

"Now, let me put a ring on it, woman!" he exclaims.

I giggle. I give him my left hand, and as he gently slides the beautiful ring onto my delicate finger, I whisper, "It's always been that way. You and me. Me and you. I get to marry my best friend."

GRANT TOOK A photo of me while I was holding up my left hand to show off my new ring. I scrunched my nose because I know how much he loves when I do that. After taking only one photo because *that's all I need*, he looked down at his phone in awe. His smile was adorable. He turned to me and said, "You're gorgeous, do you know that?"

The ring is so blinding, I could faint. Well, I could go blind. It's also a paperweight on my tiny, little finger. Set on a thin gold band are two large (giant) diamonds placed side by side. A heart diamond and a circle diamond. He explained that the heart diamond signifies our past to match the other pieces of jewelry he got me and that the circle diamond signifies our future. Infinity. Totality.

When Grant sends the photo of me to his family chat, it goes something like this:

Annie: SHUT THE FUCK UP

Annie: LANGUAGE. I DON'T EVEN CARE

Annie: OH MY GOD!!!!!!

Mom: I'll let this one slide, Annie. You look so beautiful, Ava. We love you so much.

Mom: And congratulations, Grant. Took you long enough.

Dad: What Mom said. Took you long enough, son. Wonderful news

Layla: WHY DID NO ONE TELL ME THIS WAS HAPPENING

Layla: Omg I love you guys so much. Wow. BEST NEWS EVER

Ben: About damn time, brother. Congrats, you guys. Love you both

Grant responds: Never been happier. She's finally my girl. Love you all.

My phone is in the car, so I take his phone and respond: It's Ava. Thank you for treating me like family since day one!! It makes me so excited to be a Wilder!!

Grant: You already are one

Annie: You already are one

Annie: Jinx, bitch

Layla: Yup. What they said. AVA WILDER, AHHHH

Ben: Layla, stop screaming

Ben: Welcome to the crazies, Campbell

Ben: I mean, Wilder

Mom: You've always been one of us, sweetheart.

> Since Thanksgiving dinner two years ago! We love you!

Grant kisses me, then takes my hand to lead me back to his car. "Oh no!" I exclaim.

He looks back at me, concerned. "What?"

"Look at you sweating and huffing and puffing to pull me with you. I'm so sorry you have to tug so hard. I just gained twenty pounds in my hand. You might have to start dead lifting to avoid carpal tunnel." Grant shakes his head at me and chuckles. I love, love, love teasing him. It's my favorite pastime.

Before opening the door to his car, he presses me against the side of it and smiles. He takes my hands in his and softly kisses the middle of each of my palms. I let him have his way around me, planting his delicate kisses all over my face, my ears, my neck, my nose.

"We're engaged," I say in pure disbelief.

He kisses me on the lips before saying, "You're my fiancée. My future wife. You're going to be my *wife*. God, I'm so happy, Ava, I might explode."

I cup Grant's face in my hands and smile up at him. "Don't explode, Callum Grant. We have a whole life to live together."

CHAPTER EIGHTY
GRANT

THE WEDDING

I remember it like it was yesterday.
　　Ava and I got married that July at an estate in Tuscany, Italy. She was twenty-three years old. I was bloody thirty.

The day after Ava agreed to be my wife, Annie hauled her out of our apartment to embark on the millions of wedding errands a bride ought to have. I was adamant, with Ava's excitement and agreement, that we'd get married as soon as possible. I didn't want to wait. I wanted her to be my wife already.

Ava spent the flight to Italy anxious and jittery. She was nervous, but I wasn't. I had been waiting three years for this.

I spoke at length about my fiancée at the rehearsal dinner a few days before the wedding. Ava cried. Ava spoke about me after I was done talking. Then, I cried.

I cried again when I saw her for the first time dressed as a bride. The morning of the wedding, we had a first look in the quiet garden behind the white manor. Everyone was still inside getting ready, so it was just me, Ava, and the photographer. I wore a gray tux because Ava asked me to. She said that she always loved how the color gray muted my eyes a bit. It reminded her of the softness she instilled in me that was always reserved for her.

Ava looked… There aren't any words. I became emotional the second I turned around after she tapped me on the shoulder. She looked so…*her*. She intentionally wore her hair down for me—it had grown by then—and it reminded me of the beginning. The beginning of our nearly three-year long story.

Beads and lace made up the first wedding gown that she wore. It was short sleeved, sheer at the top, but sparkly and beautiful. The gown was sophisticated and elegant, but it was also somehow quirky. It's hard to explain. All I know is that it was made for her.

The second dress was plain white satin, cut at a place above her breasts that bared her tanned neck, her shoulders, her chest. My wife looks like an angel every day, but that day, she was a dream.

Thousands of photos were taken throughout the wedding. Ava and I with her family, with my family, with our families combined. My favorites are the ones of just us. Obviously.

I kept teasing Ava and making her laugh since naturally, it's my favorite sound in the world. I think in eighty percent of our photos, Ava's head is thrown back, laughing. She looks her most beautiful authentic self that way. I love it. Those pictures are golden.

If you ask my wife what her favorite part of the wedding was, she'd say the dancing. The massive party that continued until late that night. But if you ask me? Mine isn't the dancing. Mine is a scene I picture in my head every single day. I still get the chills when I recall the vivid setting.

I remember watching Ava's arm tightly hooked around her father's. A sheer veil flowed in front of her, and in her left hand, she held a small bouquet of flowers.

She was itching to get to me.

Ava couldn't bother with the expected slow walk down the aisle toward me in rhythm with the song playing. She was antsy. David struggled to keep up with her. I chuckled with tears in my eyes.

The pastor began to speak once Ava reached me, but we barely heard him. We were focused on only each other. It was a sweet surprise when I noted what Ava added to her outfit between our first look and the ceremony.

Every piece of jewelry that I got for her since we met. She smiled when she saw that I noticed the diamonds. She gently lifted her wrist for me to see the bracelet first.

"Thanksgiving?" I mouthed. She nodded with this indescribable sunshine in her eyes.

She pointed at her neck.

"Christmas?" I mouthed. Again, she nodded. She was excited about the game we were playing.

After the wedding, Ava said she felt like she was misbehaving in a classroom. We had decided we would read our vows to each other privately. We knew that what we wanted to say was heavy and intimate and for us only, so the ceremony was our little hangout since the only thing we had to do was say two words and kiss.

She pointed at her earrings last. That was the wedding gift I gave her on our flight to Italy.

"I love you," I mouthed. She bit her bottom lip and smiled. She couldn't contain her excitement. You'd think she snorted a line, but the only drug she was on was happiness in its purest form.

We finally left our little bubble when everyone in the crowd chuckled sweetly. "It seems our couple is a little distracted," the pastor teased. Ava apologized profusely for not paying attention. It was so cute that I couldn't help kissing her head. I didn't care that it wasn't traditional. I apologized to the pastor and asked for him to continue.

"Callum Grant Wilder, do you take Ava Ruth Campbell to be your lawfully wedded wife from this day forward—to have and to hold, in good times and bad, for richer or for poorer, in sickness and in health; will you love, honor, and cherish her for as long as you both shall live?"

"I do." I was assured as anything.

He turned to Ava and asked her the same question with the names reversed. She nearly shouted. I'm not sure the pastor got the last word out before she blurted a loud, "I DO!"

The reception was Ava's favorite part of our wedding because it was pure fun, like she is. All of our closest friends and family flew in to be there to celebrate our marriage. Grandpa danced with the bride, and she finally got to meet the Wilder *and* Harrison cousins. They're all obsessed with her.

We were having the time of our lives on that busy dance floor; we didn't ever want to stop dancing.

While dancing her heart out, pressed against my body, Ava noticed out of the corner of her eye that Hannah was watching the dance floor, standing off to the side. Ava ran up to her, grabbed her arm, and dragged her over to dance with us. I smiled, hugged Hannah tightly, and kissed Ava so damn hard. My wife is fucking amazing.

I rented a villa close to the estate, so we could spend the week following the wedding with family before our four-week-long honeymoon. Ava insisted on staying since she was a Wilder now and wanted to get to know her new family.

Mrs. Ava Ruth Wilder. That's my *wife*.

My mother planned for a late lunch at a winery the day after the wedding. She wanted a chance to say a proper goodbye to our guests and thank them for flying out to celebrate Ava and me. It was so beautifully set up; it was pretty much a second wedding reception.

That morning before lunch, I woke up to the view of Ava's naked back and messy, light brown hair. My arm was draped over her waist, and her hand rested on top of mine. It was the first morning of a million more that I'd be waking up beside my wife, and that idea was surreal.

Ava hummed when I kissed her shoulder, then turned in my arms to face me. She kissed my tattoo. She does that every time I'm shirtless.

I never had to explain the arc to my wife one day. She was there when it happened.

"Hi, wife." I hugged her, squeezed my arms tightly around her body and softly sucked on her neck.

"Hi, husband," she croaked. Ava glowed differently that morning. "Is this a solicitation for sex? Because the sign outside says no solicitors."

Ava said this with her eyes closed. She wasn't fully awake yet, and she was already being weird, hoping to make me laugh.

I howled. "No, it doesn't."

"Maybe you just can't read Italian."

I tapped her freckled nose, and she scrunched it. "There's no sign," I said.

"You're just trying to bang me. Do you have proof?"

Ava teased me with the word *proof* on the daily.

She screeched when I lifted her naked body in my arms and held her like the bride she was. Ava covered her boobs and squealed, "I'm naked!"

"We're going to get you that proof." I was good at that.

"*You're* naked!" she countered.

I paused my way to the front door and shrugged. "You're right," I boasted. "I just wanted to cross the threshold again, but naked this time."

Ava giggled. "How romantic," she teased.

I did exactly that and walked back into the bedroom. I set Ava down on her feet. Her bare body was pressed against mine, skin to skin, heart to heart. She had her arms tightly wound around my waist, rested her chin in the middle of my chest, and looked up at me.

"Hi, husband."

I cradled my wife's beautiful face in my hands and stroked her hair. "Hi, wife."

"We're married." She looked at me with wonder. I'm sure I looked at her just the same.

"You ready for the rest of our life, Ava Ruth?"

She nodded. "Of course I'm ready. I'm so happy, I could cry." And she did. Ava cried the happiest tears in the world that morning.

"Am I dreaming, Grant?" she cried. "Is this real?"

I kissed the side of her head and spoke into her hair. "Yes, honey. It's real. It's the realest life we'll ever know."

EPILOGUE

AVA

The honeymoon was a European sex fest.

I wasn't mad about it. Grant wasn't either.

I did push for us to tour the three countries we were visiting. We were pretty much off the radar for six weeks. We were originally supposed to go for four, but when I woke up one morning next to my *husband* for the eighteenth time and imagined the rest of my life with him, I decided I didn't want to postpone getting pregnant.

I knew it could take time with all of the medical intricacies, so in a king-sized bed at a penthouse in Saint Tropez, it was decided. I couldn't say what time it was. We were in such pure bliss that we had no conception of time on that trip.

This one morning, I was buried in my warm cocoon of Grant's arms. I spend most nights like that, and I wouldn't change it for the world.

Grant's arm was draped over my waist, and he had his giant palm flat against my stomach. I felt the metal from his wedding band against my skin and his hot breaths in my hair.

I had imagined what it would feel like for Grant to touch my stomach because I was growing our child in there. It was like this wave of certainty came over me, and nothing else made sense. It felt right.

I was awake, but I didn't make a move because I wanted Grant to sleep. We hadn't been able to sleep more than three hour stretches before one of us mounted the other. Like I said, European sex fest.

"What are you scheming, Mrs. Wilder?" he mumbled hoarsely into my hair. His voice was happy and laced with all the love in the world. His laugh was rough but also soft. "I can practically hear your brain working."

"What is my brain saying?" I turned in his arms, kissed his tattoo, and beamed up at him. He kissed me. "I'll give you five bucks if you tell me what my brain is saying."

"Oh. That's so tempting. Five whole dollars," he said sarcastically.

I whined. I was apparently rich now, but I still whined. Grant chuckled at me.

"Come on, just guess!"

I looked up and talked to him with my eyes, and he knew. He just knew.

"You're ready?" he uttered quietly. His thick eyebrows pinched in concern.

"Yeah," I whispered. Grant was in deep contemplation while playing with my hair. He looked at me. He studied me. I just waited.

"Are you sure?" His voice was still hoarse with sleep and his natural deep octave. I nodded. "Are you saying this because I somehow pressured you?"

"No. It's because I want it."

"You do? *You* want it? You're not deciding this for any other reason? Because if it's for me, Ava, I swear—"

"It's not for you," I whispered, interrupting him. "Not entirely. I want to be a mother. I know it could take a long time, but I really want that with you. I want to start a family. I want that life."

Grant insisted we stay on vacation for an extra two weeks if we were going to start treatment as soon as we got home, which is exactly what we did.

I won't sugarcoat it. It was absolute hell.

I spent the duration of almost a month with needles jabbed into my body. I couldn't stomach giving myself the hormone injections that were required for the treatments to work, so I made Grant do them. I squeezed his hands until they turned blue every time.

The first egg collection was the hardest. They were going to create our baby under a microscope and were removing my eggs to do that. It was painful and intimidating, and I cried *a lot*.

I blamed it on the copious amounts of hormones that were now in my body, but it was also a really stressful time.

After the final step in the treatment, the embryo implantation, Grant spent the two-week waiting period chained to me. This was the hardest period for a couple going through IVF. We were just waiting around for two weeks to know whether or not it all worked; whether or not I was pregnant.

I felt so guilty when I snapped at him one morning around day nine. "Would you please stop hovering? *God*, Grant, I'm *fine*!"

All he was trying to do was make sure I felt as comfortable and supported as possible. He had listened to me and left me alone, but I needed him to know that I was at fault. That he did nothing wrong. I climbed into bed beside him later that night.

"I'm so sorry," I whispered. I was crying because I had been for the last month. "I shouldn't have yelled at you. I'm just really anxious."

"It's okay, baby." Grant pulled at my hand for me to lay down beside him and curl into his chest so I was in my cocoon again. "I love you. I always want to understand how you're feeling. Thank you for telling me."

"What if it—"

"No. Don't. That's the worst thing you could do to yourself." He pinched my chin with his thumb and index finger and lifted my face to his. He smiled softly. "Let's stay positive. We can do this. We were made for this. Happy mindset, Ava. Happy."

It worked. I was pregnant. Thirty-seven weeks and four days later, I had Grant's green-eyed baby.

Callum Harrison Wilder.

Harry is seven now. He has the shocking, green eyes and the shiny, black hair. He's in the 99th percentile for height, and I find myself in genuine awe of how genetics work every time I look at my eldest son. He's serious and curious. His brows are always furrowed because he's always deep in thought. The other day he asked me to explain photosynthesis to him. He also wanted to know how boats float. My firstborn is a little engineer.

He's Grant's *clone*.

We decided to try again when Harry turned three.

The first round failed. The second round didn't, but we still had it fairly easy. Some couples struggled for years.

Our next baby wasn't a girl who looks like Madison. Our next one was a boy. Harry was four when I had Will.

Grant William Wilder.

We were starting our own namesake tradition.

Will is… *God*, Will is *me*. Aside from his green eyes, Will is my little clone. I was so excited about that. I thought I was only ever going to birth mini-Grants.

Will is our wild one. The one who's perpetually falling because he's always climbing on something. The kid cannot sit still for a minute. He jokes with us and goofs around at any opportunity. Grant and I find ourselves howling with laughter at the funny things that he says. Grant always tells him, "Son, you are a male version of your mother." He says he's lucky that he gets not one, but two Avas now.

Grant was hesitant when I brought up having more kids once Will turned three. He was worried that I was being too hard on myself and my body, but I wanted to try again. I felt energetic and powerful. The femininity inside of me was excited for more babies. Being a mother is the best thing that's ever happened to me, and I wanted to keep going.

I will never forget my post-implantation appointment. I didn't tell Grant that I was going to the doctor that morning because I didn't want him to worry. If it succeeded, great. If not, we'd try again soon.

I gasped when I saw the screen in the ultrasound room.

That night, I was antsy when the kids came home from school. Grant prioritizes being home before bedtime, so I knew he'd get here in time to feed the kids dinner. I was dying to see him.

My husband smiled sweetly when he walked through the door. He put his phone away and kissed me really hard. The boys shouted, "Ewwwwww!"

"Hi," I panted. "What was that for?"

"You're the love of my life. I'm *married* to you. We have two sons." Grant spread his long arms opened and said, "We have this house and this life. Do you know how happy I am? This is the best life in the world."

"This is the best life in the world!" the boys echoed. It was this thing they did with their father. The three of them shouted it at least twice a day.

I was so eager to be alone with Grant that I was excited for the boys to go to bed. I walked into the kitchen to find my shirtless husband cooking at the stove. I took a picture with my phone and sent it to Chloe. I wrote: How is this my life?

She replied: You are living the dream, and you deserve it more than anyone I know. Say hi to him from me. Miss you both lots!

I wrapped my arms around Grant's strong waist. I laid my cheek against his hot skin and inhaled slowly. He placed the spatula on the spoon rest and turned in my arms. I kissed his tattoo.

"Did they go down okay?" he asked me.

"Yeah. How was your day?" *Because my day was insane.*

"It was great. What about you, honey? How were the boys today?"

I looked at Grant until we both laughed. Little boys are a handful.

"They're the best," he whispered.

"The best ever," I replied.

Grant looked at me like I was glitter. "I'm so happy," he said.

"I'm happy, too." I got on my tiptoes to kiss him. "I have something to show you."

I pulled out the picture from my jeans pocket. Grant's green eyes widened when he saw it.

"Is this…?" I bit my lip, gauged his reaction, and nodded. "We're having…?"

"Yeah," I whispered.

Grant lifted me. He spun me in circles until I was uncontrollably laughing. He squeezed me so tight and whispered how much he loves me and respects me and cherishes me over and over in my ear.

I'm due in a month.

I'm the bowling ball.

It's twins.

ACKNOWLEDGEMENTS

Firstly, I'd like to thank YOU for reaching the end of this book, thus reaching the end of Grant and Ava's story. Although it's bittersweet to say goodbye to these debut characters of mine, I had the most incredible time creating them for the last four years. I love them dearly and I thank you for loving them alongside me!

I want to give a humongous, massive thank you to Mary, Val and Julie from Books and Moods. You guys made the process of self-publishing so incredibly seamless and I can't thank you enough for your patience, creativity and guidance.

Kaitlin, thank you for being the best editor on the planet. You went above and beyond with your feedback and proofreading to ensure this book is a masterpiece. I also want to give you a shout out for bearing with my constant questions of *"How's this?"* and *"Does this sound weird?"* Thank you, thank you!!!

To my sisters—my best friends forever. Maytal, you're my go-to whenever I need a *"Your son is fine, Mima. Chill out!"* or a good, freaking laugh. Moral, you're my go-to whenever I need an emotional conversation, a venting session, or a DMC. Thank you for being that for me. And lastly but definitely not least, Michal. You're my favorite go-to whenever I need to gossip, make fun, or choke from laughter. All three of you are my favorites, you fulfill all the voids in my life, that I don't bother with a social life. I should probably do that, though. *Or not?* Anyway, I love you, I love you, I love you!! (One for each of you.)

To my parents—not much has changed since my acknowledgement in Liar but I will say the biggest thank you for giving each and every one of your children the strength, grit and power to stand up for the right thing. To be good people. To know right from wrong. To stray from being judgmental and to recognize that only God can judge us. I cherish you both more than you know. And I'm still so incredibly proud to be your daughter.

To my book girlies—Ariana, Faith, Madita, Shelli, Kimmy, Maxine, Faria, Molly, Hattie, Meagan, Kristina, Erika, Ellie, Jess, Julia, Lilly and Salma. Simply put: you girls are the *best*. Thank you for the constant support, the adorable excitement over this book coming out, exposure for both Liar and Lover and just being my fun internet friends. You all mean so much to me!

To my son—I love you. You are my life, my soul and the air that I breathe. And knowing you, you'll probably teach yourself how to read this within a few months. Hi baby!!

And lastly, to Isaac—you have no idea how terrified I was that you'd open the proof once it got to the house and read the dedication that I so desperately wanted to be a surprise. So, was it? I've known you are my person since I was fifteen years old. As soon as Ava said it to Grant, I knew that this book belonged to no one but you. I love you. You are my best friend in the world, you know me so perfectly, and there is no one else that I could ever imagine doing life with. You're my person, Isaac. Through and through.

ABOUT THE AUTHOR

Born and raised in Los Angeles, California, Mima began writing book one, The Path of a Logical Liar, sitting at a retail cashier's desk with her iPad and a portable Bluetooth keyboard. Three years and one prequel later, she's excited for the world to enjoy the continuation of Grant and Ava's story. In her spare time, Mima enjoys reading smut and perpetually adding to her TBR list. She lives in Los Angeles with her husband and son.

ALSO BY MIMA ROSENFELD

The Path of a Logical Liar